Th   ....
Support Group

...herine Jinks has won the Children's Book Council of
...stralia (CBCA) Book of the Year Award four times, the
...torian Premier's Literary Award, the Aurealis Award for
...nce Fiction and the Australian IBBY Award. She lives in
...Blue Mountains of New South Wales with her husband
...daughter.

Also by Catherine Jinks

To Die For
Pagan's Crusade
Pagan in Exile

The Reformed Vampire Support Group

Catherine Jinks

Quercus

First published in Great Britain in 2009 by

Quercus
21 Bloomsbury Square
London
WC1A 2NS

A CIP catalogue reference for this book is available from the British Library

ISBN 978 1 84724 778 0

10 9 8 7 6 5 4 3 2 1

Designed and typeset by Rook Books, London
Printed and bound in England by Clays Ltd, St Ives plc.

To Claire Haywood – your training really put me on the right track

Chapter One

Nina was stuck. She didn't know what to write next.

So far, her teenaged captive had been dragged into a refrigerated meat locker by two thugs armed with a gun and a boning knife. But Zadia Bloodstone was already waiting for them. Hanging upside-down from a meat hook, wrapped in a long, black cape and covered by a thin layer of frost, Zadia had cleverly disguised herself as a harmless side of beef. Only when she'd spread her arms wide had the crackle of breaking ice announced her presence.

Bang-bang! Two bullets had promptly smashed into her ribcage. But Zadia wasn't troubled by bullets, because her vital organs could regenerate themselves at lightning speed. Somersaulting to the floor, she'd walked straight up to the bigger thug and kicked the gun from his hand. Then she'd whirled around to fight off his friend. Within seconds, the two baddies had been knocked out – leaving a very important question unanswered.

What would the rescued boy do?

Obviously, he would be grateful. He might even be dazzled by Zadia's flawless face and perfect figure. But if he saw her sink her fangs into anyone's neck, he would also be frightened.

He would realise instantly that she was a vampire, and run for the door.

He would be unaware, at this point, that Zadia was a heroic crime-fighter who only preyed on lowlife scum.

Nina chewed away at a lock of her hair, thinking hard. She was in the middle of chapter eight. The room in which she sat was illumined solely by the glow of her computer screen; barely visible in the dimness were her brass bedstead, her Indian cushions and her lava lamp. A poster of David Bowie hung on the wall, curling at the corners. A small bookshelf contained multiple copies of *Youngblood* (*Book Two of the Bloodstone Chronicles*), by someone called N. E. Harris.

Splashed across the cover of *Youngblood* was a glamorous, slinky young girl with white skin, black hair and ruby-red lips. She wore high-heeled boots and lots of black leather, as well as an ammunition belt. Her canine teeth were long and pointed, but she was stunningly beautiful nonetheless.

She appeared to be leaping from rooftop to rooftop, her black cape streaming out behind her.

'Nina!' somebody shouted, from beyond the closed bedroom door. Nina didn't respond. She stared unblinkingly at the computer screen, still gnawing at her hair – which was thick and dark, and cut in a heavy, clumsy, old-fashioned style that didn't suit her bony little face.

It was about time, she decided, that Zadia made friends with the boy she'd rescued.

Zadia hesitated, Nina wrote, *torn between her desire to punish the wicked and her need to reassure the tall, pale, handsome teenager with the big brown eyes.*

'Nina!' a distant voice called again. Ignoring it, Nina deleted the word 'pale'. Her hands on the keyboard were like chicken's feet, all scaly and dry. Her skin was the colour of a maggot's, and her legs were so thin that her tights were wrinkled around the knees.

Her boots had flat heels on them.

'Nina!' The door burst open to admit a withered old woman in a quilted nylon dressing-gown. 'For God's sake, are you deaf? Father Ramon's outside – you want to keep him waiting?'

Nina sighed. She shut her laptop, moving sluggishly.

'All right,' she murmured. 'I'm on my way.'

'Aren't you feeling well?' the old woman wanted to know. She had the hoarse rasp and yellowed fingertips of a chronic smoker; her hair looked like a frayed clump of steel wool, and her scarlet lipstick was bleeding into the cracks around her mouth. 'Because if you're sick,' she said, 'you shouldn't be going.'

'I'm not sick, Mum. I'm fine.'

'That's what you always say, and you never are. Is your head giving you trouble?'

'No!'

'What about your stomach?'

Nina didn't reply. Instead she rose, reaching for her sunglasses – which shared the cluttered surface of her desk with a Pet Rock, a pile of vintage vampire comics, and a netball trophy awarded to the 'Junior Regional Inter-School Champions' of 1971. On a noticeboard hanging above the desk-lamp were pinned various faded photographs of laughing teenage girls.

If any of these girls was Nina, it wasn't immediately apparent. They were so sleek and glossy and bright-eyed that they could have belonged to an entirely different species.

'Are you nauseous?' her mother nagged. 'You are, aren't you?'

'There's *nothing wrong*,' said Nina, on her way out of the room. It was a lie, of course. There was always something wrong.

And her mother knew it.

'If you get sick, I want you to come straight home,' the old woman advised, as they descended a narrow wooden staircase together. 'Dave won't mind bringing you back early, if you can't stay to the end. And don't leave it till the last minute, the way you did before. Dave won't want you throwing up all over his sheepskin seat-covers again . . .'

Nina winced. It was true. She had ruined Dave's precious seat-covers. Was it any wonder that he didn't exactly beat a path to her door? Was it any wonder that she spent so much of her time in imaginary meat lockers with the stylish and vigorous Zadia Bloodstone? At least there were no uncontrollable bouts of vomiting in Zadia's world.

Nina pulled open the heavy front door of her mother's terrace house. Outside, the darkness was relieved only by the soft glow of a nearby streetlamp; stars were scattered like sequins across a coal-black sky. Yet Nina had already donned her sunglasses, which were big, heavy, wrap-around things that made her pinched face look smaller than ever . . .

You know what? This isn't going to work. I can't write about myself the way I write about Zadia. It's too weird. It's confusing. Next thing I'll get mixed up, and start making me do things that I can't actually do. Like turn into a bat, for instance. Zadia can do that, but I can't. No one can.

The plain fact is, I can't do anything much. That's part of

4

the problem. Vampires are meant to be so glamorous and powerful, but I'm here to inform you that being a vampire is *nothing* like that. Not one bit. On the contrary, it's like being stuck indoors with the flu watching daytime television, for ever and ever.

If being a vampire were easy, there wouldn't have to be a Reformed Vampire Support Group.

As a matter of fact, I was going to a group meeting that very night. Father Ramon had come to pick me up. It was a Tuesday, because all our meetings are held on Tuesdays, at 9.30 p.m., in St Agatha's church hall. And in case you're wondering why I couldn't have driven myself to St Agatha's . . . well, that's just one of my many problems. I still look fifteen, you see. I still *am* fifteen, when all's said and done, since I stopped ageing back in 1973, when I was infected. So I'd attract far too much attention behind a steering wheel. (Besides which, Mum doesn't have a car.)

As for the public transport option, Sanford Plackett has ruled that out. He's always ruling things out; you'd think he was our lord and master, the way he carries on. He's forbidden any of us to travel around Sydney on buses or trains, for instance, in case we stumble across something that Father Ramon would probably describe as 'an occasion of sin'. I suppose Sanford's worried that we might encounter a bleeding junkie rolling around on a station platform, and won't be able to stop ourselves from pouncing.

'You think you'll never succumb,' he once said to me, 'because you can't come to terms with your true nature. You refuse to concede that you're really a vampire, with a vampire's weakness. But you are, Nina. We all are. That's why we have to be careful.'

5

And being careful means not catching cabs. According to Sanford, it's too risky. Staring at the back of a cab-driver's exposed neck would be quite stressful for most of us – especially if someone's been bleeding onto the seats beforehand. Sanford also insists that no one in our group should go wandering the streets all alone. He says that we wouldn't stand a chance against the drunks and addicts and muggers on the loose out there. He says that everyone should follow his advice, because he's been around for so long and has so much experience, and because, although Father Ramon might be our group facilitator, even a priest with counselling experience can't be its *leader*. Not if he isn't a vampire himself.

That's Sanford's opinion, anyway. He's got a lot of opinions, let me tell you. And he's never shy about airing them, whether asked to or not.

He was already in the car when I reached it, because he can't drive either. People who grew up before the First World War rarely can. Back then, even doctors like Sanford didn't own motor vehicles – and he certainly couldn't risk learning to drive now. None of us could. We'd be exposing ourselves to the kind of official scrutiny that you need to avoid at all costs, when you're toting fake IDs. Most of the vampires I know have changed their identities at least once, and Sanford has done it twice, owing to the fact that he doesn't look his age (believe it or not). Despite his balding scalp and clipped moustache – despite his preference for three-piece suits and fob-watches – you'd never guess that he was a hundred and forty years old. The very fact that he's not six feet underground is a dead giveaway. And he's no different from the rest of our group, which is full of people living precarious lives, under assumed names, with forged papers.

It's a real drag, believe me.

'Hello, Nina,' he said, as I slid into the back seat of the waiting Nissan Pulsar.

'Hello, Sanford.'

'How are you, Nina?' Father Ramon inquired, pulling out from the kerb.

'Oh – you know. Nauseous. As usual.'

I didn't want to complain too much, because that's what vampires do. They complain too much. But I needn't have worried. Gladys did the complaining for me.

'I bet you're not as nauseous as I was last night,' she said, moving over to give me some space. 'I was trying to sell a timeshare, and I spewed all over the phone. At least a cupful of blood. It no sooner went down than it came back up again. I lost the sale and everything – didn't I, Bridget?'

'Oh, yes,' said Bridget, who was knitting. Bridget's always knitting. She was eighty-two when she was infected, so she can't do much else. Even climbing stairs can be a problem for Bridget, because of her hip joints.

There's only one thing worse than being a vampire, and that's being an elderly vampire with bad hips.

'Have you been taking your enzymes, Gladys?' asked Sanford, from the front seat. He craned around to peer at her. 'Every morning, before you go to bed?'

'Of course I have!'

'What about other treatments? Have you been drinking those herbal concoctions again?'

'No!' Gladys exclaimed, sounding defensive, though it was a perfectly reasonable question. Gladys goes about smelling weird, like a hippy, because she's always treating her manifold health problems with miraculous new oils or exercises or

7

meditation techniques. She even looks like a hippy, in her beads and her shawls and her long, flowing skirts. Having been infected back in 1908, she can't bear to expose her legs; ladies didn't do that sort of thing in the old days, and Gladys likes to think of herself as a lady – even though she was actually a common streetwalker. She also likes to think of herself as a *young* lady, despite her old-lady obsession with bowels and feet and joint-pain, because she was only twenty-four when she first got infected. But I'm here to tell you, she's about as young as a fossilised dinosaur egg.

'I haven't even been burning scented candles,' she whined, 'and I'm still getting that rash I told you about. The one on my stomach.'

'It might be a bad response to the supplements,' Sanford mused. 'I could adjust your levels a bit, I suppose. Have you had any dizzy spells?'

'Yes! This morning!'

'What about headaches?'

'Not since last week. But the other night one of my toenails fell off in the bath –'

At this point I could restrain myself no longer.

'Hey! Here's an idea!' I growled, my voice dripping with sarcasm. 'Let's all talk about our allergies, for a change! That'll be fun.'

There was a long pause. Father Ramon glanced into the rear-view mirror, shooting me one of those reproachful-yet-sympathetic looks in which he seems to specialise. Sanford sniffed. Gladys scowled.

'Well, what do *you* want to talk about, then?' she demanded. 'What have *you* been doing lately that's so wonderful? Watching re-runs of *Buffy the Vampire Slayer*?'

'I've been writing my book,' I said, knowing perfectly well what sort of reaction I'd get. And when Sanford removed his sunglasses briefly, to massage the bridge of his nose, I braced myself for the usual guff about how I was putting everyone at risk (even though I write under a pseudonym, and use a post office box for all my correspondence).

'Yeah, yeah, I know what you think of my books,' I added, before Sanford could butt in. 'Spare me the sermon – I've heard it all before.'

'They're not doing us any good, Nina,' he replied. 'People are scared enough already; you're only making things worse.'

'Zadia's not scary, Sanford. She gets fan mail. She's a *heroine*.'

'She's a symbol of your flight from reality.' This was one of Sanford's stock remarks. For at least twenty-five years he'd been telling me that I was stuck in the 'denial' phase of the Kubler-Ross Grief Cycle (rather than the 'anger', 'bargaining', 'depression' or 'acceptance' phases), because I had refused to embrace my true identity as a vampire. 'You feel compelled to invest vampires with a battery of super-human powers,' he said, making reference to Zadia Bloodstone, 'just so you can tell yourself that you're not really a vampire. You're living in a dream world, Nina.'

'No – *you're* living in a dream world.' I was trying to be patient. 'You talk to me like I'm still a kid, even though I'm *fifty-one-years-old*. Do you know how boring that can get?'

He did, of course. Everyone did, because I'd mentioned it often enough. It had been a good thirty years since our group's first meeting, so we knew each other pretty well by this time. We'd also covered every subject known to man, over and over and over again. It's something that tends to happen when you don't mix very much with other people.

Sometimes I look around St Agatha's vestry on a Tuesday night, and I think to myself: *If I never see any of you ever again, I'll be a happy vampire.*

'You might have lived for fifty-one years,' Sanford chided, without even bothering to glance in my direction, 'but you're still a kid at heart. You're stuck in a teenage time warp. You still think like a teen. You still behave like a teen.'

'What – you mean like this?' I said, and flipped him the finger. Gladys giggled. Father Ramon changed gears abruptly, though his voice remained calm.

'Come on, now,' he remonstrated. 'That's enough. If you want to argue . . . well, you should at least wait until the meeting.'

Then Sanford's mobile phone began to trill. While he fumbled inside his jacket, I turned my face to the window. Outside, streetlamps were gliding past, illuminating the kind of neighbourhood that I've always enjoyed looking at. House-fronts were shoved up hard against the pavement. Though the gaps between shrunken curtains and broken cedar slats I could see flickering television screens, curling drifts of cigarette smoke, and people rushing from room to room, slamming doors.

But I couldn't see enough. I never can. I always get a fleeting glimpse of normal life before it's whisked away – before I'm back in a crowded car with a bunch of vampires.

'Oh. Hello, Dave.' Sanford had found his phone, at long last. 'Yes. Yes. Dear me. That is troubling. Yes, I'll tell him.' Addressing the priest, Sanford delivered Dave's news with solemn emphasis. 'Dave says that Casimir won't answer his intercom,' Sanford announced. 'They've been trying for about ten minutes. Dave wants to know if you still have a spare key.'

'Yes, I do,' said Father Ramon. He sounded worried. 'Tell him I'll swing round.'

'Did you hear that?' Sanford addressed his mobile again. 'He said we'll swing round. Yes. Well, I hope so. All right. Yes, see you soon.'

He hung up.

I don't think anyone quite knew what to say, initially. Sanford appeared to be thinking. Father Ramon was obviously reassessing his planned route; he suddenly pulled into someone's driveway, and executed a rather clumsy three-point turn. Bridget was looking puzzled.

I couldn't even pretend to be anxious. In fact I was downright disgusted. 'Ten to one Casimir's out on the prowl,' I said at last, airing a very natural suspicion. 'I bet he's got his fangs into somebody *as we speak*.'

Boom! Instant uproar. If I had set fire to Gladys, I might have triggered a less impassioned response.

'Nina!' Father Ramon seemed genuinely horrified. 'That's a dreadful thing to say!'

'You shouldn't talk about people like that,' Bridget protested. I couldn't see her eyes behind the dark glasses that she wore, but her face was even whiter than usual. It was almost as white as her hair.

Sanford twisted around to admonish me.

'Casimir Kucynski hasn't set a foot wrong since being released,' he pointed out, in frigid accents. 'That was five years ago. Casimir's reformed, now.'

'Reformed?' I folded my arms. 'He sleeps in a *coffin*, Sanford!'

'He's doing his best, Nina. Casimir is a victim too – just like the rest of us.' Sanford's tone became pompous. 'You know you're not the only one who was infected by Casimir. If the others have forgiven him, why can't you?'

'Because he's a creep,' I replied, without fear of contradiction. Casimir Kucynski *was* a creep. Even Sanford couldn't deny it. Though Casimir might have called himself a reformed vampire, he was anything but. He would go on and on about 'the good old days', when you could buy your very own slaves and kill them with impunity. He would do the most awful things with his tongue, which was long and blue, like one of those poisonous jellyfish. He had eyes like oysters, and teeth like tombstones.

In fact, if you want my honest opinion, Casimir had been a vampire for so long that he wasn't really human any more. It's vampires like Casimir who give other vampires a bad name. But try telling that to Sanford. Even now he maintains that it's important not to draw any kind of distinction between what's human and what's vampiric. He insists that vampirism is just another form of humanity – that there's nothing inherently wrong with being a vampire. And whenever I try to contradict him, he gives me a lecture about my attitude.

'Casimir is probably sick,' said Father Ramon, playing the peacemaker as usual. 'He probably can't get out of bed.'

'That's right,' Sanford agreed. 'He might be having an adverse reaction to his supplements. It's happened before.'

I could have reminded him, at this juncture, that Casimir had also suffered adverse reactions from fanging dead rats. But I didn't speak. Instead I stared out at the passing streetscape, which was undergoing a slow transformation: the turrets, avenues, door-knockers, mailboxes and iron railings were giving way to signage, awnings, plate-glass, traffic lights and concrete barriers. Pedestrians strolled along, swaddled in winter coats. Coloured lights flashed inside a corner pub.

I lifted my sunglasses, to get a better look at the festivities. It was only going to be a quick squint.

But Sanford nearly bit my head off.

'Nina!' he squawked. 'There are headlights everywhere! Do you want your eyes to start bleeding again?'

Welcome to my world. It's the kind of place where you can't do the simplest thing without risking a full-blown haemorrhage.

God I'm sick of it.

Chapter Two

People often think that vampires live in decrepit old castles, or mausoleums, or sprawling mansions full of stained glass and wood panelling. Unfortunately, that's not the case.

Perhaps it would be, if all the vampires in this world were millionaires. But since the ones *I* know are just ordinary working stiffs (so to speak), their dwellings tend to be on the modest side. They can't afford towers or gargoyles or enormous iron gates. Some of them can't even afford a broadband connection.

Nevertheless, there are certain features that distinguish a vampire's domicile. A vampire, for instance, doesn't like picture windows. In fact a vampire doesn't like windows at all. So you're not going to find a vampire living in a modernistic glass box featuring lots of skylights and breezeways.

For the same reason, a vampire's windows are always going to be well covered. Shutters and curtains are favoured over vertical or Venetian blinds. Rubbery draught excluders are attached to most of the doors, and there's never an exposed keyhole or an unsealed letterbox.

What's more, a vampire likes to sleep somewhere special. Somewhere safe. So a vampire's abode usually contains the kind of bolt-hole that you often don't find in normal homes.

Sanford, for instance, lives in a former bank building, and sleeps in the vault. Gladys and Bridget live in an old butcher's shop, and sleep in what was once a refrigerated meat-locker. Even Dave has managed to find a skinny little duplex with a disused dark-room in it.

As for me, I sleep in the basement of my mother's big, Victorian terrace house. It's quite a nice space, really, even though Mum has had to brick up the front window, and block off the outside door. There are quite a few cockroaches, but they only come out at night, when I'm upstairs. And we use a dehumidifier to keep the damp under control.

But Casimir never had the funds to inhabit anything vampire-friendly. While the rest of us have managed to support ourselves one way or another, Casimir was always far too antisocial; he used to get by on a disability pension, augmented by the occasional gift from those of us with money to spare. As a result, he could only afford to occupy a one-bedroom flat. A *downmarket* one-bedroom flat.

The building itself was a dingy art-deco structure, all blood-coloured brick and pus-coloured paint. It stood three storeys high, on a narrow patch of mangy grass. There was a separate laundry block, as well as a two-car garage.

When we arrived there, we saw Dave's blue hatchback sitting out the front.

'Don't park too close to Dave,' I suggested, leaning forward to address Father Ramon. 'It might look too busy. Like an emergency, or something. People might get interested.'

'She's right,' Sanford agreed – to my utter astonishment. 'Park around the corner a bit.'

So we parked around the corner a bit, some distance from the nearest streetlamp. As we swept past the hatchback, I spotted Dave in its driver's seat, with Horace beside him. They had been smart enough to stay huddled in the car, instead of hanging around the front entrance.

I should probably explain, at this point, that Dave Gerace is the only vampire in our group who can drive. When he was infected, back in '73, he'd already had his licence for just over two years (having acquired it at the age of seventeen), and he's managed to renew it regularly ever since, by means of various cunning and questionable ploys. That's why he's spent the last three decades chauffeuring the rest of us from pillar to post. You have to admire him for it; personally, in Dave's position, I'd have been tempted to *run over* Casimir, instead of faithfully picking him up every Tuesday night. But Dave's so tolerant and mature. And sensible. And safety-conscious. Once I was listening to some music in his car, and when I asked him to pump up the volume a bit, he wouldn't. He said he was worried that my ears might start bleeding, the way my eyes and nose and gums often do. It's funny: to look at him, you'd think he was a teenager. But a lot of the time he acts just like my mum.

During all the years I've known him, he has never, *ever* exceeded the speed limit.

'You might want to come with me, Sanford,' Father Ramon remarked, when his own vehicle had stopped moving. He jerked at the handbrake as he turned his key in the ignition. 'Casimir might need some help.'

'Yes, of course,' Sanford replied. Then he glanced into the back seat. 'Someone had better stay with Bridget,' he added. 'She wouldn't even make it up the stairs.'

'I'll stay,' Gladys offered, in a feeble voice. 'Casimir smells, and I feel sick enough already.'

'Then I'll go too,' I said. Because the sad fact is that Gladys

16

happens to be a chronic whiner, who rarely talks about anything except her own health problems. She claims that she suffers more severely from symptoms and side-effects than the rest of us do – though I've noticed that she's never too sick to curl and colour her hair. (She's not a natural blonde, that's for sure.) At any rate, whatever the reason might be, she's not exactly a bundle of laughs.

And I was in no mood to hear about her rotting toenails.

'I want to see Casimir's flat, anyway,' I said, pushing open the back door. 'I've never been in there.'

'It isn't very exciting,' the priest observed doubtfully. He seemed to have forgotten that *any* new venue is exciting when you don't get out much. Like the rest of our group, I have to put up with a very limited existence: I never meet any strangers, I conduct most of my business on-line, and I'm frequently so ill or exhausted that I spend entire nights slumped in front of the television.

So I ignored Father Ramon, and set off towards Dave's car.

By this time it was empty. Dave and George and Horace had already climbed out, and were standing around with their hands in their pockets, waiting for us. Dave was dressed in his usual jeans and denim jacket, so he looked all right. George was wearing the kind of baggy, over-sized, swamp-coloured clothes that you see on most sixteen-year-olds these days, so he wasn't too conspicuous, despite the orange fuzz on his scalp.

Horace, however, had arrayed himself in a Gothic assortment of crushed velvet, black satin and patent leather that shouldn't be allowed, in my view. He might as well have had *I am a vampire* embroidered across the front of his watered-silk waistcoat. An outfit like that is going to get him staked one of these days; it's exactly what Boris Karloff would have worn, if he'd joined the cast of *The Rocky Horror Show*.

'You shouldn't be out in that stuff,' I muttered, as soon as I was close enough to be heard. 'Why not go the whole hog, and put on a bloody bat costume?'

'Get in the car, Horace!' Sanford snarled. He was close on my heels, and took me by surprise. Even Dave looked startled. But Horace merely lifted one side of his mouth, exposing a yellowish fang.

'Bite me, Sanford,' was all that he said.

'Is the intercom actually working?' Father Ramon quietly asked Dave, before any further comment could be made on the subject of Horace's ridiculous costume. 'Did you press the other buttons?'

'Only one,' Dave replied. 'A woman said hello.'

With a grunt, the priest pulled a bunch of keys from somewhere beneath his cassock. And Horace snorted.

'I don't know why you're so worried about *my* clothes attracting attention,' he remarked. 'Father Ramon's wearing a *dress*, for God's sake!'

'Shut up, Horace,' said Dave. He must have been quite rattled, because he rarely snaps at anyone. On the contrary, he tends to slouch glumly in the background, hiding behind his hair and his five-o'clock shadow.

Sanford always used to say that Dave was stuck in the depression phase of the Kubler-Ross Grief Cycle. But then again, Sanford was born in the nineteenth century; he thinks that any man who doesn't shave every morning is either clinically depressed or a prison inmate.

He also likes to see women wearing hats, even in the middle of the night.

18

'George, you should go and sit with Bridget and Gladys,' he said, as Father Ramon strode down Casimir's front path. 'If anything happens, they'll need somebody with them; they're not fit to take care of themselves.'

Then he followed Father Ramon, leaving the rest of us dumbstruck – because George Mumford isn't someone I'd like to have taking care of *me*. One look at his gormless, waxy, nondescript face is enough to tell you that he's not exactly the sharpest tool in the box.

But perhaps that was why Sanford had decided to get rid of him. Perhaps Sanford felt that George was much better out of the way.

Horace certainly seemed to think so.

'Yes, off you go, George,' said Horace. 'No reason why we should all head up there. We wouldn't fit in, for a start.'

'How do you know?' I was taken aback. 'Have you been inside Casimir's flat?'

Horace shrugged.

'I had to upgrade my PC, so I gave my old one to Casimir,' he revealed. '*Someone* had to get him connected.'

'To the Internet?' This was ominous news, which hadn't been debated at any of our meetings. Before I could pursue it, however, Dave beckoned to us.

'Hurry up,' he said, 'if you're coming.'

And we went.

The main entrance to Casimir's building was protected by a security door with a missing pane of glass. Beyond it, a shabby foyer contained a notice board, a light switch, and something that was either an empty planter or a very large ashtray. The carpet looked older than I am. Cobwebs fluttered from inaccessible corners of the ceiling.

19

I couldn't imagine how Casimir's coffin had been lugged all the way up to the top floor.

'Don't make too much noise,' the priest murmured, putting a finger to his lips. It was unnecessary advice. I'm sure I wasn't the only one who felt horribly vulnerable as we approached Casimir's apartment. Every creak of the stairs made us wince. Every peep-hole in every numbered door seemed to be aimed straight at us, like a loaded gun. I couldn't help worrying about nosy neighbours, or wondering how on earth Casimir had survived in such a crowded place. How had he smuggled in his guinea pigs? And by what means had he disposed of their tell-tale little corpses?

'Uh-oh,' said Horace, under his breath. I peered past him, unnerved by a muffled roar of canned laughter. Clearly, the occupants of number twelve were watching television. The walls were so thin that I could hear the clink of cutlery, and the sound of someone coughing.

Father Ramon had reached number fourteen. Even from where I was stationed, bringing up the rear, it was obvious that Casimir's lock had been tampered with.

The spare key wouldn't be needed after all.

'It could have been a robbery,' the priest said at last, his voice a mere thread of sound. 'Casimir might have been scared away if he woke up and found the place ransacked.'

'But why not call us?' I whispered. And Horace hissed, 'Let's just go in. Now. Before somebody asks what the hell we're doing.'

There was really no choice. Father Ramon pushed at Casimir's front door, which creaked open to admit us. One by one, those of us wearing sunglasses slowly removed them.

Inside the flat, total silence reigned. I couldn't even hear the humming of a fridge.

'Casimir?' said Father Ramon, hesitantly.

No one replied. It was very dark. Even so, there was enough light spilling across the threshold to show me that Casimir had taped sheets of cardboard over the windows. I could also see how bare the living room was; it contained one stool, one recliner chair, a portable TV on top of a milk crate, and a wooden desk supporting Casimir's personal computer.

'This place wasn't robbed,' Horace opined, as Father Ramon flicked the switch by the door. But nothing happened.

'Oh dear,' said the priest.

There was no bulb in the overhead socket. Vampires are extremely sensitive to artificial light; I realised suddenly that Casimir must have functioned quite well with only the TV and computer screens to illuminate his domestic environment.

That's why I offered to turn on both machines.

'I'll do it,' Dave said softly, and sidled towards them, step by cautious step. Sanford took the priest's arm.

'Just stand still, Father,' he advised, in an undertone. 'You might run into something, otherwise.'

At that instant the TV clicked on, brought to life by a jab of Dave's finger. Shots rang out and music blared; we all flinched like nervous chihuahuas. Frantically Dave scrabbled around for the remote, which he used to adjust the volume.

For some reason, however, that blast of noise had changed things. It had broken the spell cast by such a creepy, all-encompassing silence. We felt safer, and more courageous.

Horace, for example, suddenly marched towards the kitchen.

'There's no one in here,' he announced, peering into a

21

narrow, murky, unrenovated nook. 'Unless Casimir's hiding in a cupboard.'

Gently, Father Ramon shut the front door. Sanford headed for the bathroom. Dave and I peered through another door, into a space that looked pitch black from where we were standing.

'His coffin's in there,' the priest informed us. Whereupon Dave and I exchanged glances.

'You've got the best eyes,' Dave pointed out – and it was true. I have terrific night vision. Perhaps it's because I was infected at a younger age than anyone else in our group.

'I've found a candle,' said Horace, from inside the kitchen. 'Matches, too.'

But by then I was already stepping into Casimir's bedroom, where I almost fell over his coffin. It had been placed directly on the floor, you see, and lay much too close to the entrance. Upon crouching down, and running my hands over a large expanse of polished wood, I discovered an extremely handsome piece of funeral furniture with brass fittings, carved embellishments, and a lid that was divided into two parts.

I couldn't lift even one of these parts by myself.

'You'll have to help,' I told Dave, who was hovering around in a nervous manner, as if he expected something to come leaping out of the shadows. Obediently he squatted, his knees cracking.

'You don't think he's still in there, do you?' Sanford inquired, from the doorway. All at once the room was flooded with a faint, golden glow; I glanced around to see that Horace had entered, carrying his candle. He was shielding the flame with one hand, looking positively spectral in his black cape and frock-coat. His lank, oily, slicked-back

22

hair gleamed like a billiard-ball in the flickering light.

On either side of him stood Sanford and Father Ramon, their faces creased with anxiety.

'I don't know if he's in here or not,' was all I could say. 'But we'd better check, don't you think?'

Sanford gave a nod. Father Ramon made an approving noise. But Horace gestured towards a gigantic wardrobe that occupied about a quarter of the available space. Taped to one of its doors was a poster of Bela Lugosi.

'That closet's pretty big,' said Horace, uneasily. 'What if he's in there?'

'You should take a look,' Sanford suggested. Horace blinked, his face a study in consternation. Before he could think up an excuse, however, Dave and I raised the lid of Casimir's coffin.

Bang!

Then we dropped it again.

'What's wrong?' said the priest.

I couldn't reply. I had covered my mouth. Dave grabbed my arm suddenly, pulling me backwards as he straightened.

'Oh, man,' he groaned.

'What's in there?' Sanford darted forward. 'Is it him?'

'Oh, shit,' Dave rasped. At which point Horace relinquished his candle, thrusting it at Father Ramon. As the priest staggered, and I flinched, it was Horace who helped Sanford to raise the lid of the coffin again – exposing the grisly contents of that satin-lined box.

I'll never forget what we saw in there. Not ever.

A dense pile of ash lay pillowed on several folded sheets. This ash had been slightly disturbed by a puff of displaced air; a sharpened stake had also scored a deep trench through its powdery heart. But despite all this interference, there was enough shape left in the mound to tell us everything we needed to know.

The ash was so fine – so delicately moulded – that I could see Casimir's nostrils, and his earlobes, and his grin of agony.

There could be no doubt at all that he was dead.

Chapter Three

When I saw Casimir's remains lying there, I was appalled. I was shocked. I was very, very frightened. So were Dave and Sanford and Horace.

But we didn't feel bereft. That's something I have to make clear. We didn't grieve for Casimir because we didn't really like him.

It was Casimir, you see, who first brought the vampire infection to this country.

He left Europe at the end of 1907, alarmed by the growing number of people there who had been reading *Dracula*. After choosing one of the most isolated spots on earth as his destination, he disguised himself as an Egyptian mummy, lying dormant and well-wrapped for the duration of his long sea voyage. In January 1908 he arrived in Sydney, where his sarcophagus was delivered to the Australian Museum. And on the night of 23 January he was released from his temporary entombment by Horace Whittaker.

If you check out the vestry of St Agatha's on a Tuesday evening, you'll find yourself looking at a collection of vampires who wouldn't even be there, if it weren't for Casimir Kucynski. Either directly or indirectly, he was responsible for infecting every single one of us. Take Horace, for instance. Horace was an aspiring young archaeologist when he prodded at Casimir's bandages, down in that dank museum basement a hundred years ago. I've seen him in a sepia-tinted photograph, wearing a high collar and a silly hat; you almost wouldn't recognise his clear gaze, straight back and fresh face. Of course, it's possible that Horace was a bit of a reprobate even before he became a vampire, but I doubt it. I think he changed after Casimir bit him. I don't believe that the upright twenty-one-year-old in that picture would ever have considered making money off dodgy Internet scams.

Naturally, Horace claims that his money comes from a cutting-edge computer program that he designed several years ago. But I beg to differ. From some of the things that George has let drop, I figure that Horace is running an embezzlement ring out of their house. And one of these days we'll all get stung because of it.

At any rate, Horace was Casimir's first victim – though of course he wasn't the last. After attacking Horace, Casimir was able to escape from the museum and bite Gladys Blakers, who was a streetwalker at the time. In fact, before the end of 1908, Casimir had managed to infect fifteen people (most of whom are now either dead or living in Melbourne). He was not, however, directly responsible for infecting Sanford, Bridget or George. Those three suffered from secondary transmissions.

Sanford Plackett was the doctor who treated Horace a day or two after Horace became infected. In one sense Sanford was very unlucky; if he hadn't been stitching up a wound before his arrival in Horace's bedroom, Horace might not have attacked him. In another sense, however, Sanford was very lucky indeed. He had a jewel of a wife (named Maud) who was a former nurse, and who had also read *Dracula*. Together, she and Sanford quickly worked out what had happened. Not only that, but within a few months they had developed a crude 'digestive powder', which was an early prototype of the enzyme supplements that vampires take now.

You have to give Sanford his due. He might be a humourless, opinionated know-it-all, but there isn't a vampire in Australia who wouldn't have been worse off without him. It was Sanford who freed us from the necessity of drinking human blood. It was Sanford who started the Reformed Vampire movement. And it was Sanford who finally dealt with Casimir, confining him for more than sixty years in a strong-box under a cement slab. Sanford was also the one who located Gladys, Bridget and George – just in time to stop them from spreading the infection any further. Mind you, I'm not saying that *Bridget* would have bitten anyone. She was the nun who nursed Gladys at the Magdalene Hospice, after Casimir's attack, and she would have sealed herself up in a crypt rather than harm another living soul. But George was just a teenage boilermaker's apprentice when Gladys lured him into a dark alley. He was as brainless then as he is now, so he didn't know enough to stop himself from fanging other people, once he was blooded.

You won't understand about blooding, because it's a difficult concept to grasp. Basically, it's that moment when, as a vampire, you first smell fresh human blood and have to fight the urge to bite someone. Microscopic amounts of blood won't trigger the reflex; a flossing accident or razor nick won't send most vampires into a feeding frenzy, though I

27

have to admit that even grazed knees and hangnails make us feel uncomfortable. It probably takes about five millilitres of blood before the response kicks in. And then you have a choice: you can either give in to it or not.

George gave in to it once. He fanged a woman named Ethel (who was later murdered by her own family) before Sanford tracked him down and stopped him. The Placketts also looked after Gladys, and did their best for Bridget Doherty. Thanks to Sanford and Maud, there wasn't another case of infection in the whole of Australia until 1973 – when Casimir ran amok again.

In my opinion, he should never have been released from that strong-box.

I suppose you could almost say that it was Father Ramon's fault. After Maud died, Sanford was in a bad way. He was particularly upset that she had refused to become a vampire on her deathbed. So he turned to the priest for comfort. One thing led to another, until finally Sanford made his confession to Father Ramon. At which point the priest found out about the vampire buried under the cement slab.

Now, Father Ramon is a decent man. It's written all over his face. With his solid build, shaggy grey head and big brown eyes, he looks like an elderly labrador, seasoned and weary but not disillusioned. He spends a lot of time visiting sick people, organising charity collections and counselling wayward teenagers. It was therefore hardly surprising that he should have felt for Casimir, back in 1973.

Father Ramon was of the opinion that Casimir had suffered enough. So Sanford dug up the strong-box and slowly brought its contents back to life. After which that scheming, slimy, oyster-eyed Lazarus made a bee-line for the nearest pub – where Dave Gerace became his next victim.

Poor Dave had been playing a gig at one of the harbour-side hotels. He hadn't left until the early hours, by which time he'd downed just a few too many beers. In fact he was so legless that he never even realised what had happened; upon waking up in a gutter the next morning, on top of his guitar, he'd assumed that he was suffering from a really bad hangover, and had crawled home to spend the day in bed.

Luckily for his flatmates, he had lost his wallet near the site of the attack. Sanford and Horace found it there, half-hidden by weeds, the following night. So they were able to identify Casimir's victim, and pay him a visit before Dave was strong enough to do anything regrettable. I suppose they were pretty quick off the mark, really. I just wish they'd been a fraction quicker. Because if they had been, I wouldn't be writing this now.

Sanford was living with Casimir at the time, and was therefore well placed to monitor his guest's state of health. What's more, as a physician, Sanford had a keen eye for physical changes. It's normally impossible to disguise the symptoms of fresh human blood; a single mouthful can triple your strength, boosting your energy levels like a drug (or so I'm told). Dave's blood might have been adulterated by alcohol, but its effect on Casimir's metabolism was still noticeable. When Casimir returned home from his meeting with Dave, Sanford took one look at that two-faced louse and knew damn well what he'd been up to. But there was nothing to be done – not with daylight fast approaching. Forced into bed, Sanford wasn't able to lift a finger until he woke up again, by which time Casimir was raring to go. Still invigorated by the residual effects of Dave's blood, Casimir bolted. And Sanford couldn't stop him; it takes more than one reformed vampire to restrain another vampire who happens to be in Casimir's condition.

That's why Sanford was forced to pursue Casimir. That's also why he broke off his pursuit, very briefly, to call Horace and George from a public phone-box. Unfortunately, by the time reinforcements arrived, it was too late. I had already staggered out of a friend's place, unaccompanied, to vomit up the gin I'd been drinking. And Casimir had already stuck his fangs into me.

I'll tell you right now, that was my last ever drink. Though I was always a bit of a party animal in my early years, I've been as sober as a judge since 1973.

I haven't really had any choice.

So that's my depressing story. And Dave's. And Sanford's. And the rest of the group's. Is it any wonder that we weren't saddened by the passing of Casimir Kucynski? Is it any wonder that our immediate and heartfelt reaction was fear, rather than sorrow?

Because let's face it: as a vampire, the very worst thing that you have to deal with – worse than the isolation, and the indignities, and the health problems – is the fact that a large chunk of the world's population wants to kill you. *For no good reason.* (After all, if vampires were permanently attached to other people's jugular veins, the entire planet would be populated by vampires. And it isn't. Is it?) Not only that, but a large chunk of the world's population also knows *how* to kill you. Despite the vast number of stupid vampire myths floating around, most people nowadays have grasped at least one fundamental truth: to kill a vampire, you either cut off his head, plunge a stake through his heart, or stick him outside in the sun.

Apparently, Casimir had been staked.

'This is bad,' croaked Horace, who was the first to find his voice. And he rose abruptly, backing away from the coffin. 'This – this is a *slaying*.'

Father Ramon crossed himself. Sanford wiped his mouth, as if battling a sudden urge to throw up. His face was drawn tight.

'Keep calm,' he quavered. 'We have to think. We have to figure this out.'

'We have to check the wardrobe,' said Dave.

Everyone swung around to stare at the piece of furniture in question. I remember how my guts seemed to drop through the floor. I remember thinking: Is the killer in that wardrobe? If not, where is he? In the neighbouring flat? In a car downstairs? *What if he's outside, waiting for us?*

'We have to leave,' I said, hoarse with fear. And Dave's grip on me tightened.

'Shh!' he warned, as Father Ramon – our brave protector – advanced a few steps, his candle elevated, his eyes fixed on the wardrobe. But Horace stopped him. After briefly casting around for an alternative weapon, Horace had reached for the wooden stake.

'Use this!' he suggested, before his arm was knocked aside by a furious Sanford Plackett.

'There might be fingerprints!' Sanford hissed. Whereupon Horace scowled.

'*What*?' he squawked. 'Don't be so stupid!'

'It's evidence, Horace!'

'*Bite me*, Sanford!'

'Hello there!' said Father Ramon. Though his voice was steady, his hands were shaking; I could tell by the way the candle-flame flickered. 'My name is Ramon Alvarez,' he continued, addressing one of the cupboard doors. 'I'm a Catholic priest, and I mean you no harm. Why don't you come out and talk to us? We won't hurt you, I swear.'

There was no response. Not even a creak or a shuffle.

'Maybe we should fetch that stool from the other room.' Dave was talking under his breath. 'Or a knife from the kitchen . . .'

But it was too late. All at once the priest leaned forward, yanking open the door in front of him.

He jumped back just in time to dodge a long-handled spade.

It fell to the floor with a mighty *clang*, barely missing his toes. I must have screamed, because Dave began to pat me on the shoulder. 'It's okay. It's nothing,' he said, without much conviction.

Meanwhile Father Ramon had opened the second door, and the third. Behind each of them I could see jangling coat-hangers, discarded shoes, a collection of dowdy overcoats and a high shelf stuffed with shirts and towels and knitwear – but no lurking assassin. There wasn't even a muddy footprint, or a tell-tale hint of disarray among the contents of the wardrobe.

'No one's in here,' the priest said with a sigh. He bent to pick up the spade, which was encrusted with dried soil.

I wondered if Casimir had been burying his dead guinea pigs.

'Someone should call Gladys,' Sanford urged, sounding deeply shaken. 'Tell her to lock the doors and stay in the car.'

Almost without thinking, I fumbled in my pocket, searching for my mobile phone. Dave and Horace did likewise. But when Sanford plunged his hand into Casimir's ashes, I forgot about Gladys. For a moment I just stared in disbelief.

Because Casimir's face was gone. It had crumbled away beneath Sanford's touch.

'*What are you doing?*' I yelped.

'We can't let anyone find him like this.' Sanford's lips were trembling. His eyes were glistening. I'd never seen him so agitated. 'You know what will happen. We can't risk it.'

'Sanford's right.' Horace muscled in before I could object. 'Jesus, Nina, we don't want the police to see! What if they work out that Casimir was a vampire?'

I had to laugh, though it wasn't funny. Not the least little bit. 'There's a *coffin* in here, Horace!' I reminded him. 'Of course they'll work it out!'

'No they won't,' said Father Ramon, his expression grave and tired. 'They'll think poor Casimir was mentally unbalanced.' And he laid his hand gently on the coffin. 'What should be done with the ashes?' he asked Sanford. 'How should they be interred? What will the official cause of death be, in such a case?'

These were all good questions. Unfortunately, they were also hard to answer. Try telling the police that someone has turned to ash after being staked in the heart, and see how far it gets you.

'Do we have to tell the coppers?' I objected. 'We don't want them poking around. Suppose they come looking for us? Suppose they find Casimir's address book?'

Suddenly I stopped, appalled by a terrible possibility. If the *killer* had found Casimir's address book, then he (or she) might already know our names – and where we lived.

The same notion must have occurred to everyone else in that room at exactly the same instant. Because we stared at each other for two or three seconds, in absolute horror, before Dave croaked: 'Did Casimir even *have* an address book?'

Nobody knew. Not even Father Ramon. Horace began to claw at his hair.

'This is bad,' he shrilled. 'This is *bad*.'

'We have to go.' Dave was getting antsy. 'Right now.'

If he hadn't started jerking me out of the room, I would have agreed. For all we knew, Casimir's killer was in the neighbouring apartment, waiting to pick us off, one by one, as we made our exit. For all we knew, Bridget and Gladys and George were already dead.

But I hate the way people assume that I'm brainless, just because I look like a kid. I hate the way they keep pushing me around.

'And where are we supposed to go, exactly?' I demanded, shaking off Dave's hand. 'What if there *is* an address book? What if this slayer knows where to find us?' The full import of our situation hit me, then; it was like copping a bucket of water full in the face. 'Christ!' I spluttered. 'What about my *mum*?'

There was no immediate response. Even the priest was stumped; he stood dazed with shock and lost for words, exactly like the rest of us. I was thinking: *How can this be true? How can this have happened*? It didn't seem real.

Finally, however, Horace began to use his head.

'This guy is a slayer,' he reasoned, in a halting and tentative sort of way. 'If – if he used a stake, he must know his vampire lore. Which means he probably thinks that a crucifix will kill us.' When Horace discerned no spark of comprehension in the eyes of his audience, he added impatiently, 'We should go to St Agatha's. He won't be looking for us there. Vampires aren't meant to hang out in churches.'

'You're right.' I suddenly realised that we would have to start putting ourselves in the killer's shoes. 'Horace is right. We should go to St Agatha's.'

'But what about . . .?' Father Ramon didn't finish his sentence. He simply gestured at Casimir – or what was left of Casimir.

'That can wait,' said Dave. He didn't, however, inject enough urgency into his reply, which was pitched too low and phrased without emphasis. (Dave always talks as if he's ever so slightly stoned.) As a result, the priest remained unconvinced.

'What if somebody notices the damage to the lock?' he fretted. 'What if they investigate?'

'Can't be helped,' I said. And seeing him frown, I began to panic. 'We can't stay here, Father! Suppose the killer comes back? He might be watching this flat *right now*!'

I don't know whether it was my argument that persuaded him or my very obvious state of extreme distress, but Father Ramon needed no more urging. He followed Horace out of the room, which was instantly engulfed in darkness. Even so, I could just make out Sanford's huddled shape. He was crouched beside the coffin, spreading Casimir's ashes around. Something had snagged his attention.

'Come on!' I implored. 'We have to go, Sanford!'

'Wait. Give me one minute.'

'What are you *doing*?'

'Look.' He thrust his open palm under my nose. But the

light was too dim for me to see much, except a faint glint of metal. 'I think it's a bullet,' he said. 'It might even be a silver bullet. We shouldn't leave this.'

'Then bring it!' I was already halfway out the door. 'Bring whatever you want, only do it now! Quick! Because we *have to get out of here!*'

Don't ever believe that vampires are fearless. On the contrary. What happened to Casimir could happen to any vampire, at any time.

When the whole world hates you, fear becomes your friend.

Chapter Four

We weren't killed on our way to St Agatha's. There were no sinister figures lurking near Casimir's apartment block; nor were we followed by any mysterious, dark-coloured cars. During the entire trip, we didn't encounter so much as a red traffic light. And when we reached the vestry, we were able to examine Sanford's chilling discovery without fear of interruption.

It was a silver bullet, all right. A 9mm solid silver bullet.

'See? What did I tell you?' said Horace. 'This slayer's misinformed. He thinks a silver bullet is going to do more damage than a lead one. Which means that he won't be looking for us in here. Not in a church.'

'But I don't *want* to stay here!' Gladys snivelled. And Father Ramon said, 'You can't stay here. I'm sorry, but you can't. This is a place of worship. People will be in and out all day tomorrow. We can't have you cluttering up the vestry – you'll be seen.'

'There isn't a crypt we could use?' Sanford queried, without much hope.

The priest shook his head. He was occupying his usual seat, near a pile of plastic tubs full of old Christmas decorations. In fact we were all sitting where we normally did, and at first glance might have been holding our regular Tuesday-night get-together, surrounded by a familiar assortment of locked cupboards, dusty leadlight windows and piles of folding chairs.

On this occasion, however, there were no glazed eyes, slumped postures or smothered yawns. Nor was there any talk about 'owning your identity' or 'setting positive goals'. We hadn't gathered to discuss Dave's issues with his father, or Casimir's issues with the rest of the world, or my issues with having to attend group meetings in the first place. So the customary atmosphere of boredom, fatigue and resignation had evaporated; the air seemed to buzz with tension, and I remember clearly how confused we were. I remember how, as the shock wore off, most of us couldn't keep still. Bridget wrung her hands. Dave clawed at his hair, and Sanford paced the floor. I was chewing my fingernails, the way I always do when I'm on edge.

Never in my wildest dreams had I ever expected to run foul of a genuine vampire slayer. Blade and Van Helsing are fictional creations, after all; they're not supposed to be walking around in *real life*. They belong to the kind of fantasy world where vampires are dangerous, or at least very powerful. They belong to a world inhabited by hyper-evolved beings like Zadia Bloodstone – who has her own, special way of dealing with vampire slayers.

She always lures them to their doom with her cat-like grace, and husky purr.

'Okay,' said Father Ramon, assuming his customary role as facilitator. 'I guess we're all here now, so we should probably recite our Common Goal, just to kick things off. George – I think it's your turn, isn't it?'

Obediently, George took a deep breath. 'I swear,' he began, 'on all I hold sacred, that I will preserve my humanity in the face of temptation, and harm no living soul in the pursuit of –'

'Screw that,' Horace interrupted. He glared around at the rest of us. 'Forget the Common Goal. This isn't a group meeting, this is a Council of War.'

'Hear, hear,' I said. 'Something's *happened*. Casimir's *dead*.'

'But I don't understand.' Bridget whimper was barely audible. 'What kind of person would do such a terrible thing to poor Casimir?'

'Someone who believes all the lies,' Father Ramon sadly rejoined. 'Someone who's scared.'

'Someone who's read Nina's books,' Sanford snapped, and I turned on him.

'You think this is *my* fault?' I was ready to explode. 'Is that what you're saying, you *stinker*?'

'No.' The priest laid a hand on my arm. 'No one's blaming you. No one's blaming anyone.' He cut a reproachful look at Sanford. 'That wouldn't be useful.'

'You're lucky I'm here at all,' I spluttered, having suddenly experienced a flash of inspiration. 'Without me, you'd be stuffed. You'd have nowhere to go.'

'Huh?' said George. And Sanford stopped pacing for a moment, to look at me.

'Well, think about it.' I gazed around the room. 'This killer – he waits until daytime. He was too scared to attack Casimir at night, so he must believe that we have superhuman powers.' I went on to outline my theory: that the slayer, if he knew our whereabouts, would probably try the same technique with all of us. He would launch his attack during the day, when we were helpless. (Or at least, more helpless than usual.) 'But he won't be able to do it if my mum's around,' I finished. 'Because she won't let him in.'

Sanford frowned.

'Are you saying we should sleep at your place tomorrow?' he asked, and I have to admit that my hackles went up. Though Sanford's tone wasn't the least bit dismissive, he'd rejected so many of my proposals in the past that I was expecting a scornful reaction. So I braced myself for negative feedback as I growled, 'Unless you've got a better idea?'

Then the priest spoke. He sounded worried. 'It's a bit of a risk, Nina,' he said. 'This individual we're talking about – he's obviously deranged. What if he attacks your mother in an attempt to get at you?'

'He won't.' I was convinced of it. 'She won't let him in. No way.'

'But suppose he gets in regardless? He broke into Casimir's flat, remember.'

'That might have been pure luck.' In an unprecedented show of support, Sanford had decided to take my suggestion seriously. 'The security door at Casimir's had a pane of glass missing. And the whole building is probably empty during the day, while people are at work.' He stroked his moustache as he considered our predicament. 'Nina's house isn't like that,' he admitted. 'There are bars on the downstairs windows, and Estelle would be watching the doors. She'd have enough time to ring the police if an intruder tried to get in.'

Everyone stared at him, astonished. Over the years, Sanford has always been very emphatic about our need to avoid contact with the police. His thinking is that, while the authorities are duty-bound to protect us, they can't do it for every minute of every day – not against the host of weirdoes who are bound to make us their number-one target as soon as we're publicly identified.

'The police won't listen to an armed intruder,' he explained. 'Especially if he starts talking about vampires.'

'But he has a *gun*, Sanford.' The priest wouldn't be quelled. 'What if he uses it? He could do that without getting in.'

Father Ramon had a point. The gun had slipped my mind. With a gun, you don't have to be close to your victim. All you need is an unimpeded view.

The madman who had invaded Casimir's top-floor apartment could easily shoot my mother through the bars of her kitchen window.

'You know what? You're forgetting something.' It was Horace who finally broke the long, dejected silence. He wasn't addressing anyone in particular; his eyes skittered about as he glanced from face to face. 'This idiot uses silver bullets,' he said. 'Not only that, he uses a stake *and* a silver bullet. It's overkill. Nina's right. He's scared because he's misguided. Which means he won't believe that a vampire can live with ordinary people. Not without fanging them.'

Sanford chewed on his bottom lip.

'You mean –'

'I mean that he's been reading the wrong books. Like Nina's, for instance.' Before I could tell him where to stuff his brilliant ideas, Horace added, 'To this slayer, *all* vampires are unreformed, or why kill them? So we'll be safe with Nina's mum, even if he does have the address. He'll take one look at Estelle while she's putting out the rubbish, or hanging out the laundry, and he'll decide that there can't be any vampires in her house.' Upon receiving no encouragement from the rest of us, Horace finished by saying, 'You watch. I guarantee he won't even try to get past her. He won't think he has to.'

It was hard to disagree. I understood Horace's reasoning, though I wondered if we should view Casimir's killer as altogether rational. Suppose he refused to take chances? Suppose he had a 'better-safe-than-sorry' kind of approach to exterminating vampires? The fact that he'd used a bullet as well as a stake seemed to suggest that he might.

All the same, I saw no possible alternative to my mother's house. And neither, it seemed, could anyone else. Even Father Ramon had subsided; he sat gloomily rubbing the back of his neck as Bridget peered at him, seeking reassurance. Horace had folded his arms defiantly. Sanford was ruminating. Gladys was massaging her temples, eyes closed.

Dave was still inspecting the silver bullet.

'There's a stamp on this,' he suddenly observed. 'Some kind of trademark.' He raised his head. 'We might be able to trace the manufacturers.'

'And then what?' I spat. 'Tell them their product's a health hazard?' I shouldn't have been so snippy, but I was on the verge of hysteria. Dave must have realised this, because he didn't seem offended. Or if he was, he didn't show it.

He rarely does, even though I snap at him a lot. Even though I snap at *everybody* a lot. I don't mean to, and I'm not as bad as I once was, but it's hard to keep your temper when the vampires around you are finding every possible excuse not to get off their butts and *do* something.

Not that Dave's a shirker. In fact he was being extremely proactive, just then.

'If it's a mail-order business, it might have a customer list,' he remarked. 'Sometimes you can buy customer lists off a dodgy company. I've done it myself.'

'Yeah?' I figured that, since Dave ran his own mail-order business, he probably knew what he was talking about. 'You mean we can find out who bought this bullet?'

'Maybe.'

'We *have* to find out who bought it,' Sanford declared. 'If we don't, we'll be living like fugitives. We'll never know if this wretched maniac has tracked us down or not.'

'Or we could move, and change our names,' I said. Though I myself had never been forced to switch identities, most of the others had. And though I understood that the procedures for doing so were both complex and dangerous, I wasn't prepared for the groans of dismay that greeted my proposition.

'Oh, *Christ* no,' said Horace, and Sanford grimaced. Gladys wailed, 'I don't want to go through that again! Do we *have* to go through that again?'

'Not if we find this guy,' said Dave. 'If we find this guy, we can stop him.'

'How can we stop him if he's got a gun?' asked George, with unexpected perspicacity. (In general, George doesn't say much; he can barely *follow* conversations, let alone contribute to them.)

It was Horace who answered.

'Personally,' he snarled, 'I'd stop him by sticking his head in a toilet until he drowned.'

'Oh no!' Father Ramon was appalled. 'There'll be no killing, Horace. Nothing like that. Two wrongs don't make a right.'

Sanford quickly reminded us that we had faced such hostility before. Why, he himself had persuaded Horace's parents not to chop off their son's head. 'Communication is the key,' he insisted. 'We have to show this person that we're not a threat – that the media hasn't been fair to us.'

'You think someone like that will even *listen*?' I scoffed. 'What if he shoots first and asks questions later?'

'Nina, there won't be any meaningful dialogue if either participant is armed.' Sanford spoke with a kind of weary patience, like someone addressing a very small and stupid child. 'That's why we have to discover this person's whereabouts, and make sure he's not in a defensive mindset when we approach him. In fact it might be best if Father Ramon talks to him first.'

All eyes swivelled towards the priest, who shrugged and sighed.

'I suppose so,' he mumbled. At which point I cut in again.

'This is all very well, but you haven't even considered the most important question,' I said, scanning the room for input. 'Did Casimir blow his cover, or did someone hunt him down? Has he mentioned any names? Or what he's been doing?'

'Not to me,' said the priest. George shook his head. By screwing up her face, Gladys conveyed quite clearly that she had never been tempted to seek out Casimir for any purpose whatsoever – let alone a friendly chat about his daily activities.

Sanford appeared to be racking his brain.

'Casimir hasn't had his computer for long,' was Dave's comment, after an extended pause. 'Maybe we should be looking on-line.'

I have to admit, I was impressed. And I couldn't believe that the same thought hadn't occurred to me. It was so *obvious*.

'God, yes.' I rounded on Horace. 'What's Casimir been up to? You must have some idea – you gave him your computer!'

Horace squirmed in his seat, looking unbelievably shifty. At the sight of his discomfort, Dave and Sanford both stiffened, their eyes widening with alarm.

'Oh, man,' said Dave. Then he appealed to the rest of us. 'You don't reckon Casimir's been logging on to that bloody website, do you?'

It was an appalling prospect, which made us all gasp. Two weeks previously, Horace had mentioned stumbling upon a vampire website. The Net is full of vampire blogs and websites, which cater to fans of horror movies and fantasy novels. Sometimes these blogs are frequented by slightly disturbed people who dress like Horace and have an unhealthy obsession with gore. Never once have I sensed the presence of a genuine vampire amongst all the deluded, online chat about tissue regeneration and the covens of *Underworld*. On the contrary, it's all the most outrageous nonsense – and although it can be useful for someone who writes vampire fiction (like me), it's also dreadfully misleading.

I have to admit, I was always interested in Dracula movies. In fact I used to think vampires were pretty glamorous, until I met my first one. But since then I've become more and more disillusioned, as I've discovered that glamorous vampires just don't exist – except in books like the Bloodstone Chronicles.

That's why I hadn't been very interested in Horace's discovery. Not at first. (Why look for fantasy on-line when you could can produce it out of your own head?) But after hearing about the anonymous user who wanted to become a vampire, I'd changed my mind. Apparently, at least one crazy person somewhere in the world was looking for a vampire to bite him (or her). Nicknamed 'Fangseeker', this mentally unbalanced individual had provided an email address, and an assurance of complete confidentiality.

Horace had wanted to know if infecting Fangseeker could possibly be regarded as 'wrong', given the circumstances. He had seemed very disappointed when informed by Father Ramon that on no account should such a perverse desire be indulged. According to the priest, Fangseeker was clearly unhinged, and to take advantage of someone with a psychiatric illness would be inexcusable. There could be no question of reduced culpability, just because Fangseeker claimed to be a willing victim.

I could remember being quite interested in the discussion that followed. I could also remember being disgusted by Horace Whittaker's ill-concealed regret. But I couldn't remember a thing about Casimir's reaction – perhaps because I had always tried to avoid even looking at Casimir, if I could possibly help it.

'You didn't give him that web address, did you, Horace?' Father Ramon inquired anxiously. And when Horace gave a sulky nod, the priest covered his face with one hand.

'Oh, boy,' Dave moaned. Even Gladys was scandalised.

'*Horace*! How could you be so *stupid*?' she screeched, with such venom that Horace bared his canines at her.

'Are you calling *me* stupid?' he hissed. 'That's a laugh!'

'It was probably a set-up,' I interposed, having refused to be distracted by this pointless bickering. 'Someone's trying to lure vampires into exposing themselves. Don't you think?' I turned to Dave for support. 'We have to check Casimir's computer. We have to check his email.'

'How can we do that if we don't have his password?' Horace sneered, then addressed the room at large. 'Does *anyone* know Casimir's password?'

No one did. No one even knew his date of birth, or his nationality. (He'd always been very vague about both.)

'I suppose I could go and have a look around his flat,' Father Ramon finally offered. 'I'd probably be safe if I went back there during the day. But I'm not sure . . .' He hesitated, before turning to Sanford. 'What should we do about Casimir?' the priest wanted to know. 'Should we report him missing? Should we pretend that he's moved? Do you want the police involved, or not?' As we reluctantly focused our attention on this thorny issue, which hung over us like a dark pall, Father Ramon continued. 'If Casimir stops drawing his pension, or paying his rent, someone might get suspicious,' he said. 'And what if I'm spotted leaving the place? It's a problem, Sanford.'

'Yes,' Sanford conceded. 'It is.'

'As for poor Casimir . . . well, in a manner of speaking he's already entombed,' the priest finished. 'But I'd prefer it if he were laid to rest properly.'

By this time, I should tell you, the rest of us were very tired. After such a busy and emotional evening, we had lapsed into a state of torpor, and were finding it hard to concentrate. Perhaps that's why we couldn't decide what to do about Casimir.

What if the police decided to visit his flat?

'We can't let the cops get hold of Casimir's computer.' Horace was firm. 'God knows what's on his hard drive. Even if we can't sneak it out, we should destroy it. Plug it in, turn it on, and throw it into a bath full of soapy water. *That* should do the trick.'

'We can't leave those ashes, either,' I said. 'It might not be obvious what they are, but the police have all these forensic people, nowadays. They might be able to analyse stuff like that.'

'Anyway, vampire dust is very valuable,' Gladys piped up. When everyone stared at her in amazement, she was prompted to elaborate. 'Vampire dust has alchemical properties,' she went on. 'People do things with it. Curses, mostly.'

'Oh dear.' Father Ramon wrinkled his nose. He's always had an absolute horror of witchcraft. 'In that case, we shouldn't let poor Casimir fall into the wrong hands.'

Finally, after much fretful dispute, our plans were laid. Father Ramon would first collect the generous supply of emergency sleeping bags that were stored in his presbytery. He would then deliver them to my house, before returning home for a well-earned sleep. Finally, in the morning, he would proceed to Casimir's apartment, where he would destroy the computer and dispose of Casimir's ashes.

'You'll either have to dump them out the window or flush them down the toilet,' Horace recommended. 'You won't be so memorable, if you leave the place empty-handed.'

'But –'

'If you come out with anything at all, you'll look like burglar,' Horace said impatiently, dismissing Father Ramon's objections. To which Sanford's response was, 'Surely not, if he's dressed as a priest?'

Horace snorted. And I couldn't help butting in.

'Are you kidding?' I cried. 'If he's dressed as a priest, someone's bound to remember him.' I was so sure of this that I leaned over to grip the priest's arm. 'Don't wear your cassock, Father,' I begged. 'Just put on something bland.'

Wearily he agreed. Then Sanford began to delegate the various other tasks that faced us. Back at my house, Father Ramon's sleeping bags would be distributed over my mother's basement floor. Meanwhile, Dave would use my computer to track down the manufacturer of the silver bullet. Horace would also use my computer to communicate with Fangseeker, if possible. With any luck, some progress would have been made by daybreak.

If not, we would continue our search the following night. And the night after that. In fact we wouldn't give up until Casimir's killer had been identified.

'As long as he's out there, we're in mortal danger,' Sanford insisted, addressing us all in a solemn, self-important manner that – for once – didn't seem overblown or inappropriate. 'That's why we have to act as a team,' he said. 'That's why we have to work together for as long as it takes. Because if we don't, we might not get through this.'

It's funny; I hate so much about my life. I hate the cramps, and the nausea, and the boredom, and the listlessness. I hate surviving on guinea pigs, and not being able to get a decent haircut. But that night, when it came to choosing between life and death, I didn't hesitate. Not for one second.

I didn't want to end up as a pile of ashes on a bedroom floor.

Chapter Five

There's an abiding myth that vampires are afraid of garlic. This, of course, is a lie. The garlic myth was triggered hundreds of years ago, when a nameless vampire joked about not attacking some woman because she 'smelled of garlic'.

I mean, how could anyone be terrified of a culinary herb?

It's true that garlic makes vampires sick. But in that respect it's no different from bread or bacon or Brussels sprouts. A vampire's stomach isn't capable of digesting normal food; one slice of watermelon could put half a dozen vampires in bed for a week. Even stale blood can result in some pretty gruesome side-effects: not just stomach cramps and migraines, but continual vomiting, extreme dehydration, and a kind of slimy red discharge from the gums.

I've heard tell that Gladys once *begged* for a stake through the heart, after she stupidly dosed herself with horse-chestnut. The skin was peeling off her in powdery flaps, and her joints swelled up like balloons.

So it's important to be very, very careful. The only thing a vampire can absorb is fresh blood, straight from the vein (and even then, if it's animal blood, it has to be taken with special enzymes to counteract the impurities). But *you* try looking for a constant supply of live animals, and see how far you get.

It isn't easy – not unless you live on a farm.

Sanford's solution was guinea pigs. He made the choice about sixty years ago, and has stuck with it ever since. Guinea pigs are small, so their drained cadavers can be concealed without much effort. They're also fast breeders, and they aren't fussy about their food. Even more importantly, they can be kept indoors. And they're tough little things, in many ways. You don't have to be a genius to raise them.

That's why George Mumford was given the job of supplying each of us with our daily ration: one guinea pig, taken in the evening, with supplements. One guinea pig seems to be enough; as Horace often says, 'A guinea pig a day keeps Sanford away'. (If only it were true!) Thanks to George's excellent breeding programme, none of us have missed a meal for the last twenty-six years.

George moved in with Horace Whittaker some time around 1961. The residence they bought together was a spacious and solid brick bungalow with a wine cellar, a dilapidated conservatory, and six enormous bedrooms – so it was perfectly suited to raising guinea pigs. I went there once and it freaked me out; *I* certainly wouldn't want to live my life surrounded by animal pens. Nevertheless, despite all the droppings and the bad smells and the clouds of fur, it was an ideal set-up.

In fact the whole system's worked very well, right from the beginning. George discovered a new way of earning money. The rest of us secured a reliable source of live animals. And when Dave appeared on the scene, he was able to start making deliveries twice a week (for a modest payment).

There was only one drawback. Fresh blood can be messy stuff, and no one likes living in an abattoir.

You probably haven't seen a vampire fanging a guinea pig. For your sake, I hope you never do, because it's not a pretty sight. Guinea pigs tend to wriggle around, you see; since adulterated blood isn't good for us, we try not to drug them if we can possibly help it. That's why we sometimes miss the right spot, and end up with arterial sprays all over the wall. That's also why we tend to consume our meals alone, in tiled bathrooms. In fact I usually try to do it when Mum is asleep. And I always clean up afterwards.

Nevertheless, it's been hard for my mother – in all kinds of ways. Vampires make untidy house guests. They litter their domiciles with animal corpses. They stay up all night watching television, and surfing the net. They're always having medical emergencies. They're often too tired to pick up after themselves. And not all of them (let's face it) can be trusted. I mean, you only have to look at Casimir.

So although my mother is used to vampires, even *she* balked at the idea of having seven of them sleeping in her basement.

'For Chrissake,' she said, after our dire situation had been explained to her, 'this isn't a bloody hotel. Why don't you go to Rookwood Cemetery and find yourselves a nice mausoleum?'

She was only half-joking. I could hear a cranky note in her voice, and she stubbed out her cigarette as if she were squashing a cockroach.

Sanford, however, took her seriously. He has no sense of humour.

'A lot of very questionable people frequent Rookwood Cemetery, especially at night,' he said. 'Vandals and drug dealers and so forth. You wouldn't want Nina exposed to them.'

52

Mum blew a mouthful of smoke at his face. 'Nina wouldn't be exposed to anyone like that,' she retorted. 'Because Nina would be sleeping at home. As usual. I wouldn't throw out my own daughter, would I?'

'Give it up, Mum.' I wasn't feeling strong enough to sit through one of her rants. 'Either the others stay here or they all get staked. End of story.'

My mother grunted. She was sitting at the kitchen table, wearing a disgusting old nightie under her hideous quilted dressing gown. Though her dentures were in, she hadn't done anything about her hair.

My mother is only seventy-six, but at that precise moment she could have been ten years older. She's never at her best in the middle of the night.

'Well, all right, then,' she growled at last. 'I suppose I can't really say no.' From the arrangement of her features, I could tell that she was wondering how on earth it had come to this: how she, of all people, had ended up with a kitchen full of vampires. But the funny thing is that the kitchen and the vampires were a perfect match, because Mum isn't a granite-bench-top, stainless-steel-appliance kind of person. Her kitchen is all peeling linoleum and cracked tiles. It's clean, but it's not cheery. Everything that isn't black or brown is pale green, except the fridge – and that's so covered with trashy fridge magnets, you can hardly work out *what* colour it is.

In a dingy, well-worn, utilitarian environment like my mother's kitchen, vampires tend to fade into the background. They're all of a piece with the discoloured grouting, the ancient electric jug, and the baked-on grease stains in the oven.

'How long will you be staying?' Mum asked, eyeing

Horace as if *he* were a baked-on grease stain. But it was Sanford who replied.

'That depends,' he said. And Dave added, with a sidelong glance in my direction, 'The sooner we find this maniac, the sooner we can leave.'

He was prodding me, and I knew it. He wanted to start an Internet search as soon as possible.

So I hauled myself out of my chair.

'Come on,' I said. 'You'll be needing my password.'

'Wait.' Mum's voice cracked on a cough. 'Wait just a minute,' she croaked. 'No one goes anywhere until I lay down the rules.'

She went on to declare that her bedroom was out of bounds, that no one would be permitted to touch the washing machine, and that all guinea pigs were to be confined to the basement. Fanging was to take place in the bathroom *only*. No calls could be made from the kitchen phone. There would be a very strict policy about the distribution of keys, and every exterior door had to be deadlocked at all times.

'You can clean up your own bloodstains,' she finished, 'and work out a shower schedule. Two extra showers a night are the absolute limit – I'm not made of hot water. As for the lights, you can leave them off. Nina does, and I don't want the neighbours thinking I've opened a bloody backpacker's hostel.'

'But Nina has exceptional night vision,' Sanford objected. 'I'd be worried that Bridget might fall downstairs if she has to walk around in the dark.'

'Then she can stay in the basement.' Mum rose abruptly, pocketing her lighter and her cigarettes. 'In fact you can all stay in the basement, unless you absolutely *have* to be somewhere else. I don't want people banging around upstairs while I'm trying to sleep.'

Gladys pouted. Before she could start talking about her inalienable right to a daily scented bath, however, Dave was able to head her off.

'We'll try not to make too much noise, Mrs Harrison,' he promised, placating Mum with his husky voice and spaniel eyes. My mother has always had a soft spot for Dave, and you can't really blame her. To begin with, he's the sort of bloke mothers tend to like; he's neat, and polite, and soft-spoken, and he doesn't do drugs. (I mean, he *can't* do drugs; he couldn't if he tried.) What's more, he really admires my mum. His own mother abandoned him when he was two months old, so he's very respectful of mothers who stick by their kids. And to give Mum her due, she's always stuck by me. She might treat me as if I'm still fifteen, and bitch about everything I wear, and give me haircuts that make me look like Judith Durham from the Seekers, but at least she's stuck by me.

'I know I can trust *you*, love,' she assured Dave. 'It's not you I'm worried about.' And she fixed Sanford with a baleful glare, because she's never liked Sanford much. In fact from the very beginning she's regarded George as a moron, Bridget as a wimp, Gladys as a pain and Horace as a 'nasty piece of work'. (Can't say I disagree with her, there.) Sanford lost her good opinion the minute he told her to stop smoking, and as for Casimir . . . well, I'd better not tell you how she used to describe Casimir. You might be shocked. My mother's an ex-barmaid, you see, so she's picked up a lot of bad language, over the years.

Incidentally, if you're wondering how an ex-barmaid managed to afford a big old terrace house in Surry Hills, don't forget that Surry Hills used to be a real dump, thirty years ago. Besides which, until I was infected, my mother used to help pay the bills by taking in boarders. At one time we had three other people living with us: two country girls and a very shy Pakistani student.

Ordinary boarders are one thing, though; vampires are another. Reformed or not, they're still vampires. I couldn't blame Mum for being cross.

'We wouldn't ask you if we weren't desperate,' I pointed out, as she began to shuffle off towards the stairs. 'I mean, you do realise that it's a matter of life and death, don't you, Mum? You do realise how serious this is?'

'Of course I do, I'm not senile!' she snapped. 'I understand what's going on! I'm just not very happy about it, that's all.'

'Neither are we,' said Gladys, sounding resentful. Sanford, too, seemed put out.

'Casimir was killed today, Estelle,' he reminded her. 'Surely that merits a little sympathy? It was a very great shock for all of us.'

Mum sniffed. 'Should have happened a long time ago,' was her blunt rejoinder, which made Gladys gasp, Horace snicker and Dave choke.

'It could just as easily have been Nina!' Sanford protested. But my mother didn't agree.

'If you think I'd let anyone into *this* house with a stake and a silver bullet, then I don't know why you're here,' she said contemptuously. 'Nina's perfectly safe as long as I'm around. I once held off six drunken bikers with a cricket bat and a bottle of Guinness, so don't talk to me about self-defence.'

56

I can't tell you how many times I've heard about the infamous cricket-bat-and-bottle-of-Guinness affair. It's one of Mum's favourite stories. But before I could even roll my eyes, the doorbell rang.

'That must be Father Ramon,' Sanford conjectured.

It was. The priest had finally arrived. With him were Bridget, George and seven alpine sleeping bags, which were promptly carried downstairs and arranged across the basement floor. Sanford supervised this job, while Gladys complained about the smelly sleeping bags, and Mum made the priest a cup of tea.

I took Dave and Horace upstairs to my room. There I showed Horace my computer, which he hadn't seen before. To tell you the truth, he hadn't so much as set foot in Mum's house for at least twenty years; it was Dave who installed my computer, because Mum had always discouraged Horace from coming around. She's never been able to stand Horace. 'That slimy little bastard belongs in a spittoon,' was how she once expressed her feelings about him.

When he spotted my David Bowie poster, Horace smirked.

'This bedroom hasn't changed much,' he remarked. 'Anyone would think you were still fifteen.'

'Anyone would think *you* were still eight,' I snarled, as Dave settled into my office chair and booted up the machine in front of him. 'Just keep your greasy mitts off my things, will you?'

'Why do you still have a bed up here, when you sleep downstairs in an Iso- tank?' Horace queried. It was the sort of question you should never ask a vampire. It was hurtful. It was *cruel*. You might as well ask a paraplegic why she keeps her old sports equipment.

But despite the fact that Horace had hit a nerve, I wasn't about to let him know it. Instead I folded my arms and said, 'Why do *you* still bother brushing your hair, when no one would possibly want to look at your ugly mug anyway?'

Horace narrowed his eyes. Before he could think of a comeback, however, Dave interrupted us.

'Come on, guys,' he pleaded. 'Lay off. I know it's hard, but show some respect, eh?'

'For Casimir?' Horace scoffed, and Dave regarded him gravely.

'Casimir's dead, mate. We could all be dead soon, if we don't stop wasting time.' Dave shifted his attention. 'You want to log on, Nina?'

'Only if nobody looks,' I said, then glowered at Horace.

Dave got the message, of course. He averted his gaze. But I wouldn't enter my password until Horace was safely out in the corridor, because I didn't trust him. It was Horace, after all, who once terrified the rest of us by pretending to be an obsessed fan of the Bloodstone Chronicles. Having 'discovered' my street address, he kept sending me creepy letters until Mum and I were on the point of moving house. And when he finally came clean, he didn't apologise, or anything. Oh, no. According to Horace, he'd only been trying to demonstrate how risky it was, publishing books when you were a vampire.

After that, I decided never to cut him any slack ever again. That's why I banished him from the room, while I was entering my password. He was only allowed back in after Dave had launched an on-line search for silver bullets; within minutes, we were all three peering at the official website of an American company called Ranger's Inc.

You could order Ranger's Inc. silver bullets over the Internet, for fifteen dollars each plus postage.

'Here it is,' said Dave. 'Here's the trademark. This is where he got 'em – whoever he might be.'

'But who else buys them?' It troubled me that the demand for silver bullets was big enough to sustain a viable business. 'I mean, surely *every* customer isn't a vampire slayer?'

'Of course not,' Horace rejoined. For a moment I actually thought that he had something insightful to contribute. But then he drawled, 'Most of these people must be after werewolves. Though they probably wouldn't draw the line at shooting the odd vampire. What do you reckon, Dave?'

Horace has an irritating habit of teasing people as a form of stress relief. He was certainly teasing Dave, who had always maintained that werewolves might very well exist, though not necessarily in the form that populates most films and comic strips.

No one else shared this opinion. Not back then.

'Well . . . I reckon if there *are* any werewolves out there, they'd better watch out,' Dave replied. (As usual, he didn't rise to the bait.) 'Someone must be buying silver bullets, because this mob don't seem to supply anything else.'

Further investigation, however, uncovered the fact that Ranger's Inc. silver bullets were being promoted, not as ammunition, but as ideal gifts for police officers, computer programmers, and recently divorced men. It was possible to buy your silver bullet in a velvet-lined box, or attached to a silver chain. Special requests were also catered for.

'Like disguising your bullets as something else,' Horace suggested. 'You'd never be able to post them to Australia, otherwise. Would you?'

'Maybe if you pretended they were jewellery.' Dave was scribbling down a telephone number. 'Which they're mostly sold as, by the look of things. There can't be many people who buy them as ammo. Not at fifteen dollars a pop.'

'In which case, our loony should stand out like a sore thumb,' said Horace. 'He'll be ordering his bullets by the cartload.'

At this point Mum called my name, so I missed Dave's telephone conversation with the vice-president of Ranger's Inc. Instead I went downstairs to say goodbye to Father Ramon. Then I shooed Mum off to bed and arranged things in the basement. I filled it with kitchen chairs, card tables, and electronic equipment. I drew up a shower schedule and distributed cans of insecticide, in case the roaches became a problem. I even dug up a couple of old board games, a set of dumb-bells, and some movie magazines.

By the time I'd finished, I felt as if I had played four quarters of basketball. Though I could hardly stand up, however, I felt quite proud of myself. I felt that I'd exhibited a degree of energy and enthusiasm that you don't often see in a vampire.

But Dave had done even better. With just one phone call, he had managed to secure a printout of the Rangers Inc. customer list – for five thousand American dollars.

'*Five thousand?*' Horace cried, aghast.

'That's less than a thousand for each of us,' said Dave. 'I thought it was a pretty good deal.'

'But is the list even helpful?' I queried, and he looked slightly hurt, as if I'd been questioning his competence.

'See what you think,' he mumbled. 'If you ask me, it's pay-dirt.'

Upon examining the printout, I had to agree. Ranger's Inc. hadn't been doing much business in Australia during the past two years. Dave had underlined just five local orders. A Queenslander called Nefley Irving had purchased twelve silver bullets. Finian Pendergast, from Western Australia, had bought six. Two of the other customers had requested only one bullet each. And Barry McKinnon, of Wolgaroo Corner ('via Cobar, New South Wales') had ordered a hundred.

'*A hundred bullets?*' Horace exclaimed, when Dave had drawn our attention to this fact. 'What's he using, a machine gun?'

'That's got to be him,' I said. 'Don't you think? Sanford?'

But Sanford was frowning, and stroking his moustache. 'I don't know,' he replied. 'Cobar? That's an awfully long way away. That's near the South Australian border. It's not just a day trip – not for anyone coming to Sydney.'

'Then we've got a problem,' said Dave. When the rest of us stared at him, he explained that Barry McKinnon's phone number wasn't listed. 'Either it's ex-directory, or he doesn't have a land-line,' Dave reasoned. 'Which makes things pretty difficult.'

'What about the other customers?' asked Gladys. 'Did you try them?'

'Yeah.' According to Dave, Nefley Irving's number was disconnected. The Queenslander no longer seemed to be living at the address supplied by Ranger's Inc. And Finian's number had been answered by a machine. 'I didn't leave a message,' Dave concluded, in his slow, quiet way, 'because I didn't know what to tell him.' He scanned the basement, looking for help. 'Does anyone know what we're going to say to this guy?'

No one did. We hadn't got that far. After all, what *can* you say to vampire slayer?

How on earth do you persuade him to change his views?

'I suppose we'd better speak to Father Ramon before we make any final decisions,' Sanford said at last, with a sigh. 'We have to consider how to approach our suspects, now that we've narrowed down the possibilities.'

'We'll narrow them down a lot more if we make contact with Fangseeker,' Dave mused. 'The trick will be to find out where he's from. If he mentions Cobar, we're in luck.' Scratching his scrubby jaw, Dave turned to Horace. 'Why don't you go upstairs now, and send him a message?'

'At two o'clock in the morning?' Horace's tone was contemptuous. 'He'll be fast asleep, if he *is* our man.'

'It's still worth trying,' Sanford interposed. And everyone agreed.

So Horace went upstairs with Dave, to make contact with the mysterious Fangseeker. And the rest of us settled down in front of the television – because there wasn't much else we could do. Sanford suggested that we watch *30 Days of Night*, so that we could 'gain a bit of insight' into the mind of our adversary. But there are some things it's better not to know. By the end of that movie, we were more depressed than ever.

I can't tell you how sick I am of bloodsucking monsters with long yellow fingernails and no moral imagination.

'If *that's* what the killer's mind is like, then we're in trouble,' I said. And we all glanced fearfully towards the basement door. Outside it, somewhere not too far away, a ruthless murderer was lying in bed, either plotting his next act of butchery or dreaming about the last one, while we sat cowering in our underground hole as helpless as a litter of newborn guinea pigs.

Can you blame me for inventing Zadia Bloodstone? At least Zadia is in control of her life – unlike most vampires of my acquaintance.

Chapter Six

There's a scene in *The Redempionist* (Book One of the *Bloodstone Chronicles*) where Zadia is asleep in her ancient stone sarcophagus. The carved lid is fitted snugly in its proper place, because she's so strong that she never has any trouble moving it. She lies like a corpse as two blood-soaked mafia hit men lift the lid, grunting and straining under its immense weight.

Then the largest hit man leans towards her. He's holding a sharpened stake in one hand, and a wooden mallet in the other. But the blood on his shirt is still fresh; a drop of it falls on to her lush, ruby-red lips.

Suddenly her almond-shaped eyes snap open – despite the fact that it's still only half-past three in the afternoon.

I'm not proud of this scene, which is complete and utter hogwash. There isn't a vampire on earth who could be roused at 3:30 p.m., no matter what the circumstances. You could be dropped into the middle of a Viking massacre, and you'd still be as lively as an effigy on a tomb. Why? Because from dawn till dusk, whatever the time of year, a vampire is clinically dead.

If you examine me during the day, you'll see no movement whatsoever: no heartbeat, no brain activity – nothing. I look like an extremely fresh corpse. As for what I feel like . . . well, it's exactly like being anaesthetised. Exactly. You black out, and next thing you know, you're awake again. You don't dream. You don't hear things. You're not subconsciously aware of time passing. You disappear, and then you come back.

What's more, when you *do* come back, you feel just as tired as you did before you left.

So that's what happened to us all, the day after Casimir was killed. I lay down in my isolation tank, and the others zipped themselves up in their sleeping bags, and we lost consciousness until sunset. Then, just before six o'clock, we opened our eyes again. At which point we found out what had been going on during our absence.

Happily, my mother was still alive. In fact she had nothing whatsoever to report. The only person who'd come anywhere near our house was the postman, and he hadn't even slowed down. 'It was pretty boring,' said Mum, who likes to keep busy. (She's had a very active retirement so far, what with her volunteer hospital work, and her bridge club, and her pottery classes.) 'I ended up watching a lot of soaps.'

Father Ramon, however, had been fully occupied all day. To begin with, he had gone to Casimir's apartment, only to find that the police were there – having been notified of the broken lock by a nosy neighbour. While the priest had explained that he was 'worried about his friend', two uniformed police officers had inspected the broken lock, peered at the shrouded windows, and opened up the coffin. 'I hadn't done anything with the ashes, at that point,' Father Ramon admitted, when the subject was raised. 'But it didn't really matter.' The police, he said, hadn't been very concerned. After examining the coffin, they'd promptly decided that Casimir was mentally ill.

'They were very nice,' Father Ramon hastened to acknowledge, 'but I could see what they were thinking. They were thinking that Casimir might have wandered off without telling anyone, since he was obviously mad. They even asked if he could have broken the lock himself, because he'd forgotten his key.'

'So what are they going to do?' Sanford queried. 'Are they going to report him missing?'

'Not until tomorrow,' the priest replied. 'They told me to check with his friends, if he had any.' Father Ramon was looking pale and tired, as if his brush with the law had depleted him. 'The ash didn't trouble them at all,' he finished. 'One of them suggested that Casimir might have tried to fake his own death, and the other one laughed. They wanted to know if Casimir went around collecting ashes because of his illness.'

In other words, they had refused even to consider the possibility that Casimir's coffin really *did* contain his mortal remains. This was good news, of course, though it was also strangely depressing.

Personally, I find it rather hard to accept that I'm not supposed to exist.

Father Ramon went on to describe the rest of his day, which had been filled with vampire-related errands. On Sanford's advice, he had paid a quick visit to Horace's house – where he had found no broken locks or smashed windows. After feeding the guinea pigs (and selecting a few for our dinner), he had then checked Bridget's old butcher's shop on his way back home. Again, he had seen nothing suspicious. Sanford's place had yielded a similar result; like Dave's house, it bore no signs of forced entry.

This could have meant that our slayer had been busy at work all day. Or it could have meant that he didn't have our addresses. As Sanford pointed out, it was too soon to tell.

'We can't go home yet,' he declared. 'We should wait until the weekend, at least. Unless we find him beforehand.'

'And if we do?' I queried. 'What happens then?'

There was no immediate reply. My mother fished in her pocket for a cigarette; she was sitting at the kitchen table, opposite Father Ramon, with a half-drunk cup of tea in front of her. Bridget was perched on another chair, knitting. Gladys was absent-mindedly rearranging fridge-magnets, while Sanford paced and Horace yawned.

The whole room smelled of Mum's shepherd's pie, which was baking in the oven. I used to love shepherd's pie. I used to love fried fish, too. And ice cream. And coconut cake. But nowadays, even a whiff of cooked food just makes me feel slightly ill.

'If we do find him, then we should persuade him to see the error of his ways,' Sanford said at last, going on to concede that Casimir's killer might have to be restrained while he listened to reason. Bridget fretted about this; she wondered aloud if we should also provide refreshments, as a gesture of goodwill. And I was about to say something caustic along the lines of 'Why not just buy him flowers and chocolates while we're at it?' when a creaking, thumping noise indicated that someone was descending the stairs.

Soon Dave appeared at the kitchen doorway. He looked depressed, but that was nothing unusual. With his slouch, his pallor, and his mournful dark eyes, he always looked depressed.

We gazed at him in a state of high expectation.

'No message,' he reported.

Sanford sighed. My own stomach contracted; I didn't know whether to be disappointed or relieved. Mum said, 'Huh?'

'There's nothing from Fangseeker.' Dave propped himself against the door-jamb. 'Horace didn't get a response.'

'To what?' Mum asked, and I told her about our attempt to lure the on-line vampire fan into revealing something about himself. As I was doing so, George sidled into the kitchen. He was carrying a plastic bag; his expression was sheepish.

There were blood-spots on his khaki sweatshirt.

'Bathroom's free,' he muttered, when I had finished speaking.

We all exchanged glances.

'Who's next?' asked Horace. Receiving no reply, he climbed down from his stool. 'Then I'll go,' he announced. 'Unless anyone's feeling dizzy?'

No one was. My mother reminded him that there was a roll of zip-lock bags in the vanity cupboard, where he would also find the sponges and disinfectant. At this point she was on the verge of lighting up, because she normally doesn't worry about smoking around vampires. (It's not as if we'll die of lung cancer, after all.) But then she remembered about Father Ramon, and put her cigarette away.

'Incidentally,' Horace drawled, as he rearranged his black lace cravat, 'in case you make any decisions while I'm not here, just remember: I won't be going to Cobar. So you'll have to look elsewhere for a volunteer.'

Then he left the room, while the rest of us were still trying to work out what he meant.

The penny dropped soon enough, though. After a

moment's reflection, it dawned on me that Cobar *would* have to be our next step. Since one of our chief suspects was living on the west coast, and the other had vanished, Barry McKinnon of Cobar was now our most accessible target.

Cobar. As I inspected the pinched, pathetic faces encircling Mum's kitchen table, I realised that there wasn't a vampire in sight who had travelled more than a handful of kilometres in the past thirty years.

I tried to picture any vampire of my acquaintance making a trip to the outback, and failed. Vampires congregate in cities for good reason. It's not just because there's less direct sunlight in a built-up area; it's also because of the anonymity provided by an urban existence. After all, Sydney is full of junkies and alcoholics and creative people who don't sleep, rarely eat, and like wandering around at night. But in the dusty streets of a country town, where the shops all close at 5 p.m. and everyone knows everyone else's business, a vampire is going to stand out like a polar bear on Bondi Beach.

'Couldn't we just write a letter?' I proposed, appealing to Sanford. 'I mean, I realise this Cobar guy doesn't have a listed number, but surely we don't have to travel all the way to his house? Especially since he probably isn't even *in* Cobar. He's probably still here in Sydney, searching for us.'

'I wouldn't count on it.' To my surprise, Dave sounded quite authoritative. 'He might have come and gone. That might be why he didn't try to kill anyone today.' A pause. 'Unless – you know – he just wasn't in the mood.'

'But –'

'It's not *that* far, Nina. I checked. Cobar is only about a day's drive from here.'

'And I don't know if a letter is the best way to handle this,' Father Ramon interjected. 'The man who bought those bullets might not be the man who killed Casimir.' He went on to point out that if our letter should mention vampires, and was delivered to the wrong man, then we might simply be making things worse for ourselves.

Sanford agreed.

'Yes, we have to careful. Very, very careful,' he said. 'And fast, too. If we write a letter, it will take at least a week to get a reply.' He pursed his lips as the sound of a high-pitched squeal filtered down from the bathroom. 'What's more,' he added hurriedly, 'we can't be sure of the outcome. We don't know if this fellow in Cobar can read. We don't know if he's still living at the same address, or if he gave away some of his bullets. We don't know anything, really.' Sanford had been contemplating the polished tips of his sensible brown shoes; now he raised his head, and surveyed his dumbstruck audience. 'There's no alternative,' he concluded. 'Someone will just have to travel out there and investigate.'

I wish I could tell you that I reacted to this proposal like Zadia Bloodstone. I'd like to report that I nodded curtly and said, 'Count me in', adopting the kind of power stance that you can only pull off if you have a belt full of guns, grenades and nunchakus.

Unfortunately, I didn't do anything of the sort. Instead I thought about getting stuck on a country road at sunrise. I started wondering how much light would filter into a locked car-boot. And then I realised what was happening.

I was thinking like a vampire.

While the physical side of a vampire's transformation only

takes about thirty-six hours, the mental change is always a much more gradual process. Slowly you stop resisting. Slowly you lose your edge. You cease to engage with the outside world, as your feelers retract. Your interests become hopelessly circumscribed; your energy trickles away. In the end, you only care about the state of your stomach and the latest episode of some moronic television series.

It occurred to me that, if I wasn't careful, I would turn into a vampire. I mean, *really* turn into a vampire. Not physically, but mentally. Psychologically.

Even so, I couldn't bring myself to volunteer for any kind of road trip. And neither could Gladys.

'That's crazy!' she blurted out. Even my mum grimaced.

'Bit of a tall order, isn't it?' she said. 'Hotel rooms get cleaned every morning, and the blinds are always broken. I wouldn't stick Nina in a hotel room – not unless it had a bloody big safe in it.'

'What? Oh, no.' Sanford was adamant. 'There's no question of *that*. No, no, we couldn't risk using a hotel.'

During the pause that followed, everyone glanced towards the priest. I remember thinking that he was the perfect spokesman – that one look at his sober cassock and creased, pouchy, compassionate face would surely be enough to calm the fears of even the most rabid slayer. Besides which, he could drive a car. *During the daytime.*

He was the obvious choice of emissary.

Feeling all eyes upon him, Father Ramon ran a hand through his silvery thatch. 'You want me to go? Is that it?' he said. And there were nods all round.

'You can't make him go by himself,' Mum flatly objected. She stood up, then went to remove her shepherd's pie from the oven. 'You don't know *what* he'd be up against. It wouldn't be right. It wouldn't be fair.'

'Of course not.' Sanford's manner was stiff. 'I wasn't suggesting anything of the kind. Naturally, someone else would have to go with him. Someone who can drive, for instance. Someone like Dave.'

'*Me?*' said Dave, in faltering tones. Catching his eye, I thought he looked scared. Like a kid. Like a vampire.

Then all at once he squared his shoulders.

'Okay,' he rasped. 'I'll go.'

The rest of us gaped at him in astonishment. Before anyone could comment, however, Horace reappeared with a zip-lock bag full of dead guinea pig.

'Where do I put this?' he wanted to know.

While Mum was explaining that all guinea pigs had to be placed in the freezer until garbage-collection night, I slipped from the room. It was an act of pure cowardice. Being small, I was an obvious candidate for the outback road trip. Not only did I convey a distinctly harmless impression; I could also be folded into a car-boot or suitcase during the day.

It was a prospect that appalled me.

So I muttered something about taking my turn, and went to fetch a guinea pig from under the stairs. I won't tell you exactly what I did with that guinea pig, because after so many years I've mastered the art of detaching myself from the whole, repugnant procedure. I'll listen to my iPod. Or I'll take the radio into the bathroom with me, and concentrate on a talk-back show. Or I'll imagine something beautiful: like Zadia kissing a tall, handsome, teenage boy, for example, amidst the crystalline formations of the cave in which she sleeps.

That night, however, I couldn't distract myself from the misery of my situation. I remember stooping over the bath, with a dead guinea pig in one hand and a plastic bag in the other. Bloody drool was dripping from my mouth. My hair was matted with blood and saliva. I was a mess. A joke. And not only that: I was useless. I'd ducked for cover while Dave had stepped up to the plate. For years I'd been accusing the others of being typical bloody vampires, and now that the chance had come to act – to be *involved* – I had piked. I'd done what most vampires would do: which is, of course, nothing.

It flashed into my mind that maybe Casimir was better off dead. I thought: *What's the point of living, if you're a vampire?* I felt so pitiable. So *victimised*. Nevertheless, while it seemed monstrously unfair that someone should be attacking powerless invalids like me, I could also understand the sense of revulsion motivating Casimir's killer. After all, vampires made *me* sick. How could I blame other people for having the same response? I was in the unfortunate position of resenting behaviour that I could understand perfectly.

For several minutes I plunged deeper and deeper into an emotional black hole. Then, with an enormous effort, I hauled myself out again. I made a decision.

Like Zadia Bloodstone, I summoned up all my failing strength and prepared to do battle. Only I wasn't wrestling with a drug cartel or a protection racket.

I was fighting the infection in my veins.

'I'll go,' I said, upon re-entering the kitchen. 'I'll go with Father Ramon.'

Everyone stared. Sanford frowned. Dave slowly rubbed his unshaven jaw, as he always does when he's troubled.

'Oh, no you won't,' said Mum. She had just slapped a plate

of shepherd's pie in front of the priest. 'You'll stay right here.'

'I'm going, Mum,' was my firm rejoinder. 'It'll be good for me.'

'*Good* for you?' Mum exclaimed. 'It'll be the bloody *death* of you!'

'No, no.' Sanford once again surprised me by leaping to my defence. 'Not if we use a truck, it won't. The risk of exposure will be minimal.'

'A truck?' I echoed. 'What truck?'

It was promptly explained to me that the priest would be hiring a truck for his journey: a truck with an enclosed storage compartment at the rear, in which vampires could safely be stowed throughout the sunlit hours of the day. As long as this storage compartment was properly sealed – and fully secure – it would be the perfect solution to our difficulties.

'We could even line the interior with black plastic,' Sanford remarked, as my guts unclenched slightly. *Thank God*, I thought. *They won't be putting me in a car boot.*

'It'll cost a bit, though,' Horace protested. And there followed an argument about funding, because he didn't want to shell out any more cash. I'm afraid we have this kind of argument quite often. Gladys doesn't earn very much, you see, and neither does George. Bridget augments her pension by making handicrafts for a local gift-shop. (They're mostly knitted animals and quilted place-mats.) Dave isn't exactly rolling in money, either, though he tries to do his bit. And despite the fact that I manage to get by, it's not as if my books are runaway best-sellers. I mean, it's not as if I'm *Stephanie Meyer*, or anything.

Sanford and Horace are by far the richest members of our group. But after they had spent several minutes bickering about who was going to hire the truck, I couldn't take it any more. 'Let *me* pay,' I said. 'Since I'm the one who'll be using the damn thing.'

'And me,' Dave added. 'Since I'll be going as well.'

Two passengers, however, would be the absolute limit. According to Sanford, there would only be enough room for three people in the cabin of the truck. And even then, it would be a tight squeeze.

'Which is another reason why Nina is such a good candidate,' he said. 'She's small, she's childish and she's not intimidating. If it's a question of laying someone's fears to rest, she's a much better prospect than Horace or George.'

Talk about a backhanded compliment. 'Gee, thanks,' I growled. But no one paid any attention. I don't think my mother heard me at all; she was busy trying to convince Sanford that Bridget looked even more harmless than I did, what with her sparse white hair and rickety limbs and tranquil blue eyes. Who could ever view Bridget as a threat? But Sanford wouldn't hear of sending Bridget. ('You know perfectly well what her hips are like,' he said crossly.) And no one else was on Mum's side, either.

Not even me.

'I'll be all *right*, Mum,' I insisted, though I still had grave doubts about the entire undertaking. 'I'll have a sleeping bag, and it'll only be for a couple of days. I'll be fine.'

My mother doesn't take kindly to being contradicted. Her lips thinned, and her eyes narrowed. After swallowing a mouthful of shepherd's pie, she insisted that she herself should go.

But I shook my head.

'You have to stay here, in case the killer shows up,' I retorted. 'Besides, I don't want to sit on my arse while other people do all

75

the work, and take all the risks. I'm not a child. I'm a responsible adult, with something positive to contribute.'

In other words, I wasn't your typical vampire.

You might believe that my head was full of Zadia Bloodstone when I volunteered for the trip. I'm quite sure that everyone else did. Horace even muttered something about my 'strapping on the old skean dhu' (referring to the Scottish dagger that Zadia customarily employs). But I wasn't thinking about Zadia at all. I was thinking about Casimir.

Casimir had been a typical vampire – the quintessential vampire, in fact. And look what had happened to him! Whereas I . . . well, I was different. I was active and empathic and dependable and involved. I wasn't anything *like* Casimir.

It's funny what lies you tell yourself, when you're scared to death.

Chapter Seven

For my trip to the country I packed the following items: one toothbrush, one tube of toothpaste, one comb, two sets of underwear, two pairs of tights, two jumpers, two skirts, and as many blouses as I could stuff into my old Globite suitcase. I also took my pink coat, my sunglasses, my woolly beret, and all my various supplements.

My guinea pigs, however, travelled in their own hutch.

There had been a lot of discussion about the advisability of taking guinea pigs. On the one hand, guinea pigs are dirty and troublesome, and require constant feeding. On the other hand, they're a much safer option than farm animals. When Horace wondered if Dave and I should perhaps start fanging sheep, the suggestion was vetoed. 'Do you seriously think that Nina would have the strength to chase a sheep around a paddock?' Sanford scoffed. 'I've seen her lose her breath after climbing three flights of stairs.'

So in the end Father Ramon loaded four guinea pigs into the back of his rented truck, together with a wooden hutch, some old newspapers, and a bag full of food pellets and lettuce leaves. Though we were all slightly worried about the storage compartment's inadequate ventilation, we had to concede that it would certainly help to muffle any tell-tale squeaks or squeals.

'I mean, it's not as if those animals are going to live very long,' Horace pointed out. 'And if they suffocate before they're fanged, so what? No one's actually going to starve to death as a consequence.'

Sanford grunted. He doesn't approve of missed meals – not after seeing what six decades under a concrete slab can do to a vampire. When Casimir was finally released from his underground confinement, back in 1973, he looked just like a bog-mummy. He couldn't even blink for a week. His tongue was kippered, his teeth were loose, and his eye-balls had shrunk to the size and consistency of dried peas. It was a month before he could string three words into a basic sentence.

Whenever the rest of us lose our appetites at the prospect of fanging yet another unfortunate guinea pig, Sanford always drags out his 'before-and-after' photographs of Casimir.

'If the situation gets desperate,' Sanford advised me, 'then a pig is your best alternative. Better than a sheep or a cow. But steer clear of rodents; they're nothing but trouble.'

'I know that, Sanford. Don't worry.' Standing by the front door, surrounded by apprehensive, whey-faced vampires, I was suddenly desperate to go. I'd had my fill of Sanford's ponderous counsel. Even a trip into the unknown seemed less arduous than sitting through yet another lecture about speed limits or bad mobile reception. 'Goodbye, Mum,' I said, stepping forward to give her a hug. 'Don't you worry, either. I'll be back before you know it.'

My mother didn't reply. She didn't have to; her rickety frame was stiff with disapproval, even as she patted me on the back.

When I let her go, she folded her arms and hunched her shoulders.

'It's all right, Mrs Harrison.' Dave must have been under the impression that a lump in my mother's throat had rendered her speechless. He can't have seen the angry glint in her eye. 'Nothing will happen to Nina. I'll take good care of her.'

I couldn't suppress a snort, and even George looked doubtful. It was hard to see Dave as a bodyguard. Despite his shaggy hair and impressive height, he's always been remarkably unassertive – not to mention squeamish. In fact he's the only one among us who's ever risked public exposure by illegally purchasing human blood from a hospital orderly. And he did this, not because stale human blood is a better option than the fresh animal variety (it isn't), but because he's never been too happy about those nasty, messy sessions in the bathroom.

I suppose, when you think about it, he's quite a sensitive person in many ways. In fact it's probably no coincidence that he stopped playing his guitar after he was infected. Something about a vampire's life managed to 'block his creative flow' (as Sanford once put it). As far as I'm concerned, you have to be pretty sensitive to have a creative flow at all, let alone a blocked one.

'Yes, you mustn't fret about us.' Father Ramon tried to sound reassuring as he laid a hand on Mum's shoulder. 'Your job is to take care of yourself. Mind you don't open the door to anyone while we're gone. Not even if they're collecting for a charity.'

'Oh, I won't,' Mum assured him.

'We'll be back on Sunday,' said the priest, who was determined not to disrupt the parish schedule any more than he had to. 'By that time,' he added, 'I'll have worked out what to do with Casimir's ashes.'

'Good,' said Mum. She wasn't happy about the two bulging plastic bags that were now squirrelled away in her laundry cupboard. Only Father Ramon could have persuaded her to take them (after he'd dragged them out of Casimir's apartment, that morning); if *Sanford* had tried to give them to her, she would have thrown them right back in his face. 'Because I don't want that creature lying around here,' she continued. 'Not even in the rose-beds. I wouldn't trust him as far as I could spit.'

'Mum – he's dead,' I assured her, for perhaps the tenth time. 'Casimir's *dead*, now.'

But she still looked unconvinced. And I suppose it's understandable, really – since dead vampires are few and far between.

'Here,' said Sanford, pressing the silver bullet into Father Ramon's hand, 'don't leave this behind. You might need it.'

'Oh. Yes.' The priest sounded faintly apologetic. 'I almost forgot.'

'We'll ring you if we get any response from that Internet maniac,' Sanford went on, 'though if he hasn't replied by now, I don't suppose he will. And Horace will keep an eye on the Internet, just in case there's any mention of Casimir's passing.'

A brief silence fell as we all contemplated the dreadful possibility of global exposure. After all, there was nothing to stop our adversary from plastering photographs of his handiwork all over the World Wide Web. (Except, perhaps, the fear that he might be risking attack from the hoard of super-vampires peopling his imagination.)

'As long as no one posts our addresses,' Dave mumbled.

Horace made a dismissive noise.

'That slayer doesn't know where we live,' he insisted, with the kind of arrogant assurance that makes other people want to kick him in the crotch. 'We would have seen him, if he did. He would have tried to break into someone's house, but he hasn't – even though it's been two whole days. If you ask me, he's gone back to where he came from.'

'Nobody *did* ask you, Horace,' Mum snapped. And Sanford patiently reiterated that we couldn't be sure of anything until the weekend, since a lot of people worked during the week.

'But Casimir was killed on a Tuesday,' Horace began, before Gladys interrupted. As usual, she wanted to complain about something.

'I *have* to be home before Monday,' she whimpered. 'I'll lose my job, otherwise. They only gave me one week's leave, and I almost didn't get that.'

She went on to grumble about the shower schedule, but no one was very sympathetic. Gladys can keep griping for hours on end, so it's best not to encourage her.

'Do we have to discuss this now?' I objected, cutting her off in mid-whinge. 'We'll never get *anywhere* at this rate.'

'Yes, we shouldn't linger,' Father Ramon agreed. 'It's going to be a long trip, and the sooner we get there, the sooner we'll get back.'

When I picked up my suitcase, it was like a signal. There was a sudden burst of activity. Father Ramon pulled open the front door. People fumbled for their sunglasses. George murmured something about taking good care of the guinea pigs, while Bridget produced three woollen scarves that she'd knitted the previous night. 'Just in case you get cold on your trip,' she explained, in her whispery voice.

Sanford insisted on carrying my case to the truck, even though he isn't much stronger than I am.

To be honest, although we referred to it as a truck, the vehicle parked in the street was actually a small removals van, with 'Saxby's Hire & Haul' painted on its fluorescent orange sides. According to Father Ramon, Saxby's hadn't been able to offer him a more muted shade, because fluorescent orange was the company's official colour.

'We'll probably be noticed anyway, out in the country. No matter what we're driving,' he'd said. Nevertheless, he'd replaced his cassock with a dark grey jumper and a pair of jeans, to make himself a bit less conspicuous.

Dave and I were also wearing our most harmless-looking clothes. We didn't want anyone to think that we were junkies, or university students, or creative nonconformists – let alone vampires. We didn't want to attract attention.

'Well . . . goodbye, then.' I blew a kiss at my mum, who had accompanied Sanford out of the house. Then I waved at the others – at Bridget and Horace and Gladys and George – who were still hovering on the threshold, peering at me through their sunglasses. 'Take care of yourselves, and we'll see you on Sunday.'

'Don't do anything stupid,' Mum warned, as I climbed up into the van's rather smelly cabin. 'Just do what Father Ramon says.'

'I will.'

'Maybe you should take a cricket bat, or something,' she fussed. But Father Ramon shook his head.

'How are we going to persuade anyone that we're harmless, if we're carrying cricket bats?' he said gently. 'Believe me, Estelle, I'll be very careful.' He looked over to where

Dave was loading luggage into the back of the van. 'Perhaps you could take the first shift, Dave, and let me grab a few hours' sleep,' he concluded.

Dave had no problem with that. He caught the keys that were tossed to him, and locked up the storage compartment. Meanwhile Father Ramon exchanged a few words with Sanford, before hoisting himself into the seat next to me. Then Dave slid behind the steering wheel.

Doors slammed on both sides of the cabin; I found myself suddenly hemmed in. For a moment Dave sat thoughtfully contemplating the dashboard, as Father Ramon lifted his hand to Sanford.

'Keep in touch,' said the priest.

'I will,' Sanford promised gravely.

At which point the engine roared and the headlights flicked on. When Dave released the hand-brake, I knew that there was no going back.

I was on my way.

'*Bye, Mum!*' Frantically I flapped my hand, leaning across Father Ramon to catch my last glimpse of her. It could have been quite a traumatic moment, but Father Ramon was very smart. Before I could even digest the fact that I was off on a perilous mission, he shoved a street directory into my hands.

'I'm going to be asleep,' he said, 'so you'll have to navigate. You need to get us on to the motorway. Once we're across the mountains, you'll be needing *this* map.' He began to unfold an enormous sheet of paper. 'Can you see it properly?'

'Oh, yes.' Even the feeble glow emanating from the dashboard dials was enough for someone with my highly developed night vision. 'Which road are we taking? This one here?'

'That's right.' The priest traced his finger along a wavering red line, rattling the stiff paper as he did so. 'We'll be going through Dubbo, towards the Barrier Highway.'

'Dubbo!' I stiffened. 'That's where my dad came from!'

It was a reflexive comment, with nothing emotional about it. But the two men exchanged glances over the top of my head.

'Uh – yes.' The priest's delivery was hesitant. 'Does that bother you, Nina?'

'No. Of course not.' I was surprised that he would even ask, because we had discussed my father often enough in our group meetings. For your information, my father was a waste of space. He left Mum the minute he heard that she was pregnant, and died two years later in a car crash. According to Mum, he'd been driving under the influence, and had run headfirst into a telephone pole.

'It's no big deal,' I assured the priest. 'My dad never meant anything to me – you know that. He was just some bastard who didn't have the guts to hang around after he got my mother knocked up.'

The words were barely out of my mouth before I realised that I'd dropped a huge clanger. But then I made it even worse by trying to correct my mistake. Hurriedly I assured Dave that I wasn't accusing *him* of being a bastard, like my dad. 'I mean, it wasn't the same for you, was it?' I said haltingly. 'You were much younger than Dad was, and – um – well, you were only seventeen, weren't you? Just a kid, really. Not old enough to be a father, even if that girl's parents had actually let you be one, which of course didn't happen.' When Father Ramon nudged me in the ribs, I made a clumsy attempt to shift topics, inquiring if Dave had brought along any compact discs. (Being a dealer in second-hand music, he tends to like a soundtrack when he's driving.) 'I don't mind *what* you play, as long as it doesn't put you to sleep. Ha-ha,' was the best that I could manage.

Sometimes I wonder how other people put up with me.

Dave produced a crooked half-smile. 'I don't think Father Ramon will get much sleep if we play any of my CDs,' he observed, without taking his eyes off the road. It was a grisly moment. God, I felt bad. Because if there's one thing that Dave regrets more than anything else, it's the way he abandoned his pregnant girlfriend, some thirty-odd years ago. Not that it was entirely his fault. She was only sixteen, and her parents moved her away (out of Dave's reach) when they discovered that she was pregnant. Apparently she wrote to him once or twice, but by then he'd dropped out of school to play in a band; his life was all sex and drugs and rock 'n' roll, at that stage, and he didn't write back.

Maybe he would have, eventually. Maybe, if he'd been given a few more years, he would have matured enough to start behaving like a real dad. Maybe he would have tried to forge a connection with his son or daughter – who now, oddly enough, must look twice as old as Dave does.

But then Casimir showed up near that harbourside hotel. And by the time Dave started to feel remorse for what he'd done, it was too late. He was already a vampire.

The rest of us have tried telling him that a lot of young blokes find it hard to shoulder parental responsibility. We've reminded him that he hasn't dumped a girlfriend for more than three decades (that he hasn't, in fact, even *had* a girlfriend since 1973). We've even pointed out that he shouldn't feel bad for not making peace with his own dad, who was a selfish, abusive, alcoholic dickhead.

Poor old Dave, however, seems to have a permanently inflamed conscience about his past. Nothing will ever lessen the guilt he feels about deserting the mother of his unborn child. And what makes it even worse is the fact that he can't have any more kids, because vampires aren't capable of reproducing. Not in the normal way, at least. We can only pass on our infection.

It's a pretty dismal state of affairs for every one of us. But Dave has always found it particularly depressing. Even certain pieces of music tend to set him off. I remember he once took me to the Tuesday meeting, when Father Ramon's car was being fixed, and Marianne Faithfull began to sing *As Tears Go By* on the radio. Dave immediately plunged into such a black mood that everyone else talked about it for the entire meeting. Father Ramon speculated that Dave had abandoned his old girlfriend in the flesh, but not in the spirit. Sanford observed that, in Dave's mind, she probably represented the Unattainable Past. Horace stressed the importance of getting over someone who was probably a grandmother by now, and who wouldn't look twice at a weedy, listless, wax-faced vampire anyway.

Personally, I didn't play a big part in that discussion. I was feeling too miserable, for various reasons that I won't go into. And Dave didn't say much either, because he never discusses his old girlfriend if he can possibly avoid it. That's one reason why I pegged him for a broken-hearted romantic casualty, quite early on. That's also why I shouldn't have mentioned my dad to him, on the way to Cobar. Sometimes I can't help thinking that Dave blames *himself* for what Dad did. It's very odd.

Disheartened by Dave's continuing silence, I sought help to clear the air. I appealed to Father Ramon.

'Is that right, Father? Would you prefer it if we didn't play any music?' I asked, in pure desperation. And the priest nobly came to my rescue.

'Oh, don't worry about keeping *me* awake,' he said. 'I can sleep through anything. I've slept in puddles. I've slept through earth tremors. I've slept beside the world's noisiest two-stroke engine –'

'In South America?' I inquired, and he nodded.

'When I was doing mission work,' he acknowledged. Occasionally he'll provide you with titbits about his eventful youth, talking about gunfire during a funeral, or floods in a slum, or how he once had to perform an exorcism. But he clearly wasn't about to recount anything of interest that night. On the contrary, having decided that he'd done his level best to improve Dave's spirits, he yawned and arranged himself for a nap, placing Bridget's folded scarf under his head.

'Wake me at four,' he said. 'We need to make sure that you're all wrapped up before daybreak.'

Then he sniffed, wriggled, cleared his throat and closed his eyes.

For a few minutes after that, Dave and I didn't speak. There didn't seem to be much point, since he was in one of his morose moods, and I had run out of distracting ideas. Together we gazed out at the unfolding vista of glowing shop-fronts, deserted side-streets, fast food outlets, bus-shelters, traffic islands, nature-strips and tail-lights. Car yards began to proliferate; the road became wider. I could no longer see into people's living rooms, which were shielded by screens of foliage. Illuminated signs warned us about approaching exits, as the lanes in front of us multiplied.

Then suddenly great walls of concrete reared up on either side of our route. And I realised something that prompted me to break the extended pause.

'You know what?' I said softly. 'This is all new. I've never seen this before, have you?' When Dave shook his head, I looked out again a landscape that was undeniably and inescapably foreign, filled with wonder at the scale of what I'd missed. 'I haven't been this way in thirty-five years,' I breathed, as Dave nervously checked the rear-view mirror.

But there was no one behind us.

Chapter Eight

I'll never forget that trip to Cobar. It was a revelation. Once we'd left the city behind, the space outside our truck became endless. A cloudless, starry, immeasurable expanse arched above us. Densely wooded hilltops stretched on forever. The road ahead seemed infinite as it unfurled like a black-and-white ribbon in the glow of our headlights.

Barrelling along, I was filled with a strange and unfamiliar sense of freedom. I suppose it's common enough to feel this way when you're on the move, but you have to remember that I normally don't get out much. Even the air that wafted through our open windows had a wildly invigorating freshness to it.

After crossing the mountains, we reached the edge of the Great Western Plains. And I couldn't suppress a cry of wonder as I gazed down at a view that most people wouldn't have been able to see, in the middle of the night.

'Wow!' I exclaimed. 'Just look at that!'

'Uh – yeah.' Dave's tone was distracted, because he'd reached a very steep slope that was hard for him to navigate.

'Do you think there's a lookout somewhere?' I asked. 'Do you think we could stop?'

'Maybe. I dunno.'

'We ought to stop soon. It's important to take a break every two hours when you're driving.' I glanced at him doubtfully. 'Besides, you're not used to long hauls like this. You must be getting pretty tired.'

'I'm okay.'

'Are you sure?'

'I'm sure.'

'When did you learn to drive one of these things, anyway? Did your band have its own bus, or what?'

'We had a van,' Dave revealed.

'With graffiti all over it?' I always liked to hear about Dave's short-lived musical career. Before I was infected, all I really wanted to do (besides marry David Bowie) was get into a hotel and see a genuine pub band. Now that this ambition had been well and truly torpedoed, I was eager to hear more about Dave's experience as a rock-and-roll guitarist.

The trouble was, he preferred not to discuss that stage in his life. I always used to wonder if it reminded him too much of his former girlfriend.

'We had stickers on our van, not graffiti,' he mumbled.

'Oh yeah? What did they say?'

'Dumb things,' he replied, looking vaguely embarrassed. 'You wouldn't want to know.' Then he flicked an uneasy glance at the priest.

But Father Ramon hadn't been disturbed by our chatter. Clearly, he *was* able to sleep through anything; in fact he didn't even wake up when we narrowly avoided hitting a fox on the road. Though Dave braked hard, and I yelped, and the engine stalled, Father Ramon slumbered on peacefully.

After that, I didn't bother keeping my voice down. I felt free to exclaim at the moonlit views, and to complain about potholes, and to comment on the farmhouses that we passed. Dave didn't say much. He's never been a hugely talkative person, and driving in the country must have been quite a challenge after thirty-five years spent pottering around suburban backstreets. At last, however, he proposed that we discuss our plans.

'We haven't decided what we're going to tell this Barry McKinnon guy,' he observed. 'If we show up on his doorstep, and he's actually there, what's the procedure? Do we mention those bullets straight off? Do we explain how we found him? Or do we go in undercover, so we can search his house when he's not looking?' Dave's long face grew longer as he contemplated this last scenario. 'I suppose we could pretend that we've broken down,' he said, 'and ask to use the guy's toilet.'

'Yes. I suppose we could do that.' For the first time I really focused on the task ahead; until that instant, I had been more concerned about our journey than our destination. I tried to imagine the mysterious Barry, who lived in the middle of nowhere without a phone. I tried to imagine knocking on his front door at ten o'clock at night.

I tried to picture a welcoming grin – a friendly reception – and I couldn't.

'This is going to be hard,' I muttered.

'You're not wrong.'

'What do *you* think we should do?'

'I dunno.' Dave scratched his jaw. 'Hard to say, until we get there.'

'If we see garlic and crucifixes all over the place, then we'll know where we stand,' I remarked, and he gave a sour little smile.

'Yeah. That would make things a lot simpler. Scarier, but

simpler.'

'We could tell the truth, in that case. We could just introduce ourselves, and explain why we're no threat. I mean, it'll be pretty obvious, even to a fanatic.' I peered down at my fluffy pink coat, and my chewed fingernails, and my wasted legs in their wrinkled tights. 'We look so feeble and hopeless.'

Dave grunted. Something about the timbre of that grunt made me turn my head to study his expression.

'What?' I said. And he sighed.

'Well – I was wondering if it might turn out to be a problem,' he confessed. 'The way we look so harmless, I mean.'

'Why?'

'Because he might not believe that we're vampires.'

'But –'

'Just think about it, Nina. We can't fly. We can't turn into bats. We aren't a bit like Zadia Bloodstone. How are we going to prove who we are? Unless we fang the guy.'

It was a good point. As I turned it over in my mind, I realised that someone brought up on a diet of Bram Stoker might have trouble accepting the dismal reality of our condition. Even if that person *did* believe in vampires.

'What about these?' I said, tapping one of my canines. 'These should do the trick, shouldn't they?'

But Dave shook his head.

'I dunno,' he replied. 'They're not especially big. Not like the ones in the movies.' He gave a sniff. 'You could open a can of fruit juice with those fangs in *Underworld*.'

'So what do you suggest, then?' Anxiety always makes me irritable – and when I'm irritable, I often resort to sarcasm. 'Are you saying that one of us should volunteer to lie out in the sun?'

'Come on, Nina.' His tone was patient. No matter how hard I prodded him, he would never get riled; I figured he simply didn't care enough to waste his energy on a sharp retort. 'I'm not saying that,' he murmured. 'I just think we should be prepared.'

'In case our killer doesn't believe Father Ramon?' I asked, jerking my chin at the priest. As Dave hesitated, I had a flash of inspiration. 'Even if this guy doesn't think we're vampires, he'll think we're vampire supporters. And any vampires with friends like us *must* be harmless,' I argued. When Dave didn't answer, I gave a shrug. 'Maybe you don't agree,' I said, turning away from him, 'but whatever happens, you ought to shave. Without all that hair you won't look so suspicious.'

Dave's mouth twisted. 'Gee, thanks,' he said dryly.

'It's true. Scrubby chins are for B-grade villains. You must have noticed.' Then I spotted the fuel-gauge dial. 'We're getting a bit low on petrol, Dave.'

'I know.'

'We'll have to stop at the next town.'

Luckily, the next town boasted an all-night service station, with a well-lit convenience store attached. As we pulled up beside a vacant pump, I stared in astonishment at the gigantic road train that was sitting nearby. Never before had I been so close to such a large vehicle.

It felt as if we'd parked next to a cruise liner.

'Have you done this before?' I inquired of Dave, overwhelmed by all the bright lights, big trucks and oily smells. Dave must have understood that I wasn't thinking clearly – that I was confused by the unfamiliar surroundings. Because he said, very kindly, 'I've got my own car, Nina.'

'Oh. Yeah. Of course.'

'Do you think we should wake Father Ramon?'

We both surveyed the priest, who was still snoring away. It seemed a shame to disturb him. 'He probably wouldn't thank us,' was my conclusion, and Dave agreed with it. But when he reached for the door-handle, I caught his arm.

'Do you think – I mean – can I go too?'

He hesitated.

'Come on, Dave. Please? I haven't been to the shops for *months*.'

You may be wondering why I had to ask permission – and why Dave seemed so reluctant to oblige. The reason is simple: I hadn't been blooded. And although I've already mentioned blooding, I didn't really explain how important it is. You see, once you give in to that first impulse, and fang someone, you're in trouble. You could fall off the wagon again at any time. According to Horace, the memory of that initial buzz stays with you; you're like a heroin addict, or an alcoholic. But if you resist, you'll never face the same degree of temptation ever again. Resistance gets easier and easier. That's what Sanford says, anyway, and I believe him. After all, he's had a hundred years of experience.

Horace was blooded just before he bit Sanford. Gladys was blooded at the Magdalene hospital; she fanged Bridget after a woman gave birth nearby. Bridget herself was blooded when she witnessed an accidental knife-cut in the convent kitchen. But unlike Gladys, Bridget stood firm.

And she wasn't the only one.

There are many theories as to why some vampires withstand the urge to infect people and some don't. Sanford maintains that he never succumbed because he had the support of his wife. He says that Bridget was able to control herself owing to her a very strong religious faith; she was accustomed to fighting what she called 'the Devil's snares'. And Dave was lucky. His blooding took place the morning after he was infected, while he was staggering home. Though he passed another Saturday-night casualty on his way – a man who was bleeding from a split lip – Dave was still strong enough to ignore his own sudden, irrational desire to attack the guy's jugular vein.

That's why Sanford doesn't worry about Dave the way he worries about Horace and Gladys and George, who aren't allowed to go anywhere unless they're accompanied by another, more reliable vampire. Gladys, for instance, has to take Bridget with her everywhere. Sanford and Dave are meant to be keeping a close eye on George and Horace. Casimir was always a special case; he wasn't supposed to appear in public unless he had at least *two* sponsors in attendance. (That was the rule, though he obviously wasn't following it before he died.)

As for me, I was always the odd one out – because I'd never even been tempted. And when you've never been tempted, you're treated like an unexploded bomb.

You get people looking at you the way Dave looked at me that night, under the blazing lights of a service station in the middle of nowhere.

'Well . . . I dunno,' he said. 'There won't be much to see. Just lollies and junk. Maybe a couple of stale meat pies . . .'

'Five minutes. That's all I want.'

But Dave shook his head.

'It's the sunnies,' he objected. 'Both of us wearing sunglasses, in the middle of the night. They're going to think we're here to rob the place.'

'No they won't. They'll just think we're wankers.'

'Wankers can cop a lot of flack, mate. We don't want to draw attention to ourselves.'

'Oh, come *on*.' I was getting annoyed. 'In case you haven't noticed, you could easily pass for a junkie after a bad week in jail.' Seeing him swallow, I added, 'Not that I'm any improvement, but let's face it: you don't need *me* to attract attention.'

'We'll ask Father Ramon,' he decided, then reached over to jog the priest awake.

'*What*? No!' I tightened my grip on Dave's arm. 'Are you out of your mind?'

'Nina –'

'Just check out that bloke over there!' I said, pointing. 'He's much stranger than we are. If anyone looks like an armed robber, it's *him*.'

The truck driver in question was huge, bald and wearing only a fox-fur waistcoat on his top half. A skull was tattooed across his scalp, and pictures of jellyfish adorned his bulging biceps. One narrow thread of beard ran along his left jaw line, up over his top lip, and around to his other ear.

As he vanished into the shop, I offered up my final, clinching argument.

'Anyway,' I declared, 'you can't leave me here by myself. Not without a sponsor.'

'Father Ramon –'

'Might have a nose-bleed,' I finished, in triumphant tones. 'It's against the rules, Dave. You *know* that.'

'Okay, okay.' Dave sighed. 'I'm too tired to argue. Let's get this over with.'

He climbed out of the truck, and I followed him. It was unexpectedly cold; I found myself jigging from foot to foot while I waited for him to fill up the tank. Believe it or not, the changing numbers on the petrol pump fascinated me. So did the tyre-servicing equipment, and the window-washing squeegee, and the cage full of gas cylinders. It doesn't take much to interest a person of my limited experience.

When I finally entered the shop, I was drawn first to the magazine rack, then to the rather impressive muffin display. Until that moment, I hadn't realised that cranberry and walnut muffins even existed. It was also hard not to exclaim over the vast array of iced teas in the fridge, but I managed to restrain myself.

I didn't utter a single word until Dave had finished paying the bleary-eyed man behind the counter. This man was obviously so exhausted that I doubt he would have raised an eyebrow if a T-rex had walked in and purchased a bag of popcorn. Two pallid vampires wearing sunglasses didn't faze him in the least.

'Wait,' I said, as Dave began to nudge me towards the door. 'Look. It's an inflatable neck pillow. Do you think Father Ramon might need a neck pillow?'

'I think he might need a neck *brace*, if we're not careful,' Dave warned me – and I soon saw what he meant. The bald trucker, who had preceded us out of the shop, was now standing near our bright orange van. His arms were folded, and there was a frown on his face. With him was another huge truck driver with grey hair and a beer belly. The two men were engaged in a muttered conversation as they stared at the back of the van.

Father Ramon was still asleep.

'Don't stop,' Dave advised, under his breath (because I had pulled up short at the sight of Baldie's glower, and Beer Belly's broken nose). 'Let me do the talking.'

'No,' I whispered, 'let *me*. They won't punch me.'

'Shh!'

Upon approaching our van, we quickly realised why it had attracted an audience. Now that the petrol pump beside it wasn't humming away, the shrill piping of distressed guinea pigs could be heard quite clearly. I have to admit, it did sound odd.

Beer Belly seemed only mildly intrigued, but Baldie was scowling. 'They're guinea pigs,' Dave explained, with a sickly grin.

Beer Belly retreated hurriedly; I had a feeling that he was embarrassed. Baldie sniffed.

'They're fine,' I assured him, before Dave could continue. 'It's a big cage. They just don't like travelling, that's all – they're very neurotic.' Hoping to persuade this hulking, tattooed animal lover that the guinea pigs were cherished pets (rather than tomorrow's breakfast), I added, 'They're mine. Their names are Torquil, Huntingdon, Arabella and . . . um . . . Sanford.'

Perhaps I came across as being a bit odd, what with my sunnies, my bleached complexion, and my list of romance-writer names. The trucker peered at me as if I'd just told him that I had two hearts.

'Come on,' said Dave, who'd pulled open the driver's-side door. He didn't exactly shove me back into the cabin, but he certainly applied a lot of pressure to my elbow. 'The sooner we get going, the sooner we can let 'em out, eh?'

I was astonished to see that Father Ramon hadn't moved.

Sliding into the seat next to him, I was assailed by a sudden, terrible fear that he might be in a coma – or worse – and shook him furiously.

He woke with a start, mumbling something about rosters. Then his eyes focused.

'Nina,' he croaked. 'Are we there yet?'

'No.' I glanced into the rear-view mirror just as Dave joined us, slamming the door behind him. Like me, he peered up at the mirror.

We saw that Baldie was moving away from us.

'Thank Christ,' said Dave, and slumped against the steering wheel. In a matter of seconds, all the nervous energy seemed to drain from his limbs; his head drooped, his shoulders sagged, his lungs deflated as he heaved a great sigh of relief. 'That could have been a disaster.'

'What could have been a disaster?' the priest demanded, and I had to explain that someone had heard our guinea pigs.

'But it's okay now,' I said. 'Isn't it, Dave?'

'I guess.'

'Nobody's going to call the RSPCA, or anything. It's not illegal to put guinea pigs into the back of a removals van.' When Dave didn't rally – when he remained with his forehead propped against the steering wheel – I regarded him with some concern. 'Are you all right?' I asked him, conscious of a nauseous sensation in my own stomach. 'Are you feeling sick?'

'I'm feeling wiped out.' He raised his head to address Father Ramon. 'Can you take over now? I need a break. I didn't realise how tiring this would be.'

'Yes, of course,' the priest replied. And he swapped seats with Dave, while I watched Baldie drive away in his enormous semi-trailer. I was concerned that he might be heading west, and that we might continue to encounter him at other petrol stations, or on the kind of narrow, lonely, two-lane roads that you often see in horror movies about serial killers.

We were lucky, though. When he reached the highway he turned right, and I saw that he was heading in an easterly direction.

We turned left, continuing on towards Cobar.

Chapter Nine

Dave was soon feeling well enough to drive again. But he wasn't behind the wheel for very long. We were already through Dubbo when I checked the time, and realised that we had less than half an hour in which to protect ourselves from the deadly approach of sunrise.

So we pulled off the road, before clambering out on to the dry, red earth.

As we opened the back of the van, the guinea pigs warbled accusingly. Though still alive, they were in a foul mood. Father Ramon suggested that their cage be moved to the front seat; he wouldn't mind the noise, he said, because it would help to stop him from dozing off.

'We could put a towel underneath them,' he added, but Dave shook his head.

'It's all right, Father,' Dave replied. 'They won't keep *us* awake. Nothing ever does.'

Fortunately, the sleeping bags were already unrolled, and tied down like cupboards or pianos. Had they not been secured, Dave and I might have bounced around like ping-pong balls every time the van hit a bend or a pothole. We might never have reached our destination in one piece. But we emerged unscathed from the final leg of the trip, which ended outside a place called the Miner's Rest Motel.

Needless to say, I was unconscious long before our arrival. I missed the unforgettable sight of a desert dawn. I missed the kangaroos that fled from our approach, their grey backs bobbing above the sandbanks. Though I heard about these things later, from Father Ramon, I might have been six feet underground for all the impression they made on me. Lying in the back of the van, with my alpine sleeping bag zipped up over my face, I must have listened to about ten minutes of rattles and jingles and high-pitched squeaking before I blacked out.

Next thing I knew, we weren't moving any more. Silence reigned.

It can often take a minute or so to recover your wits, after a day's blackout. But the instant I heard Dave groaning, I knew where I was – or at least, where I *should* have been. And I began to struggle out of my sleeping bag.

The guinea pigs were still with us, scratching around in their cage. It was very dark, and very cold; the only light came from my wrist-watch. In its pale-green glow I could see that the van's double doors were tightly shut, and that my suitcase was still sitting where I'd left it.

Beside me, Dave coughed.

'Are you all right?' he whispered.

'I think so. What about you?'

'No worse than usual.' He certainly didn't look his best, as he peered at me with bloodshot eyes through a tangle of hair. 'Should I ring Father Ramon? Or should we have breakfast first?'

I was startled by this suggestion. Our original plan had been to use Father Ramon's motel bathroom for our meals;

102

we had even brought our own cleaning equipment, and a set of burgundy towels that wouldn't show bloodstains.

'I figure we could probably hose all this off,' Dave continued quietly, gesturing at the sheets of black plastic that surrounded us. 'Instead of trying to sneak animals into a motel room.'

'Let's just work out where we are first,' I replied, and he shrugged.

Then he fumbled for his mobile phone.

I can't pretend that I wasn't anxious as we waited for a response to Dave's call. There was no telling what might have happened during the past twelve hours; for all we knew, the van in which we were confined might have been impounded by the police, or parked outside a pub, or abandoned on an outback highway. We couldn't be sure of anything until we had spoken to Father Ramon.

I remember offering up a silent prayer that nothing bad had happened, because Dave and I were hardly in a fit state to deal with lawyers or hospitals. Dave obviously had a killer headache, to judge from the way he kept kneading his temples. And I felt as if I were about to throw up.

When Father Ramon answered his phone, my nausea eased a little. But only a little.

'Yeah, it's me,' Dave rumbled. 'Yeah, we're fine . . . no . . . yeah . . . okay. Good.' He broke the connection, his face a mask of relief. 'We're right next to the motel room, and there's no one else around,' he reported. 'We'll be out of here in a second.'

Sure enough, he had hardly finished speaking before a creak and a thump announced that Father Ramon was unlocking the back of the van. All at once the doors swung open. I groped for my sunglasses as artificial light flooded our dingy compartment.

The guinea pigs immediately began to complain, in very shrill voices.

'Get them inside, quick,' muttered Father Ramon, who was standing in front of a blue door with a number on it. 'We don't want anyone to see.'

'I was just thinking – about breakfast –' Dave began. The priest, however, wouldn't be delayed.

'*Hurry!*' he begged.

So I grabbed my suitcase, ignoring a slight touch of dizziness as I scrambled out into the fresh air. Dave threw a towel over the guinea pig cage. But he had his own luggage to carry, and it was Father Ramon who finally smuggled the guinea pigs into our motel room, with many a nervous backward glance.

Because the door of the room was positioned directly behind our van, we didn't have a long way to go. As far as I could see – from my fleeting glimpse of it – the Miner's Rest motel was just a long line of rooms facing a car park, with an office at one end and a small, fenced-off pool at the other. But I wasn't given a chance to inspect the place very closely. Within seconds I had been hustled into a shabby sleeping area that boasted red brick walls, a brown carpet, and two queen-sized beds sitting under a framed photograph of the Eiffel Tower.

My heart sank as I gazed around at the wood veneer cupboards and the broken vertical blinds. This was the first motel room that I had ever experienced, and it was a grave disappointment. After watching so many lifestyle holiday programmes, I had been expecting a spa bath, at the very least.

'Is this all?' I said. 'It stinks.'

'It's better than the back of the truck,' Dave rejoined, dumping his bag on the carpet. 'Do you want to go first, Nina?'

'Oh. Right. I guess.' My gaze travelled from the quivering cage under the burgundy towel to the red brick wall behind it. 'How soundproof are these rooms, do you think?'

'I'll turn on the TV,' Father Ramon offered. 'Don't worry, Nina. There'll be time enough to talk once you and Dave have done what you have to do.'

And he settled down to watch a fuzzy news bulletin.

I won't revolt you with a description of my breakfast, or of the mess that I had to clean up after I'd finished. I'll just say that, for once, I didn't feel too bad about what I'd done – because the bathroom already had mouldy grouting, smelly drains and a dust-clogged extraction fan. When I complained about the housekeeping to Father Ramon, however, he simply shrugged.

'I've seen worse,' he replied. He was sitting on one of the beds, which had obviously been slept in; I soon discovered that he'd spent the whole afternoon napping, after a morning devoted to reconnaissance.

It seemed that Wolgaroo Corner was located about forty-five minutes to the north of town, along an extremely rough dirt road.

'I went to the office and asked for directions,' he explained, once Dave had finished in the bathroom. 'I said that I was a friend of a friend of Barry McKinnon, just passing through. And you know what the receptionist did?' Father Ramon paused, but Dave and I just stared at him blankly. So the priest continued. 'She gave me this,' he said, displaying a crumpled sheet of paper. 'It's a photocopy of a hand-drawn map. With Barry McKinnon's house *marked in red pen*.'

I was confused by his tone.

'You mean the receptionist drew all over it?' I queried, wondering why he found this so surprising.

'No, no.' Father Ramon spoke slowly and carefully, in the manner of someone transmitting vital information. 'I mean that she had a whole pile of maps to the McKinnon house. They were sitting under the counter.'

'A whole *pile* of maps?' Dave echoed.

'That's right. And when I asked her if Barry McKinnon had a lot of visitors, she laughed. And winked.'

'She *winked*?' I was astonished. 'Why would she do that?'

'I don't know. The phone rang, then, and she had to answer it.' Father Ramon dragged his fingers through his hair. 'I was so floored, I just . . . well, I just left. It seemed so odd. I had to go away and think.'

The priest went on to admit that he hadn't questioned the woman again, because he'd been worried about drawing attention to himself. 'So I went to have a look at the place, instead,' he revealed. 'I wanted to get a feel for the layout while there was still light enough to see by.'

I blinked. Dave frowned.

'Wait a minute,' I said. 'You mean you drove to Wolgaroo Corner? In the *truck*?'

'Yes.'

'This *morning*?'

'I didn't speak to anyone. I didn't even stop,' Father Ramon assured me. 'I just wanted to be certain that we knew what to expect before we went in there after dark. It's always a good idea to check your exits.'

I stared at him in amazement. Sitting on the unmade bed, all rumpled clothes and untidy grey hair, he looked the same as usual. But it occurred to me that Father Ramon wasn't your average priest. Providing pastoral care for a group of vampires requires more than just compassion and a sense of duty. It also requires a taste for adventure.

I wondered if the excitement of his early years in South America had given him a daredevil streak. I wondered if ordinary parish work was becoming a bit of a bore.

'Wow,' said Dave feebly. I said nothing. It bothered me that I would never, in a million years, have considered going anywhere *near* Wolgaroo Corner – not on my own. I just didn't have the guts.

'It's a great big spread,' Father Ramon related. 'You can only just see it from the road.' He explained that he had slowed down upon reaching a steel-drum mailbox and a five-bar gate; from that point, a long driveway had led to a collection of buildings and one or two trees, way off in the distance. 'Pretty flat,' he said thoughtfully. 'No livestock that I could see. But lots and lots of vehicles.' He raised his eyes from the patch of carpet that he had been contemplating, then fixed them on Dave. 'That's what I found so odd,' he confessed. 'The number of cars that were parked near the house.'

'How many?'

'Oh – at least fifteen.'

'*Fifteen?*' I squawked. And Dave said, 'It's like that in the country. People just leave their old rust buckets lying around when they're ready to upgrade –'

'No, no.' Father Ramon shook his head. 'These were all good cars. I wasn't very close, but I could see they were mostly recent models. Some of them looked brand new.'

There was a long pause as Dave and I processed this infor-mation, trying to work out what it meant. A pile of maps. A congregation of cars. A conspiratorial wink. What did they all add up to?

'Could there be a party tonight?' I proposed at last. 'I bet they have really enormous parties out here, which go on for days and days.'

'Then why didn't the receptionist warn me?' Father Ramon objected. 'Why didn't she say, "Oh, I don't know if it would be a good idea to drop in on Barry right now, what with the party and everything"? Why did she just wink like that?'

Dave suggested that we might be visiting someone with a bit of a reputation. He speculated that Barry McKinnon's parties might be notorious – full of drinking, drug-taking, and the kind of wild behaviour that you can only really get away with out in the country, where you don't have nosy neighbours breathing down your neck. I wondered aloud if Barry McKinnon might even manufacture his own illegal drugs, and throw a party for his best customers once in a while. Then Father Ramon said that, as long as we weren't about to crash the fifth anniversary of a Vampire Extermination Club, Barry's houseful of guests would prob-ably work to our advantage.

'If he *is* our man, he won't try anything nasty in front of his friends,' the priest declared, sounding for all the world like someone from the Army Reserve.

Dave agreed. I didn't know what to think; I was beginning to feel very anxious. It had been years since I'd encountered a large and noisy crowd of people. I had a sudden vision of drunk teenagers cutting themselves on smashed glass – in fact I could clearly remember something of the sort happening at the last party I'd ever attended. It had been held in a big old house full of university students, none of whom I'd met before. But a friend of mine had known somebody who lived there, so I'd gone with her. (I had a reckless streak, in those days, though you wouldn't think so now.)

I'm pretty sure a boy stuck his fist through a window, that night. I seem to recall seeing a bloodstained tea-towel wrapped around his arm, before I staggered outside to throw up. After that, of course, I never went to another party. Because Casimir caught up with me, in a murky back lane.

'Maybe we ought to wait till tomorrow night,' I said, troubled by my memory of the bloodstained tea-towel. But Father Ramon didn't think much of this idea. He was keen to be back in Sydney for the Sunday-morning service, if possible. And Dave was convinced that there would be safety in numbers.

'We might even be able to crash this thing without anyone knowing that we weren't invited,' he said, speaking with the thoughtful air of someone accustomed to gatecrashing. 'Especially if we take some beer.'

In the end, though, we decided that our motives would look questionable if we slunk into the house like spies, and were later discovered. Barry might believe that we had come for the sole purpose of attacking him.

Besides which, Father Ramon wanted to wear his clerical collar.

'Our whole aim is to appear completely honest,' he said. 'People tend to trust priests, but not when they sneak into parties disguised as laymen. Everything has to be above board. We should go there and say that we're making inquiries about a silver bullet.'

'A silver bullet that we found at a friend's house,' I added, suddenly struck by an inspired notion. 'A friend who's disappeared.'

'Yes.' The priest gave a nod. 'We're just three honest people searching for some answers. That's how we'll approach this thing. As for how we proceed from there . . .' He shrugged. 'I suppose that will depend on what we find out.'

It was as good a plan as any. I certainly couldn't think of a better one. But before we left I decided to give my mother a ring, just to make sure that Fangseeker hadn't been identified. (He hadn't.) I also wanted to reassure her that I was fine, and to satisfy myself that she was fine, too.

She was. According to Mum, no one had bothered her during the day. There had been no lurking strangers or wordless phone calls. At present, she told me, Horace was trawling the Internet for phrases like 'I killed a vampire', Bridget was knitting, Gladys was having a bath and George was feeding the guinea pigs.

'It's Sanford who's driving me mad,' Mum complained. 'He can't seem to settle.' As if to prove her point, Sanford suddenly addressed her in the background; I heard a short, sharp exchange before Mum relinquished the phone. When Sanford's voice exploded in my ear, I quickly surrendered my own receiver to Father Ramon.

The last thing I needed was another one of Sanford's lectures.

'Yes? Who? Oh, Sanford. Yes. Yes. Yes. Oh, yes.' The priest's patience astounded me. 'No. Yes. No,' he murmured. 'Yes, of course. We were just about to leave. There seems to be some kind of party going on over there . . .'

As Sanford was given a full report, I followed Dave out to the van. By now it was nearly nine o'clock. Across the dusty road that skirted the car park stood a line of small, shabby houses made of asbestos cement sheeting and corrugated iron. Peppercorn trees rustled in the wind. A battered white utility truck drove past, bristling with antennae. The starry sky seemed so huge that it had a strange kind of weight to it, as if it were pressing down hard on the stunted landscape.

The air was as sharp as an ice-pick.

'Have you been to the outback before?' I inquired of Dave, very softly.

'Yeah,' he answered. 'Once. When I was touring.' He lifted his chin, staring up at the Milky Way. 'Amazing, isn't it?'

'Kind of . . . scary, too. Don't you think?'

Dave looked at me. Then he glanced back at the door to our room. Then he said, 'We'll be all right. I've got a deterrent.' And he reached into the pocket of his jeans.

I don't know what I was expecting. A gun, perhaps? A flick-knife? Something fairly intimidating, at any rate.

Imagine my disappointment when he produced a very small bottle of perfume.

'You want us to smell so nice that they can't bear to kill us?' I demanded. That's when he produced one of his rare, slightly downcast smiles.

'It's Windex,' he rejoined. 'With pepper and chilli powder. It's for squirting in people's eyes.'

'Oh.'

'You can take it, if you like. I've got a Swiss army knife, as well.' Dave passed me the elegant little atomiser. 'It looks harmless, but it will come in handy if anything goes wrong.'

I have to admit, I was impressed.

'That's really brilliant, Dave.'

'Thanks.'

'I should have thought of that myself.' It annoyed me that I hadn't; once again, I had demonstrated a woeful lack of initiative. 'Does *he* know?' I asked, jerking my chin at our room.

Dave shook his head as he climbed up into the front of the van. I could understand his reluctance to inform the priest, though I doubted very much that Father Ramon would confiscate my innocent-looking perfume bottle. As for the Swiss army knife, you could hardly call it a *weapon*. It was more of a tool.

I was trying to imagine holding off an armed psychopathic killer with a corkscrew and a squirt of spiked Windex when it occurred to me that these two items weren't our only means of defence. But I could hardly bring myself to say so. In fact I'd been sitting inside the van for several minutes before I finally muttered, 'Dave?'

'Yeah?'

'If anything *does* go wrong, would you . . . that is, if you had to protect yourself . . .'

As I trailed off, he regarded me from behind a pair of opaque lenses.

'Would I fang someone, you mean?' he said.

'Yes.'

We gazed at each other wordlessly. Then he opened his mouth. Before he could reply, however Father Ramon suddenly appeared – and you don't discuss topics like that in front of a normal person. It isn't polite. After all, poor Father Ramon would soon find himself sitting right next to us, in a small enclosed space, speeding through the night across an empty wasteland. No one in this kind of situation wants to hear that the two vampires with him are prepared to use their fangs, if necessary.

That's why I never did learn how Dave felt about defensive fanging. It's also why I had to make a certain moral decision all by myself, in private and without assistance, as we headed along a bumpy, unsealed road towards Wolgaroo Corner.

You can discuss these subjects all you like in a group meeting, but it doesn't prepare you for the moment when you actually have to make a choice.

Chapter Ten

The moon was full. That's why it wasn't as dark as it could have been. Even if our headlights hadn't been pushing back the shadows, I would have spotted quite a few things, I feel sure. I would have seen the fences, and the saltbush, and the small, furry creature that skipped out of a dry creek bed as we passed. I might even have spied the bleached animal-bones that lay scattered beneath a lone desert tree like fallen magnolia petals.

Not that I was much interested in the scenery. Not for long, at any rate. Because we had barely cleared the outskirts of town, leaving behind the last telephone pole and dusty, unoc-cupied shopfront, when we caught sight of two glowing red dots in front of us.

Someone else was on the road to Wolgaroo Corner.

'Do you think that's Barry McKinnon?' I asked, peering through the windscreen. I wasn't really expecting a reply, and I didn't get one; in fact nobody said anything for about ten minutes after that, probably because we were all becoming increasingly nervous. It was Dave who finally spoke, after he'd glanced into the rear-view mirror.

'Uh-oh,' he mumbled. 'Look.'

I looked, and saw the reflection of two blazing lights.

'There's a car behind us,' he continued, quite unnecessarily. Then he opened the passenger-side window and adjusted the wing-mirror next to him. 'I can't figure out what make it is,' he said.

'Well . . . they can't *both* be Barry McKinnon,' Father Ramon observed. 'And I doubt that he has many neighbours – not all the way out here.'

'It's a party. I told you,' was my contribution.

We fell silent again, dividing our attention between the vehicle up ahead and the one to our rear. At last a distant cluster of buildings became visible, bathed in electric radiance; within seconds, the tail-lights preceding us had veered off to the left.

'There's that gate I told you about,' said Father Ramon. 'Should I drive straight in, or should we park down the road a bit, and walk?'

'Are you kidding?' Dave sounded apprehensive. His hands shook as he rolled up the window. 'We can't go in on foot. Outback farms always have packs of vicious dogs. Not to mention snakes.'

'Snakes don't come out at night,' I said scornfully. 'They're cold-blooded.' I did, however, agree that we should drive straight in. 'Otherwise people will think we have something to hide.'

So when we reached the gate, Father Ramon turned left. We immediately clanged over a cattle grid, which stretched between two whitewashed gateposts. Dust still hung in the air, thrown up by the tyres of the car we were following. Somewhere a dog barked.

'See? What did I tell you?' Dave commented, under his breath.

I couldn't see any dogs, at first; just the glare of arc-lights, an assemblage of concrete water-tanks, and a long, low residence that seemed to be constructed almost entirely out of fly screens. The vehicles parked near this building ranged from filthy old Land Rovers to gleaming luxury rental cars. There were more than fifteen of them, I noticed.

Lots more.

'This is a really big bash,' I said, in sheer amazement. The closer we drew to the house, the clearer it became that no one very neat or cultivated lived there. Paint was peeling off the walls. Old animal skulls were nailed to every available post. Bits of junk were strewn all over the place: discarded tyres, rusty petrol drums, chewed bones, even a gutted lounge chair. But there wasn't a hint of decoration. No streamers or balloons fluttered from the eaves. No fairy-lights illumined the fences or outbuildings.

If it was a party, I decided, it was a very strange one. Because the people who were climbing out of their cars and hurrying towards a gate at the rear of the house didn't smile or greet each other. Nor were they carrying bottles of wine, or brightly wrapped presents. They all seemed to be men, and they were dressed in dull, dirty colours, with caps or hats pulled down low over their eyes.

'You know what?' Dave said uneasily. 'I don't like the look of this.'

'No.' The priest had braked. 'It feels a bit . . . illicit.'

'You'd better move,' I suggested. 'We're blocking the road, here.'

Obediently Father Ramon steered us towards a vacant patch of gravel that lay between a parked campervan and a tin shed. The campervan's driver had to step out of our way

116

as we glided to a standstill; he kept his head lowered and his shoulders hunched. Watching his rapid retreat, I decided that my sunglasses might not be a problem after all.

'Everyone seems so *shifty*,' I remarked, then glanced at Dave. 'You're going to blend right in, with that two-day growth.'

'Yeah – but *he* isn't.' Dave gestured at Father Ramon's clerical collar. 'I don't know if they're going to welcome a Catholic priest with open arms, do you? Unless someone keels over suddenly, and they need the last rites.'

'I'll put on my jumper,' said Father Ramon.

The jumper certainly helped, though it couldn't conceal his patient, candid, kindly expression. Even without his cassock and dog-collar, Father Ramon retained a priestly air. But there was nothing we could do about that. He wouldn't wear his sunglasses because it was too dark, and the only hat in his possession had a Latin motto embroidered on its crown, directly under a sacred heart of Jesus.

'You'll just have to stand behind Dave,' I advised him, in a low voice. Then we jumped down from the van and joined a kind of straggling queue, which had formed in front of a young but grim-faced man posted beside the back gate. This man seemed to be collecting tickets, or tokens. He was large and sunburned, with a vicious scar on his cheek; his oily blond hair had been combed straight back from his forehead.

Something about him made my stomach churn.

'Do you think that's him?' I breathed, plucking at Father Ramon's jumper. 'Do you think that's Barry McKinnon?'

The priest shrugged, just as Dave jabbed me with his elbow. Being so small, I had to peer around the enormous gut of the man in front of me before I could see what was happening at the head of the queue – where the scar-faced man was retrieving a silver bullet from almost everyone who passed him by.

I gasped.

'Follow the track . . . just follow the track,' Scarface droned, as the bullets dropped into his open palm, one by one. There was a contemptuous edge to his voice. 'Thanks, mate . . . yeah. Just follow the track.'

'What are we going to do?' I whispered. 'Are we going to speak up, or what?'

'Shh,' said Dave.

Now the fat man ahead of us was surrendering his silver bullet. 'Hullo, Dermid,' he said, and Scarface gave a cool little nod.

'G'day, Russell.'

'Where's your dad? Up at the pit?'

'He's busy,' Dermid replied. 'You'll see 'im soon enough.'

'Good turnout, eh?'

'Yeah.' Dermid was getting impatient. His pale eyes flickered in my direction. 'Not bad.'

'Hope there's enough room for us all,' Russell added. 'I wouldn't want to miss anything.'

'You won't,' Dermid said shortly. 'Just follow the track.'

A sudden low growl alerted me to the wide-bodied, muscle-bound dog sitting beside him. I couldn't tell you what breed of dog it was – only that it had big teeth and a broad, ugly head. But one glimpse of those teeth was enough to get rid of Russell. He sauntered through the gate and waddled off down a narrow dirt track, towards another collection of arc-lights in the distance.

Dermid fixed his gaze on me again. I sensed that I was an

118

unexpected (and possibly unwelcome) sight. But before he could say anything, Father Ramon spoke up.

'Good evening,' the priest declared. 'My friends and I were hoping for a word with Mr Barry McKinnon. About this.' And he displayed our silver bullet, holding it between his thumb and forefinger.

Dermid blinked. Confusion replaced the hostility in his eyes; he frowned as he glanced from the priest's face to mine, and back again. Something clearly didn't make sense to Dermid. Our silver bullet had thrown him.

I braced myself, convinced that he was about to interrogate us. Luckily, however, I was wrong. Footsteps crunched on the gravel behind me; the line was lengthening, and time was running out. After a brief pause, Dermid shrugged.

'Yeah. Right. Whatever,' he growled, reaching for the bullet in Father Ramon's hand. 'Dad'll be along any minute. He'll talk to you then.'

'But –'

'You gotta gimme that. You can't just keep it.' Dermid yanked the bullet from Father Ramon's slackening grip. 'Just follow the track. It's a five-minute walk – you need to stay between the green lights.'

'Yes, of course,' said Father Ramon. If I hadn't poked him in the ribs, he probably would have stood there asking questions for another ten minutes. As it was, I had to nudge him forward to escape the swelling crowd at our heels.

Something about my presence still baffled Dermid, who leered and winked when he caught my eye.

'Enjoy yourself, love,' he drawled, in mocking tones. 'Just follow the track.'

So I did – as quickly as possible.

'You know what? I shouldn't be here.' This was painfully obvious to me by now. 'We've crashed a stag party, I reckon. Maybe he thinks I'm the stripper.'

'Shh!' Dave took my arm. Ahead of us lay two long strings of green lights; placed about a metre apart, like a pair of emerald necklaces, they marked the edges of our designated route. Beyond them, on slightly elevated ground, a brightly illuminated crowd of people had gathered around a wire fence. I could hear the murmur of massed voices, swelling occasionally in response to another noise – a kind of clanging thud.

'What's *that*?' I hissed. 'Did you hear that?'

'Ah, Christ,' said Dave, just as the priest stopped short. Dismay was written on both their faces.

'It's a pit,' whispered Father Ramon.

'Yeah, I know.' Dave was barely audible. 'But we can't make a fuss. Not now. Just keep moving.'

'Why? What's the matter?' I pleaded. 'What's going on?'

'A dog fight,' Dave rejoined, very softly. 'Or a cock fight. Something like that.'

'Blood sports,' the priest murmured. 'They're illegal.'

'This is really bad timing,' said Dave.

He pulled at my arm and we stumbled forwards. Shuffling footsteps to our rear announced that another, larger group of people was gaining on us; clearly, we would soon be over-taken. I tried to make sense of what I'd just been told. Dog fighting? It had been in the news, lately. Someone, some-where, had been arrested for training dogs to kill each other.

'You mean there's dog fighting *here*?' I demanded. Whereupon Dave's grip tightened.

'Shh! Keep it down!' His voice buzzed in my ear. 'We can't

make a fuss. It's too risky.'

'We have to find Barry McKinnon,' said the priest.

All at once we were standing in a warm pool of light, having reached the wire fence. Not that we could see much of this fence, which was already ringed by large male bodies. A line of broad backs confronted me, severely restricting my view of the main attraction (whatever that was). The range of clothing was unexpected; leather jackets alternated with pastel knits, hooded sweatshirts, tailored coats and bulky anoraks. A hum of conversation filled the air, punctuated by the odd yelp of laughter.

You could feel the excitement building.

'Excuse me.' Father Ramon was fearless. He leaned forward to tap the biggest shoulder in our immediate vicinity. 'Do you know where Barry is?' he asked. 'Barry McKinnon?'

Several heads turned, revealing several impatient frowns, and a couple of curious stares.

'Nah, mate. Sorry,' came the reply.

So the priest moved on. Dave and I pursued him, keeping very close together. I was conscious of how sturdy and strong everyone looked. Even the older men had a vibrant, robust, highly coloured appearance. They jostled each other for a place at the fence, grunting and pointing.

As Father Ramon circled them, I tried to work out what they were pointing at. A hole, certainly; a very large hole (about the size of a public swimming pool), which lay directly at their feet. But what was *in* the hole?

'Um . . . *okay.*' Suddenly an amplified voice rang out, piped through a hidden speaker. '*You've got five minutes. This is your five-minute warning. Thank you, gentlemen. Five minutes.*'

A crackle was followed by a click – and then everyone rushed the fence. I was caught up in a kind of stampede; Dave and I were forced apart. Next thing I knew, I was wedged between two well-padded torsos. Someone was shoving against my spine. The pressure was so great that I was propelled forward, until I found myself being squeezed through the very small gap that separated the two men in front of me.

But I couldn't go any further. Not with a wire net in the way.

'Nina? Nina!' cried Dave, from somewhere close by. I opened my mouth to respond. Before I could do so, however, I glanced down – and saw, at last, what everyone had been pointing at.

Just beyond the fence lay a deep, tiled pit that looked almost like an empty swimming pool. Maybe it *had* been a swimming pool, once; there was certainly a drainage outlet at the bottom. But your average swimming pool doesn't have razor wire threaded around its rim, or an iron hatchway punched through one of its sides.

Nor does it usually contain a fierce, hairy, panting animal about the size of a bear.

I was in such a state of shock, by this stage, that it took a while for the truth to sink in. As I stared at the creature's mangy pelt, pug snout and ferocious snarl, I registered every feature without really understanding what it meant. Only when I tried to find a label for this bizarre collection of characteristics did I realise that I couldn't.

I didn't know what the strange beast actually *was*.

'Nina!' Dave had managed to pummel his way through the crowd. He grabbed my arm. 'Come on, quick!' he said.

'No.' I clutched at the fence, winding my fingers through it. 'Wait.'

'But –'

'Look! Down there!'

The creature was pacing; it kept close to the walls of the pit, moving with its head down. It had a peculiar, uneven lope and very long limbs, but I couldn't see any tail. When it drew near, its little tufted ears became visible – as did its glaring green eyes. A pattern of pink-and-white scars over one flank didn't improve its appearance, which was ugly enough.

Saliva dripped from a huge set of fangs.

'*Two minutes,*' the public address system declared. '*This is your two-minute warning.*' To my surprise, the rasping, amplified voice didn't stop there; it seemed eager to whip up more enthusiasm. '*You should all know our champ, by now. For those who don't, Reuben here has won his last eight bouts and managed to chalk up two kills in the process. Which means, of course, that he's odds-on favourite to win!*' A roar of approval greeted this announcement. '*But we shouldn't underestimate our contender, Orlando. Because he's a feisty little bastard who's been training up with the very best pit-bulls that we could throw at 'im. And let me tell you, gents – not one of them pit-bulls is alive today!*'

As the crowd cheered, I turned to find Dave beside me. He was gawping at the creature in the pit.

I had to drag his head down before I could put my mouth to his ear.

'What is it, Dave?' I hissed. 'Could it – I mean – it's not a wolf, is it?'

He didn't reply. From his blank expression, I deduced that he was lost for words.

'*It's Orlando's first time up against the champ,*' our master of ceremonies continued, '*but let's not forget that Reuben's taken a few hard knocks, lately. So there's every chance we're gunna see a* nice, long bout. It took Reuben an hour and forty-five minutes to wipe out the last contender – maybe this time he'll have another fight on his hands.'

'*GIVE'EM A SMELL!*' shouted the man to my right. And some of his neighbours took up the refrain: '*GIVE'EM-A-SMELL! GIVE'EM-A-SMELL!*'

That was when I remembered the silver bullets.

'Dave.' I yanked at his shoulder with such force that I almost pulled him off balance. 'You don't think – it's not a *werewolf*, is it?'

'*You want me to give'em a SMELL, do ya?*' our master of ceremonies concluded. '*All right then, gents – since you asked – let's give it up for our new contender, the one and only, the fresh and feisty, ORLANDO!*'

At which point the hatchway sprang open.

Chapter Eleven

The growl I heard then was like something out of a nightmare. It was savage and resonant; I could feel it through the soles of my feet.

'Oh, man,' Dave muttered.

The second beast – Orlando – was even bigger than the first, with a thicker, blacker pelt and a longer snout. For such an awkward-looking animal it was surprisingly quick, and displayed remarkable agility as it jumped through the hatch into a blaze of electric light. Almost immediately, however, it froze. Its gaze locked on the creature called Reuben.

They surveyed each other from opposite ends of the pit, their hackles raised, their teeth bared.

Slowly – very slowly – they lowered their heads.

'*GARN!*' someone yelled, making me jump. '*GARN, YA MONGREL!*'

Strident music suddenly blared from the loudspeaker, drowning the throb of Reuben's disturbing growl. Orlando began to slink around the side of the pit, edging towards Reuben with undisguised hostility. But Reuben didn't move.

Orlando stopped again.

'You don't want to see this,' said Dave, forgetting to keep his voice down. The words had hardly left his mouth when the two beasts sprang at each other. One of them gave a horrible, high-pitched yelp.

A howl, no less horrible, erupted from the audience.

What happened next is engraved on my memory. There was a snap of teeth and a weird kind of squawk; the two heavy shapes came together with a *thud*, throwing up wisps of fur and sprays of saliva as they rolled around. Like dogs, they led with their jaws. Unlike dogs, however, they used their limbs in a way that I found absolutely terrifying – perhaps because it so looked fluid. So *human*. Their claws were as sharp as their fangs.

Suddenly they were up on their hind legs. Reuben was biting Orlando's neck. But after another flurry of movement – after a thrashing, convulsive jerk – they were apart again.

And bright blood was spilling on to pale blue tiles.

Dave must have reacted before I did. He was already dragging me away from the fence when the smell hit me, practically knocking me off my feet. It was like being struck by a train; there's no other way of describing the sensation. For thirty-odd years I'd been expecting the sort of response a normal person would have to the smell of freshly baked bread. Instead, I thought that I was going to die.

If you've ever been on the verge of drowning, you'll understand the desperate, frantic, primitive need that overwhelmed me. If you've ever had chicken pox, and experienced the urge to scratch – if you've ever had a cold, and felt a cough coming on – if you've ever suffered from a bursting bladder, then you'll have an inkling of what it was like. My teeth were aching. My mouth was parched. I couldn't think or make choices; I couldn't even *see* properly. My peripheral vision faded away, as I zeroed in on the nearest person. The nearest throat.

I could taste that throat. I could smell it. The salt. The iron.

But I couldn't reach it. Something was preventing me.

'Nina. *Nina!*' For an instant I thought that the words were being spoken inside my brain. They sounded as slow as treacle. 'Nina, look at me. It's Dave. Nina?'

I saw his face. It gradually came into focus. The shadows receded slightly, and I was conscious of my own sore neck muscles.

He was standing behind me. With one hand he was pulling my head around, forcing me to gaze up at him. His free arm was wrapped around my waist.

'Ow,' I croaked.

'Do you know who I am? Nina?'

'Yeah . . .'

'Don't fade out on me. You have to concentrate. Who am I?'

You won't believe this, but I couldn't remember. Not at first. It didn't seem to matter any more.

'What is it?' demanded another familiar voice. And I couldn't put a name to that one, either.

The response from above me was hard and sharp.

'Get back! Right back!'

'But –'

'She's not *herself!*'

And then something clicked in my mind.

Dave.

'You're Dave,' I slurred. His fingers were digging into my jaw. 'Let go.'

I sensed the change in him instantly. His expression shifted. His grip relaxed.

'Nina?' he said. 'Are you all right?'

'You're hurting me. Let go.'

127

He released my chin, his eyes glinting behind smoky lenses as they searched my face.

'Do you know where we are, Nina?'

I had to think for a moment. It was difficult – like wading through honey.

'We . . . we're outside,' I stammered. 'In the outback. With Father Ramon.' I caught my breath. 'Near the pit!' I gasped. 'And the fight!'

'Shh.'

'Oh my God!'

'It's okay. You're okay, now.' He adjusted his position to enfold me in both arms, as if I needed to be restrained. His chin dropped on to my shoulder. 'Just give it a minute.'

'Is she all right?' asked Father Ramon, who must have been standing much too close. I glanced to my left and saw him hovering against a backdrop of tightly packed bodies.

'She'll be fine,' Dave insisted, his breath tickling my ear.

'What happened? Was she . . .?' The priest trailed off, unable to pronounce the dreaded word. Dave nodded.

'Yeah,' he said gruffly.

Father Ramon sucked air through his teeth. 'But I thought . . .?'

'Yeah.' Dave's reply was a broken mumble. 'It's only meant to happen with human blood.'

There was a long pause. Father Ramon crossed himself. Dave swallowed; I could hear him doing it, because his cheek was rammed against mine.

Somewhere in the back of my brain, I understood the full implications of what he had just said. At that precise moment, however, more pressing matters were occupying my thoughts.

'I'm going to be sick,' I bleated. And then I threw up.

For the next minute or so, I was too distracted to notice what was going on around me. Hanging over Dave's arm, I regurgitated my entire breakfast – which by then was thick and black, like tar. Poor Dave can't have enjoyed himself, though he was very cool and nice about it all. He stopped me from collapsing on to the ground, and held back my hair with the skill of a nurse's aide. He even took my glasses off, to prevent them from falling straight into the sticky, rancid mess.

When I'd finished, Father Ramon passed me a handker-chief.

'Oh, Nina,' he said. 'I am sorry.'

'Yeah. So am I,' a harsh voice interposed. 'That's *private property* you just spewed on. Why not take a bloody crap, while you're at it?'

Dave started; I felt the shudder. But I didn't raise my head until after I'd wiped my smeared mouth, and put my sunglasses back on.

There was no point risking a haemorrhage.

'So your girlfriend didn't like the show, eh? I figured she wouldn't.' This remark helped me to place the voice, which belonged to Dermid McKinnon. 'At least she won't mind missing the rest, though,' he added, as I peered around at him. 'Dad wants to see youse all. Back at the house.'

'Oh – ah – yes,' said Father Ramon, who didn't seem very enthusiastic. He gestured at me. 'The only thing is, my friend's not well . . .'

'She can clean up in the house. We've got a bathroom.' Dermid was straining to be heard above the pounding music and the crowd's enthusiastic cheers. In the glare of the lights

129

I could pick out every flaw in his sun-whipped complexion, and every stain on the dirty bandage that encircled his wrist. 'She won't want to stay here, I can tell ya. It's a bloodbath already, and it'll only get worse.'

As if to prove his point, one of the creatures down in the pit gave a screech that sounded like the emergency brakes on a speeding train. Dave winced. I pressed his arm.

'Could we . . . could we just go?' I begged, whereupon Dermid waved a peremptory hand.

'Come on,' he ordered. 'You want to go? Let's go. Dad doesn't have much time – he's got a business to run.'

'We didn't come about this, you know,' Father Ramon assured him, pointing at the crowd. 'This doesn't interest us. We're here to discuss another matter entirely.'

'Well, good. Let's get on with it, then.'

Even in my shell-shocked condition, I was alert enough to feel afraid. What we'd just seen in the pit was almost certainly illegal; if the McKinnons were scared of being arrested, they might very well try to silence us. Unfortunately, however, I wasn't fit enough to walk unaided, let alone run. My head was splitting. My knees were like cotton wool. I had to be supported during our trip back to the house, which took place under Dermid's watchful eye.

It was Dave who propped me up as I shuffled along. He kept one hand wedged beneath my armpit and one hand cupped around my elbow. Behind us, the yells and yowls gradually receded. And though I was thankful to be escaping such an ugly noise, I also became conscious of the huge, enveloping silence that lay ahead.

It signified an emptiness – an isolation – that didn't bode well.

'We've been seen,' I whispered to Dave. (Father Ramon

was haranguing Dermid, so I assumed that I wouldn't be overheard.) 'People know we've come here. Lots of people.'

Dave sniffed. He obviously wasn't reassured.

For a few minutes we staggered on without speaking, while I struggled to find the right words. It's hard to explain how I felt, just then. Confused, of course, but the confusion was lifting. Sick, naturally. Horrified. Scared. And grateful – so grateful that Dave had been with me. That he was *still* with me, despite my recent conduct.

'Dave?' I squeaked at last. 'Did I do anything really . . . really bad?'

'No.' He shook his head. He knew what I was talking about.

'I think – I remember trying to jump someone –'

'You didn't.'

'Because you stopped me.' Tears welled in my eyes. 'You stopped me, Dave. Thank you. Thank you so much.'

'Don't worry. You're okay, now.'

'It was awful.'

'I know.' He paused. 'It was.'

'I can't believe it didn't affect you. All that blood . . .'

'Oh, I felt it,' he murmured. 'Believe me, I felt it. Just not the way you did.'

'How did you stop yourself?' I couldn't imagine having the strength. 'What happened, did you hold your breath, or something?'

'I saw your face.' His tone was flat. He had to lick his lips before continuing. 'You weren't there any more. When I saw that, I couldn't think about anything else.' He heaved a shaky sigh. 'It was like seeing you dead. No – worse. It was like – like –'

'Like seeing me turn into Casimir.' I can't tell you how

distraught I was. If Dave had kneed me in the gut, it would have been less painful. For thirty years I'd been able to ignore the truth, because I had never really *felt* like a vampire. Not like a vampire in the traditional sense, at any rate; not like one of those ravening, mindless, deformed monsters on the silver screen, with their bloodstained mouths and screeching cries and razor claws.

For thirty years I'd been telling myself that I was different, somehow – until, at that moment by the pit, I had behaved exactly like every vampire I'd ever condemned.

'Hey. Don't cry.' Alerted by my snuffles, Dave squeezed me in such a comforting way that I nearly lost it. Only by clenching every muscle did I manage to avoid throwing myself on to his chest, like a crazed groupie. 'It might have been hard, but you did it,' he said. 'That's the important thing. You held back.'

'Because *you* were there!' I whimpered, and he shrugged.

'It was the same for us all,' he replied softly. 'None of us did it without help. And from now on you'll find the whole thing much easier to handle.'

'Hey!' It was Dermid. When I looked over my shoulder, I saw him pointing. 'See that light?' he demanded, 'That's the kitchen door. You can go straight through there, and the bathroom's on your left.'

'Aren't you coming in?' Father Ramon queried, with obvious surprise.

'Nah, I gotta get back to the pit,' said Dermid. 'These things don't run themselves, y'know.' He waved the rest of us towards the house. 'Go on. Dad'll be along in a minute.'

So Dave and I stumbled forward, through the back gate. From there it was perhaps half a dozen metres to the kitchen door, across a cement patio littered with firewood, auto parts, rolls of chicken wire and dead pot plants. As I checked to make sure that Father Ramon was keeping up, I noticed that Dermid had begun to retrace his steps.

But he hadn't washed his hands of us. On the contrary, he repeatedly glanced back to monitor our progress – and I realised that we wouldn't be able to depart unseen.

'He's watching us,' I informed Dave, very quietly.

'Then we'll have to head straight through,' said Dave, in equally hushed tones. 'We'll go inside and leave by the front entrance. Then we'll double back to the van.'

'Can you do that, Nina?' Father Ramon asked. He was directly behind me. 'Can you walk that far?'

'If she can't, I'll carry her,' said Dave. 'Because we have to get the hell out of here. *Now*.'

And he pulled open the kitchen door.

I suppose we should have worked out that there'd be someone inside, waiting for us. As soon as Dave crossed the threshold, he was bailed up. I heard a click, turned my head, and spied a short, weathered, nuggetty man aiming a rifle directly at Dave's left ear.

Dave stopped – so abruptly that the priest bumped into him.

'Oh no!' cried Father Ramon 'Please – wait – I'm a priest –'

'And I'm an atheist,' the armed man spat. I recognised his cramped country vowels, having heard them already over the public address system. His appearance matched his voice; it was compressed but strangely formidable. Where he wasn't bald, his ash-grey hair had been clipped like a shorn sheep's. His rubbery features looked squashed, and he didn't have much of a neck. Yet his broad shoulders, big hands and broken nose were intimidating – as were his scars, and his empty blue eyes.

'We didn't come here to cause trouble!' Father Ramon quavered. (By this time he was holding his hands in the air.) 'Believe me, we didn't know anything about this event –'

'But you do now.' The armed man lowered his weapon slightly, to prod Dave in the ribs. 'Thing is, I'm busy. I've got a show to run. We'll talk later.' He jerked his chin. 'Downstairs. Go.'

'But –'

'*Move!*'

You can't argue with a rifle, especially when you're feeling sick. From where I was standing, the barrel of that thing seemed enormous. Like the mouth of a cannon. Of course, I knew that nothing discharged from it could possibly kill Dave. But I also knew that a bullet in the chest wouldn't improve his quality of life, either.

The thought of seeing him a permanent invalid, wheezing and choking through tattered lungs, almost made me throw up all over again. To be honest, I just . . . well, I couldn't bear it.

'Even if you shoot us, it won't make any difference,' I began, almost incoherent with panic and distress. 'You – you don't understand who we are –'

'*Nina!*' Dave's urgent reprimand silenced me at once. He kept his arm clamped around my shoulders as we shuffled towards a rough-cut hole in the kitchen floor. I can't tell you much about that kitchen, because I was more interested in the gun. Nevertheless, I did get a vague impression of pineapple-print curtains, unwashed dishes, old newspapers, dog bowls, dog leads, pliers, bones and rat traps. (It was

134

pretty obvious that no females were living in the house.)

'Are you Barry McKinnon?' The priest seemed determined to keep talking; I was awed by his ability to do so. 'Because if you are, I assure you, we simply came here to make inquiries about your silver bullets –'

'Later,' the man barked. 'We'll discuss it later.'

'So you *are* Barry?'

'Not to you, mate. To you I'm Mister McKinnon. Now get down there, and we'll work things out when I'm done.'

The staircase didn't inspire confidence. Someone had obviously sawn through the linoleum and thrown together a single flight of stairs using whatever timber happened to be lying around. Upon gingerly making my way to the bottom step, I found myself in a brick-lined basement with several doors leading off it. These doors resembled the hatch in the tiled pit outside; they were all thick and heavy and made of iron or steel, painted yellow, and they were reinforced with enormous bolts. I couldn't help wondering if Barry had used recycled prison doors, because they looked very old.

One of them was standing open.

'In there,' said Barry. He was bringing up the rear, his gun resting between Father Ramon's shoulder-blades. 'Go on.'

'In *there*?' The priest sounded appalled, and I understood why. The whole set-up was like something out of a horror movie. 'But what on earth –'

'Just *do* it!' Barry growled.

Even then (believe it or not) the little bottle of spiked Windex didn't so much as cross my mind. I'd completely forgotten about it. Perhaps I was still groggy from the blooding – or perhaps I'm not one of those people who react quickly and heroically to adverse circumstances.

Not like Zadia Bloodstone.

Anyway, the fact is that I allowed myself to be herded into Barry McKinnon's underground cell like a brainless farm animal, without uttering a single word of protest. The first thing I spotted, upon passing through the open door, was a stainless steel toilet without a seat. The second thing was an unmade bed. The third thing was a barred gate, clamped across an opening on the other side of the room.

Beyond the solid iron framework of this gate stretched a long, dark corridor. And from the somewhere down one end of this corridor echoed the faint sound of distant cheering.

Aghast, I stared at Dave.

'Right,' said Barry. 'I'll be back in a couple of hours.'

Then he pushed Father Ramon over the threshold, shut the door, and drew the bolt.

Chapter Twelve

For at least fifteen seconds no one spoke. Finally Dave said, 'This is a tank.'

When I looked around, I saw that he was right. We were standing in what appeared to be a huge, concrete drum – the kind normally used to collect rainwater. I'd seen quite a few of them so far, on my trip into the outback; they were generally sitting beside some farmhouse, half-buried in the earth.

'It must be connected to that pit,' I remarked dully. 'By an underground passage.'

Father Ramon gave a sudden start, then began to grope around in his pockets. When he produced his mobile phone, however, his shoulders drooped.

'No signal,' he lamented. I reached for my own mobile, just to check – and my fingers closed over the forgotten perfume bottle.

'Oh, hell!' I pulled it out. 'Oh, damn! My spray! I'm so sorry!'

'We can still use it,' was Dave's opinion. And the priest said, 'Use what?'

'It's like mace,' I explained. 'For self-defence. I can squirt it in people's eyes.'

'As a last resort,' Dave added, seeing Father Ramon wince.

'I know it would be dangerous, what with the gun and everything.'

All at once I felt dizzy. When I wobbled over to the bed, however, I discovered that it wasn't very comfortable. The sheets smelled bad, the blankets were filthy, and the rusty old springs squeaked like distressed guinea pigs. Nevertheless, it was better than the cold, hard, concrete floor.

'It's half-past eleven,' the priest observed. 'When did he say he'd be back? In a couple of hours? That'll be one-thirty.'

'We have to get out,' said Dave.

'We have to think.' Father Ramon put his hands to his temples. 'Just let me think.'

I couldn't think. My brain felt numb. I was still trying to process what had just happened – what I'd just seen. The pit. The creatures. The basement.

The blood.

My gaze travelled slowly around the oddly shaped room, from one item to the next. There was an overhead light and a wall-mounted heater. A power cable had been taped across the ceiling; it disappeared through a small, irregular hole in one wall. There was also a pile of old paperback books, and a plastic drink bottle. Various bits of torn clothing were scattered around.

It all looked pretty innocuous at first glance. But then I spied the manacle and chain attached to a bolt in the floor.

'Someone lives here,' I said.

Dave grunted.

'A person. Not an animal. There's a toilet.' I started to shake. Even my lips were shaking. 'You don't think it's like the Roman Empire, do you?'

'What?' Dave stared at me in confusion.

'You don't think they actually feed human beings to those things out there?'

Even as I spoke, the distant clamour of massed voices swelled to an appreciative roar. Our eyes swivelled fearfully towards the barred gate. Then Dave said, 'Nina, those things out there *are* human beings.'

'But –'

'They have to be. You were blooded. That only happens with human blood.'

'So you're quite sure, are you?' Father Ramon was doing his best to stay calm. 'You really believe that those creatures are werewolves?'

'Why not?' Dave said. He had removed his sunglasses. 'Nina and I are vampires.'

I wanted to point out that we weren't vampires like Zadia Bloodstone; we couldn't fly, or turn into bats, or walk through a hail of bullets. Whereas the things outside appeared to be genuine shape-shifters.

But I couldn't summon up the energy to speak.

'And you think they've actually been living in here?' Father Ramon glanced around at the meagre furnishings. 'As prisoners?'

'If you can call it living,' said Dave.

The priest rubbed his mouth. 'Of course we might be wrong,' he allowed, though not with much conviction. 'There are people who build underground homes in the desert, to keep cool. This room might be for casual workers who come here during the hotter months.'

Dave snorted. Even I was unimpressed.

'You don't chain your workers to the wall,' Dave argued, and Father Ramon couldn't disagree. In the silence that followed, another bloodthirsty roar from beyond the barred gate made us all flinch.

It occurred to me that we might have been left in the tank for a reason. What if, when the fight was over, Barry McKinnon decided to open that barred gate? What if the victorious werewolf retreated back into its lair – and found us waiting? If that happened, an atomiser full of Windex wouldn't be enough to defend us.

'We've left our luggage at the hotel,' Dave pointed out suddenly, in hoarse accents. 'We've booked a room. When someone starts searching for us, the trail will lead straight here.' He turned to Father Ramon. 'I mean, you *asked* about Barry McKinnon, didn't you? You asked the receptionist.'

'And she winked,' said the priest, pulling a long face. 'She might be a friend of his.'

'Yes, but even if she lies, we talked to other witnesses. Out there by the pit.'

'Who probably won't want the police to know what they've been doing,' was Father Ramon's glumly expressed view. Dave's response was to bend over, propping his hands on both knees. Suddenly he looked exhausted – and very sick.

'Come and sit down,' I entreated, patting the vacant stretch of mattress beside me. Poor Dave couldn't move, though; not without help. Father Ramon had to take his arm, and lower him onto the bed.

I recognised all the symptoms of a blinding headache.

'Okay, listen.' As the priest addressed us both, he flicked a nervous look at the door. 'I'm sure these people will have the sense to let us out,' he said, very softly. 'But if the worst comes to the worst, we mustn't forget that there are three of us. We should be able to defend ourselves.'

'Against *those* things?' I couldn't imagine what he expected us to do. 'Did you see their claws? And their teeth? They could easily bite our heads off. *Easily.*'

'Perhaps they could, at present,' he conceded. 'But there may not be two of them by the time they're done. And even the winner might not be in great shape.'

He was right. We all peered at the gate, analysing the noises that were drifting through its bars. We heard a raucous chanting. We heard moans of disappointment. And we heard a startled canine yelp, as if a very large dog had just received a nasty shock.

'Maybe we can hit it over the head when it comes in,' said Dave. Gloomily he surveyed his surroundings. 'Except that there's nothing in here to hit it *with*.'

'The bed?' I suggested. The bed, however, was bolted to the floor – and the heater was out of our reach. Obviously the McKinnons didn't want to give their captives anything that even remotely resembled ammunition.

'We could stick Dave's knife in its neck,' I began, confident that I would be able to find the jugular on anything. At which point Father Ramon gasped.

'Oh! Wait!' he cried, fumbling in his pockets. After a few seconds, he produced a box of matches. 'Windex is flammable, isn't it? I'm sure it is,' he said.

Dave and I stared. 'What are those for?' I demanded. 'You haven't started smoking, have you?'

'I like to carry them on me,' the priest explained, 'just in case any votive candles burn out.'

'Oh.'

'We've sheets here, too. And books . . .'

After a whispered discussion, we decided that we would

141

drench one of the sheets in Windex. Then, if a werewolf did burst into the room, we would ignite the Windex and fling the flaming sheet over our feral opponent's head.

Dave wanted to try the same trick on Barry McKinnon. But Father Ramon didn't approve.

'He hasn't hurt us, Dave,' the priest objected. 'You want to set him alight the second he comes in? What if he's decided to let us go?'

'Then he won't come in, will he?' Dave rejoined. 'He'll just open the door.'

'He might want to discuss things first.'

'Oh, *please*.' I couldn't believe my ears. 'He's got a *gun*, Father.'

'She's right,' said Dave. 'The minute we see his gun, we'll know what he really wants to do.'

'We need to get him before he gets us,' I insisted. 'And if Dermid's with him . . . well, maybe Dave should use his knife on Dermid.'

'While you grab the gun, Nina.' Dave was nodding. 'Father Ramon can throw the sheet, you can go for the gun, and I'll stab Dermid.'

'It's all right, Father.' I could see that the priest was about to protest. 'Even if I do get shot, it won't be fatal. You're the one who has to watch out, not me.'

This was a typical Zadia Bloodstone remark. It's the sort of thing that looks pretty good on paper. But the fact is, I couldn't say it like Zadia Bloodstone. My voice trembled as I thought about copping a bullet in the gut. While an injury like that wouldn't trouble Zadia, it could easily ruin *my* life.

The prospect made me feel sick all over again.

Even so, I was able to hold two corners of the soiled,

greyish sheet that Father Ramon dragged off the bed. He sprinkled Windex on to the centre of this sheet while Dave held the other two corners; the sheet was then placed midway between the door and the gate, ready for use.

When my atomiser was empty, Dave wrapped it in a blanket and stamped on it. He then distributed the resulting bits of glass, sharing them out between the three of us. According to Dave, they were better than nothing. 'You never know,' he said. 'They may come in handy.'

Though I couldn't imagine fending off a ravenous were-wolf with a tiny sliver of perfume bottle, I tucked one jagged shard into my pocket. From the pit, a savage roar was followed by a high-pitched squeal. Father Ramon immediately pulled off his jumper, exposing the dog-collar that he wore underneath.

'They might think twice about harming a minister of the church,' he conjectured.

By this time Dave was back on the bed, with his head in his hands. I wondered if he was feeling well enough to answer a question.

'Do you think the stories are true?' I asked. 'Do you think werewolves turn back into human beings when the sun rises?'

'Who knows?' Dave mumbled.

'There's a full moon tonight,' I went on, 'so *that* bit must be true.' Another troubling thought crossed my mind. 'Do you think they're just like us? Do you think they spread the werewolf infection when they bite people?'

'Maybe,' said Dave.

'What happens to a vampire who gets bitten by a were-wolf, anyway?' In *Underworld*, as far as I could recall, such bites were supposed to be fatal – but *Underworld* was just a fantasy. It wasn't real. 'And what happens if a vampire bites a werewolf? Would it have any effect?'

'Don't ask me.' Dave didn't seem particularly interested. 'You're the one who writes *Dracula* spin-offs.'

'It might have some effect,' I continued, thinking aloud. 'It might be worth a try.'

'Nina – we won't be fanging anyone if we can help it.' Dave lifted his head. 'You know what Sanford always tells us. If you give into that urge –'

'– it'll harm you as much as it harms your victim,' I finished, impatiently quoting Sanford. 'I realise that. But what if it's a choice between psychological damage and total dismemberment? What if those things try to *eat* us, Dave?' (My panic was mounting.) 'Shouldn't we at least bite back?'

'Before you do, you might want to cast an eye over this,' said Father Ramon. He had picked up one of the books. 'Someone's been reading *Harry Potter*. And Philip Pullman. And Terry Pratchett.' He cast a troubled glance in my direction. 'I'd be very surprised if any of these books belonged to the McKinnons,' he added. 'They look like teenage reading, to me.'

Dave groaned. I was struck dumb. Father Ramon squatted down to examine the other books, but found no name scribbled inside them. I watched him leaf through one battered volume after another. The minutes ticked by. I checked my watch; it was already ten past twelve.

By two o'clock, the mob outside was still howling enthusiastically – and I was half-dead from the strain of waiting. My nerves were shredded. The longer we sat there, the less likely it seemed that we would ever have the strength or speed to carry out our ambitious plans. In fact the very sight of Father

Ramon filled me with a sudden, overwhelming sense of despair; he was actually reading *Harry Potter and the Half-Blood Prince*, as if he had nothing better to do.

'Maybe we should tell the McKinnons that we're vampires,' I blurted out at last. Seeing Dave's jaw drop, I hurried to demonstrate that I wasn't going mad. 'They might not kill us if they think we're worth money,' I said. 'We could offer them some kind of media deal.'

'I dunno.' Dave's tone was doubtful. 'What makes you think they'd go for the publicity? I didn't see any posters up in town.'

'They'll be making quite enough money from their were-wolf fights,' Father Ramon quietly remarked, looking up from *Harry Potter*. 'If you tell them who you are, Nina, you might spend the rest of your life as a captive, forced to fight against other vampires.'

'Or you might be digging your own grave,' Dave morosely pointed out. 'There aren't many people who'd think twice about killing a vampire.'

'If I were you, I'd only reveal who you are as a last resort,' the priest concluded.

No one spoke again for a while after that. The noise from the pit became louder and louder. Dave had to lie down. Father Ramon rose and began to pace the floor, his attention divided between the sinister barred gate and his book. He obviously found the distant crowing just as ominous as I did.

Then all at once silence fell. He stopped in his tracks. We stared at each other, listening hard.

Once a relaxed murmur became audible, I knew. We both knew.

'It's finished,' he hissed.

145

'Oh my God.' I jumped up. 'Oh my God, oh my God!'

'Give me that sheet,' the priest whispered. But Dave said weakly, 'It's all right. Don't panic.'

'Don't *panic*?' I couldn't believe my ears. 'They might send those werewolves back *in* here, Dave!'

'I don't think so.' Dave had been lying with his arm draped across his bloodshot eyes. Now he uncovered them, and scanned the room. 'Just look at this place,' he murmured. 'There are no scratches on the paint. No bite marks on the door.' He flapped a listless hand. 'If those things out there ever got in here, they'd tear the place apart. And they haven't.'

'There's always a first time,' Father Ramon objected. Dave, however, shook his head.

'It would be too messy,' he replied. 'You can't hose this place off – there's no drain in the floor. Not like there is out there.'

'You think we'll be forced into the *pit*?' I squeaked.

'Not if I can help it,' he assured me. But since he was on his back, in bed, with a raging headache and a pasty complexion, I didn't find him very convincing.

Father Ramon fetched the sheet. I went to stand near the door, while Dave sat up and pulled out his Swiss army knife. No one said anything; we were concentrating too fiercely on the sounds drifting into our cell.

Five minutes passed. Then another ten. As the minute hand on my watch slowly measured out a complete circumference, I passed from a state of near hysteria to one of acute anxiety – until the length of our wait took the edge off my fear. Weren't the McKinnons *ever* going to return? What on earth was happening?

'Oh, man,' Dave eventually remarked. He was still sitting on the bed, as if he couldn't find the strength to get up.

'What?' I prompted, after he failed to continue. And he lifted his face to address me.

'I was just thinking,' he croaked. 'Suppose no one comes down here until after sunrise?'

I gasped.

'Suppose the McKinnons get here and find the pair of us dead to the world?' Dave continued. 'We won't be able help Father Ramon. We won't be able to do a thing.'

'Oh, but . . .' I checked my watch, for perhaps the hundredth time that night. 'We still have a good two hours, at least. Anyway, he *said* he'd be back soon.'

'But what if he isn't?' Dave closed his eyes for a moment. 'What if something's cropped up?' he faltered. 'What are we going to do if the McKinnons walk in and decide that we're already dead?'

I had no idea. My mind was a blank. And Dave must have had the same problem, because he slumped forward mutely, massaging his eye-sockets.

It was Father Ramon who supplied an answer to Dave's question.

'I tell you what *I'm* going to do,' the priest announced. 'I'm going to pretend that I killed you both.'

Dave snorted.

'I mean it.' Father Ramon's tone was perfectly serious. 'I'll say that I smothered you to save myself.'

'What are you *talking* about?' Dave groaned, and I exclaimed, 'That's stupid!'

'No, it's not. It's our best chance.' Lowering his voice, the priest began to argue his case. 'We're only in danger because the McKinnons are worried that we'll tell the police what they've been doing here,' he said. 'But if I have *your* deaths on my conscience, I won't be telling anyone about anything. Will I?'

He went on to explain that he would write a confession, which he would offer to Barry as insurance. Then he would drive away with our 'corpses', promising to remain silent about the McKinnons' activities as long as the McKinnons remained silent about the cold-blooded murders that he had committed to save his own skin.

'I'll demand that you be thoroughly wrapped up before we take you outside,' he finished. 'I'll pretend that I'm worried about people seeing you.'

'But –'

'It'll work, Nina. I'm sure it will. In fact it's our only hope.' He frowned at me. 'What else are we going to do? What else can I possibly say? Can *you* think of anything?'

I couldn't. Though I tried and tried, I was unable to come up with an alternative plan.

I was still racking my brain when, at 6:57 a.m., I suddenly blacked out.

Chapter Thirteen

I woke up at 5:29 p.m., and didn't know where I was.

That's always a terrible feeling. It hasn't happened to me often, thank God, but it's one of those nasty events more likely to befall a vampire than a normal person (unless, of course, you're a normal person who's a drunk or a drug addict). For a second or two I lay in total confusion. My face was covered, and it was very dark.

Then something moved beside me.

'Who – who's that?' I quavered.

There was a brief silence.

'Nina?' came the muffled response.

'Dave?'

'Shh!'

I could feel him struggling, and when I tried to raise my arms, I understood why. Something was binding them. I was wrapped up like a mummy.

So was Dave, to judge from the way he was thrashing about.

After a moment's blind panic, I realised that my bonds were fairly loose. I was able to bend my elbows and slide my hands up until they were level with my shoulders. Then I tugged and clawed at the shroud that enfolded me, working away until I'd dragged it off my eyes.

I found myself staring straight up into Dave's shadowy face.

'We're in the van,' he whispered.

'What?'

'Shh!' He was kneeling beside me, plucking at the rope that encircled my chest. Frantically I began to wriggle out of my cocoon, which had a familiar smell; apparently someone had rolled me up in the Windex-covered bed sheet.

'Where's your phone?' Dave hissed.

'I don't know . . . let me see . . .' I thrust aside a great swag of cotton, before searching the pockets of my coat with unsteady hands. 'It's gone,' I informed him, very quietly.

'So is mine,' he breathed. 'Someone's taken them.'

'Are you sure this is *our* truck?'

'I'm sure,' said Dave, and when I looked around, I had to agree with him. Though my wristwatch didn't provide much illumination, I could still make out the double doors in front of me, and the sheets of black plastic that lined every other visible surface.

'What do you think?' I asked, in hushed tones. 'Do you think Father Ramon's trick worked?'

I was referring to the priest's fake homicide scenario. Dave must have understood that, because he shrugged.

'I dunno,' he softly replied. 'Maybe.'

'Except that we don't have our mobiles,' I fretted. 'Why would he have taken them away?'

Dave didn't answer; he was already crawling towards the only exit, leaving a dim tangle of rope and fabric behind him. As I groped around for my sunglasses (which seemed to have vanished, along with my phone), he gave one of the doors a tentative push.

To my utter astonishment, it swung open.

'Shit!' Dave jerked back, sucking air through his teeth. All at once he was silhouetted against a silver-gilt landscape of stones and saltbush. My heart sank when I saw the corner of a tin shed. Clearly, our van was still parked where we'd left it.

'Shh,' Dave warned, placing a finger to his lips. He thrust his head outside, glancing around with great caution. At last he gave me a thumbs-up signal.

When I hesitated, he beckoned urgently.

'Quick!' he muttered. 'Before anyone sees us!'

'But where are you going?' I was confused. 'Isn't Father Ramon supposed to be driving us away? Shouldn't we be waiting right here?' Seeing him frown, I added, 'We were all wrapped up, just like he promised. The plan must have worked.'

'If the plan had worked, we'd be back home by now,' Dave retorted, under his breath. 'And we'd still have our mobile phones.' He craned his neck once more, scanning our immediate vicinity. 'I think we should check things out before we decide what to do. Otherwise we might end up making a big mistake.'

He was right. I could see that. So I followed him out of the van and helped him to close the door, as quietly as possible. A stiff breeze soughed through the branches of a nearby peppercorn tree, masking the crunch of our footsteps.

Dave put his lips to my ear.

'I'm going to sneak around and make sure that nobody's in the driver's seat,' he buzzed. 'You keep an eye out.' Before I could protest, he was edging along the side of the van, keeping its bright orange bulk between himself and the McKinnons' kitchen window. I recognised this window

151

because it was all lit up; a golden glow poured through the familiar pineapple-print curtains drawn across it. Apart from the moon, it was the only source of illumination in an area that must have been about half the size Switzerland.

I was feeling a little woozy, at this point. Nevertheless, I had the presence of mind to notice that our van was no longer surrounded by other vehicles. I could see only a dirty white utility truck parked nearby, next to a plum-coloured four-wheel-drive that fairly bristled with antennae and bull-bars. I was trying to memorise the truck's number-plate when the pineapple-print curtains suddenly disappeared. Someone had snapped off the kitchen light. Within seconds, a screen door banged as Barry and his son emerged from the house, talking loudly.

But by that time I had already ducked out of sight, so I didn't witness their exit. I only heard it.

My retreat was so abrupt that I ran headlong into Dave, who seized my arm and dragged me behind the tin shed. Though I'm convinced that we must have stepped on loose gravel and dry sticks, we didn't alert the McKinnons. They were too busy arguing with each other about who was going to drive the van.

In the end, Barry prevailed. He secured the van for himself, while Dermid agreed to drive the truck. Not once was Father Ramon mentioned by either man. As engines fired and doors slammed shut, I pinched Dave's elbow. I suppose that I was seeking reassurance, but I didn't get it. The look on his face made my stomach lurch.

Like me, he must have been wondering if Father Ramon was dead.

'Just wait,' he whispered. And that's what we did. We stood

152

there, frozen in the shadows, until our van and the McKinnons' truck had roared off into the night. Only when the sound of their engines was just a faint and distant hum did we finally emerge from our hiding place.

But even then Dave remained cautious.

'There might be someone else inside,' he muttered, squinting towards the house. I did the same.

'Are we – I mean – do we actually need to go inside?' I queried. It was little more than a rhetorical question, because I knew that we didn't have much choice. Father Ramon might still be in the house, along with a phone, or a gun, or even the key to the remaining vehicle.

Outside the house, there was nothing. Nothing as far as the eye could see.

Dave cleared his throat. 'We'll arm ourselves,' he suggested gruffly, stooping to pick up a piece of discarded fence-post. 'You take this. I'll find something else.'

'We shouldn't use the same door.'

'What?'

At long last my brain was beginning to function. 'We should split up,' I proposed, in a very small voice. 'I'll go to the front door first. If someone's inside, he'll be concentrating on the front door –'

'Which means that I can sneak in the back, through that open window over there.' Dave didn't seem to approve of my plan. In the faint wash of moonlight I could easily make out his troubled expression. 'I dunno, Nina,' he said. 'I dunno if we should split up. You'll be all on your own . . .'

'So will you,' I rejoined. 'And you must be feeling just as sick as me.'

'Yeah, but –'

'It's our best chance.' I was convinced of this. 'Anyway, all the lights are off. I don't think anyone's inside.'

'Except maybe Father Ramon,' Dave mumbled. We exchanged another long, anxious look. Then Dave handed me the fence-post.

'Okay,' he said. 'You try the front door. I'll find an axe or something, and go round the back. This place is bound to be knee-deep in things you can hurt people with.'

'Dave?'

'What?'

I swallowed before speaking. 'Where do you think the werewolves are?'

My question hit him like a punch. His whole body drooped. It was apparent that the werewolves had momentarily slipped his mind.

I felt bad about jogging his memory.

'They must have changed into people by now,' I said, making a feeble effort to comfort him. 'And if they haven't, they'll be locked up somewhere. Even Barry McKinnon wouldn't let them roam around loose.'

'Oh Christ, Nina.' Dave put out a hand, propping himself against the corrugated wall of the shed. His voice was ragged. 'I dunno. I dunno what we're going to find in there. Maybe we should just start walking.'

'No.' That was out of the question. 'We can't. It's too risky. The sun might rise before we get anywhere.' I took a deep breath, and squared my shoulders. 'Let's just get this over with,' I exhorted, with a courage born of pure desperation. 'Before Barry comes back.'

I can't pretend that I waltzed up to the McKinnons' front door with steely eyes and a kick-ass attitude, like Zadia

154

Bloodstone. In fact, to be perfectly honest, I nearly didn't make it at all. At one point I froze in my tracks, too scared to take another step. But the thought that Father Ramon might be bleeding to death somewhere underground finally propelled me forward; after a brief, internal struggle, I somehow made myself cross that creaky veranda, and turn that tarnished doorknob.

When the latch clicked, I couldn't have been more surprised. It had never occurred to me that the McKinnons would drive away *without locking up their house*. Perhaps people in the country are more honest than people in the city. Or perhaps securing your property is the kind of thing that you forget to do, when you're about to get rid of two human corpses.

I gave the door a gentle shove, wincing as its hinges squealed.

'Nina?'

If I had died of shock, right then, it would have been Dave's fault. As it was, I almost fainted. He had armed himself with a shovel, and his big, shaggy, ill-defined figure would have terrified even Zadia Bloodstone, had she found it waiting for her.

I suppose he must have been on the point of letting me in.

'For God's sake!' I hissed. 'You practically gave me a heart attack!'

'Sorry. The back door was unlocked.'

'Is anyone here?'

'Not that I can see.'

'Have you checked downstairs?'

'Nope.'

'What about the bedrooms?'

'I had a quick look. They're empty.'

'Are there any lights on?'

Dave shook his head.

'Then we're safe,' I decided. 'If you're a normal person, you don't walk around in the dark.'

'Let's check downstairs,' he said.

I followed him along a high, dim corridor lit by two dangling bulbs. The rooms that we passed obviously hadn't been painted (or even cleaned) in years, and they were full of really horrible things: animal skulls, pig-shooting magazines, bloodstained clothes, chewed apple cores. There had been no attempt to match curtains, repair blinds, or make beds.

The whole place smelled bad.

'Right,' whispered Dave, upon reaching the kitchen. 'I'll check the basement while you stay here and keep watch.'

'There's a light on down there.'

'Yeah. I can see that.'

'Be careful, Dave.' My voice cracked; I didn't want to be left on my own. 'Don't open any doors unless you know what's behind them.'

'It's okay,' he assured me. 'I'm not brave enough to do anything stupid.'

Then he began to descend the staircase.

My gaze didn't linger on him. Instead it skipped from the grubby green cupboards to the peeling wallpaper; from an overflowing garbage-bin to a china bowl full of silver bullets. When I spotted the empty wooden knife-block, I wondered if I should search the room for a weapon that was slightly more efficient than my fence-post.

But I didn't want to make too much noise, crashing through drawers full of cutlery. The ticking of the clock on the wall was loud enough. What with that, and the sighing of the wind, and the humming of the refrigerator, I found it hard to listen for approaching vehicles.

The sudden swell of a murmured conversation underfoot made my job even more difficult. Though I strained to catch the words, I couldn't make them out. As far as I could tell, the tone of the dialogue was excited rather than fearful. Nevertheless, my nerves were stretched to breaking point by the time a muffled voice said, 'Nina? Are you still up there?'

'Dave!' I cried. 'Are you okay?'

'I sure am,' Dave answered. 'And so is Father Ramon.'

I couldn't even respond to that. My throat closed up as tears sprang to my eyes. It's funny how things hit you, sometimes: things that knock you sideways because they're such revelations. The fact that you're really a vampire, say. Or the fact that you care about someone a great deal, and you didn't even know it.

The relief that flooded me was so overwhelming that I nearly dropped my fence-post, and had to lean against the kitchen table.

'Nina? What's wrong?' Dave's head had appeared, popping out of the hole in the floor. 'Are you feeling sick?'

'No. I'm fine.' Though I wasn't, of course. 'What are we going to do now? Look for a key?'

'We don't have to. They didn't lock the cell door. They just bolted it from the outside.' Having reached the topmost step, Dave moved aside to make way for Father Ramon. 'We'd better not turn on any lights, Father. Just in case the McKinnons come back and see them from a distance.'

'Oh, I don't think they'll be coming back any time soon,' Father Ramon replied, before he, too, began to emerge from the hole in the floor: first his head, then his shoulders, then his torso. He didn't look any different; there were no bruises on his face or rips in his clothes, and his thick grey hair was no more dishevelled than usual.

He didn't see me until I moved towards him.

'Nina!' he said with a smile. 'You're okay, are you?'

'Yes. Oh, yes.' I was about to fling my arms around him when I heard an unexpected creak. And my heart seemed to do a back-flip.

Someone else was mounting the stairs behind Father Ramon.

'*Who's that?*' I yelped.

'Don't worry. It's all right.' The priest stepped forward, inserting himself between me and the stranger. 'It's only Reuben.'

My jaw dropped.

'Reuben won't hurt you,' Father Ramon added quickly. 'He didn't before, and he won't now. Reuben – you remember Nina, don't you? She's not dead, as you can see. Or maybe you can't.' He gave an embarrassed chuckle. 'I'm afraid it's a bit dark in here.'

You might be wondering what I did, upon being formally introduced to my very first werewolf. I'm afraid that I didn't do anything much. I just stared and stared, with my mouth hanging open.

Because Reuben was gorgeous.

It's a mystery to me how that mangy, skulking, ill-formed beast from the pit could have turned into such a beautiful boy. Not that he looked particularly well-groomed, or anything – far from it. His clothes were soiled and torn. His fingernails were dirty. Dried blood was smeared across his

158

neck and chest, and was soaking through the bandage that had been wrapped around his left forearm. I doubt that his hair had been cut in years; it was a mane of snarled, disorderly brown curls that hung down to his shoulders. If he hadn't been so young, he probably would have been sporting a beard down to his navel, instead of the scrubby growth that covered his chin like moss.

But despite being unkempt, unshaven and thoroughly uncared for, Reuben was still the most stunning guy I'd ever seen. Though he wasn't very tall, his proportions were perfect. So were his teeth, and his nose, and his high, sculptured cheekbones. He had enormous green eyes ringed by jet-black lashes, and a lean, wiry, muscular build. Though adorned with many scabs and scars, his hands were as finely modelled as his face, with long fingers and strong wrists.

What I most admired about him, however, was his vibrancy. You could tell at a glance that he wasn't a vampire, because no vampire ever had such a warm olive complexion, or such luminous eyes. No vampire ever moved in such an energetic way, as if he could barely restrain his enthusiasm or his impatience. Even when he was standing still, Reuben seemed restless. You could almost feel the nerves twitching under his skin.

When he scrutinised me, his whole head lunged forward – and I have to admit that I fell back a few steps. I suppose that I still nursed a lingering, irrational fear that he was going to pounce like a panther.

'You look better standing up,' he remarked, squinting through the shadows. I glanced at Father Ramon, in mute appeal. Because Reuben wasn't making any sense.

'That was Reuben's cell, downstairs,' the priest explained.

'He came back in there after you fell asleep. After he . . . when he was himself again.'

Only Father Ramon could have put it so delicately. Dave was a little more blunt.

'What about the other werewolf?' he asked. 'Shouldn't we be letting *him* out, as well?'

The priest hesitated, as Reuben swung around to confront Dave.

'His name was Orlando,' Reuben said harshly. 'And I killed him.'

'Oh.' Dave cringed, though I don't suppose anyone saw him do it except me. Not in that light.

'I killed him and then I ate him,' Reuben continued. There was so much raw anger and self-disgust in his voice that I could hardly bear to listen. 'I don't remember doing it, but I saw what was left of him afterwards. When I woke up.'

'Don't think about that now,' Father Ramon advised. 'We'll talk about it later. Right now we have to go.'

'Yes. Let's get out of here,' I whimpered. But Reuben scowled.

'I'm not going anywhere,' he spat, with more venom than I would have thought possible. 'I'm staying right here. And when those bastards come back, I'll kill them.'

'No, no.' The priest laid a hand on Reuben's arm. 'You mustn't do that. It might seem like the right solution, but it isn't.'

'If I don't kill them, they'll come after us!'

'Reuben . . .' Father Ramon's tone was the same one that he always uses at our group meetings, when he's trying to reason somebody out of a black mood. 'I'm sorry to be so frank,' he gently admonished, 'but haven't you killed enough people already?'

Believe it or not, this was exactly the right thing to say. Reuben seemed to crumple. His shoulders sagged. A sob burst out of him.

'It's not your fault,' the priest continued. 'I understand that.'

'I can't – I can't –'

'You're not to blame for what's happened in the past,' Father Ramon assured him. 'But if you kill the McKinnons, the sin will be on your head. Not on theirs.'

'We have to go,' said Dave. 'Really. We have to go *now*.' Tentatively he addressed Reuben. 'Listen, mate – about that four-wheel drive parked outside. Do you happen to know where the keys are? Cos if you don't, we're going to have to start walking.'

Reuben sniffed. He wiped his damp cheeks, spreading some of the dirt around. Finally he looked up at Dave.

'I don't need keys,' he replied hoarsely. 'Not when it comes to car engines.'

Then he pushed past us, bounding towards the kitchen door.

Chapter Fourteen

It's hardly surprising that Reuben Schneider knew how to hot-wire a car. Until the age of fourteen, he'd led a very disorderly life

His mother should never have had any children. Of the seven sons she bore (to three different men), one is now dead, one's in jail, one's a drug dealer and one has mental health problems. The eldest son, Dane, is twenty years older than Reuben; when the boys' mother died of an alcohol-related disease, Dane and his wife invited eight-year-old Reuben and his twelve-year-old brother Jessie into their home. But Reuben and Jessie were pretty wild. They drank and smoked and sniffed the odd can of petrol. They stole cars and went for joy rides. Sometimes they vandalised the empty shops that were becoming more and more common in the main street of their small country town, which was slowly wilting at the edges, like a week-old lettuce in the fridge.

So no one was much surprised when Reuben was found lying naked in a paddock one morning, with no memory of how he'd arrived there. He'd been drinking quite heavily the evening before, because his older brother Callum had come to town – and Callum was always happy to buy beer for teenagers. Since Reuben and Callum and Jessie and their friends had all got drunk too, it was generally thought that they must have played a practical joke on Reuben.

No one connected Reuben's lost night with the six dead sheep that were discovered on nearby farms the next day, with their throats torn out and their entrails gone. Everyone blamed wild dogs for the slaughter. Everyone, that is, except Barry McKinnon. Because Barry knew a lot about werewolves. He knew things that most people don't know.

He knew, for example, that werewolves are born, not made. Unlike vampires, werewolves don't spread their infection. That's why werewolves are so rare. They come from a particular gene pool that originated in Spain or Portugal, and they're always seventh sons. In fact one of the South American countries used to provide a cash payment for every seventh son born, just to prevent these babies from being killed by their parents. I can't remember which country it was (Argentina, perhaps?), but if you want to know more, you can look it up on the Internet.

Of course, seventh sons aren't as common as they used to be. At least not in Australia, or Europe, or North America. That's why you'll find more werewolves in countries like the Philippines and Brazil. Nevertheless, it sometimes happens (even in Australia, or Europe, or North America) that a boy, upon entering puberty, suffers an adverse reaction to a certain stage in every lunar cycle. If he's lucky, he won't end up dead by morning. (Apparently unrestrained werewolves are often killed by fox-baits or pig-shooters or hypothermia – because lying naked in a frosty paddock can be fatal.) If he's *extremely* lucky, his parents soon work out what's going on, and take steps to protect him. They might lock him up or pump him full of tranquillisers when they're expecting a full moon.

They might shield him from the public gaze.

But if he's very unlucky indeed, someone like Barry McKinnon will get to him first. And that's quite likely, because the Barry McKinnons of this world know exactly what to look for.

I should explain how Barry managed to capture his were-wolves, so you'll understand why Reuben found himself in such a predicament. First of all, Barry used to make a point of listening to regional news broadcasts from across the country. Whenever he heard a story about stock losses blamed on dingos or feral dogs, he would head straight for the scene of the attack. Then, upon reaching his destination, he would start to make inquiries. He'd hang out in pubs and check the local papers, trying to find out if any teenaged residents had been 'playing up'. By masquerading as a youth worker with engine trouble, he would not only buy himself a few days in town; he would also have an excuse for his interest in the problems of young people – problems such as unexplained absences at night, sudden displays of aggression, blackouts, moodiness and mysterious injuries. Sometimes he would ask about the number of children in a particular family, though for the most part he wouldn't even have to. If there were seven sons, this unusual fact would often be volunteered without encouragement.

By the time he'd left the area, Barry would have narrowed down his search. He would have identified his quarry's name, address and customary hang-outs. Armed with this information, his son would pass through town soon afterwards, driving a panel van that had been rented with a fake ID. Dermid would be in and out of the place so quickly that he would rarely attract any kind of attention.

But when he left, he would take with him a drunk, stoned, hog-tied or otherwise incapacitated werewolf, concealed in the back of his panel van.

According to Reuben, the McKinnons had used this technique at least twice before they kidnapped him. Other werewolves had been acquired in other ways. One Filipino boy had been purchased from his grandfather and smuggled into the country. One fully grown werewolf had been tracked down somewhere in the wilds of northern Australia – where he'd been living a miserable, isolated existence, drinking himself to death. In neither case had the friendless werewolf been reported missing.

'*I* probably was, in the end,' Reuben remarked. 'But everybody would have thought I'd run away. Like Callum ran away. I was always saying I'd run away.'

At this stage in his narrative he had to stop, overcome by some memory or emotion that caused him to turn his head and stare out the window. We were well past Cobar by then, driving hell-for-leather towards Sydney in the McKinnons' four-wheel-drive. Our luggage had been left behind at the Miner's Rest motel; we had decided not to return there, in case the staff were friends of Barry McKinnon's.

Besides, as Dave repeatedly pointed out, we had to get back home as quickly as possible – preferably before the sun came up.

Father Ramon was at the wheel, because he was the only one of us still in possession of a driver's licence (not to mention a mobile phone and a credit card). Dave had offered to sit beside Reuben in the back. I don't know why, exactly. It's possible that Dave didn't trust Reuben. Or perhaps Dave wanted to sit as far away from the headlights as possible, since

I was the one who had managed to score Father Ramon's sunglasses. Poor Dave's eyes were completely unprotected; we could only hope that, if he shut them on those rare occasions when we encountered an oncoming vehicle, he wouldn't start bleeding from his tear-ducts.

'You can notify your brothers just as soon as we've sorted things out,' Father Ramon advised Reuben, in an attempt to offer some kind of comfort. 'As I mentioned before, Dave and Nina and their friends would prefer not to have dealings with the police. They wouldn't want to become involved in any official measures that you might take against the McKinnons. But once we've laid our plans, you'll be able to go straight back home.' Glancing into the rear-view mirror, the priest addressed Dave. 'While you were asleep, I told Reuben all about your . . . um . . . difficulties,' he finished. 'I had to.'

Dave grunted. Reuben turned. He had a way of throwing his entire body into every movement, expending vast amounts of energy on the simplest little action.

'Yeah,' said Reuben, seizing on the topic of our 'difficulties' like a starving leopard tucking into a wildebeest. 'I didn't believe him, at first, but then I thought – why not? If I'm a werewolf, why can't there be vampires? Especially since you can't fly, or nothing.'

'No,' Dave murmured. 'We can't.'

'And you don't go round biting people, either. Is that right?'

'That's right,' I piped up, craning around to emphasise this all-important fact. 'We're *reformed* vampires. We've never attacked anyone. Have we, Dave?'

Dave shook his head. Reuben's sudden crack of laughter had an almost hysterical edge to it; his mood was volatile, and he couldn't seem to keep still. He was constantly scratching and squirming and tugging at his clothes and hair. I could see why Dave looked uneasy, though he must have felt sorry for Reuben. How could you *not* feel sorry for someone who's been locked in a concrete tank for five years? I mean, it obviously wasn't Reuben's fault that he had an incendiary streak.

All the same, I couldn't deny that he was an unsettling person to have around – exciting, but unsettling. Like a smoking volcano.

'Reformed vampires,' Reuben cackled. 'That's good. I wish *I* could reform myself. But I can't.'

'Are you sure?' said Father Ramon. He didn't mean to imply anything; of that I'm quite convinced.

Nevertheless, Reuben frowned.

'Of course I'm sure!' he snapped. 'That's good. How can I stop myself if I don't even know what I'm doing? I never remember a *thing*! Not one, single, bloody thing!'

'Yes, of course,' said the priest, in a soothing manner. Whereupon Dave quickly changed the subject.

'I'm getting a signal,' he observed, tapping at the screen display on Father Ramon's mobile phone. This was exciting news. So far, we hadn't been able to make any calls, because the McKinnons didn't have a land line – and because Wolgaroo Corner was too remote for anything but satellite phone reception. Finally, however, we had strayed into an area with mobile coverage.

Dave immediately began to punch my mother's number into the keypad.

'Who are you calling?' I demanded. 'Are you calling my mum?'

'Yeah,' Dave replied. 'She must be pretty worried –'

'Here! Give it here!' I tried to grab at the phone, desperate to hear my mother's voice. 'Please, Dave? Let me talk to her.'

Dave submitted without protest, and I jammed the little device to my ear just as Mum said 'Hello?' at the other end of the line.

'Mum?'

'Nina?'

'It's all right,' I croaked. 'We're all right, Mum.'

'Where the hell –?'

'I know! I'm sorry. You wouldn't *believe* what happened! It was *awful*.'

'Where are you?' She cut me off. 'Are you coming home?'

'We're on our way. But it's going to take a while.'

'Nina.' Dave had leaned forward. 'Did you have any identification on you?'

'What?' I couldn't believe that he would even *think* of interrupting me at such a time. 'Dave, I'm talking to my mother-'

'Were you carrying any identification?' He spoke so sharply that I stared at him in amazement. Usually he's not prone to snapping and sniping. 'It's important,' he insisted. 'Was there anything in your pockets that had your address on it?'

'No,' I answered, as realisation dawned. If the McKinnons knew where to find us, we were in big trouble. 'Hang – hang on, Mum. Dave just asked me something.'

'They never looked in *my* wallet,' Father Ramon suddenly volunteered, referring to the McKinnons. 'They don't know *my* address.'

'But they know mine,' Dave growled, then plucked the phone from my hand. 'Mrs Harrison? I need you to go to my house *right now* and pick up my laptop. My laptop and my address book. They're both on my desk.' He fell silent for a few moments, listening to Mum's objections. 'Yeah, I realise that,' he finally continued, 'but it's not the slayer I'm worried about. It's someone else – someone who *does* know where I live. And I don't want him tracking down the rest of us.' During the pause that followed, he began to gnaw at his bottom lip. 'What do you mean?' he said at last. 'What phone call?'

I glanced fearfully at Father Ramon.

'When was that?' Dave inquired, before clicking his tongue at my mother's response. 'You're kidding. Shit. Well, you did the right thing.'

At this point I signalled my desire to have the phone back. Dave, however, ignored me.

'No,' he went on. 'No, it wasn't the slayer, it was – it was someone else. Bloke called McKinnon. We've got his car, and he's got our truck. Let's just say it's a long story –'

'Give me that!' I exclaimed. 'Let *me* tell her!'

'Hold on, Mrs Harrison. I'll let Nina fill you in.' Dave passed me the phone, having recognised the futility of any further resistance. Unfortunately, it was too late. We had already lost the signal.

'Never mind,' said Father Ramon, who could see that I was upset. 'We'll be in range again soon.' He looked up again, catching Dave's eye in the rear-view mirror. 'I should have fetched your laptop when I went to check your house,' the priest said ruefully. 'I just didn't think. Naturally I assumed that if someone had taken Casimir's address book, it wouldn't do any good to worry about yours.'

'You were right,' said Dave. 'It wouldn't. If this loony has one address, he'll have the lot.'

'If *who* has one address?' Reuben demanded. He must have felt that he'd remained silent for long enough. 'Who are you talking about? Are you talking about Barry McKinnon?'

169

The priest assured him that we weren't. Dave mumbled something to the effect that it was a long story. I said to Dave, 'What was all that about a phone call?' And Dave hesitated.

He's never liked delivering bad news.

'Your mum got a call about fifteen minutes ago,' he revealed at last. 'Some guy told her that he'd found your phone, and wanted to send it back. He asked for the address.'

I gasped. Reuben hissed.

'She didn't give it to him,' Dave added quickly. 'She thought it might be the slayer.'

'She thought it might be the *what*?' Reuben yelped. But no one replied. I was too busy fighting the urge to panic, while Dave and the priest were turning things over in their heads.

'It sounds as if Barry might be looking for Nina,' was Father Ramon's verdict. 'The question is: has he got back to the house already?'

'I dunno,' said Dave. 'It's been at least an hour since we left, so . . .' He shrugged. 'It depends where he was planning to go with that van.'

'Do you reckon he might come after us?' I quavered. And Reuben gave a snort.

'Of *course* he'll come after us! I'm worth *money* to the McKinnons!' Seeing my confused look, Reuben began to splutter with impatience. 'You just don't understand!' he complained, then began to lecture Father Ramon. 'They'd never have let you go. If I hadn't killed Orlando, you'd be dead by now. I know how they think.' He tapped his forehead. 'I bet you *anything you like* they wanted to put you in the pit with me, next full moon, so the punters would have a show to watch. That's if they couldn't get another werewolf in time.'

'Oh, no,' said the priest.

'Oh, yes,' said the werewolf. 'They're animals. They call *me* an animal, but they're the real animals.'

He went on to declare that if the McKinnons had been planning to release Father Ramon, they never would have used our orange van as a hearse. Clearly they had decided to dump the two 'corpses' they'd been saddled with, then dispose of the van and return to the house in their utility truck. But they had waited for nightfall to ensure that their activities wouldn't be noticed.

'Ten to one they reached their dump site, opened the van doors, and found you both gone,' said Reuben, his gaze skipping from my face to Dave's. 'So now they probably reckon that someone *else* musta taken you. Because they won't be thinking that you walked off by yourselves. They won't believe that you're still alive.' Another explosive honk of laughter burst out of him. 'I saw you myself, and you looked dead to me,' he informed Dave. 'Really dead. No pulse or nothing.'

'But who could possibly have taken us?' I queried, causing Reuben to roll his eyes.

'A frienda yours! Who else? Someone who was hiding near the house when they left.' His rapid-fire delivery was nearly as exhausting as the way he kept bouncing around on his seat. 'Those bastards will be shit-scared,' he announced. 'They'll figure that whoever broke into the van musta broken into the house as well. To save this bloke.' He jerked his chin at Father Ramon. 'That's why they'll be trying to work out where you all live. They'll be wanting to track us down – you and me, Father. And this mystery guy they think let us out.'

'But I've confessed to murder,' Father Ramon protested.

171

'It's obvious that I won't be reporting them. Wouldn't they just prefer to let sleeping dogs lie?'

'Aw, cripes. Don't you *listen*?' Reuben was almost beside himself with frustration at our failure to grasp the essentials. 'I told you, I'm worth money! *Big* money! Last week they told me that some Yank promoter had offered them *a hundred thousand dollars* for me! And they turned him down! Because they can make more money off the punters!' He revealed that each of the men we'd seen converging on Wolgaroo Corner the night before had paid at least $1500 apiece to receive a silver bullet in the mail. 'That's basically $1500 a ticket,' Reuben announced. 'Not to mention the bets that come in from people who can't make it on the night.'

'So this is a big business?' asked Dave.

'Oh, yeah. Especially in America.' When Reuben fixed his attention on me, the effect was rather like being caught in a force-field. It was hard to look away, he was so dazzling. 'Can you see why they're going to come after us? No matter what?'

There was a long, pensive silence, which Father Ramon eventually broke.

'Maybe we *should* go the police,' he murmured, without taking his eyes off the road ahead. 'I mean – this is outrageous. Something like this shouldn't be allowed to happen. And if the McKinnons are as dangerous as Reuben says they are –'

'We can't go to the police,' I interrupted. 'You know what will happen.'

'We'll be lynched,' Dave agreed. 'There'll be a million slayers, instead of just one. They'll start clubs. They'll form vigilante groups.'

'We can't go to the police.' Reuben's support was completely unexpected. When the rest of us stared at him, he

172

grimaced. 'If the police find out about me, they'll lock me in a bloody zoo!' he exclaimed fiercely.

'Oh, I don't think so,' the priest began. But Reuben had his own ideas about the rest of the world, and he wasn't about to discard them.

'It's true!' he cried. 'The police will think that I'm some kinda wild animal! Everyone always does!' His voice cracked. 'Orlando's own grandfather used to keep him chained to a tree! He used to feed him scraps and pigswill!'

'Reuben.' Dave cleared his throat. 'Listen, mate –'

'No one's ever going to shut me up again! Not *ever*! Not in a zoo or a loony bin or anywhere else! Do you hear me? I'm going to *kill* anyone who even tries!'

By this time Reuben was shouting and slamming his fists down onto his knees. I suppose that I should have been scared, but I wasn't. After thirty-odd years of group therapy, I knew enough to hear the pain behind the anger. I could detect the fear that Reuben was trying to conceal.

And I felt deeply sorry for him.

'You mustn't worry about us,' I said, before he could launch into another round of threats and accusations. 'We understand how it is for someone like you. We're vampires, remember? *Everyone* hates vampires.' It was tough, having to say this aloud – especially to a stunner like Reuben – but I couldn't fool myself any longer. I was a vampire, through and through. 'The good thing is that there's a lot of us,' I continued, 'and we're in the same boat as you are. So we can help each other. We can figure out some way of defending ourselves without going to the police.' As he peered at me through the dimness, I couldn't help being struck by the amount of heat that was coming off him. Vampires don't exude much heat. We're chilly and cold-blooded, with dull cheeks and purple fingers. 'Reuben, believe me, we're no danger to anyone,' I finished. 'Just look at us. We're sick. We're feeble. We're comatose during the day. We couldn't lock you up if we tried – you'd make mincemeat out of us.'

'No, I wouldn't.' He sounded sullen. 'You think I'm an animal, but I'm not. As a matter of fact, I'm a vegetarian –'

'That's not what I meant,' was my hasty assurance. 'I only meant . . . well, there's no way we can make you do anything that you don't want to do. Not us. We don't have what it takes.'

For some reason, this particular argument struck a chord. Reuben's scowl yielded first to a pensive expression, then to a slow and sweet (though slightly crazed) little smile.

'I dunno about that,' he said. 'If you wanted me to take you dancing, I reckon I would. And I *hate* dancing.'

I have to admit that I was gobsmacked by this remark. It was completely unexpected. Vampires don't normally attract even the most backhanded compliments – especially not from a hot guy like Reuben. Of course, he hadn't seen anything even remotely female for a very long time; after five years of total deprivation, even a colourless, anorexic vampire with a lousy haircut must have looked good to him.

I didn't know how to respond, and was still racking my brain for a suitable answer when Dave spoke for me.

'We don't go out in public if we can help it,' he flatly declared. 'Especially not where there are lots of people.' Disregarding my gasp of outrage, he concluded with a Sanford-like putdown. 'You wouldn't want to tire her,' he said. 'Physically she's not very strong.'

'Oh.' Reuben pulled a funny sort of face that I couldn't interpret. His smile slipped sideways. 'Right. Gotcha.'

He would have dropped the subject, then, if it hadn't been for me. But I wasn't about to let anyone belittle me as if I were a six-year-old child – not to a brand-new acquaintance. *Especially* not to Reuben, who had enough energy for two people.

'Vampires aren't allowed to have any *fun*, you see,' I snapped, glaring at Dave. 'Not according to some experts in the field.'

'I didn't say that.' Dave was trying to be patient. He kept his voice very quiet and even. 'All I said was –'

'Vampires have to sit around watching TV all night. When they're not working at boring jobs, or cleaning bathrooms.'

'Nina –'

'I'm not a complete idiot, Dave. I do understand that I'm living with a handicap. I just prefer to pretend that I'm not, occasionally – if you *don't* mind.'

'Uh – speaking of handicaps,' Father Ramon interposed, before Dave could defend himself, 'what are we going to do if we don't reach Sydney by daybreak? Because we won't be able to hire another van in the middle of the night, and this car is all windows.' As I surveyed the vast expanse of tinted glass that surrounded us, the priest reviewed our options. 'Perhaps our best bet is to start searching for a hotel with very dark rooms. Or a twenty-four-hour service station that sells extremely big cool boxes,' he said. 'But whatever we decide, we'd better be quick. Since this might take quite a bit of planning.'

He was right, of course. We needed a couple of bolt-holes, as soon as possible.

Otherwise Dave and I wouldn't last all the way to Sydney.

Chapter Fifteen

It was Reuben who came to our rescue. As an aspiring motor mechanic, he had noticed that our vehicle's spare tyre was mounted over its rear bumper. He had therefore concluded that there might be some extra storage room under the cargo floor.

He was right. There was. And this dark, stuffy little compartment was just big enough to accommodate Dave – as long as he remained in a foetal position. What's more, when we checked the load space behind the back seat, we discovered an enormous steel toolbox sitting on top of the cargo floor. This toolbox was promptly put at my disposal. Once emptied of all its clattering contents, it wasn't a bad place to sleep; cramped and grimy, perhaps, but absolutely lightproof.

All the same, I kept hoping that I wouldn't have to use it. Every time Father Ramon stopped for a toilet break, or slowed down to pass through a slumbering country town, I would tap my feet and gnaw at my thumbnail. Buying petrol became an ordeal, not just because we didn't have an ignition key, but because I grudged every moment that we spent distracting dozy service-station attendants while Reuben got our engine running again.

It wasn't until we reached the mountains that I finally

admitted defeat. We weren't going to reach Sydney before daybreak. So I took off my coat and crawled into the stinking toolbox, while Reuben shook his head in wonderment.

'You couldn't pay me to do that,' he said. 'How can you do that?'

'I don't have much choice,' was my sour retort, which didn't seem to faze him in the slightest. With his customary vigour he swung around to address Father Ramon. 'Won't she suffocate? How's she going to breathe?'

'I don't breathe. Not during the day.' It did occur to me, however, that the few minutes of consciousness preceding my blackout might be a bit uncomfortable, once I was sealed inside my small and airless resting place. We therefore decided that Reuben should sit near me, in the back of the vehicle, until my breathing stopped. Then he would quickly shut the toolbox lid.

'What happens if you *do* get caught in sunlight?' was one of the questions that he asked me, as I lay waiting for the inevitable. 'Do you get burned, or what?'

'Kind of.'

'Are you sure? I mean, how do you know what'll happen if you've never even tried to go out in the sun?'

'It happened to a friend of a friend,' I replied. In fact, it had happened to the vampire I mentioned earlier: the one named Ethel, who was infected by George Mumford. After her own family exposed her to the sun, Sanford had been forced to clean up the mess. And ever since then, he's been firmly opposed to publicity of any description. 'It's a kind of cellular breakdown. All your peptide bonds dissolve.'

'Oh.' Reuben didn't ask what peptide bonds were. Maybe he was scared of looking stupid. I have to confess that I didn't really know what they were myself. I was just passing on what Sanford had told me. 'So you haven't seen daylight since . . . when?' he inquired.

'Since 1973.'

'Man.' He sounded awe-struck. 'And I thought five years was bad!'

'You mean they *never* let you out? Except at night?' I couldn't see his face from down in my box, so I don't know why he fell silent at this point. Perhaps he was speechless with fury. He might have been fighting back tears, or distracted by something on the road. Whatever the reason, he didn't immediately respond.

And by the time he did, I'd already blacked out.

When I woke up, it was the worst awakening of my life. I felt stifled, as if I barely had the room to inflate my lungs. There were cramps in every limb. My head was pounding.

But Reuben had kept his promise to leave the toolbox latch unfastened. With a single shove, I managed to free myself. The lid fell back, the air rushed in, and I sat up like a jack-in-the-box, coughing and moaning.

It was several seconds before I realised that I wasn't in a car any longer.

'Dave?' I rasped, looking around. My toolbox had been dumped on the concrete floor of a garage, between the McKinnons' four-wheel-drive and a grey saloon that I recognised as belonging to Father Ramon. The garage itself was full of cobwebs. Junk was piled high against the walls; in the dimness I could just make out a rusty tricycle, a wooden stepladder, a roll of carpet, a lampshade, a wardrobe, a fireguard and a stack of vinyl records.

Suddenly I heard a thump from inside the McKinnons'

vehicle – and it occurred to me that Dave must still be in there, tucked beneath the cargo floor. 'Oh! Wait! Hang on!' I cried, surging to my feet. Almost at once, however, I fell down. After being folded beneath my chin for so long, my legs weren't being very cooperative. 'I'm on my way! Don't panic! I'll be with you in a jiffy!'

But by the time I was more or less upright, Dave had already crawled out of the car. He too was having trouble with his legs; he hung off the tailgate as he waited for his knees to stop trembling.

'How are you?' he asked.

'Okay. I guess.' Considering what I'd been through. 'I need breakfast, though. How about you?'

'I'm all right,' he said hoarsely, glancing around. 'This is Father Ramon's garage.'

'Are you sure?'

'Yeah. I recognise those.' He indicated the pile of dog-eared album covers. 'I brought them here for a charity sale. He obviously hasn't sold them yet.'

'I'm not surprised. Old Air Supply records? Who on earth would buy those?'

'Lots of people,' he rejoined, sounding slightly miffed. 'They're collectables.'

I gave a snort. 'Well, it's good to know that there are sadder things in life than being a vampire,' I said. 'You could be someone who collects old Air Supply records.'

Now, if there's one thing Dave hates, it's musical intolerance. Although he's generally a quiet sort of person, you can always get him talking by claiming that one band or song is intrinsically better than another band or song. His mail-order business caters to a wide range of tastes, you see, so he doesn't believe in what he calls 'stylistic elitism'. It's a real crusade, with him. He insists that there's a place for every kind of music in this world.

But before we could get involved in yet another endless argument about the merits of 'easy listening' radio stations, I moved unsteadily towards the only exit: a pair of large, dilapidated wooden doors. Though tightly shut, they had been left unlocked, and I was pulling one of them open when Dave warned me, in a hushed voice, to be careful.

'We don't know what might be out there,' he murmured, much to my surprise.

'But we're back in Sydney. We're at Father Ramon's,' I pointed out. 'We've probably been left here because you have to park in the street at my mum's.' Someone had obviously decided – sensibly enough – that it would be unwise to emerge from beneath a cargo floor within plain sight of any passing pedestrian. 'Anyway, the McKinnons don't know this address, remember? They didn't get Father Ramon's ID.'

'I still think we should be careful,' Dave stubbornly insisted. He made me wait as he rummaged around in the piles of accumulated junk, until he was finally able to present me with an old golf club. For his own weapon he chose a spanner that had originally been stored in the McKinnons' toolbox.

Then he led me out of the garage and across a stretch of crumbling asphalt, straight to the back door of Father Ramon's presbytery.

Like the church next to it, this house was built just before World War One, out of maroon bricks and grey slate. It's a depressing sort of structure, with dark rooms and damp problems. Nothing in it seems to work properly. The roof leaks, the plumbing's too old, and the dining room floor has been damaged by termites. Father Ramon's always sticking tiles back on the wall with super-glue, when he isn't sealing cracks in the brickwork.

Personally, I loathe the place – even though it's exactly the sort of gloomy, old-fashioned house that most people would expect a vampire to inhabit. I've done my best to avoid it over the years because the sight of its dour façade never fails to make my heart sink. But on this occasion I was quite eager to get inside – so eager that I didn't notice one odd thing about the windows at the back of the house.

Dave did, though. He said very quietly, 'Why aren't there any lights on?'

I stopped in my tracks.

'Could he be asleep, already?' Dave continued. 'He didn't get a wink last night, with all that driving.'

'Maybe he's at my place,' I suggested, before realising how unlikely this was. 'No,' I added. 'He wouldn't go away and leave us by ourselves.'

'Anyway, his car's still here,' said Dave, trying the handle on the back door. It yielded to his pressure. And as he pushed it open, we smelled the gas.

I should probably explain that the back door of the presbytery leads directly into a ramshackle sunroom, which has become a dumping ground for donations of various kinds. Dave and I had to thread our way through teetering piles of tinned food and old blankets before we reached the kitchen, where we turned off the gas burners and threw open the windows. We had to hold our breaths, of course; if we'd been normal people we probably would have passed out. Fortunately, however, vampires don't need much oxygen to survive.

I only started to cough when I called Dave into the dining room.

'Look at this!' I cried, too shocked to remember that I shouldn't be inhaling. Someone had left a heater running on 'HIGH', having positioned it so that it was sitting under a heap of crumpled nylon that was probably a tablecloth. You didn't have to be a genius to work out what was going on. Clearly, I was staring at a makeshift slow fuse, designed to ignite the gas in the air just as soon as the nylon began to burn.

It was a trick that wouldn't have worked if Father Ramon had been able to afford new appliances. But his heater didn't have a safety cut-off mechanism, and his stove was so old that you could turn on the gas for as long as you liked without triggering an electric spark, or even having to hold down a knob.

As for the wiring in his house, it was ancient. I had to pull the heater's plug straight out of the wall socket, because there was no 'ON–OFF' switch.

'Jesus!' Dave spluttered, upon staggering into the room. By this time I had pushed aside the dusty velvet curtains that hung across the windows. And while I battled with sticky casement hinges, Dave whisked the tablecloth out of harm's way.

Soon we were both draped over the windowsill, sucking in great lungfuls of fresh night air.

'Okay,' Dave finally gasped. 'We should check the rest of the house . . .'

'Who did it?' I asked. 'Could they still be here?'

'I dunno.'

'They wouldn't risk staying, would they? They must have got out.'

'Could they have turned on other heaters?' Dave said. For a moment we stared at each other. Then Dave dashed towards the living room and I made for the office.

But we were lucky. No additional heaters had been left on downstairs. Father Ramon's office was dark and silent. The bathroom smelled of nothing but mould. The living room contained little of interest except a few dirty glasses and what looked like the contents of Father Ramon's pockets: his car keys, his wallet, his box of matches and his sunglasses.

Dave took the keys, the wallet and the sunglasses.

'This is bad,' I croaked. 'He wouldn't have gone anywhere without his wallet.'

'We'll look upstairs,' said Dave. As I followed him to the first-floor landing, I held my breath; not because the gas was bothering me (it wasn't), but because I was listening hard for any creaks or cracks or murmurs that might suggest we weren't alone.

All I could detect, however, was a deathly hush – together with a very faint whiff of natural gas.

'Do you know where Father Ramon sleeps?' I whispered, peering at the array of dark-brown doors that opened off the landing. Dave shook his head. So we tried each of the six doors in turn, beginning with the one to our far left and working in a clockwise direction.

The first door led to a linen closet stuffed with towels and mothballs. Behind the second was a room containing two camp beds, an empty clothes rack, and nothing else. It wasn't until we reached the third door that we stumbled upon another human being. He was lying on a double bed beneath a flowered quilt, and he wasn't Father Ramon.

Though he didn't move when we peeled the quilt off his face, he was still breathing.

'Hello?' said Dave, shaking the recumbent body. '*Hello?*'

'Who is this?' I demanded. 'Do you know him?'

'No.'

The sleeping man was short and plump. He had very big ears, and mouse-coloured hair that was thinning on top. Because his mouth was open, I could see all his fillings.

He wore a striped shirt under a beige V-necked jumper that didn't match his trousers.

'What's wrong?' I asked, when no amount of poking and prodding served to waken him. 'Is he drunk?'

'Or drugged. Or sick. Or knocked out,' said Dave.

'This is weird.'

'Yeah.'

'There's nothing in his pockets,' I said, causing Dave to rub his jaw.

'I don't like the look of this,' was his muttered verdict. 'We should call Sanford. Sanford's a doctor.'

'But who can it be? Is it one of those homeless guys?' Father Ramon, I knew, often provided beds for people in crisis: evicted families, abused children, sick vagrants. 'Maybe there's something wrong with him. Maybe that's why he's here.'

'Maybe,' said Dave, before heading off to search the next bedroom. I hesitated, frantically wondering if there was some kind of first aid that I should be employing. What were you supposed to do with an unconscious person, anyway? Roll him on to his side? Slap his face? Try to feed him coffee?

'Nina!' Dave called, from the very next room, and I reluc-

184

tantly abandoned the sleeping stranger. When I reached Dave's side, he was standing beside Father Ramon's bed, staring down at the priest's motionless form.

'He's breathing,' Dave announced, before I could even ask. 'He's alive but he won't wake up.'

I can't tell you how frightening it was, to see Father Ramon lying so still. He's always been such a calm and gentle man that you forget how full of life he actually is, what with his warm eyes and expressive face and sympathetic manner. Seeing him reduced to an unresponsive lump . . . well, it was a big shock. A bad shock.

'We'd – we'd better get Sanford over here,' I stammered, reaching for the phone on the gunmetal filing cabinet that served as a bedside table. Dave, however, grabbed my arm.

'No!' he said. Much to my surprise, he insisted that we should take Father Ramon to Sanford, rather than bringing the doctor to the patient. This didn't make much sense to me. After all, Sanford was conscious, and able to walk.

'He could catch a cab,' I argued. 'It wouldn't be that much of a risk – not for Sanford. Or you could go and get him.'

'Nina, we can't stay here. Suppose the McKinnons did this? Suppose they turn up again?'

'But the McKinnons don't *have* this address!'

'How do you know? They might have got it from the hotel in Cobar. Besides, who else could it possibly have been?'

'The slayer?' I submitted. And Dave inclined his head.

'Maybe,' he had to concede. 'Either way, they might come back. We'll be safer at your mum's house.'

'I guess so.'

'We'll take Father Ramon's car,' Dave went on slowly, wrestling with the logistics of our situation. 'I'll drive it straight up to your mum's door.'

'What about Reuben? Where's he gone?'

'I dunno. Let's have a look.'

But Reuben wasn't anywhere to be found. When Dave and I checked the last two rooms, we discovered only a sparse collection of thrift-shop furniture.

'You don't think *Reuben* did this?' I said, once Dave and I were back on the landing. 'We *rescued* him, for God's sake!'

Dave shrugged.

'It just doesn't make sense!' I leaned against a door-jamb. My stomach was beginning to bother me, and all the stress was making me light-headed. 'We told Reuben we weren't going to turn him in! He might be unstable, but he's not a fool! Why would he do something so stupid?'

'I don't think he did,' Dave replied, after a moment's thought. 'If he had, he would have tried to kill us, too. Because he knew where we were.'

'You're right.' I couldn't help being impressed by Dave's deductive powers. In fact I was beginning to realise just how quick he really was, under that quiet, laid-back façade of his. 'It can't have been Reuben, then.'

'He's either run off or he's been kidnapped.'

'By the McKinnons?'

'Yep.'

A sudden chill ran down my spine. It wouldn't be long before my nausea was out of control. I recognised the symptoms; I was heading for a crash.

I needed a fresh guinea pig and a good, long rest in a darkened room.

'How could the McKinnons have found this place?' I queried, struggling to remain focused. 'They didn't take

Father Ramon's ID. Do you really think they got his details from the hotel register?'

Dave sighed. 'I dunno,' he said.

'It's not as if he's listed in the phone book,' I went on fretfully. 'Unless there's some kind of Catholic priest register that you can look up?'

'It doesn't matter.' Dave's tone implied that I was fussing over inessentials. 'What matters is that we get out of here. Fast.'

'And the homeless guy?' I was referring to the stranger in the spare bedroom. 'What are we going to do about him?

'We'll take him with us.'

I blinked. 'But we can't!' I exclaimed.

'We have to.' Dave was insistent. 'If we leave him here, he might die.'

'But we don't *know* him, Dave!'

'Father Ramon does.'

'If that fat man wakes up in a strange house, he'll freak! He might call the police, or something! He'll certainly call them if he wants the McKinnons arrested for drugging him, and where's that going to leave us?'

Dave sighed. 'It's a risk,' he acknowledged. 'Thing is, if he wants to call the police, he'll do it no matter where he wakes up. Unless Father Ramon asks him not to. He might listen to Father Ramon.' Seeing my tortured expression, Dave pleaded his case more urgently. 'We can't leave the poor guy here, Nina. He could choke on his own vomit or something – like Jimi Hendrix. And what if the McKinnons come back? They'll kill him for sure.'

'But he'd be in *my house* . . .' I said feebly, frightened at the thought of a domestic invasion. Dave put his arm around my shoulders.

'We'll take this one step at a time,' he recommended. 'First we have to get Sanford on the case. He's a doctor. After that, we can work out our next move.' When I failed to respond, he added, 'We've gotta be quick, though. Because I'm starting to feel a bit crook.'

The implication was clear. If we didn't hurry, Dave wouldn't be well enough to drive. And if that happened, we'd be stuck – since we couldn't exactly load Father Ramon into the back seat of a taxi.

'Okay,' I said. 'You fetch the car. I'll call Sanford.'

'Tell him –'

'I know what to tell him. I'm not stupid.' It was mean of me to snap at Dave, when he was being so nice. I'm not sure why I did it – fear, perhaps? But before I could apologise, something occurred to me: something so dreadful that I actually reeled, and almost dropped my golf club. 'You don't think – I mean, whoever did this . . .' I had to take a deep breath before continuing. 'What if they know where Mum lives?'

'They don't.' Dave hastened to reassure me. 'Remember what your mum told us? The McKinnons asked for an address, and she wouldn't give it to them.'

'But what if it's *here* somewhere? What if there's an address book in the office with my name inside? What if they heard you call me Nina, back at Wolgaroo?'

Dave stiffened. Our gazes locked.

Then we turned, simultaneously, and bolted for the nearest phone.

Chapter Sixteen

I'm going to cheat a bit now. I'm going to tell you something that wasn't known to me until long after it actually happened.

You see, while Dave and I were out cold in Father Ramon's garage, Nefley Irving was climbing through Dave's kitchen window.

Let me introduce you to Nefley first. At the time of which I speak, he was a postal worker. Don't imagine that he served behind a counter, exchanging gossip and counting out change; his job was in mail sorting, so he didn't have to interact with many people at all. And this was just as well, because he'd never been very sociable. In public he was shy and timid, hovering on the fringes of every conversation – unless that conversation dealt with horror movies, psychics, or paranormal phenomena. Nefley always had a lot to say on *those* topics: so much, in fact, that he could become very boring to listen to. The world of the paranormal was his obsession. He spent most of his free time reading books about ley lines and alchemy and demonic possession, watching films about shape-shifters and witchcraft, and researching occult subjects on his computer.

Needless to say, he wasn't married. Nor did he have a girl-friend. In fact he didn't have any friends at all, except the ones he'd made over the Internet. To some of these Internet friends he'd expounded his theory about the role of Evil on earth: how Evil was a kind of spiritual waste product that had to be collected in certain 'vessels', so that it wouldn't spill out and contaminate everything. Some of these vessels were inanimate: rocks and weapons and houses. Some of them, however, were human beings.

There were also 'Hemihoms', who were supposed to be half-human, half-animal. According to Nefley, they were the most dangerous vessels of all, because they contained a concentrated mixture of conscious and unconscious evil. Vampires, he told his Internet friends, were Hemihoms. And they were a danger to the entire human race.

At this point you must be thinking that Nefley was out of his mind. But he wasn't. There are lots of perfectly sane people who create their own weird philosophies, and Nefley was no different. Nor was he particularly violent or cruel. On the contrary, he wanted to be a hero. He wanted to be a warrior fighting for Good against Evil.

His problem was that he didn't have anyone sensible to talk to.

When he posed as 'Fangseeker' on the Net, Nefley was still living in a kind of fantasy world. But Casimir's response changed all that. For the first time Nefley realised that he was in actual, physical danger, and it scared him. He wondered what would happen if he refused to meet with Casimir after all. Suppose the vampire became angry, and tried to track him down regardless? Suppose Casimir was a computer expert?

Faced with this awful possibility, Nefley devised a 'honey-trap'. This he did after consulting one of his geeky Internet contacts, who probably took it for granted that they were both engaged in an on-line role-playing scenario. Upon discussing Casimir's unexpected approach, they agreed that Nefley should arrange to meet the vampire at an all-night coffee-shop in the middle of town. But Nefley wasn't to make contact with Casimir. He was to monitor Casimir from a distance until the vampire grew impatient and went back home. Then Nefley would pursue him, in the hope of discovering Casimir's lair.

So when Casmir did show up, at the designated place and time, Nefley was waiting in his car. And when, after thirty minutes, Casimir finally left the coffee-shop, Nefley followed him home. As luck would have it, Casimir even checked his mailbox before disappearing inside – thus revealing his exact address.

The broken pane of glass in the building's front door sealed Casimir's fate. Once Nefley had spotted it, he realised that a break-in would be easy to carry out. He could offer no valid excuses for shirking his duty to protect the world from Evil – especially since Casimir was such a small, hunched, withered, pasty, shuffling creature. Faced with a strapping great vampire in tip-top condition, Nefley might have had second thoughts about attacking him. Even Nefley, however, didn't find Casimir intimidating.

On the contrary, Casimir conveyed the impression of being verminous, like a cockroach. And it isn't hard to squash a cockroach.

At the time, Nefley worked on Saturdays. But he received every Tuesday off in lieu. So he broke into Casimir's flat on a Tuesday, knowing that fewer neighbours would be around during the week. He took with him a pair of gloves, a stake,

191

a crucifix, several cloves of garlic, a can of lighter fluid, a box of matches, and a pistol loaded with silver bullets.

As it turned out, Casimir's corpse-like appearance made killing him far easier than Nefley had anticipated. It was like spearing a waxwork dummy. There wasn't even any mess to deal with; after his mission had been accomplished, Nefley simply closed the coffin and departed. But he picked up Casimir's address book on his way out – and spent the rest of the week poring over it, whenever he had a minute to spare.

He knew that he would have to determine whether Casimir's friends were vampires or not.

By Sunday he was ready to act. That afternoon, he approached Sanford's house and knocked at the door. When no one answered, he checked around the back. And when every window proved to be heavily fortified (because it was, after all, a former bank branch), he proceeded to the next house on his list – which happened to be Dave's.

I've already mentioned that Dave lives in a skinny little duplex with a basement darkroom. This house is stuck into the side of a hill; you reach the front door by climbing a steep flight of stone stairs, and you reach the back door by turning into an alley that runs behind the house, then pushing through a rusty gate. Because Dave's garden is massively overgrown with choking vines and unpruned bushes, Nefley was invisible to any neighbours who might have glanced outside at approximately two o'clock that Sunday afternoon.

In other words, no one raised the alarm.

Nefley soon located an unlocked window, which gave him access to Dave's kitchen. From there he penetrated the rest of the house, including the basement darkroom. But the dark-room was empty. No one lay in Dave's modified sun-bed, which is tucked between great piles of second-hand records in cardboard boxes. Nefley poked around for a while without any luck.

He was making his way back upstairs when the doorbell rang. It was a terrific shock. For perhaps five minutes he stood frozen on the third step from the bottom, holding his breath. Then he heard the sound of a window being pushed open. I'm not sure if he realised that someone was climbing through the same window that he'd used. All I know is that he bolted for the front entrance, trying to avoid whatever threat was looming out the back.

He wasn't aware that there were two intruders, and that one of them – Barry McKinnon – had remained by the doorbell. Nefley suddenly found himself face to face with a man who appeared to be a legitimate visitor.

So Nefley lied to protect himself.

'I'm – I'm a friend of Dave's,' he stammered, in an attempt to account for his presence. 'Is it Dave you're looking for?'

'Yeah,' said Barry, before shoving him inside.

As soon as Barry closed the front door behind them, it occurred to Nefley that if Dave *were* a vampire, he wouldn't be receiving visitors in the middle of the day. At almost the same instant, Barry asked if Dave was about.

'No,' Nefley replied, in his squeaky voice. By this time he understood that he was in trouble. Barry's tone was menacing, and his hard, pale eyes were empty of emotion. What's more, he had Dermid backing him up; when Nefley looked around, he glimpsed Dermid's hulking silhouette, framed in the kitchen doorway.

'He wouldn't be with that priest, would he?' Barry continued, as Dermid stood blocking the light. 'Big bloke.

Grey hair. Ramon something.'

'Ramon Alvarez?' said Nefley, who was familiar with the name. He had found it in Casimir's address book.

Barry and Dermid exchanged a quick glance.

'That's him,' the older McKinnon confirmed. 'Where does he live, do you know?'

Nefley promptly recited Father Ramon's address, hoping to ingratiate himself with the two McKinnons, and perhaps secure a safe passage out of the house. But they weren't finished with him. Not by a long shot.

'And Reuben?' Barry asked. 'Where's Reuben?'

Nefley wasn't acquainted with anyone called Reuben. He said as much to Barry, who didn't believe it for one moment. The McKinnons seized Nefley's gym-bag, which contained a stake, a crucifix, a pistol and a box of silver bullets.

When Barry laid eyes on those silver bullets, he immediately jumped to the wrong conclusion.

'I think you might know who Reuben is,' he sneered, as Dermid put a knife to Nefley's throat. The two McKinnons then searched Nefley's pockets, consulted his driver's licence, and forced him into their utility truck, which was parked in the street outside. Despite his strenuous denials, they were convinced that Nefley had been hiding behind a bush somewhere, watching and waiting, as they drove the orange removals van away from Wolgaroo Corner. They decided that he must have been the one who'd rescued Father Ramon. It was therefore obvious to them that he must also be hiding their runaway werewolf. And they wouldn't believe anything he said to the contrary.

Not even after they'd searched his flat, and found no one there.

By this time they must have realised that they were dealing with a rather strange sort of person. For one thing, Nefley kept babbling on about the Undead. For another, his entire flat was full of garlic and pentagrams and crucifixes and posters of Buffy the Vampire Slayer. If they hadn't been so intent on their need to locate Reuben, they might have stopped to wonder what the hell was going on.

But they didn't. Instead, having drawn a blank at Nefley's apartment, they dragged him off to the presbytery. Their plan was to use him as a kind of Trojan Horse, gaining access to Father Ramon's house by making Nefley knock on the door for them. They assumed, you see, that he had been working in league with Father Ramon. They wouldn't believe that Nefley and the priest had never even met.

The McKinnons' ruse only worked because Father Ramon is accustomed to having lost souls turn up on his threshold at all hours of the day and night. If he had checked through his peephole and spotted the McKinnons, he would never have let them in. But he didn't know the man who was hovering on his front veranda. And he saw enough of Nefley's shaking hands, damp brow and tortured expression to conclude that he was looking at a desperate case: an addict seeking counsel, perhaps, or a sinner wishing to unburden himself of some terrible secret.

So Father Ramon opened his door, just as he's opened his door to a hundred other forlorn supplicants. At which point the McKinnons (who had been waiting out of sight) hurled themselves at him like a couple of attack dogs.

I should tell you, at this point, that they had come to Sydney fully prepared for a showdown. Their truck was stocked with a .22 rifle, several sets of handcuffs, a syringe full of anaesthetic, a bottle of back-up tranquillisers, and lots of nylon rope – enough to sedate and secure at least ten people. What's more, they had also taken Nefley's handgun, and his stack of silver bullets. So poor Father Ramon didn't stand a chance; the McKinnons had him hog-tied on the floor before he could say 'Boo'.

And then, of course, they went looking for Reuben.

It was unfortunate that Reuben happened to be asleep upstairs at the time. If he'd been awake and alert, they might not have been able to subdue him. Knowing Reuben, the very sight of Barry and Dermid would have enraged him to the point of apoplexy; he would have tried to tear them apart. But when the McKinnons finally tracked him down, Reuben was snoring in one of the spare bedrooms. They had the barrel of the .22 shoved into his ear before he'd even opened his eyes.

He woke up to find himself already handcuffed, with Dermid sitting on his legs and Barry measuring out a stiff dose of anaesthetic. 'You know the drill, mate,' said Barry, before plunging a loaded syringe into Reuben's left buttock.

The McKinnons spent about fifteen minutes upstairs with Reuben. Meanwhile Nefley and Father Ramon lay in the living room, gagged, handcuffed, and forcibly drugged. Nefley blacked out quickly; despite his generous gut and double chin, he isn't a big man, and he'd been given a generous dose of knockout drops. The priest, however, succumbed more gradually. He was still conscious when Barry wandered past, growling into his mobile phone.

It just so happened that Barry was talking to an American millionaire named Forrest Darwell – the same man who had offered to buy Reuben for a hundred thousand dollars.

Darwell ran his own illegal werewolf fights in Colorado. He had been visiting various countries in the southern hemisphere, looking for more 'stock', and had been most impressed with Reuben's fighting ability. But Barry had refused to sell Reuben for less than half a million dollars. And since Darwell wasn't willing to pay that much, he'd flown to the Philippines in search of cheaper options.

Now he was Barry's last hope. The McKinnons were on the run; a hostile group had discovered their nasty little secret, and news of the discovery might very well have leaked out. As far as Barry was concerned, Wolgaroo Corner was no longer safe. He wanted to start afresh somewhere.

To do that, however, he needed money. And Reuben Schneider was not only the McKinnons' most valuable asset; he was also a walking time bomb. Testimony from the abused werewolf would be enough to put Barry in jail for life. That was why Reuben had to be prevented from approaching the police with his story. It was also why the McKinnons were fully prepared to kill Father Ramon. Even if he didn't go to the police (having apparently committed a double homicide), the priest was still a potential witness. There was nothing to prevent him from getting drunk, one night, and spilling his guts to a loose-lipped friend. He had to be silenced somehow, or the McKinnons would never rest easy.

As for Nefley Irving – well, Nefley had got in the way. He'd been in the wrong place at the wrong time. The McKinnons had sent at least three people to their deaths, in the pit at Wolgaroo; they weren't particularly worried about one extra corpse, especially since their plan was to make everything look like an accident. They'd been intending to kill Father Ramon with a fake overdose of tranquillisers, until Barry saw what passed for a stove in the presbytery kitchen. Then it became obvious to him that the entire house could be blown up. In Barry's view, no investigator would ever suspect arson once it was established that Father Ramon had been using fifty-year-old appliances. And any traces of foul play would be turned to ash in the subsequent fire.

You may recall that when Dave and I found Father Ramon, he was in bed, asleep, with no ropes or handcuffs restraining him. This was part of Barry's carefully thought-out scheme. Once the priest had lost consciousness, he was freed from his bonds and carried upstairs, where the McKinnons left him lying with his quilt tucked under his chin. It was all meant to look perfectly innocent. Even if Father Ramon wasn't burnt to a crisp, the smoke or the gas would certainly kill him. And the pill bottle left by his bed would convince any suspicious detectives that he had dosed *himself* with barbiturates – or so Barry was hoping. As far as Barry was concerned, every base had been covered.

But he was wrong, of course. For one thing, he didn't check the garage. For another, he neglected to lower his voice during his conversation with Forrest Darwell. The priest heard every word that Barry uttered – and therefore became privy to several important facts. After listening to one side of a prolonged and heated negotiation, Father Ramon learned that Reuben was being sold to someone called Darwell, for a great deal of money. Father Ramon also discovered that Mr Darwell would be returning to Australia on a plane that was scheduled to arrive in Sydney the next morning, at half past eight. The 'delivery' of Mr Darwell's purchase would then be arranged over the phone.

Until that time, however, the McKinnons would have to

hide out somewhere.

It was lucky that Barry decided to discuss the alternatives with his son as they untied Nefley Irving. 'Gimme his keys,' Barry said to Dermid, unaware that Father Ramon was still conscious. Barry went on to explain that the keys would give them access to Nefley's flat. 'We'll hole up there tonight,' Barry decreed, 'and piss off early, before anyone comes sniffin' around.'

'I dunno.' Dermid sounded unconvinced. 'Couldn't we just sleep in the truck?'

'What? All three of us?' Barry sneered. 'We'll have the kid, dozy.'

'Oh. Yeah.'

'If I take this guy's wallet, no one'll know who he is,' Barry declared, as he pocketed Nefley's identification. 'And if he doesn't end up totally barbecued, they still won't figure out his name until we're long gone. Don't worry. I've got it all sorted.'

You can imagine how Father Ramon felt, upon hearing this. He remembers thinking vaguely: *They're going to set us on fire. I have to get up.* But his eyes were already closed, and a deadly numbness was creeping over him. He couldn't move. He couldn't speak.

The last thing he heard, before he went under, was Dermid's loudly voiced complaint about Nefley's flat. 'All that bloody Goth stuff gives me the creeps,' Dermid grumbled. 'I hate that stuff. How am I going to sleep in a room full of skulls and crosses and shit? I'd have to be as sick as this little psycho.'

Then darkness descended, and the nagging, nasal monologue simply faded away.

Chapter Seventeen

You've probably worked out by now that Nefley Irving was the mysterious stranger upstairs in the presbytery. He wasn't a homeless person at all; he was Casimir Kucynski's murderer. But Dave and I didn't realise that. So we loaded him into Father Ramon's grey saloon, which Dave had parked near the back door of the presbytery.

Then Dave drove the saloon to my place, wearing Father Ramon's sunglasses. I sat in the front passenger seat – shielding my eyes from the glare of passing headlights – while our two unconscious passengers made snuffling noises behind us. We reached our destination at seven-fifteen. Dave had barely pulled up to the kerb when a flock of people started to spill out of Mum's house: Mum and Sanford, Horace, Gladys, George. I had phoned Sanford just before leaving the presbytery, to make sure that everything was all right back home, so he knew what to expect.

When he reached the car, he immediately plunged inside it to get a better look at its drugged occupants.

'Where's that bottle of pills?' he barked at me, without even saying hello. I shut the front passenger door, then passed him the little plastic vial that I'd found by Father Ramon's bed. Though I'd already told Sanford that the vial wasn't labelled, he wanted to inspect it anyway.

He tucked it into his pocket just as Mum threw her arms around my neck.

'Thank God!' she wheezed. 'Thank God you came home!'

'It's okay, Mum. I'm fine.'

'What a nightmare!'

'Yeah. It was.'

'I won't let it happen again, darl. Not *ever*. No more bloody wild-goose chases for you.'

'What the hell is going on, anyway?' asked Horace. He was still dressed in his ridiculous black cape and frock coat; I realised that no one else had changed so much as a pair of socks since Tuesday, either. 'Who's the bald bloke?' he added. 'Have we worked that out yet?'

'No,' said Dave, slamming the driver's door. 'But we have to get him inside, no matter who he is. Just give me a hand; I can't do this on my own.'

'Yes, both of you take care of our guest,' Sanford instructed, from the back of the car. 'George, you can help me carry Father Ramon.'

'And make it quick,' my mother added. 'Or we'll have the whole neighbourhood out here, stickybeaking.'

She promptly hustled me into the house ahead of Gladys – who had already started to whine about the cold night air. Bridget was waiting for us in the vestibule, leaning on a cane. She greeted me with a paper-dry kiss and an inquiry about my health.

'You don't look well,' she quavered. 'Your colour's not good.'

I refrained from pointing out that my colour was never good, even at the best of times. Instead I muttered something

201

about missing breakfast the previous night.

'Yeah, we heard about that,' said Mum. 'Father Ramon told me you had to leave the guinea pigs. I'll get you one right now, shall I? And your supplements, as well.'

Instead of answering her question, I asked one of my own. 'So you've talked to Father Ramon?' I queried. 'Since we got back?'

'Oh, yeah.' Mum made an impatient gesture. 'He rang this morning, soon as he got home. He would have come straight over if he hadn't been worried about leaving you two. We must have talked for two hours, I reckon. He told me everything.' At that moment Sanford appeared on the threshold, shuffling backwards with his arms wrapped around Father Ramon's chest. And my mother's face crumpled. 'I don't understand it,' she said hoarsely. 'We were on the phone, not long ago, and now look. What the hell could have happened?'

'We'll find out soon enough,' Sanford wheezed, pausing at the foot of the stairs. 'He might wake up with a headache, but at least he *will* wake up. This doesn't look like an overdose – all his vital signs are normal.' He nodded at George, who was supporting Father Ramon's legs. 'Can you keep going? It's not much further.'

'Put him in the spare room,' was Mum's recommendation. 'I've changed the sheets.' Then she watched as Dave and Horace staggered through the front door, bearing our mystery guest. 'I suppose you'd better put this one in Nina's room,' she decided, much to my dismay.

'But *Mum*,' I cried, 'that's *my* bed!'

'You don't use it, though, do you?' said Horace, in an deliberate attempt to bait me. When I rounded on him, he smirked.

'As a matter of fact, I *do* use it! I just don't sleep in it!'

Having put him in his place, I turned back to my mother. 'How am I going to write if there's a strange man in my room?' I wailed.

It was Sanford who tried to reassure me. Though he was halfway up the first flight of stairs, he stopped to peer over the banister rail. 'Don't worry,' he said. 'These two will be up and about soon. If I were you, Nina, I'd have a shower and a meal. They might be awake by the time you're done.'

'You think so?' I cast a doubtful glance at the limp body that Dave and Horace were carrying. 'They look pretty out of it.'

Sanford didn't reply. He was probably too breathless to utter a word; it can't have been easy, dragging Father Ramon up all those stairs, and Sanford wasn't in the best of health. As for poor Dave, he barely made it to the first-floor landing. Driving home had been bad enough; that final ascent nearly finished him off. After dumping his burden on to my bed, he lay down next to our anonymous visitor and groaned.

'Oh, man,' he complained. 'I feel like my skull's about to split apart.'

My mother clicked her tongue in sympathy. 'You should never have gone away,' she said. 'Both of you should never have gone.' Then she rummaged in my chest of drawers for some clean clothes, while I stood staring at the two guys draped across my duvet.

They couldn't have been more different. Dave was tall and thin and long-haired. The stranger was short and fat and balding. Yet they both shared at least one characteristic: they both looked as if nothing short of an earthquake would shift them.

'This was a big mistake,' panted Horace, surveying the

203

intruder. 'What are we going to say to our friend here when he wakes up? He'll have a heart attack. I guarantee it.'

'*You* won't be talking to him,' I rejoined. 'In fact you won't be allowed anywhere near him, looking like that.' As well as his satin cape and velvet frock-coat, Horace was wearing laced-up leather trousers tucked into knee-high boots with stacked heels. 'He'll *definitely* go to the police, if he sees that outfit.'

'We'll let Father Ramon talk to him,' Mum said, pushing a wad of clean clothes into my hands. 'He'll listen to Father Ramon. They know each other, don't they?'

'I'm – I'm not sure.' It suddenly occurred to me that the overweight stranger might be a friend of Reuben's. 'He didn't have any ID on him.'

'But he's definitely not the werewolf?' asked Horace.

'No.'

'Are you sure?' Anticipating a scornful reply, Horace raised his hand defensively. 'I realise he doesn't *look* like the werewolf, but if your friend can turn into a wolf, he might be able to turn into other things, as well. He might have several identities. Have you thought of that?'

I hadn't. And I realised that Horace could be right. After all, what did we really know about werewolves? It was possible that we were just as misinformed about them as normal people were about us.

'If *I* was running away from a pair of thugs,' Horace continued, 'then the first thing I'd do is disguise myself.' He nodded at the unconscious man in the beige jumper. 'Maybe this is a disguise.'

'If it is, then the McKinnons would have seen it before,' said Dave. Though he appeared to be half-dead, he had obviously been listening. 'Unless Reuben can change into a different shape every time, and what are the chances of that?'

'What are the chances of finding a werewolf in the first place?' Horace retorted, at which point my mother took charge.

'We can discuss this later,' she said. 'Right now Dave needs a rest, Nina needs a bath, and Sanford needs to suss things out. Everyone else can clear off downstairs until we're ready to have a proper meeting.' She gave Horace a prod with one bony finger. 'Go on. Get. You're not needed.'

'But what about these McKinnons that everyone's so worried about?' Horace demanded, still breathing heavily from his recent exertions. 'Are they going to show up here, or not? Does the werewolf know where to find us? What are we supposed to do if he does?'

'We'll *discuss it later*!' Mum snapped. And we did, though not for an hour or two. In the meantime I filled my stomach, cleaned a few tiles, and had a long, hot soak in rose-scented water, while Sanford examined his new patients and Dave nursed his throbbing head. Then Sanford decreed that Dave ought to get some blood into him, quick smart; I had to vacate the bathroom in a hurry, so that Dave could fang a couple of guinea pigs. Poor Dave: even after a substantial meal he still felt too sick to clean up the mess he'd left behind. Gladys took care of that, though not willingly. She bitched and moaned about the injustice of it all until I was ready to stick her head in the toilet.

We didn't sit down to confer until about nine o'clock, by which time I was feeling rather peaky. Nevertheless, I was determined to participate in our group discussion, which took place in the living room. Mum was in attendance, of course, since it was her house; she sat smoking on the piano stool. Dave was also present, sprawled across Mum's recliner. Gladys and I were crammed together on the love seat opposite him, while George shared the daybed with Horace. Sanford was there as well, pacing back and forth, but Bridget wasn't; she had been asked to watch over our mystery guest, just in case he woke up. (As Sanford had so rightly pointed out, even the most confused and hysterical person was bound to be calmed by the sight of Bridget placidly knitting away in a bedside rocking chair.)

It was Sanford who opened the meeting, with a call to order. But I was the one who kicked things off.

'We have to do something about Reuben,' I said.

George frowned. 'You mean the fat man upstairs?' he asked.

'She means the werewolf,' Gladys mumbled. And Horace said, 'Who *might* be the fat man upstairs.'

'I don't think so.' Dave had been cradling his head in his hands. Now he glanced up, uncovering his bloodshot eyes, 'I don't think the McKinnons would try to kill Reuben. He's worth too much money. He told us that.'

'And what makes you think he told you the truth?' Horace drawled. 'In fact, what makes you think *he* didn't leave the gas on?'

'No.' Dave was adamant. 'If he'd tried to kill Father Ramon, he would have tried to kill us too. But he didn't. Even though he knew where we were.'

'Are you sure he would have known *how* to kill you?' Horace countered. Whereupon Dave sighed.

'Everyone knows how to kill us, don't they? Isn't that part of our problem?' He turned to address Sanford. 'I'm sure that

Reuben was kidnapped. The McKinnons somehow got hold of Father Ramon's address. But they couldn't afford to leave any witnesses, which is why they tried to burn the place down.'

'And now they'll stop bothering us,' said Horace. When everyone stared at him, he languidly waved his hand. 'They got their werewolf back, didn't they? They killed all the witnesses – or so they think. If you ask me, they'll go home now. Unless we start bothering *them*.' He pulled one of his wily faces. 'I mean, I'm sure your werewolf is a *really lovely* fellow, Nina, but we've got our own problems. There's still a vampire slayer out there, in case it's slipped your mind.'

'Yes, and we can't even go home!' Gladys chipped in. 'I can't even do my job any more! Who cares about some were-wolf? It's *us* we should be worrying about!'

During the brief pause that followed, I scanned the room. Mum and Sanford were looking thoughtful. George was biting his bottom lip. Gladys sat with her Indian shawl wrapped tightly around her hunched shoulders, brooding, while Horace watched me from beneath lowered eyelids.

I realised that Reuben meant nothing to them, either as a person or as a cause. Even Mum was thinking like a vampire, after so much time spent in vampire company. I could under-stand it, too; when you're ill, and scared, and tired, and when every little thing is a big effort, you don't want to worry about other people, with other problems.

But I'd met Reuben. I'd talked to him. I'd even tried to put myself in his shoes – because that's what a writer always does. On the long drive back to Sydney, I'd been turning things over in my head. And it seemed to me that Reuben might very well free us from the trap in which we were caught.

'As a matter of fact, I *am* worrying about us,' I told Gladys. 'What happened to Reuben could easily happen to me or to you. He's been treated like an animal because some people don't think he's a human being. Does that sound familiar?' I turned to Dave for help, but it wasn't forthcoming; he sat with his eyes closed, massaging his scalp, the very picture of misery. So I ploughed on unassisted. 'Reuben's in the same boat as we are,' I said. '*Exactly* the same boat.'

'Except that he can live a normal life for most of the year,' snarled Horace.

'Yes! He can! Which is *great*!' I cried. 'Imagine how useful it would be to have him around! He could go out in the sunlight! He could shop and drive and deal with plumbers!' Seeing Dave's head jerk up in surprise, I backed off a little. 'Which isn't to say he'll do that, necessarily,' I had to admit. 'But it's something to consider. Maybe if we help him, then he'll help us. And he *can* help us. In all kinds of ways.'

'By being ornamental, for instance,' Horace slyly remarked. 'I hear he's a bit of a looker.'

'Is he?' For the first time, Gladys perked up. 'Who told you that?'

'I did,' said Mum. Her tone was defiant. 'I asked Father Ramon if this bloke had . . . well, you know. Hair coming out of his ears, and so forth. But Father Ramon said he's a very nice-looking lad. Very handsome.'

'Except when he's got fangs and fur,' Dave muttered. At which point Sanford calmly observed that, however handsome and helpful Reuben might be, the fact remained that he wasn't the sort of person you'd want to have in your house during a full moon.

'From what you told me earlier, Nina, I get the impression

that your friend basically turns into a wild animal. Isn't that true?' he said.

'Well – yes, but –'

'And these McKinnon people are even worse,' he went on. 'They're dangerous. After what happened last time, do you really think that any of us should be returning to Wolgaroo Corner? Because I don't.'

'Sanford –'

'It's a noble thought, Nina. I commend you for it. But Horace is right – we have more immediate concerns. Someone wants to kill us, and he has to be stopped.'

'That's right! He does! And *Reuben could help us to stop him*!' I leaned forward, fists clenched. 'Don't you see? Reuben would be *more* than a match for someone like that – someone who sneaks around killing people when they can't defend themselves! Reuben could wipe the floor with him. Isn't that right, Dave?'

Everyone looked at Dave, who grunted. Then Mum said, '*I* could wipe the floor with him too, y'know. I once held off six drunken bikers with a cricket bat and a bottle of –'

'Guinness. Yes. You've told us.' I tried to keep the groan out of my voice. 'But we can't ask you to do everything. Poor Father Ramon never gets a break, and neither do you, Mum. If we help Reuben, maybe he'll shoulder some of your load.' Without waiting for a reply, I swung around to confront Sanford. 'You keep saying that vampirism is just another form of humanity,' I exclaimed, 'yet you're happy to sit here and let other people suffer! Is *that* what a real human being would do? How can we ask normal people to care about us, and respect us, and treat us properly, when we don't even try to stop a pair of criminals from hurting people who aren't vampires? Don't you think we have to shoulder at least *some* responsibility for the rest of the world?'

During the subsequent pause, Mum cleared her throat. Dave scratched his jaw in a sheepish sort of way, while Sanford stroked his moustache.

Horace snorted.

'Zadia Bloodstone rides again,' he sneered, exposing one discoloured canine tooth.

I'd had just about enough of Horace.

'I wasn't talking to *you*!' was my caustic rejoinder. 'I wouldn't expect *you* to agree, because you're a coward and a blowhard and a typical bloody vampire with no guts and no backbone! I wouldn't ask you *flush a toilet*, Horace, because you couldn't even manage that! You're useless! You're a *waste of space*! And the only reason you go around wearing those stupid clothes is because without them you'd be invisible!' As he opened his mouth to protest, I let him have one final barrage. 'But if you want to get staked,' I rapped out, 'go ahead! Wear your stupid clothes! Do us all a favour! At least we won't have to put up with you any more!'

There followed a deathly hush. George gaped at me. Sanford slowly shook his head. Gladys blinked, then cast a surreptitious glance at Horace to check his reaction.

At last Sanford spoke.

'I'm not surprised that you're feeling angry, Nina,' he said carefully. 'You've been through a lot over the past few days, and it must have been traumatic. But you're dumping a very toxic load of unprocessed fear on the nearest available target, and it isn't fair. It isn't fair on Horace. He's not responsible for the way you feel right now.'

'Sick to the stomach, you mean?' I snapped – and would

have said more if Bridget hadn't suddenly called down the stairs to us.

'Sanford!' she cried feebly. 'Estelle! Can you come up here, please?'

Sanford gave a start. As he hurried towards the doorway, Mum slipped off her piano stool with a grimace. (Her knee was bothering her; I could tell.)

'What is it?' Sanford boomed. 'Bridget? What's wrong?'

'Nothing. Nothing's *wrong*,' she assured him. By this time I had joined Sanford in the vestibule, and could just make out Bridget's spectral face, hanging over the banisters above us.

'I think Father Ramon's friend is waking up,' she announced, straining to project her cracked little voice. 'He's mumbling and thrashing about.'

'Sedatives,' Sanford confirmed, in a distracted sort of way, as he moved upstairs. Before I could follow him, however, he tossed a string of instructions at me, and I stopped in my tracks.

'Go and make some tea,' were his orders. 'Bring it on a tray. Just you – no one else. We don't want to scare him.'

'What about the rest of us?' asked Horace, who had appeared in the living-room doorway, alongside my mother. 'What are *we* supposed to do?'

'Keep watch. Help Dave. Stay quiet.' Sanford was about to recommence his climb when something made him hesitate. He opened his mouth, shut it again, then stiffened his resolve and spoke his mind. 'But if you really want to be useful, Horace, you can do something about those clothes,' he urged. 'Cover them up with a raincoat or something. Nina's right; you're simply making trouble for us in that outfit, because . . . well, to be perfectly frank, it's irresponsible. And

211

while I can understand your need for attention, I don't approve of the way you're putting our lives in danger.'

I don't know who was more astonished by this outburst: Horace or yours truly. But I do know that we were both rendered speechless until long after Sanford had disappeared into my room – where our nameless guest, who was emerging from his drug-induced stupor, had begun to make muffled, incoherent, undeniably panic-stricken noises.

'Irresponsible?' Horace finally spluttered. '*Irresponsible?*' He put his hands on his hips. 'I tell you what's irresponsible,' he yelled after Sanford, 'and that's bringing a complete stranger into this house!'

Then he stamped off into the kitchen before I could think of anything to say.

Chapter Eighteen

I've been trying to put myself in Nefley Irving's shoes. I've been trying to picture what he saw when he woke up in my bed.

First he would have seen those stupid rainbow stickers on the ceiling. Then he would have spotted my David Bowie poster or my lava lamp. Then he would have found himself staring up into Bridget's face, which is blanched and puckered but not particularly terrifying – not unless you have a phobia of old people. In fact I can't understand why Nefley should have been so scared. Even Sanford isn't *that* repellent. I mean, his moustache might be a little off-putting, and his three-piece suits can make him look like an undertaker, but he certainly doesn't give the impression of being someone who would happily break your arm.

So why was Nefley sweating bullets when I walked in with my tea tray? It wasn't as if we'd given him our names at that point. In fact Sanford hadn't done much more than check Nefley's pulse, and murmur reassurances. 'It's all right,' I heard Sanford say, as I entered the room. 'Calm down. You've been drugged. But there's nothing to worry about – no one's going to hurt you.'

'They tried . . . I've gotta . . . why is . . .' Nefley couldn't seem to string three consecutive words together.

'Shh. You're safe now,' said Bridget, patting his hand. 'How are you feeling? How's your head?'

'Would you like a cup of tea?' Sanford inquired, having registered my appearance. 'Thanks, Nina,' he continued. 'You can put those over there.'

I set down the tea tray without comment, then glanced up to see that our visitor had turned green. He really had. It wasn't just a figure of speech after all. I could definitely make out a green tint around his mouth, and under his eyes.

'Are you feeling sick?' asked Sanford, who must have noticed Nefley's colour change as well. 'Do you want to go to the bathroom?'

Nefley nodded frantically, his lips welded together. He threw off the bedclothes, swung his feet to the floor and made a lunge for the nearest exit – reeling against the door-jamb as he did so.

Being no stranger to nausea myself, I didn't think this behaviour especially odd. But I couldn't work out why he recoiled from my touch as I tried to lead him towards the bathroom. And I certainly didn't expect him to bolt the bath-room door after he'd ducked inside.

'That's weird,' I said, just as Sanford emerged from my room.

'What's weird?' was his automatic response.

'He's locked himself in,' I replied. 'What if he needs help? How are we supposed to reach him?'

Sanford frowned. Then he tapped on the bathroom door with one knuckle.

'*Hello?*' he said, raising his voice. '*Are you all right in there?*'

But he received no answer.

'Maybe he thinks we're in league with the McKinnons,' I speculated. 'Maybe he's scared.' I put my ear to one of the door panels, listening for any tell-tale sounds of retching or gasping. Instead I heard the scrape of a window being opened.

'What is it?' Sanford was alerted by my sudden frown. 'What's he up to?'

'I don't know.' When I tried to peer through the keyhole, a draught like a cold needle made my left eye water. I couldn't see a thing. 'He might need some air, I suppose.'

'Let me look,' Sanford instructed.

At that instant, Father Ramon spoke from the threshold of the guest room. 'Where's Reuben?' he croaked.

Sanford and I both jumped like startled rabbits. We whirled around to find that Father Ramon had struggled out of bed. Though his face looked as if it needed ironing, and he was using the door handle to support himself, there could be no doubt that he was on his way to a full recovery.

Bridget gave a little crow of delight. She had been following Sanford, and had only just shuffled into view.

'Father?' she said. 'Are you all right?'

'Where's Reuben?' the priest slurred, ignoring Bridget as he addressed me. 'Did they take him?'

'Did who take him?' I was confused. 'The McKinnons, you mean?'

'*Where is he?*' asked Father Ramon, then staggered slightly, as if the force of his own question had knocked him off balance.

'We don't know.' Sanford answered before I could. 'He might be the one in the bathroom. We're not sure.'

The priest blinked. 'What?' he mumbled, and I could

215

sympathise with his perplexity.

'*I* don't think it's him,' was my contribution. 'Horace thinks that Reuben might have become someone else, but I don't think so.'

'There's an overweight man in the bathroom,' Sanford informed Father Ramon. 'About five foot six, maybe thirty years old, clean-shaven, receding hairline. He was upstairs at your place. Asleep.'

'Is he a friend of yours, Father?' Bridget inquired. Whereupon the priest turned his head slowly to stare at her.

He looked stunned.

'That's not Reuben,' he said at last. 'That's Nefley. The McKinnons brought him to my house.' He screwed up his face in an expression of unadulterated bafflement. 'Did they really walk off without him?'

A heartbeat's silence was broken by a shattering noise. *E-e-e-CRUNCH!* I heard a shriek, too, ahead of the final impact. And somehow I knew instantly what had occurred.

Our guest had fallen into the alley between my mother's place and the house beside it.

'Oh, my God.' Sanford threw himself against the bathroom door. It was a stupid thing to do. I was already quite sure that Nefley had hit the ground; we wouldn't have been able to reach him through a first-floor window. So I hurtled down to the vestibule, where I met Horace.

'That crazy fool –' he began.

'I know.' Cutting him off, I tried to push past. 'He must have jumped.'

'He was climbing a downpipe!' Horace corrected, flapping a hand towards the room he'd just left. 'You can see him through the window! He pulled the pipe off the wall!'

216

'*Don't go outside!*' Sanford snapped at us both, from the top of the staircase. Then he, too, made a rapid descent, clutching his medical bag. 'Don't anyone go outside unless I say so!' he instructed, before raising his voice. '*Estelle*! Are you there?'

'I'm here.' Mum appeared on the living-room threshold, with Dave at her heels. 'He's still alive. You can hear him groaning.'

'Come with me,' Sanford barked. He glanced over his shoulder to where Father Ramon was progressing unsteadily downstairs, step by careful step. 'Can you manage, Father? Don't push yourself.'

'I can manage,' the priest avowed. 'I have to talk to Nefley.'

'You'll need the keys, first.' I thought it worth reminding people, at this juncture, that our side-alley was secured by two high metal gates, one at each end. 'They're in the kitchen.'

So everyone charged towards the kitchen, heading for the back door. Even George and Gladys joined in; they had managed to tear themselves away from the skinny little window in the western wall of my mother's living room, from which it was possible to glimpse Nefley's twitching, whimpering form if you pressed your cheek firmly against the glass.

But very few of us advanced beyond the kitchen. Sanford held firm; he wouldn't let anyone accompany him outside except my mother and Father Ramon, just in case there was a lot of blood lying around. 'I want the rest of you down in the basement,' Sanford decreed, 'except you, Dave. I might need you for something.'

'What about me?' I wasn't about to be overlooked. 'I've

been blooded too. Didn't you know? And I passed the test.'

This would have been big news at any other time. It would have been the subject of exhaustive discussion during at least six consecutive meetings of our support group. Even now, it was received with a discernible gasp; had Bridget not been thumping her way slowly down the stairs, she would have given me a congratulatory hug, I feel sure.

'It's true,' said Dave, as people looked to him for confirmation. 'I was there. She did it.'

'Why didn't you tell us before?' Gladys demanded.

'I don't know.' It was a good question, which I couldn't answer. 'There was too much else happening, I guess.'

'Well, now – that's excellent.' Sanford hovered near the back door, clearly desperate to be on his way, yet feeling obliged to acknowledge my achievement. 'I suppose, in the circumstances, you might be usefully employed up here,' he went on. 'But the rest of you need to be downstairs, because we'll be bringing the patient inside. And I don't want to take any risks.'

It was a reasonable sort of request, in the circumstances. Horace, however, wasn't pleased.

'What the hell did you do to that poor bloke, anyway?' he snapped. 'Did you *push* him out the window?'

Before Sanford could reply, Father Ramon spoke for him. 'No one pushed anyone,' the priest quietly insisted. 'Nefley tried to escape because he knows you're vampires. And he's very, very scared.'

During the stunned silence that greeted this announcement, Father Ramon turned on his heel. Then he vanished outside – leaving the rest of us goggle-eyed and slack-jawed. Even Sanford couldn't move for a few seconds. It was my mother who finally broke the spell that had been cast, by jangling her keys.

'Wait! Father!' she cried. 'I have to unlock that gate!'

She limped after him, hampered by an arthritic knee, as Sanford brought up the rear. Though I attempted to pursue them, Dave stopped me.

'Don't,' he said. 'Sanford's right. The smell might be a problem.'

'But this doesn't make sense.' I was flummoxed. 'How could a complete stranger know that we're vampires? Did Father Ramon tell him?'

'Maybe no one told him.' Seeing my blank stare, Dave spelled things out for me. 'He's called Nefley, Nina. Think about it. How many people in the world are called Nefley?'

You can probably blame a deep-seated fatigue for my slow reaction time. The impact of recent events must have left me a little duller than usual; I was still pondering when Horace suddenly gasped.

'He was on that customer list!' Horace exclaimed. 'Nefley Irving was! He bought those silver bullets, remember? He was *next on the list after Barry McKinnon.*'

'And he recognised my name.' At last I saw what Dave was getting at. 'He knew it, Dave. Nina. He heard it and he turned green.'

By now, evidently, Gladys was feeling ill-used. 'What are you talking about?' she whined. 'Will someone please explain what's going on?'

'He's the slayer.' Horace rounded on her. 'That fat guy out there on the ground. He killed Casimir, and he stole Casimir's address book.'

Gladys caught her breath. George clapped a hand over his

mouth. But before I could remind Horace that all we had so far was circumstantial evidence, a sudden screech sounded from the alley.

The shock of it galvanised Dave.

'Quick,' he said. 'You three get downstairs.'

'But –'

'*Go on, Horace*! You know the rules!' As everyone gawked at him – astonished to hear him throw his weight around – Dave seized my arm. 'Come here,' he ordered, then dragged me over to the living-room window. Through it, I could see Father Ramon crouched over Nefley, trying to offer comfort. Sanford was preparing a syringe. Mum was speaking to our uninvited guest quite roughly.

'For Chrissake, you moron, will you *calm down*? I'm not a bloody vampire – look.' And she flipped her dentures out of her mouth. 'Thee?' she said. 'No teeth! Let alone fangth!'

Nefley, however, continued to emit feeble protests, which doubled in strength when Sanford stuck a needle in his thigh. It occurred to me that if the neighbouring house hadn't been a business address – if it had contained a sleeping family, instead of a collection of empty offices – we would have been in trouble.

'It's all right,' Sanford attested, his voice muffled and unclear. 'You've broken your arm . . . there doesn't seem to be any spinal damage, though I can't be sure just yet . . .' He looked up. 'Dave? Can you hear me?'

'Yeah,' Dave replied, nodding energetically and moving his lips in an exaggerated way, as if he were talking to a deaf person. 'I can hear you.'

'We need some kind of stretcher,' Sanford told him. 'Get a sleeping bag and stick an ironing board inside it – can you do that?'

'Sure,' said Dave. He immediately went to retrieve a sleeping bag from the basement, while I fetched Mum's ironing board. But he wouldn't let me go with him when he delivered these items to Sanford. 'There are too many people in the alley as it is,' Dave said, before loping outside. I had to wait by the fridge, nursing a headache, until the whole rescue team came staggering into the kitchen. Nefley was in their midst, strapped to a makeshift stretcher.

He smelled of fresh blood.

I have to admit, I found that smell very difficult to endure. It made me slightly dizzy; I had to lean against the fridge and clap a tea-towel over my nose. But I didn't lose control. I didn't forget who I was, or what I was supposed to be doing. Dave had been one-hundred-per-cent right: the second time was much easier than the first – especially with Dave there, and Sanford, and Father Ramon. Just looking at them helped me. Dave did appear to be slightly affected, though his livid cheeks and faltering step might have been the natural result of overexertion, rather than a response to the smell of blood. As for Sanford, he was taking it all in his stride. His voice was firm and his manner brisk as he explained to me that he had fashioned a temporary splint out of a large screwdriver from Mum's garden shed.

'But I'm going to have to set the bone, once the swelling's gone down,' he declared. 'And I can't do that without my plaster-kit. I have everything I need except my plaster-kit.' He glanced from Dave to Father Ramon. 'Someone will have to get it from my house.'

'Not if we call an ambulance,' said Mum.

Sanford shook his head. 'We've been through this a thousand times, Estelle,' he reminded her, with the air of someone dismissing a subject once and for all. 'It wouldn't be *just* the ambulance – it would be the rest of world as well. The best we could hope for would be some kind of quarantine. The worst . . .' He shook his head as his gaze drifted down towards Nefley, who was beginning to lose consciousness. 'Well, it doesn't bear thinking of.'

'I understand what you're saying,' Father Ramon interposed. 'But don't you think, all things considered –'

'No.' Sanford was adamant. 'I've seen what can happen, Father. You weren't there in the old days. You don't know what people will do. Now who's going to bring me my plaster?'

Mum raised her hand. She would catch a cab, she said, and fetch whatever was needed. But Father Ramon refused to allow it; he insisted on going himself.

'This is your house. It's where you belong,' he told her. Then he turned to Dave. 'How did you get here, Dave? Did you use my car?'

Dave nodded.

'In that case, if you give me the keys, I'll drive to Sanford's myself,' the priest continued, before fixing his attention on Nefley Irving. 'Hello? Nefley? Are you awake?' he inquired.

'Ah-ngh,' said Nefley, struggling to focus.

'Nefley?' Father Ramon poked him in the gut. 'Where do you live? Can you tell me that? What's your address?'

'Ummmm . . .'

'*Nefley!*' When the priest began to slap Nefley's cheeks, I think everyone else was just as surprised as I was. Sanford, in particular, reacted sharply.

'He's *sedated!*' was Sanford's outraged protest – which Father Ramon ignored. And just as well, too, because the next slap elicited an answer from Nefley. He mumbled a Parramatta address, and something about a spare key under a peg basket, before shutting his eyes again.

Father Ramon immediately cast around for paper to scribble on.

'Sabel Avenue,' he repeated, snatching up the notebook that Mum keeps beside the telephone. 'Sabel Avenue . . .'

'What's so important about Sabel Avenue?' asked Dave. And Sanford said, 'He can't be moved. Not yet. He can't be taken home until he's in a stable condition.'

'I'm not going to take him home.' Father Ramon wrote down Nefley's address, tore the sheet of paper out of Mum's notebook, and tucked the folded slip into his pocket. Then he swung around to confront the rest of us. 'I'm going to find a public phone box,' he said, 'and I'm going to make an anonymous call to the police, informing them that two men currently residing at that address are holding a teenaged boy against his will.'

Everybody stared.

'I have to do it,' he went on. 'I have to do *something*. Because if I don't, I won't be able to live with myself.' He surveyed the ring of thunderstruck faces surrounding him. 'Unless anyone has any objections?' he finished.

Chapter Nineteen

When Father Ramon left Mum's house, about ten minutes later, he took with him a list of required medical equipment and the key to Sanford's front door. But he didn't have permission to call the police.

Not, at least, until his plan had been thoroughly discussed by a full meeting of the Reformed Vampire Support Group.

'The second you make that call, we'll have to resign ourselves to possible exposure,' Sanford had told the priest. 'Because if the McKinnons are arrested, they'll talk. And next thing you know, the police will be on our doorstep, and we'll be answering questions about Nefley and Casimir and our forged identity papers. That's why every one of us has to be in *total agreement* as to whether this is our best option.'

'Which it isn't,' had been my view. 'Not for Reuben, it isn't. He doesn't want the police to know anything about him.'

But my proposal that we liberate Reuben ourselves had been shot down in flames. Even Father Ramon had warned me that a rescue attempt would be far too risky, because the McKinnons were armed.

As for Sanford, he'd rejected the whole idea.

'We're not in one of your books, Nina,' he'd said, before turning to Father Ramon. How long, Sanford had inquired, were the McKinnons intending to remain at Nefley's apartment? Two hours? Three?

'Until about seven or eight o'clock tomorrow morning,' the priest had advised him.

'In that case, we'll have plenty of time to think things through.' Sanford's gaze had dropped to Nefley's motionless bulk. 'For instance, we can't even *consider* calling the police until we decide what we're going to do with this fellow.'

There are occasions when Sanford simply won't budge, no matter how hard you push him. Father Ramon must have realised that he would be fighting a losing battle, because he decided not to argue. Instead he promised to wait. Then he quaffed a very strong cup of coffee and drove off in his battered grey car, having refused to swallow even one of Sanford's pep pills. 'I'll be all right to drive,' he declared, dismissing Sanford's worries about residual sedation and slow reflexes. 'Anyway, it isn't very far. I'll be back before you know it.'

We had to satisfy ourselves with this assurance, because we had other things to fret about. There was Nefley, for example; he had to be carried up to the guest room. There was the problem of the bathroom door, which had been bolted from the inside. And there was the looming question of what we were going to do when Father Ramon returned.

Would we, or would we not, try to save Reuben?

I won't bore you with an account of how Dave and George and Horace and Sanford finally managed to manoeuvre Nefley back upstairs. Let's just say it was a job and a half. Getting the bathroom door open was no cinch, either; it had to be kicked repeatedly until the screws on the bolt gave way, taking large splinters of the door-jamb with them. ('For

Chrissake,' Mum groaned, when she saw the damage, 'why didn't you just knock a couple of holes through the wall, instead? At least I would have got a three-way bathroom.')

But the greatest problem of all was deciding what to do about Reuben. Nefley, we knew, wouldn't be nearly as much of a challenge; everyone agreed that he might be *persuaded* to stop hating vampires, especially if he saw how nice Bridget was.

Unfortunately, however, this approach wouldn't work with the McKinnons. A loaded gun, I insisted, was about the only thing that they would understand.

'Which is why we have to rescue Reuben,' I begged. 'Which is why we can't just walk away. Because if we do, it will mean we're just as cruel as Barry is.'

'I dunno if it's cruel to be scared of getting your head blown off,' Dave remarked, in cautious tones. 'Cowardly, perhaps, but not cruel.'

We were sitting in the basement, on an assortment of kitchen chairs. Not all of us were present; Mum was with Sanford, tending to her uninvited guest, while George was in the bathroom, vomiting. But Horace had come down, as had Dave, and Gladys, and Bridget. In fact it was Bridget who reacted most strongly to my graphic description of Reuben's miserable life.

'I do think you're right, Nina,' she said. 'I do think it would be wrong to abandon someone who's being treated like that, no matter who they are.'

'Of course it would.' Conscious of an overwhelming sense of apathy in the room, I renewed my attack with more vigour. 'This is a turning point for us. We have to decide: are we good people or bad people? If we're good people, we have to do the decent thing.'

'But would a werewolf do the decent thing for *us*? That's what I want to know,' Gladys grumbled. 'What if we rescue him, and he turns around and eats someone?'

I was about to accuse her of being deliberately obtuse when Dave interrupted. 'This isn't about mounting a rescue attempt, Gladys,' he said patiently, from behind his hair. 'This is about whether or not Father Ramon should call the police.'

'Oh, is it?' Horace sounded perplexed. 'I thought a rescue attempt was one of our options.'

'Horace is right,' I agreed. 'We should at least *consider* a rescue attempt. It would be our only way of keeping the police out of things.' I didn't have to explain that if the police discovered our secret, we might be exiled, or confined, or experimented on, or – even worse – end up like that vampire who was scraped off her own back steps, after her family had shut her out of the house. (According to Sanford, her clothes had been buried along with her, because so much of her had soaked into them.)

But Dave was shaking his head.

'There's no telling what the police will do, Nina,' he countered. 'Even if they're tipped off, they might never find their way here. We don't know what the McKinnons are likely to tell them. Our names might never crop up.' When I glared at him, he fingered the stubble on his jaw – but wouldn't back down. 'The anonymous phone call would be much less risky than the rescue option,' he continued. 'If we're voting, I'd vote for the phone call.'

'So would I,' said Bridget.

'I wouldn't.' Gladys was scowling. 'I don't see why we have to get involved at all. This is our *future* we're talking about!

Just because Nina's in love with this werewolf –'

'I am not!'

'– doesn't mean we have to reveal ourselves, and flush a hundred years of hard work down the toilet.'

'I am *not* in love with Reuben!' The accusation made me feel sicker than ever. Especially when Horace smirked, and Gladys sniffed, and Dave quietly scratched his nose, eyes cast down. 'It's got nothing to do with Reuben! It's all about *us*!'

'Then why are you so keen to waltz in there like Zadia Bloodstone, and earn his undying gratitude?' Horace asked slyly. He was in his element; he always loves needling people. 'Sounds like you've got a bit of a crush to me. Eh, Dave?'

Dave didn't answer; he was still staring at the floor. I was furious at his lack of response, and vaguely alarmed, as well. I certainly didn't want *Dave* thinking I was in love with Reuben.

Bridget leaned over to pat my arm.

'Don't pay any attention, dear,' she murmured. 'You know how Horace likes to tease.'

'I'm not teasing her.' Horace's injured expression was utterly bogus, and made me want to punch him in the mouth. 'I'm simply stating a fact. If Nina isn't in love with that werewolf, why would she want to take such a huge risk?'

'Because it *wouldn't* be such a huge risk!' I spluttered, at which point Dave lifted his head. He was frowning.

'Nina, they have guns,' he reminded me. 'You heard what Father Ramon told us. How can we fight them if they're armed?'

'Maybe we wouldn't have to,' I said, raising a hand before he could speak. 'Listen. Just think about it. The last time they saw us, Dave, we were dead. *Dead*. They think we're dead, you and me. So how are they going to react when we walk in on them?'

During the silence that followed, I scanned the room – and saw at once that I'd made a big impression on Horace. He was sitting bolt upright, and the sneer had been wiped clean off his face.

'Nefley mentioned a spare key,' I went on. 'A spare key under a peg basket. Suppose we found it, and sneaked in, and confronted Barry McKinnon? Ten to one he'd be half-asleep, at this hour –'

'And we could say that we're the Undead!' Horace interjected, his eyes sparkling. 'We could talk in a monotone – *you* know – like zombies. *You cannot kill us, Barry. We shall always return.*'

'Oh, please.' Dave's tone was a mixture of alarm, derision and disbelief. But Horace ploughed on regardless.

'You could wear some of my clothes!' he suggested. 'It would scare the living daylights out of them! You could slick your hair back!'

'For God's sake, Horace.' Gladys didn't bother to hide her exasperation. 'Don't be such a fool.'

'This isn't a movie, mate,' Dave warned.

'But it could still work!' I avowed, desperate to win his approval. 'We'd have the element of surprise, don't you see? Barry wouldn't be expecting us. We'd sneak in. He'd be confused. He wouldn't know how to react –'

'Of course he would. He'd shoot us.' Dave seemed to have no doubts on that score. 'You've seen what they're like, those two. They're animals. I don't care *how* confused they are; they'll shoot first and ask questions later.'

'I'm sure Sanford and Father Ramon wouldn't want us

doing anything dangerous,' Bridget piped up. 'I'm sure they'd agree with Dave. Someone could get badly hurt. It wouldn't be sensible.'

'And what happens afterwards?' Dave added. 'What are we supposed to do with the McKinnons once we've got Reuben out of there? Ask them nicely to go home?'

It was a good question. I hadn't really considered that side of things.

As I lapsed into thought, Horace cocked his head.

'Kill them?' he proposed, with obvious relish.

'No!' I rounded on him. 'Of course not! We're not murderers!'

'In that case, they'll come after us. They won't just walk away.' Dave leaned towards me. 'They've got my wallet, Nina. They *know my address*.'

'But they don't know mine!'

'You can't be certain of that.'

'Yes I can. Father Ramon didn't tell them. He said so.'

'But what about Nefley Irving?' Slowly and clearly, with a kind of laborious determination, Dave kept blowing my arguments out of the water. 'Maybe they got your address off Nefley. He might have found it in Casimir's address book. Along with your phone number and everything else.'

'You mean those two McKinnon people know where *we* are?' Gladys exclaimed. And I glared at her.

'Of course not,' I snapped. 'Why would Nefley Irving tell them where I live?' Then I turned back to Dave. 'They're not his friends, Dave. They tried to kill him, remember?'

'If they tried to kill him, they might have twisted his arm as well,' Dave replied. 'They might have *forced* the address out of him – he doesn't look like a guy who'd need much forcing.'

230

'But –'

'Wait. Just wait a minute.' Gladys sat up straight. 'Are you saying that fat man upstairs knows *my* address?'

Horace heaved an impatient sigh.

'That's what we were talking about before,' he said. 'Don't you listen? The man upstairs is the one who killed Casimir.'

'We think,' Dave amended.

'Which means that he probably stole Casimir's address book.' Horace ignored Dave, fixing his attention on Gladys. 'So, yes – he probably does know where you live. And where *I* live, as well.'

'Which means that those other men might know, too? The men with the guns?' Gladys demanded.

Horace shrugged. Dave said, 'Maybe.'

Gladys surged to her feet.

'Then we *have* to call the police! Right now!' she cried. 'Before those gunmen show up here!'

Dave and Horace exchanged glances.

'I doubt they'll do that,' was Dave's opinion.

'Why should they?' Horace agreed. 'They've got their werewolf. They don't need to come looking for us.'

'But they *might*!' wailed Gladys. 'We have to call the police!'

'I'm sure we will.' Blinking, Bridget looked to Dave for confirmation. 'I'm sure that's what we're going to do. Isn't it?'

Dave hesitated. His eyes swivelled in my direction.

Then his brow creased.

'What's the matter?' he said.

I didn't reply. I wasn't able to. If I had, I would have vomited all over the basement rug.

It was one of those occasions when you can't make

polite excuses, or withdraw discreetly. Instead I jumped up, clapped my hand over my mouth and ran upstairs. I reached the bathroom just as George was emerging from it, and nearly knocked him over on my way to the toilet bowl. What happened next isn't something you want to hear about. All I can say is that I've experienced much worse; when you've spent nearly three hours straight with your head in the toilet, a ten-minute session doesn't seem so bad.

Mum heard me, of course. She always does. She came in, held back my hair, wiped my face, then led me off to my bedroom when I was done. 'Just have a lie down,' she recommended. 'You'll be fine in a moment.'

'I feel so awful . . .'

'I know you do.'

'It isn't fair.'

'You're right. It isn't.' Mum knew the drill. Having tucked me into bed, she draped a damp washcloth over my forehead and turned off all the lights. At the door she encountered Sanford.

'Just leave her alone,' Mum warned him. 'She's been overdoing it.'

'She's not in any pain?'

'She'll be fine.'

'How's your tummy, Nina?'

'Go away,' I moaned – because I hate having people hover over me when I'm sick. Mum gave it up long ago; she understands that if I'm left to myself, and don't have to fight off suggestions about hot-water bottles or extra pillows, I'll be up and about soon enough. That's probably why she ushered Sanford away from the threshold of my room, and why she closed the door with such authoritative, 'out-of-bounds' firmness.

Unfortunately, I was too depressed to be grateful. I kept remembering Reuben's lopsided smile, and his bewildered anger, and his irrepressible vitality. To most of the others, Reuben was just an abstract concept. They didn't see him as a flesh-and-blood human being. They didn't realise that turning our backs on Reuben would be like tying up a dog, then leaving it to starve.

That's how *I* felt, anyway.

I wondered if Dave was experiencing a similar sense of obligation. I wondered if he would vote in favour of an anonymous tip-off. Bridget would. The priest would. Gladys probably would – unless Sanford frightened her into submission with gory tales of sun exposure. As for Horace . . . well, it was impossible to tell what *he* would do. Except twit me about Reuben, of course, just to get up my nose.

That was another thing that really, really depressed me: the fact that people might think I was in love with Reuben. The fact that *Dave* might think I was in love with Reuben, just because Horace had been shooting his stupid mouth off.

'*Sssst! Nina!*'

It was Horace. He'd pushed open the door and stuck his head into my room; when I turned to squint at him, the rest of his body quickly followed his head.

'Are you awake?' he whispered, leaning against the door so that it softly clicked shut behind him. 'Can you talk, or are you sick?'

'What is it?' I mumbled. 'What do you want?'

'It's not what *I* want. It's what *you* want,' he rejoined. And I stared at him in sheer perplexity.

'Wh-what?'

'Nina . . .' Stealthily he approached the bed, his black cape swishing around his ankles. Before I could order him to keep his distance, he knelt down on my woolly bedside mat, thrust his face into mine, and hissed, *'We've got to go and rescue Reuben!'*

Chapter Twenty

'What?' I said vaguely. 'What do you mean?'

'We have to get Reuben back ourselves,' Horace insisted. 'We *have* to!'

'Why?'

'Because . . .' He hesitated, glancing at the door. 'Because I can't afford to get involved with the police, Nina.'

'None of us can,' I pointed out. But he shook his head.

'No, I *really* can't. More than anyone else,' he assured me.

'Why?' The question was hardly out of my mouth before I realised why. 'You've been running a scam,' I concluded, without waiting for an answer. 'Some kind of Internet scam. I knew it. I *knew* it.'

'As a matter of fact, you don't know anything,' he retorted. 'And the less you know, the better.'

'For God's sake.' I turned away from him, peevishly rubbing my eyes. 'What's the matter with you, Horace?'

'The matter with me is that I have to pay rates! Unlike *some* people who live with their *mothers*,' Horace snarled. Then he recalled that he was trying to be persuasive, and quickly changed his tone. 'Sorry,' he said. 'Sorry, it's just that I'm . . . well, I'm a bit worried. I could go to *jail*, Nina.'

He went on to explain that, even if the police were called,

they might not pay any attention. 'What if they think Father Ramon's a lunatic?' he continued softly. 'Or what if they get there too late?' It was more than likely, he added, that one of the McKinnons would drive by the presbytery, just to make sure that it had burned to the ground. And if they saw that it hadn't? 'They'll take off,' he opined. 'They'll be gone before the police even get to Nefley's place.'

'I – I suppose so.' Despite my fuzzy head, I could understand Horace's reasoning. 'But Dave was right, Horace – even if we do manage to rescue Reuben, the McKinnons will come after us –'

'No, they won't.'

'Horace –'

'*Not if we tell them we're vampires.*'

I peered up at him, floundering.

'What?' I croaked.

'Nina, they think you're dead. You said it yourself.' The relish in his voice was all too obvious. His eyes glittered. His teeth gleamed. 'If they see you, and they see *me*, and we play things right, they'll be too scared to come after us.' He gestured at his outfit – at his cape and boots and frock-coat – with the air of somebody clinching an argument. 'If you like, I can lend you my cape,' he offered.

'But . . .' I was very tired. I wasn't thinking clearly. 'But what about the guns?' was my next objection. 'It's probably true, what Dave said. We might not have a chance to say that we're vampires. Barry will shoot first and ask questions later.'

'Only if he can see what he's shooting at.'

'Huh?'

'You've forgotten something.' He rubbed his hands together, like a super-villain on a cartoon show. 'Everyone

236

has. You're so caught up in how we can't fly or shapeshift or go out in the sun that you're not focusing on what we *can* do.' Suddenly he leaned forward, grabbing my wrist. 'We can see in the dark, Nina,' he reminded me. 'If the lights are off, Barry won't shoot first. He won't know what's going on. We will, though. We'll have that gun off him before he can say "Dracula".'

'Who will?' I queried, disengaging myself. 'Who are you talking about? You and me and who else?'

There was a pause.

'No one,' Horace replied at last, trying to sound nonchalant. 'Just us.'

'By *ourselves*?' I should have turned him down right there and then. I probably would have, if I'd been in good health. The trouble was that I felt confused; despite my reservations about Horace, I could see his point. The police might *not* respond. The McKinnons *might* leave early. And Horace's plan of attack didn't seem utterly unrealistic.

'Have you asked anyone else?' I inquired. 'What did Dave say?'

'What do you think?' Horace waved his hand dismissively. 'Dave wouldn't listen. Neither would Sanford. They're both too scared – not like you. You have *guts*.'

'So has Dave,' I objected. My mind started to wander. I thought about Dave advancing into the McKinnons' basement, and climbing the presbytery stairs ahead of me. I remembered watching him square his bony shoulders before he went to check the front of the orange van. Though he might have been tall, he wasn't that strong; he had the same brittle-looking wrists and hesitant, shuffling tread as I did. Yet over the past few days, he had demonstrated the most enormous courage – unlike certain other vampires of my acquaintance.

You couldn't help admiring him. At least, *I* couldn't.

'Nina, we don't have much time,' Horace urged. 'It's now or never.'

'But –'

'Sanford and your mum are shut away in the guest room. Everyone else is down in the basement. When Father Ramon gets back, it'll be too late.' His fingers closed on a handful of duvet; the muscles in his neck were taut. 'We can't mess around, Nina. It's your decision. Do you want to save Reuben or not?'

'Of course I do.' The implied criticism annoyed me. 'But how are we going to get there, if Dave won't drive us?'

'We'll take a cab.'

'A *cab*?'

'You've been blooded, haven't you? It'll be fine.' Releasing the bedclothes, Horace whipped a mobile phone out of his pocket. 'I'll book one. We can pick it up around the corner. I've got plenty of cash.'

'It's a long way, though –'

'Come *on*, Nina! Will you or won't you?' he demanded. 'I can't go by myself – the McKinnons don't know me. They don't think I'm dead.'

'All right, all right.' Throwing off my duvet, I sat up. Immediately my head began to swim. 'Oh God. I hope I can do this.'

'Of course you can.' Horace passed me my boots. 'You'll be fine. We'll look out for each other. And when we've freed the werewolf, he can deal with the McKinnons himself.' Horace gave a snort of amusement as I lurched to my feet.

'That's something else Dave hasn't considered: how the McKinnons are supposed to come after us if the werewolf has bitten their legs off!'

'Reuben won't do that,' I weakly protested. 'He *can't* do that – not right now. He's got teeth just like everyone else, except when it's a full moon.'

Horace, however, wasn't listening. He had dialled a taxi service, and was quietly ordering a cab. I was impressed that he knew what to do; it's not as if vampires go around ordering cabs every day of the week. I was also amazed that he could remember Nefley Irving's address, which had completely slipped *my* mind.

I was having a hard time trying to remember anything – even the fact that Horace should never, ever be trusted.

'All right,' he finally declared, snapping his mobile shut. 'Are you ready? Are your boots on?'

'Yes.'

'Where are your sunglasses?'

'Uh – I don't know.' I had to think for a moment. 'The McKinnons took them.'

'Don't you have a spare set?'

'No.'

'What about your mum? She must have a pair.' After a brief wait (during which I struggled to recall something – *anything* – about my mother's sunglasses), Horace said, 'Would they be in her purse?'

'Probably.'

'Then we'll pick them up on our way out. Her purse is on the hall table.' He took my hand. 'Just follow me. And keep the noise down. We don't want anyone hearing us.'

By now you must be wondering if I'd gone mad. I don't

blame you, really; to have gone in a taxi with Horace – let *alone* on a rescue mission – was something I wouldn't normally have done. Don't forget, however, that I still hadn't fully recovered from what Sanford would have called my 'gastric upset'. I was groggy and disoriented. I was also afraid of the police. And though I wasn't completely convinced that Horace and I could pull it off alone, I did believe that his scheme might just work.

Creak. Cre-e-eak. It was astonishing that no one heard us, as we crept down the old wooden stairs. I can only assume that somewhere behind the closed door of the guest room, Mum was receiving instructions from Sanford – instructions so exhaustive that she missed our stealthy footsteps. (Normally she has the ears of a lynx.) Upon arriving in the vestibule, Horace fished around in Mum's handbag while I reached for my yellow coat. But Horace stopped me. He shook his head.

Only after we had slipped out the front door, holding our breaths at the *snap* of the deadlock, did he feel secure enough to speak.

'You wouldn't have scared anyone in that coat,' he muttered. 'The blouse is bad enough, but that coat makes you look like Tweety Bird.'

I was too listless to protest, or to accuse *him* of looking like Darth Vader. Instead I followed him around the corner into the next street, shading my eyes from the overhead lights.

As soon as we were at a safe distance from the house, he turned to give me my mother's sunglasses.

'This is where I said we'd be,' he explained. 'In front of number one. I hope we don't have to wait long – Father Ramon might be back any minute.'

'Horace.'

240

'What?'

'These are prescription lenses.' I'd completely forgotten. 'Mum's short-sighted.'

'For God's sake!'

'I can't wear these. I won't be able to see a thing.'

At that precise moment, two beams of light swept across the footpath. They heralded the sudden appearance of our taxi, which rounded the corner behind us and slid gracefully to a halt not far from where we stood. Luckily I was still wearing Mum's sunglasses; if I hadn't been, the glare would have burst the blood vessels in my eyes. But when the vehicle pulled up, Horace had to guide me towards it. Otherwise I probably would have fallen over.

I might as well have been squinting through a couple of very thick slabs of toffee.

'Whittaker for Parramatta?' the driver asked, as soon as Horace had opened the rear door.

'That's us,' said Horace. He pushed me inside, then slid in next to me. The door slammed; the car began to move.

Even through the distorting prescription lenses that were perched on my nose, I was able to see how well protected the driver was. A thick, transparent plastic screen curved around him, preventing easy access from any of the passenger seats. This screen, I assumed, had been erected as a precaution against attacks by thieves or crazy people – but it would be just as effective against vampires like Horace.

I wondered if it would also act as a kind of noise filter, blocking out conversation.

Probably not, I decided.

'You should close your eyes, if those glasses are bothering you,' said Horace, completely disregarding the driver's close proximity. I shook my head.

'No,' I rejoined. 'You close *your* eyes. And I'll take *your* glasses.'

'But –'

'You're the one who can't control your impulses, Horace – not me.' Though I didn't actually use the word 'blooded', he knew exactly what I meant. And he wasn't happy about it, either. At any other time he probably would have told me to go jump in the lake. On this occasion, however, he had to comply, lest *I* refuse to cooperate with *him*.

So we swapped sunglasses, just as the driver addressed us from behind his screen.

'Going to a party?' he wanted to know.

Horace and I exchanged glances.

'Uh – not really,' Horace said at last, speaking for us both. (I was completely tongue-tied.)

'Ah.' The driver nodded. 'Just been, have you?'

'N-o-o . . .' Horace sounded bemused. 'Why?'

'Oh – I figured you must have won first prize, that's all,' the driver cheerfully observed. 'It's the Addams family, right? Gomez and what's-her-name. The daughter.'

I blinked. Horace scowled.

'*Gomez*?' he expostulated. 'What do you mean, *Gomez*? I don't even have a moustache!'

'Maybe you're thinking of Grandpa Munster,' was my wary suggestion. I wouldn't normally have become involved in a conversation about sixties sitcoms, even though it's a very vampire-ish kind of subject. (Dave and Gladys and Horace are always arguing about who played what character in *My Favourite Martian* and *The Twilight Zone*.) But I was so completely out of my depth, at this point, that I seized on

242

such a harmless and familiar topic with gratitude.

It stopped me from thinking about the dangers that lay ahead.

'Grandpa Munster!' Horace was outraged. 'I don't look *that* old!'

'Hang on – who was Grandpa Munster?' the driver interposed. 'Was he that Frankenstein guy with the green face?'

'No!' yelped Horace. 'Grandpa was a *vampire*. I'm supposed to be a *vampire*. Can't you see that?

'Oh, yeah. Yeah. Stands out a mile.' The driver might have been humouring us. Or perhaps he really did believe that Horace looked like a vampire. At any rate, he seemed anxious to change the subject. 'I tell you what, though, don't ever go anywhere as a mummy,' he advised. 'I went to a costume party last month as a mummy, and I nearly brained myself when one of my bandages got caught on a door handle . . .'

He went on to recount some of his more farcical party-related exploits, while Horace sulked and I tried to concentrate. I have to admit, it was difficult to muster my thoughts. The driver's stories were very distracting – though they also had an oddly calming effect. When someone's rattling on about blocked toilets, collapsing marquees, and penis-shaped birthday cakes, it's hard to convince yourself that you're in a life-or-death situation.

Perhaps that's why, instead of focusing on more important issues, I found myself wondering why Horace had 'plenty of cash'. As far as I was aware, he didn't deal in cash; he ordered his groceries, paid his bills, and transferred his money on-line. In fact he'd often remarked that electronic banking was a godsend to every vampire who didn't keep bankers' hours.

When the driver eventually finished his narrative, I turned to Horace and said quietly, 'Where did you get the cash?'

'What?'

'*Where did you get the cash*?' I repeated. 'You didn't send Mum out for it, did you?'

'No.'

Something about his slippery, sidelong glance made me suspicious; I was struck by a sudden misgiving.

'It's not *Mum's*, is it?' I squeaked. 'You didn't steal it from her, did you?'

'Of course not!' Horace's denial left me unconvinced. Sure enough, after a brief pause, he added, 'It's a loan – I'll pay it back.'

'*Horace!*'

'I'll pay it back! I've got plenty of money!' At that instant his mobile tootled, and we both fell silent. It was obvious that someone at Mum's place had finally noted our absence.

'That's yours, is it?' the driver queried, after listening to several electronic renditions of the chorus from 'Hey, Big Spender'.

'Yes,' said Horace.

'Aren't you going to answer it?'

'No,' said Horace – rather rudely, I thought. The driver must have thought so too, because he didn't say anything else for some time. Neither did his passengers. Though I would have liked to tear strips off Horace for raiding my mother's purse, I was acutely conscious that every accusation levelled at him would be overheard by a total stranger. And I didn't want that.

In fact I didn't want to be in the taxi at all. That unanswered phone call had shocked me out of my daze; I'd begun to have serious doubts about Horace's strategy. But I couldn't discuss my misgivings in front of the driver. And if I told him to return home, there would be hell to pay. Horace would kick up such a stink that we'd probably be thrown out of the car.

So I decided to put my foot down just as soon as we reached Nefley's flat. That's when I would refuse to help Horace after all. Instead I would make him order another cab, and we would sneak away before the McKinnons spotted us.

Unless, of course, we were lucky. I was willing to mount a rescue attempt if the McKinnons weren't around. Or if they were too drunk to move. Or if they had mislaid their guns.

But I wasn't about to risk my neck otherwise.

'Here we are,' said the driver. With a start, I realised that he was slowing down. 'What number is it?'

'Oh – ah – just stop here,' Horace replied. As the cab pulled over, he fumbled in his pocket. 'How much do we owe you?'

I didn't catch the driver's response. I was too busy peering out at a street lined with nasty red-brick apartment blocks (most of which appeared to have been built in the 1960s), and wondering which of them contained Nefley Irving's residence. Only when Horace raised his voice did I notice what was happening inside the car.

'Is this a *joke*?' Horace was saying. 'You can't be *serious*!'

'That's the fare, mate.'

'But it's extortionate! It's highway robbery!'

'*For God's sake, Horace.*' I was appalled. The last thing we needed was a full-blown public confrontation. I had a vision of people spilling out of nearby doors and hanging out of nearby windows. 'Just pay him the fare!'

'I can't.'

'*What?*'

'I don't have enough money.' As my jaw dropped, he wailed, 'How was I to know it would cost so much? I don't *catch* cabs!'

'It's all right,' the driver calmly informed us. 'You can put it on your credit card.'

'No, I can't,' said Horace. 'I didn't bring my credit card.' He turned to me. 'Do you have a credit card?'

'Of course not!' I couldn't believe what I was hearing. 'I didn't bring *anything*, Horace! Not even my coat!'

'Then you're in trouble,' said the driver – less calmly, this time. 'Because either I drive you to where you can get some money, or I'm calling the police right now.'

'No!' I exclaimed. 'Don't do that!'

'Wait,' stammered Horace. 'I've – I've got an idea. Hang on.' He began to punch a series of digits into his mobile keypad.

My own inclination was to turn around and go home. There would be credit cards at home, even if there was no cash. And if the worst came to the worst, other people could help pay for our trip.

Besides, I was becoming less and less enthusiastic about Horace's proposed rescue scheme.

'What are you doing?' I demanded of him. 'Who are you calling?'

'Dave,' he replied.

'*Dave?*'

'I'll ask him to bring us some money.'

The sheer nerve of this manoeuvre left me speechless. I wouldn't have dared ask Dave to drive all the way to Parramatta, just to bail me out of a tight spot. And I soon found out that Horace shared my reluctance – because when the ring-tone sounded, he presented me with his mobile.

'You talk to him,' Horace suggested. 'He'd do anything for you.'

The audacity! I gasped. I choked. I couldn't find the right words; what do you say to someone like Horace? But before I could tell him where he should stick his bloody phone, headlights flashed in the rear-view mirror.

I glanced around to see Dave's car heading straight for us.

Chapter Twenty-one

Dave's hatchback cruised past, then pulled over to the kerb a few metres ahead of us.

I immediately jabbed Horace in the ribs.

'It's Dave!' I squeaked.

'I know,' Horace rejoined.

'Go and get some money! Quick!' was my advice, which Horace rejected.

'No – *you* go,' he said. Clearly, he didn't relish the prospect of asking Dave for anything. 'I'll stay here.'

'All by yourself?' (What I meant, of course, was: all by yourself with an exposed neck in front of you?) 'I don't think so, Horace.'

He gestured at the plastic screen that separated him from the driver, as if to say 'it'll be fine'. But I shook my head.

'Not an option,' I firmly decreed. 'You go, and I'll wait.'

'We can both go.'

'No, you can't,' the driver interrupted. He turned to look at us. 'I'm not having you both take off in your friend's car.'

'Here.' I divested myself of Horace's sunglasses. 'Take these, and give me back Mum's. Or you'll break your neck before you get there.'

Horace sighed. Then he swapped sunglasses and climbed

out of the cab. I tried to watch as he shuffled towards Dave's hatchback, but Mum's prescription lenses wouldn't let me; they blurred and distorted everything I focused on. So I shut my eyes and waited.

At last I heard footsteps approaching. They were obviously Dave's, because as soon as they stopped, he began to speak.

'Sorry about that,' he said gruffly, almost in my ear. 'Bit of a mix-up. How much do we owe you?'

I opened my eyes, and saw that Dave had leaned down to address the driver. By squinting, I could just make out the wad of notes that was changing hands. While the two men completed their transaction, I pushed open the rear passenger door.

Like a visually impaired person, I practically had to feel my way out of the cab.

'Okay,' Dave continued. He tucked something into his pocket. 'Thanks, mate. Have a good one.'

'What's up with all these sunglasses?' the driver demanded in reply. 'Who are *you* supposed to be, anyway?'

'He's supposed to be a rock star,' I supplied, knowing that Dave wouldn't understand the question. Then I slammed the door and stumbled off the road.

I was finding it hard to keep my balance.

'What's wrong?' Dave asked, upon joining me. 'Are you feeling sick, still?'

'I can't see. These are Mum's sunnies. They've got prescription lenses.'

'For God's sake, Nina . . .'

'I'm sorry.' I was, too. 'I'm really sorry, Dave.'

'Here.' He pressed another pair of sunglasses into my hands. 'Put these on.'

'What about you?'

'I've got a spare set in the glove box.'

'Dave, this wasn't my idea –'

'Later.'

By then our cab was on the move again. I was able to see its red tail-lights disappearing into the shadows, thanks to Dave's trendy Ray-Bans. His blue hatchback was sitting, dark and motionless, some distance from the nearest streetlight – so he didn't need my assistance to reach it, despite the fact that his eyes were unprotected. He managed quite well on his own, without tripping or haemorrhaging or bumping into a tree.

But when he arrived, he nearly had a heart attack. Because Horace wasn't waiting for us.

'What the . . .?' Dave yanked open the hatchback's front passenger door, as if expecting to find Horace curled up in a footwell. I scanned our immediate surroundings.

There wasn't a human being in sight.

'He can't have gone off by himself!' I exclaimed, as Dave extracted a pair of sunglasses from his glove box. 'He can't be that stupid!'

'Don't bet on it,' Dave growled. Having shielded his eyes, he was able to survey the row of brick apartment buildings that occupied one whole side of the street. 'Which one is it?' he asked. 'Which one is number seventeen?'

'I don't know.' The words were barely out of my mouth when a shifting shadow caught my attention. 'Look!' I yipped. 'Over there!'

'Quick,' said Dave. He set off at a pace so rapid that I had a hard time matching it. We passed several driveways before we reached a small front garden stuffed with cypress pines, behind which lurked a narrow, four-storey structure called 'Grandview'. Halfway down the side of this building, a modest entrance foyer opened off the driveway. A separate row of garages stood hard against the rear fence.

I couldn't see any sign of Horace. But then again, there wasn't much light to see *with*. Dave had begun to slow down, in an attempt to tread more quietly; he must have been worried about the ground-floor windows. Like me, he must have realised that we would look just like burglars to anyone who happened to glance outside at such an ungodly hour, alerted by the scrape of footsteps on cement.

Perhaps that's why he suddenly decided to switch off his mobile.

'Around the other side,' he breathed, when I caught up with him. I nodded. It was likely that Horace had concealed himself behind the building – or so I thought. And I was right, too. Because as we turned the first corner, we almost ran into him.

He'd pressed his nose flat against a ground-floor window-pane. Though the sound of our approach made him start, he didn't seem to mind being interrupted. On the contrary, he greeted us with enthusiasm, grinning and beckoning when he saw who we were. He wanted us to share his discovery.

But Dave wouldn't cooperate. Instead he shook his head and beckoned to Horace, who jabbed urgently at the window with his index finger. I couldn't help myself; I had to find out what Horace was pointing at.

He moved aside to give me a better look. The pale strip of light that illuminated his left cheek was spilling through a gap left by a broken blind-slat; upon peering through this narrow slot, I found that I had a very good – if circumscribed – view of the living room beyond.

This room was lit by the soft glow of a large television, which stood on a low credenza beside the front door. Facing the door was a shabby old couch, and draped across the couch was Barry McKinnon, fast asleep with his mouth open.

There was a pistol on his lap.

'Do you know him?' Horace whispered.

I gave a nod. 'It's Barry,' I replied, under my breath.

'Good.' Horace lifted one hand, displaying a keyring with three keys attached. 'The kitchen's through that doorway behind him. And the back door leads into the kitchen. I had a look.'

'You found Nefley's peg basket.' It was a statement, not a question. In response, Horace grinned and winked. Beyond the window-glass, murmurous voices were interrupted by the tinny sound of gunshots. Obviously, the TV was tuned to something violent.

By this time Dave was beside me, so I yielded my place to him. Then I dragged Horace's head down until his ear was level with my mouth.

'Where are the others?' I hissed.

He shrugged. 'Not in the kitchen,' he assured me, 'and that's all that matters. If we sneak through the kitchen, and surprise this one, we'll have his gun before the other one can do a thing.'

'But what if Barry hears us?' I objected, in hushed tones.

'Are you kidding?' Horace cocked his thumb at the pane of glass. 'He's got the TV turned right up. He wouldn't hear a fire alarm, let alone a footstep.'

'You can't be serious.' At last Dave weighed in. Hustling us away from the window, he addressed us with as much force

252

as his low-pitched delivery would allow. 'That other door must lead to a bedroom. Dermid could be in there with his rifle. What if he comes out and starts blasting away?'

'He won't, if we're aiming the handgun at him,' Horace rasped. And I said, in a whisper, 'If they start shooting, it's going to cause a big commotion. They won't want that. They won't want anyone calling the police, Dave.'

'That's right.' Horace gave his firm (if muted) support to my opinion. But Dave was unconvinced.

'They'd be long gone before the police got here,' he pointed out. 'They might decide to take the risk.'

'So what?' Horace was becoming too loud; he caught himself, and continued more softly. 'Even if they start shooting, it's not going to kill us.'

'Please, Dave.' Suddenly I found it impossible to contemplate walking away without Reuben. To do something so feeble – so flaccid and pathetic – would be hard to live with. Even a bullet in the gut might be preferable to a never-ending sense of worthlessness.

Being a vampire was bad enough. Being a skulking, cowardly, apathetic vampire would be hideous.

'We can't just go,' I pleaded. 'Not without trying. Now that we're here, we can't run away with our tails between our legs.' As Dave wrestled with conflicting emotions (which were written all over his chalk-white face), I tried to make him agree with me. Because if Dave agreed with me, then I was probably right. 'They think we're dead. They'll be wetting themselves.'

'Yeah. Plus there are three of us, and only two of them,' Horace added.

'It's Reuben, Dave. *Reuben*. He might be chained up. He's

not an animal. He doesn't deserve this.'

'Why don't you go in the back with Nina, and I'll listen outside the front door?' Horace suggested. From Nefley's keyring he removed one key, which he offered to Dave. 'That way, if he bails you up, I can jump him from behind.'

'Please? Dave? I really think we can do this.' Oddly enough, I was feeling much better; my stomach wasn't bothering me any more, and my head was remarkably clear. It was as if the prospect of imminent danger had cured me. 'I don't want the police finding out about us,' was my final argument, which seemed to have an impact. Dave sighed. He dragged his fingers through his hair. Then he glanced over his shoulder at the apartment building.

'I dunno . . .' he muttered.

'We'll go in without you,' warned Horace. 'Nina through the back, and me through the front.'

'Nina's not going *anywhere.*' On this point Dave was adamant, though careful not to raise his voice (which had a slightly desperate edge to it). 'I'll go in first, and – and Nina, you can stay here.'

'I'm not staying here.'

'Yes, you are,' he insisted. 'If something goes wrong, you can call for help. I'll give you my phone.'

'I'm *not staying here by myself.*' It's hard to sound determined when you're speaking so quietly, but I did my best. 'If you leave me here, I'll just follow you anyway!'

'It would be better if she came along,' Horace advised. 'She looks more like a zombie than you do – no offence, Nina.'

'Gee, thanks.'

'It's a *good* thing,' said Horace. 'You'll scare them. Especially if you're wearing my coat.' He began to remove his satin cape, exposing the velvet frock-coat underneath. 'And Dave can put on my Dracula cape,' he proposed, under his breath.

'Okay, listen.' Abruptly, Dave decided to capitulate. He took the keys that Horace had been attempting to force on him. It was clear, however, that he wasn't about to let anyone else call the shots. 'This is what we'll do,' he murmured. 'I'll go in first, and surprise Barry, and take his gun. If he wakes up, I'll say something as a kind of signal, and you . . .' He jerked his chin at Horace.' . . . you can come in through the front door, and distract him just long enough for me to throw a punch. Okay?'

As Horace executed an enthusiastic thumbs-up sign, I stared at Dave in astonishment. 'Do you actually know how to *punch* people?' I asked. And he swallowed.

'I'm aware that you're not a big vampire fan, Nina, but we're not all *completely* useless,' he muttered, before returning to the subject of Barry McKinnon. 'If we get inside without disturbing him, then you and I can take his gun into the bedroom and see what's happening there,' Dave continued, still addressing me. 'Maybe Dermid's asleep too. Maybe they're both dead drunk. I sure hope so.' He accepted Horace's cape, which he draped around his shoulders. 'Right – let's get this over with, before I change my mind. Did you bring any rope with you?'

'Rope?' echoed Horace.

'Or wire, or something. To tie people up with.'

'Uh . . .' When Horace and I exchanged guilty glances, Dave rolled his eyes. But nothing more was said. Having wordlessly expressed his impatience with us, Dave turned on his heel and made for the back door of Nefley Irving's apartment.

It was the last in a line of eight doors, each opening onto a narrow strip of concrete. These doors were overshadowed by the first- and second-floor balconies, and were positioned directly opposite eight matching rotary clothes lines – which had been planted in a row beside a dilapidated paling fence. I wondered if the poor light was to blame for Grandview's grubby and dispirited appearance. Or did everything look just as bad in the daytime?

Nefley's peg-basket was sitting under his kitchen window, between the back steps and the garbage bin.

'Ssst!' As I caught up with Dave, I grabbed his arm, alerting him to the fact that I was speaking. If I hadn't, he might not have heard me; my voice was a mere thread of sound. 'Do you know how to use a gun?' I asked him.

'Not if I can help it,' was his cryptic (and almost inaudible) response. After scanning the other windows for signs of life – and finding none – he focused his attention on Nefley's, which was shut but not screened. Beyond it, a murky room full of cupboards was faintly visible, though even *I* couldn't identify many of the objects strewn around on top of them. The light was much too poor.

Nevertheless, I could tell that no one was in the kitchen. We would be able to slip in unobserved, because the door to the living room was shut.

Dave took a deep breath. We both removed our sunglasses. For a moment he held my gaze; we stared at each other mutely, poised on the edge of what was shaping up to be a possible disaster. I remember thinking: *Thank God Dave's here.* And it crossed my mind that I should probably come out and say something while I still could – something along the lines of how important he was to all of us, and how grateful I was for everything he'd done, and how terrible it would be if he got hurt. But I couldn't. There really wasn't enough time. Anyway, I was kind of hoping he might say something to me, first.

He didn't, though. Instead he slowly and carefully inserted his key into the Yale lock on the back door.

We were very fortunate. The door didn't squeak as it swung open. I decided that Nefley must have been oiling its hinges; he'd certainly been mopping his kitchen floor, since the soles of our shoes didn't peel noisily off ancient, sticky spillages. There were empty pizza boxes and dirty glasses beside the sink, but I had a feeling that the McKinnons were to blame for those. To judge from his up-to-date calendar and gleaming splashbacks, Nefley wasn't the kind of person who would go to bed without washing his dishes.

The chatter from the television was much louder than it had been outside, masking the soft *click* of the back door closing. We passed a knife-block on our way to the living room. When I reached for a knife, however, Dave shook his head. 'No,' he mouthed. I was puzzled, at first; my heart was pounding like a jackhammer, and I couldn't see why Dave should want to deprive me of even the most basic weapon.

It wasn't until he'd tapped his canine tooth, and struck a 'Mr Universe' pose, than I finally understood. Vampires were supposed to be strong. A knife would send the opposite signal: it would suggest that we *needed* weapons. And it wouldn't provide much protection against a gun, in any case.

I could see Dave's point. It made a lot of sense. All the same, as he turned the doorknob, I would have given anything for a concealed weapon.

Even a perfume bottle full of Windex would have been better than nothing.

Chapter Twenty-two

'Well, you c'n take your punk-ass outta here, or I'll blow your goddamn head off!'

Someone on TV unleashed a machine gun just as Dave pushed open the door to the living room. If any hinges squealed or floorboards creaked, the noise was drowned by an explosive *rat-tat-tat-tat*, which didn't seem to disturb Barry McKinnon in the slightest. Barely visible over the top of the couch's headrest, his balding scalp remained motionless despite the sudden barrage of automatic gunfire.

Step by cautious step, Dave approached the couch. I hung back, my nervous gaze flicking between his receding figure and the bedroom door. Even in my state of acute anxiety, I was astonished at the number of vampire books and vampire posters that Nefley Irving had managed to accumulate. (No *Bloodstone Chronicles*, though; as I said before, I'm not exactly Ann Rice.) His crucifix collection was pretty awe-inspiring, too. But I didn't like the sharpened stakes that were stacked up against one wall. They were just plain creepy.

I remember holding my breath. I remember thinking: *If I throw up now, we're dead meat.*

Then all at once there was a flurry of movement.

'FREEZE!' Barry yelled, whirling around. Suddenly Dave

was looking down the barrel of a gun. At that same instant, however, Barry recognised us. I could see it on his face; his features sagged, his eyes bulged, his jaw dropped. Disbelief paralysed him, just long enough for Dave to gain control.

With a magnificent display of self-possession, Dave took another step forward. He probably would have presented a fairly chilling spectacle even if he *hadn't* been wearing the black cape; his bleached complexion, shaggy head and mournful, dark-ringed eyes were straight out of a manga comic book. Nevertheless, I was staggered by his courage. And for the first time ever, it occurred to me that Zadia Bloodstone wasn't such a fantastical creation after all. Because let's face it: I was standing in the presence of a genuine, top-grade, real-life hero.

This became even more obvious when Dave opened his mouth.

'It's no use trying to kill me, Mr McKinnon,' he declared flatly. 'Because I'm already dead.'

He'd hardly finished speaking before the front door rattled. As Horace began to make his entrance, Barry was momentarily distracted. His eyes flickered, his head turned, and in that split second Dave lunged, swatting the firearm out of Barry's hand.

Luckily, no bullets were discharged. There was merely a loud *thud* when the gun hit the floor. I immediately pounced on what I regarded (with good reason) as our only chance of success – though my hands were shaking so badly that I almost dropped the weapon again after picking it up. Then, while Dave wrestled with Barry, and Horace burst into the room, I aimed the gun at Barry's right ear.

At which point Dermid appeared in the bedroom doorway.

'Drop it!' he cried, training his rifle on me.

Everyone froze. It was like one of those stand-offs that you see in the movies; there was such a *cinematic* air about it all that I could hardly believe what was happening. Since then, I've often wondered if people behave the way they do in the movies because it's what actually occurs, or if they resort to cliché in real life because it's what they've seen in the movies.

A bit of both, perhaps.

'You can't kill us,' Dave said hoarsely. 'You could unload a hundred bullets into us and it wouldn't make any difference. Not even if they were made of silver.'

'Because we're already dead,' I wanted to say. But I couldn't. Though the words formed on my lips, I couldn't force any air through my larynx. I could hardly breathe, let alone speak.

Then Barry growled, 'She hasn't cocked the gun.'

He was lying, of course. He'd cocked it himself, before pointing it at Dave. And it was still cocked, as I discovered soon afterwards. At the time, however, I couldn't even tell if it was loaded. I was a complete novice when it came to guns.

Barry must have seen this. He must have been relying on it. His comment threw me, and my hesitation could have been fatal. It *would* have been fatal if Reuben hadn't come to my rescue. I've no doubt whatsoever that Dermid was about to shoot me when Reuben barrelled into him from behind.

Though Reuben's ankles were bound together, and his wrists were tied behind his back, he had managed to roll across the bedroom floor and launch himself at Dermid's knees. I found out later that Reuben had been feigning unconsciousness up until then. That's why the McKinnons hadn't chained him to any fixtures or fittings. That's also why, upon hearing Dave's voice, Dermid had jumped to his feet, grabbed his rifle and run out of the room without a backward glance.

I was lucky that Dermid didn't fire his gun. We all were. It slammed on to the floor just before he did; in fact he landed on it, and probably would have picked it up pretty quickly if Reuben hadn't bitten him on the calf. That bite made Dermid scream. And as he kicked out, maddened by pain, Dave darted forward. His fingers closed around the rifle.

Barry couldn't do anything to help. Not with a pistol pressed against his skull. When he made no attempt to stop Dave, I realised that I'd been lied to – that the firearm in my clammy grip was both cocked and loaded. So I remained in position, my gaze riveted to Barry's damp, red face. The fact that he was sweating reassured me. It meant that he was frightened, or at least very anxious.

I didn't see Dave grab the rifle. I did, however, hear him ask Horace to free Reuben. Whereupon Barry spluttered, 'What the hell is going on?'

'It's quite simple,' Horace rejoined, having disappeared somewhere off to my right. (I couldn't follow his progress; my attention was fixed on Barry.) 'If you're interested in preserving your immortal soul, you'll walk away and you won't look back. Or we'll drain every drop of blood from your veins.'

'Eh?' Barry looked confused rather than scared. It wasn't a promising reaction.

'We're vampires,' I intoned. 'You're messing with the Undead.'

In hindsight, I know that I must have sounded like a complete lunatic. Barry certainly thought so. He scowled angrily. 'For God's sake!' he snarled.

'They must be friends of that geek,' Dermid gasped, from somewhere down on the floor. 'More Dracula weirdos . . .'

'We're not,' insisted Horace. 'We're vampires. Real vampires.'

'Jesus.' Barry's contempt was scathing, his disbelief almost palpable. I was suddenly enraged.

'You saw us!' I reminded him. 'We were dead, remember?'

'No, you weren't. Because here you are,' said Barry. Then Reuben spoke.

'There's more wire in the bedroom,' he panted. 'I'll get it, if you like, and we can do the other one as well.'

This sounded so much like a death threat that I couldn't help glancing around in dismay. But Dermid hadn't been garrotted. Instead he was lying face-down beneath Horace Whittaker, while Horace bound his hands with the same length of cord that had once restrained Reuben.

I'd barely registered this fact when Dave cried, 'Freeze!' Turning my head, I saw that Barry had been about to take advantage of my momentary lapse in concentration. But with Dermid all trussed up, Dave was now free to point his rifle at Barry – who immediately raised his hands.

'Don't move,' Dave warned. 'If you do, I'll shoot.'

'Listen.' Barry adopted a wheedling tone that I, for one, found wholly unpersuasive. 'You're obviously not tree-hugger welfare types,' he acknowledged, as if bestowing a huge compliment on us. 'So what are you looking for? A piece of the deal?'

'No!' I snapped. 'We want justice for the persecuted!'

Barry ignored me. Having decided that Dave was in charge, he addressed himself exclusively to Dave. 'If it's a cut of the fee you're looking for, mate, you won't get it without us. Our source doesn't know you. He won't trust you. He won't pay up unless we're around.'

'We don't want your blood money!' I shrilled, without eliciting so much as a blink out of Barry. He was still watching Dave, who once again had Dermid in his sights.

Dave swallowed, then said, 'All we want is for Reuben to walk out of here a free man. Unmolested. If you can promise that, then we'll be satisfied.'

'What do you mean?' Barry's dawning outrage seemed quite genuine. His colour deepened from red to puce. His eyes narrowed. His voice sharpened. 'Are you out of your mind? He's not a bloody man, he's a werewolf! He's a danger to society!'

'*You're* the danger to society, you murdering bastard!' Reuben shouted from the bedroom. Barry, however, pretended not to hear.

'Do you know how many people that creature's killed?' he spluttered. 'If you let him walk free now, you'll have a lifetime of murders on your conscience! He's a bloody *animal*! Can't you see that? You can't trust him! You can't trust *any* of them!' Suddenly he caught his breath; Reuben had appeared in the bedroom doorway, carrying a loaded syringe. 'Keep him away from me!' Barry yelped. 'Don't – don't you let him near me!'

'Oh, shit,' Dermid quavered – and I could understand why. In all my life, I've never seen anyone look as dangerous as Reuben did just then. He was wearing an absolutely *fiendish* expression; his eyes were like chips of cold, green glass, and his clothes were spattered with dried blood. He was breathing heavily.

For the first time, I spotted the wolf's face lurking behind the human one.

'Now, hang on . . .' Dave began, torn between his desire to stop Reuben and his need to keep Dermid under surveillance. I had a similar problem. Mesmerised by the slow menace of Reuben's advance, I allowed my gaze to leave Barry's profile.

Crunch!

Next thing I knew, I was on the ground. Barry had pushed me. He was reaching for the gun that I'd just dropped. But he didn't have a hope, because Reuben leaped on him, growling – and the impact of it shook the whole room.

'*Stop!*' Dave yelled. I retrieved the pistol, rolling out of Reuben's way as he jabbed his needle into Barry's left buttock. Barry roared. He bucked against the weight on his back, successfully dislodging Reuben. And when Horace rushed to join the fracas, Dermid saw his chance.

I don't believe that Dermid was trying to escape. It's more likely that he wanted to kick the gun out of my hand. Though his own hands were bound, no one had yet tied his feet. He was therefore struggling to rise when Dave (whose attention had been diverted to Reuben's struggle with Barry) suddenly realised what was about to happen.

'Don't even think about it!' Dave remonstrated, aiming his weapon at Dermid's heart.

That was when somebody thumped on the floor of the flat above us.

We all fell silent. Everyone froze, as six pairs of eyes swivelled towards the ceiling. There was a long pause.

Finally Horace broke the spell.

'Oh, shit,' he said. 'We're disturbing the neighbours.'

I lowered my gaze just in time to see Dermid spring into

264

action. Taking advantage of the momentarily lull, he jumped up and charged like a bull, trying to headbutt Dave in the stomach. It was a clever move. Once he'd ducked past the end of Dave's gun-barrel, Dermid was simply too *close* to shoot at; had Dave been a fraction slower, Dermid would probably have knocked him off his feet – and smashed a few of Dave's ribs into the bargain. But Dave was very fortunate. Acting out of pure instinct, he swung the rifle-butt at his assailant's skull.

The result was a glancing blow that dropped Dermid in his tracks.

Poor Dave looked almost as stunned as his victim. 'I – I had to!' he stammered, appealing to the rest of us. 'I had to do *something!*' By this time Horace was sitting on Barry's head, so I doubt very much that Dermid's sufferings were visible to his father. It was the injured man's groans that wrung from Barry a muffled and rather groggy collection of curses.

'Shut up,' said Reuben. Then he kicked the base of Barry's spine, stepped over his spreadeagled body, and crossed to where Dermid lay, curled up in a foetal position on the carpet.

Dermid's hands were still tied behind his back. His eyes were screwed shut, and he was grunting and gasping – '*Ahhh! Ahhh! You bastard!*' – so he wasn't aware of Reuben's approach. But I certainly was. And when I saw the half-filled syringe in Reuben's hand, I was moved to speak up.

'Wait!' I protested. 'What *is* that?'

'Same stuff they used on me,' he rejoined, before plunging the needle into Dermid's thigh.

Dermid screeched. I flinched. Dave snapped out of his trance and said, 'What are you *doing?*' He was reaching for Reuben's arm when Nefley's first-floor neighbour started to thump on the ceiling again.

'They'll be knocking on the door in a minute,' Horace observed sourly.

'No, they won't.' Reuben spoke with complete confidence, raising his voice above Dermid's whimper. 'They won't have to. These two will be out cold in a second, and then everything will calm down.'

'You mean you've drugged them?' I demanded. Reuben turned his head to grin at me. (It was a lupine sort of grin.)

'Why not?' he said. 'Do you have a better idea?'

I didn't, unfortunately. Neither did Dave, who was starting to show distinct signs of wear. His chalky, sunken-eyed, hapless appearance suggested that he had fallen victim to a touch of nausea. In fact he looked much sicker than Dermid, despite the fact that a large bruise had begun to blossom on Dermid's brow.

I suppose we were lucky that the wound wasn't bleeding. At least we didn't have fresh human blood to contend with, on top of everything else.

'Hey!' Horace exclaimed, sounding surprised. He was peering down between his legs at Barry's motionless figure. 'He's asleep! This one's asleep!'

'I told you it wouldn't take long,' said Reuben, who remained crouched over Dermid, intently watching every twitch of the injured man's face. 'Now we can do what we like with 'em.'

'What do you mean?' I couldn't help being alarmed by his tone. Dave also seemed apprehensive.

'Can't we just leave them here?' he murmured.

Horace gave a snort. 'They'll be found,' he scoffed, 'and then they'll come after us. We don't want that.'

'We can drop 'em down a well,' Reuben submitted, in a measured and thoughtful manner that was far more frightening – in my opinion – than the most uncontrolled rant. He was still staring at Dermid. 'Or we can shoot 'em with that rifle. Or maybe we can starve 'em to death, slowly, over a coupla weeks.'

Dave and I exchanged a despairing look. All at once I felt exhausted; my second wind had well and truly worn off. In fact, of the three vampires in that room, only Horace impressed me as having even a trace of energy left in reserve.

'I don't care *what* we do with them,' Horace remarked, 'as long as we do it somewhere else. We have to get them out of here now, before the neighbours start complaining in person.'

'You're right.' Reuben nodded at Horace, then glanced up at Dave. 'He's right. Didja bring a car?'

Dave was so worn out that he had to think for a moment. It was Horace who replied.

'Of course we brought a car!' he said crisply. 'But we're not all going to fit into it. Not unless we stick someone in the boot.'

'I know just the man,' growled Reuben. By this time, however, the wheels were starting to turn in *my* brain. I had identified an obvious flaw in Horace's proposal.

'Whoa,' I said. 'Wait. We can't just haul a couple of unconscious bodies out of here. Not if the people upstairs are watching. They'll call the police for certain.'

No one tried to argue with me. It's impossible to argue with truth, after all. Abruptly, Dave crossed to the couch and collapsed on to it; he was starting to shake, poor thing, as the full impact of his recent heroics suddenly hit him. Reuben frowned. Horace chewed on his bottom lip.

'They can be drunk,' Dave muttered at last. He was sitting with his head in his hands.

'What?' said Reuben.

'We can drag them out as if they're drunk.' Dave uncovered his face. He described how he and Reuben could lift Barry up between them, pretending that he was legless but not actually out cold. 'What we have to do is stagger and make jokes,' was Dave's suggestion. 'As if we've got nothing to hide. Trying to sneak out would be the worst thing – it would look suspicious.' He sighed as he once again heaved himself to his feet, moving slowly and awkwardly, like an old man. 'I'll leave Barry and Reuben in the car, and then come back to help Horace with . . . with the other one.' For some reason, he was reluctant to pronounce Dermid's name. I don't know why.

Perhaps, when you hit a man with a rifle butt, the guilt is easier to bear if you depersonalise him afterwards by referring to him as 'the other one'.

'Can't we just follow you?' Horace asked. He had also risen, having satisfied himself that there was no need to sit on Barry any more. 'I mean, Nina could help me with Dermid – couldn't you, Nina?'

'No.' Dave shook his head. 'Nina will bring the rifle.'

'But –'

'She can hide it under this cape,' Dave concluded, before passing the cape and the rifle to me. I suddenly found myself with two loaded firearms – though not for very long. Horace quickly relieved me of the pistol as Dave and Reuben wrestled with Barry's unwieldy limbs.

Then Dave told Horace to turn on the lights.

'If anyone comes knocking while I'm not here,' advised

Dave, reeling slightly under the weight he'd just shouldered, 'you should say that Nefley's been having a party. And he wouldn't be having a party with the lights off.'

'Depends what sort of party it is,' Horace observed, under his breath. But the rest of us ignored him. We had other things on our minds.

'What if they actually want to talk to Nefley?' I asked Dave. 'What should I tell them?'

'Tell them . . . I dunno.' Dave had run out of answers. It was Reuben who came to his rescue.

'Tell 'em that Nefley's too drunk to talk,' Reuben suggested cheerfully. Despite his somewhat battered appearance, he exuded an aura so vibrant and vigorous that it made every vampire in the vicinity look wan – as if he'd sucked all the vitality right out of us. 'Who *is* this Nefley guy, anyhow? Is he a frienda yours?'

'No,' Dave replied shortly. Dismissing the subject, he then turned to Horace. 'Don't make trouble for Nina,' he instructed. 'She's the one who should be talking to the neighbours. In fact I don't want anyone laying eyes on you. Understand?'

Horace pulled a face. But he also nodded, and that nod was enough to satisfy Dave – who moved towards the front door, trying to match his pace with Reuben's. The two of them were just about to make their exit together, on either side of Barry's limp form, when Horace asked, 'Where are we going, by the way?'

Dave stopped. 'Where do you think?' he said, before yanking the door open. He was referring to my mother's house, and my heart sank as I contemplated her reaction to yet another bunch of unwelcome guests. But I didn't say anything. I didn't even wish him good luck.

Instead I shut the front door behind his retreating back, flicked on the overhead light, and wordlessly occupied myself with various minor chores: picking up the empty syringe, for example, and donning the satin cape. Horace didn't make any kind of effort to help me. Instead he stood peering down at Dermid, who was beginning to snore.

'What are we going to do with this pair when we get them to your house?' Horace finally asked.

'I dunno.'

'Does Dave really believe that Sanford can *counsel* them into submission?'

'I don't know, Horace!' His sarcastic tone was getting on my nerves. 'Maybe you should have figured that out yourself, before you decided to come here!'

I might have continued in the same vein, if a sharp rapping sound hadn't interrupted me. Catching my breath, I stared at Horace. Then we both glanced towards the kitchen.

Someone was knocking on the back door.

'Oh, no,' I breathed, because I knew full well that Dave hadn't returned. For one thing, it was too soon – and for another, he had a key.

'Quick.' Horace gave me a push. 'Quick, go and answer it. Before they call the police.'

'My cape –'

'That's okay. It's meant to be a party.' He began to roll Dermid towards the bedroom. 'Just don't let them in, whatever happens!'

I did as I was told, too panicked to think straight. I rushed into the kitchen. I answered the knock. On Nefley's back steps I encountered a short, heavy, middle-aged woman in a

270

dressing gown, whose angry expression dissolved into one of surprise when she saw me.

'Who are you?' she queried

'Ah – um – I'm a friend of Nefley's.'

'Is he here?'

'Yes, but –'

'Then tell him, be quiet. All of you be quiet.' Her English was heavily accented. 'It's too late. Three o'clock. Not fair.'

'I know. I'm sorry.'

'Too much banging. Too much shouting. You tell him that.'

'I will.'

The woman sniffed. I suspect that she had more to say, and would have said it if she'd been able to express herself with greater fluency. But her English wasn't good enough. So she swung around and marched off, heading for one of the other flats. And it was at this point, suddenly, that my mind went *click*.

I realised that I had left Horace Whittaker alone with a non-vampire.

Chapter Twenty-three

When Horace heard me enter the living room, he raised his head.

His mouth was full of blood.

Blood trickled down his chin and dripped onto his cravat. Smears of blood were visible under his nose, around his jaw, on his fingers. His pupils looked enormous, like railway tunnels. As I stared at him – paralysed with shock – he wiped his bloody lips on his sleeve.

'It's the only solution,' he said, thickly and hoarsely. 'If they're vampires, they won't come after us. They won't be *able* to. Problem solved.'

My gaze drifted down to where Dermid lay, on his side. The fang marks weren't visible from where I stood; all I could see was the big, purpling bruise on his forehead. Then the smell reached me – that unmistakeable smell of fresh human blood, straight from the jugular – and I had to get out. Fast.

I stepped back into the kitchen and slammed the door. My legs were starting to shake. A tingling in my teeth prompted me to move my right hand, firmly and deliberately, away from the doorknob. Placing both palms flat against the painted surface of the door, I leaned against it, propping myself up. For several seconds I didn't move. I just stood there, braced against the pounding of my own pulse, licking my lips over and over and over again. My mouth was so dry that I could almost *feel* the gums receding.

I didn't even turn around when Dave unlocked the door behind me.

'What's wrong?' he whispered, moments after I'd heard the scraping of footsteps, and the *snick-snick* of a latch. My sense of relief was indescribable. For one thing, it was Dave who'd entered, and not some vampire-hating friend of Nefley Irving's. (I had forgotten that Horace still had the front-door key, so I'd been expecting Dave to come through the foyer instead of the kitchen.) For another thing, I knew that I was no longer at risk of any vampirish behaviour. With Dave around, there wasn't a chance that I would succumb. He had stopped me before, and could easily do it again.

'Oh my God.' He caught his breath. 'Is that – ?'

'I'm sorry. I'm so sorry.' My voice cracked on a sob. Looking over my shoulder, I saw that Dave was aware of the smell. Though faint, it was still discernible – at least to a vampire. No doubt it had drifted through the keyhole, or under the door. 'Someone came around the back,' I quavered. 'A neighbour. I had to talk to her in here . . . I forgot about Horace . . . I'm so *sorry* . . . '

'Jesus.' Dave's hands were pressed to his brow. Despair and horror were written all over his face.

'It was so quick,' I said. 'Two minutes at the most . . .'

'I shouldn't have left you.'

'What are we going to *do*?'

'Get out of here,' he croaked. 'All of us. Now.'

'But –'

'You have to help me. We have to help each other.' There

was more than a hint of panic in his tone. 'Please? Nina? I – I can't do this by myself.'

'You won't have to.' All at once I regained control over my own impulses. My vision cleared. My hands stopped trembling. There was something about his lost expression that stiffened my spine and drove away every ominous sign of impending delirium. 'The trouble is, I left those guns with Horace,' I reminded him. 'If he decides that he doesn't want to come . . .' And I trailed off, remembering what Sanford had always said about the effect of fresh human blood on a vampire's energy levels.

Dave swallowed.

'The sooner we tackle him, the better our chances will be,' was his strained response.

'Couldn't you call Sanford?'

'Too late for that.'

Then it occurred to me: what if Horace had already left through the front door? What if he was *heading for Dave's car*? If Horace had decided to search for another target, Reuben would be the obvious choice.

'Dave,' I said, 'what about Reuben?'

We stared at each other in sheer dismay. Then, as Dave lunged for the door, I yanked it open – and we burst into the living room, shoulder to shoulder.

Dermid was still lying motionless on the floor. But Horace was nowhere to be seen.

'Oh God . . .' I croaked.

'Stay here. Don't move.' Dave didn't waste time on superfluous instructions. He charged into the foyer, shutting the front door behind him, and I was left feeling slightly winded. For a moment I just stood there, gathering my scattered wits.

Then it occurred to me that Dermid might need my help.

You may recall that I had never, until that time, witnessed what Sanford likes to call a 'transformation'. The last one I'd experienced had been my own – and I didn't remember much about that. So I approached Dermid anxiously, not really knowing what to expect. I was afraid that he might be having a fit of some kind.

Happily, he wasn't. When I squatted beside him, Dermid didn't so much as flutter an eyelid. He wasn't even twitching, let alone foaming, and every muscle in his body seemed completely relaxed.

But he was a terrible colour. I noticed that straight away. His complexion was livid, and his fingernails were a nasty, greenish shade. As for the fang marks on his throat, they were already turning black. I remembered *that*, all right: how my own bite mark had become the most frightful, festering wound, full of pus and dead flesh and strange, reddish powder.

The recollection made me feel ill. Nevertheless, I ignored my heaving stomach and started to examine Dermid's bruise. Since the TV was still tuned to a noisy cop show, I didn't hear any retching sounds. And if I had, I probably would have assumed that the on-screen action had shifted to a pub, or maybe a rehab clinic.

When I went to fetch a damp towel for Dermid's neck, I was completely unprepared to find Horace in the bathroom.

'*Horace?*' I halted on the threshold, staring down at his hunched form. He was drooling into the toilet bowl. 'What's wrong?'

He didn't reply. I don't think he was capable of speech, at that point – and I couldn't understand it. Fresh human blood is supposed to make you feel better, not worse.

'Did you stick your finger down your throat, or something?' I demanded.

He lifted his head, gazing up at me with bleary, bloodshot eyes.

'Drug,' he gasped.

'What?'

'He's *drugged*.'

'Oh.' The penny dropped. Of course! Dermid's bloodstream was full of anaesthetic. 'You mean the drug's making you sick?'

'Grrggh.'

I can't pretend that I was sympathetic. On the contrary, I was relieved.

'Good,' I said. 'I'm *glad* it's making you sick. I hope it makes you even sicker.' Almost hysterical with fear, shock, and righteous indignation, I really let him have it. 'I hope you rupture something, Horace! I hope you're in bed for a week! Don't you realise what you've *done*? You've *infected* someone!'

'It was your idea,' he responded hoarsely.

'*What*?'

'Zadia Bloodstone always fangs the bad guys,' he pointed out – then gagged, and turned his face away.

He was still vomiting when I heard the back door open again. This time, however, I wasn't taken by surprise. In fact I hurried out of the bathroom, keen to reassure Dave that Horace wasn't rampaging through Sydney, in search of more victims to chew on.

Imagine my astonishment when Father Ramon walked into the living room.

'Father?' I squeaked, but he didn't seem to notice. Instead

he crossed himself, his attention riveted to the body on the floor.

Dave was hovering just behind him.

'You'll have to take this guy too,' he said to the priest. '*And the rest of them.* I'll start driving round the neighbourhood, to see if I can spot Horace.'

'Dave,' I began, but was roundly ignored.

'He can't have got far,' Dave continued, still addressing Father Ramon. 'Even if he is firing on all cylinders –'

'*Dave.*' I raised my voice. 'Horace is still here.'

The two men goggled at me.

'He's in the bathroom. Throwing up,' I revealed. 'He's had a bad reaction to the tranquilliser.'

Dave's whole body slumped. Father Ramon closed his eyes, heaving a sigh so deep that it made him stagger.

'Thank God,' said Dave. 'Thank *God.*'

'Did you just get here?' I asked the priest, who promptly informed me that he'd arrived back at Mum's place only to be sent straight to Nefley's. Sanford would have come too, if he hadn't been setting Nefley's broken arm. As for Mum, she had actually been tricked into staying.

'We asked her to fetch a hammer from the shed,' Father Ramon admitted, in regretful tones, 'and I left while she was still out the back. Sanford didn't want her involved. Not at her age.'

'No.' I could understand that. 'She'll be mad, though.'

'She'll be furious,' Father Ramon agreed, and for an instant we both gloomily contemplated the sort of welcome we could expect when we returned to confront my mother. Meanwhile, Dave disappeared into the bathroom. He emerged again before I could pursue him, supporting a very sluggish and submissive Horace – whose bloodstained teeth caused the priest to blanch and cover his own mouth.

For someone who had just slaked an ancient, instinctual thirst, Horace looked surprisingly ill. His gait was unsteady, his face was swollen, and his expression was dazed. It was clear that he would need help, and that I was the one who would have to help him – since Dave and Father Ramon would be fully occupied with Dermid. Dave told me to leave the rifle. He announced that Reuben, Barry and Father Ramon should stay well clear of Horace, who would be travelling in Dave's car. Then, having outlined his escape plan, Dave bent down to retrieve the handgun – which he tucked into his belt.

This gun was surrendered to me only after we left the flat. As instructed, I guided Horace all the way to the blue hatchback, where I shoved him into its front passenger seat. I then positioned myself directly behind Horace, while Dermid was being strapped in next to me. It was Dave who did the strapping. Since Father Ramon had to be protected, he was sent straight back to his own car once Dermid had been safely deposited in Dave's smaller, more modest vehicle. I should tell you, by the way, that all this was done in complete silence. Neither Dermid nor Barry was able to talk, and the rest of us were trying very hard not to attract attention. Even Horace kept his mouth shut – presumably because he was scared of what might happen if he opened it.

He was still pretty sick, you see.

Dave passed me the pistol just before we set off. He asked me to shoot Horace in the back of the head if Horace so much as reached for the door-handle. 'I know it won't kill him,' Dave added, 'but it should at least slow him down a bit.' To this day, I don't know if he was being serious. (It's hard to tell with Dave, sometimes.) All I *do* know is that Horace was appalled.

'You can't do that!' he slurred. 'That's . . . Nina, you ask Sanford . . . that's not allowed . . .'

'Oh, shut up.' I almost *wanted* to shoot him in the back of the head, after seeing what he was capable of. And Dave seemed to share my feelings.

'We're not interested in what you think,' he informed Horace, his voice creaking with the effort of restraint. 'What you've done is bad enough.'

'I did the right thing,' Horace insisted, fumbling his vowels.

'Just give it a rest, mate.'

'I did!' bleated Horace. 'If you fang the bad guys, they're not a problem any more!'

'What do you mean, they're not a problem?' I couldn't believe my ears. 'Don't you know what this means, Horace? It means that we're going to have to put up with *Dermid McKinnon* in our support group!' I paused for a moment, to let this dreadful prospect sink in. 'It's bad enough being stuck with *you*,' I finished, 'let alone Dermid McKinnon!'

At first I thought that Horace had been struck dumb by this reminder, until I saw his head loll forward. Then I realised that he'd dozed off, and that my argument hadn't silenced him after all.

It was Dave who reacted.

'Oh, man,' he groaned. 'You're right. We'd *have* to let Dermid join – it would be against the rules not to.'

'Unless we change the rules.'

'What a nightmare.'

'I'm sorry, Dave.' This needed to be emphasised, in my opinion; Dave had to understand how sorry I really was. 'I should have known not to trust Horace. He probably planned this whole, stupid escapade just so he could fang someone.'

'Maybe.'

'I was sick. I wasn't thinking. I'd never have done it, otherwise – not even for Reuben's sake.'

'Yeah, well . . .'

'You believe me, don't you?' It was desperately important that he did. I couldn't bear the thought of Dave looking at me the way he'd looked at Horace. 'The minute my head cleared, I decided not to do it. I was about to go straight back home, only . . .' I paused.

'Only *I* arrived, and you persuaded me to take a chance,' Dave finished. His tone was level. 'If I hadn't agreed, none of this would have happened. It was my fault as much as anyone's.'

'No. It wasn't.'

'I was showing off,' he lamented. 'I'm always showing off. It's crazy. I must be out of my mind.' He flipped on his indicator, then pulled away from the kerb. 'I have to stop *caring*, or I'll end up shot full of holes.'

Needless to say, I was mystified. There's maybe one person in the entire universe who's more self-effacing than Dave, and that's Bridget. I couldn't imagine why he had suddenly accused himself of showing off.

But before I could air my objections, he told me to ring Sanford.

'I forgot to turn on my mobile,' he confessed, clumsily passing me his phone with one hand as he steered with the other. 'There'll be a million messages on here, and they'll all be from Sanford. You've got to call him back. Tell him what's happened.'

'*Me?*'

'I'm driving.'

'Couldn't Father Ramon – ?'

'He's driving too.' Dave glanced up into the rear-view mirror, his eyes shielded by his sunglasses. 'Would you rather do it over the phone, or face to face?' he said grimly. 'Your choice, Nina.'

Naturally, I chose the first option. I knew that, while breaking the bad news to Sanford would be hard enough over the phone, it would infinitely more difficult face to face. Though Sanford didn't often lose his temper, it was most unpleasant when he did; I fully expected a thunderous dressing-down if I arrived back home without giving him time to work off his initial outrage. By calling him up, I was hoping to avoid everything but the tail-end of the storm.

He answered immediately, on my first ring.

'*Hello? Who's that?*'

'Uh – Sanford?' I mumbled. 'It's Nina.'

'*Nina? What's happened? Where are you?*'

'We're heading home. Look –'

'*Who's with you? Is Father Ramon with you?*'

'Yes, and so his Reuben. And Horace. But –'

'*What about Dave? Is he all right?*'

'Listen. There's some bad news.' I took a deep breath, conscious that Dave was listening intently to my side of the conversation. 'Horace fanged Dermid.' I finally forced it out. 'Dermid McKinnon. We're bringing him in – and his dad, as well. They've both been tranquillised.' Hearing nothing at the other end of the line, I waited for a few seconds. At last I said, 'Hello?'

The pause dragged out for a while longer, until Sanford

eventually stammered, '*You – you can't be serious.*'

'I am. I'm sorry.' In an attempt to sugar the pill, I hastily continued. 'The good news is that Dermid's blood was full of anaesthetic, so Horace isn't hard to control. I mean, he's actually asleep at the moment. He's not out fanging people or anything.' Sanford's stunned silence convinced me that he wasn't reassured. 'But I guess we'll have to be careful when the drug wears off,' I had to concede, in a lame and halting fashion. 'With Dermid, too.'

'*Oh my God.*'

'I'm really sorry, Sanford. I was feeling so sick, I wasn't thinking straight. And then Barry turned out to be asleep, and we thought we had a good chance.' Ignoring Dave's wince – which was reflected in the rear-view mirror – I added, 'It would have worked out really well, except for Horace. He completely screwed things up.'

'*For God's sake.*' Sanford sounded more astonished than angry. '*What's wrong with you? Are you mad? You know what Horace is like!*'

'Yes, but –'

'*How could you do this? Where's Dave? Is he there?*'

'He's driving,' I replied, as Dave hunched his shoulders. 'He can't talk right now.'

'*This is a disaster. A complete disaster. Do you understand what's going on? You've spread the infection. You've created another vampire.*'

'I know. I'm sorry.'

'*You're* sorry? *Is that all you have to say?*'

'I didn't mean to –'

'*You didn't mean to what? Disobey your mother? Ignore all the rules? Put everyone at risk by pursuing some selfish fantasy of superhuman power in an ignorant dream-world?'* The initial shock had clearly subsided; Sanford was beginning to fire off his first volleys. *'You've never had to attend a transformation – you've no idea what it entails –'*

'Sanford? You're breaking up.'

'Because of your adolescent infatuation with this werewolf –'

'Can't hear you! Be there in a minute! Bye!'

I broke the connection.

'Not good?' said Dave, as I returned his mobile.

'Not good.' I delivered myself of a full-body sigh. 'He was just gearing up, by the sound of things.'

'Then he should be over the worst of it before we get there.'

'Maybe. I hope so.' But I wasn't about to bet money on it. 'Dave?'

'What?'

'Um . . . did Horace ever ask you to come to Nefley's place with us?'

Though Dave lifted an eyebrow, his expression was hard to read behind the inscrutable expanse of his wraparound sunglasses.

'What do *you* think?' he replied.

'No?'

'Of course not.'

Bloody Horace, I thought. *What a* liar *he is!*

Chapter Twenty-four

The drive back home might have been grim, but at least I wasn't in Father Ramon's car. He later informed me that Reuben spent the entire journey vilifying Barry and Dermid. In fact Reuben's threats became so vicious that when we all arrived at Mum's place, he was told not to go anywhere near the McKinnons; instead he was forced to stand apart with his hands in his pockets, while both cars were being unloaded.

'Are you sure you don't want me to help?' he queried, as Dave and I wrestled with Dermid's limp form. I'm convinced that Reuben wasn't intending to kick anyone in the head. I daresay he genuinely wanted to be useful. But Dave turned him down flat.

'You can keep well clear,' Dave said shortly. 'This guy isn't safe for you to touch.'

'He's not reformed,' I added, by way of explanation. Whereupon Reuben cleared his throat.

'The priest told me this was your idea,' he announced, his eyes glittering in the darkness. 'This whole rescue deal. He told me I've got you to thank, Nina.'

'Uh . . .' I glanced at Dave, but he was halfway inside the car by then, and his face was hidden. 'Actually, I wasn't the only one . . .'

'It took a lotta guts,' Reuben continued, as if he hadn't heard me. His expression was grave, his demeanour uncharacteristically calm. Nevertheless, I could feel the banked-down heat radiating from his tense, wiry figure. 'What you did – I mean, you risked getting yourself killed. Just to save my life.'

'Not really.' I was feeling very uncomfortable, by this stage. 'It's pretty hard to kill a vampire.'

'I still owe you. Big time. Because you're the one who didn't give up.'

'Well – okay. Thanks. But don't tell Sanford that,' I begged. 'He's mad enough as it is.' And I glanced over to where Sanford was busy with Horace, who was so heavily drugged that he couldn't make his own way into the house. Neither could Barry, of course; Father Ramon was having to drag him up the front steps.

At the top of those steps I could see my mother, framed in the vestibule doorway. Her arms were folded.

'Who *is* this Sanford guy, anyhow?' Reuben wanted to know. 'And why should he be mad at you?'

'Oh . . . he's just a vampire,' I said vaguely, distracted by Mum's threatening demeanour. 'And he's always mad at me.'

'Not while I'm around,' Reuben declared. His tone had an edge to it. 'If anyone starts tearing strips off *you*, Nina, I'll do the same to them. You won't ever regret what you've done for me, swear to God.'

Mystified and bemused, I shook the hand that he thrust in my direction – conscious all the while of Dave's wordless disapproval. Not that Dave was *impolite*, exactly: just rather aloof. And he wasn't the only one. I soon realised that nobody else was warming to Reuben either, despite his many attractive qualities. And this became even more obvious when we all piled into the vestibule.

It was a tight squeeze. Though George and Gladys were shut up in the basement (well away from any tempting cuts or nosebleeds), there still wasn't enough room for everyone. Yet despite the lack of space, Bridget and Sanford and Dave seemed to shrink away from Reuben, as if from something radioactive.

I suppose it doesn't take much to alarm a vampire; you just have to look as if you could kick down a door, or throw a punch. Reuben certainly conveyed this impression. And the fact that he was a known werewolf made things ten times worse.

'Uh – this is Reuben, everyone,' Father Ramon announced, after a brief and awkward silence. 'Reuben, I don't think you've met Sanford, or Bridget, or Estelle. Estelle is Nina's mother. This is her house.'

'Hi' said Reuben, gruffly.

Bridget's response was a timid half-smile. Sanford grunted. As for Mum, she didn't seem interested in Reuben at all. Instead she fixed me with a stony glare. 'You've got some explaining to do, my girl,' she said. And I braced myself for a tongue-lashing of biblical proportions.

It was Father Ramon who came to my rescue.

'Not now,' the priest broke in. 'Let's sort things out first. Where are we going to put these three, for a start?' He surveyed the unconscious bodies cluttering up Mum's vestibule. 'We can't just leave them lying here.'

'You're bloody right, we can't!' Mum exclaimed. 'I've already got one upstairs – I don't want any more! There aren't enough beds in the house for all of them! And what's going to happen when they wake up?'

It was a good question. It certainly galvanised Sanford, who wrenched his gaze away from Reuben's teeth and began to fire off orders. Thanks to Sanford, we suddenly stopped dithering around. We started to organise ourselves.

Firstly, Bridget agreed to take Gladys home – because we were no longer at risk of being attacked by Nefley Irving. It was felt that Gladys, especially, should be kept well away from Barry and Reuben, since we didn't want another unfortunate fanging incident. And when Father Ramon offered the two women a lift, he was told to go back to the presbytery as soon as he'd dropped them off. 'Have a good, long sleep,' was Sanford's advice, 'and don't come back until you're feeling refreshed.'

'I'll try,' said the priest, running his hands through his hair, 'though it won't be easy. I have a parish meeting at eleven, but I can always postpone that until next week.'

'Oh, we'll have everything worked out by next week,' Sanford assured him, then turned to Dave with another set of instructions. Dave was given the unenviable job of driving George and Horace over to Sanford's place, where Horace would be locked in the old bank vault for a while. ('Just to be on the safe side', as Sanford put it). Meanwhile, Sanford would remain at Mum's house; he wasn't yet in a position take charge of Horace, because he had Nefley and Dermid to look after.

Dermid, especially, would need round-the-clock care.

'Transformations are never pleasant,' Sanford explained, 'but there are certain measures I can take to make things easier for everyone involved.' These measures would include the application of poultices, the elevation of the feet, and absolutely no painkillers of any kind. Some form of coun-selling would also be advisable. 'Which means, in essence, that I'll be extremely busy,' Sanford observed, 'and won't have any time for Horace in the immediate future. So you, Dave, will be responsible for making sure that he remains isolated – and restrained, if necessary – until tomorrow night. Can you do that?'

Dave blinked. 'I guess . . .'

'It's vitally important that he doesn't have access to any non-vampires. Even Father Ramon will be at risk. Horace is sick in the head right now – you understand that, don't you?'

Dave nodded. He seemed resigned. But Mum wasn't about to knuckle under so easily.

'Can't they *all* go to your place?' she asked Sanford. 'Why am *I* the one who ends up with a houseful of hostages?'

'Because somebody has to be here during the day, to nurse Dermid McKinnon,' Sanford repeated, in long-suffering accents. 'As for Nefley, he can't be in the same house as Horace.' Breaking off, Sanford suddenly glowered at me – and inquired, in waspish tones, what I was intending to do with Barry McKinnon. 'He'll be waking up soon, and I'd like to know what your plans are.'

It was a nasty moment. Needless to say, I had no idea what to do with Barry. I hadn't given the matter any thought. And as I glanced around, cringing beneath a barrage of accusing and expectant looks, I realised that no one else knew what to do with him either.

Even Mum was giving me the hairy eyeball.

'I – I guess we'd better tie him to the spare bed,' was the only recommendation that I could come up with.

'And then what?' asked Mum. 'He can't stay in the

288

guestroom for ever.'

'No. I realise that.'

'Who's going to tell him that his son's a vampire?' Father Ramon gently inquired, whereupon a kind of pall settled over everyone – except Reuben.

'*I* will,' he piped up, with a fair degree of relish. But his offer was roundly ignored. When Sanford finally spoke, it was as if Reuben didn't exist.

'Once Barry finds out that his son is a vampire, he might become more amenable to persuasion,' was Sanford's theory. 'He might reassess his priorities, and abandon some of his prejudices.'

'Do you think so?' Dave seemed doubtful. 'You don't think he'll just want to shoot Dermid, as well?'

'Not necessarily. Not if we talk to them both.' As Reuben opened his mouth, Sanford pressed on. 'In fact that should be our tactical approach. We have to *communicate* with these people, and find a common point of reference. We have to persuade our enemies to become our friends. Don't you agree, Father?'

The priest hesitated. It was Dave who said, 'Barry McKinnon doesn't strike me as an open-minded kind of guy.'

'He's a total bastard!' I burst out, just as Reuben cleared his throat.

'No offence,' he muttered, from one dim corner of the vestibule, 'but you're fooling yourselves if you think you can *ask* that piece of shit to do the right thing. I've tried. It doesn't work.'

Again, there was no immediate response – and I found myself feeling sorry for Reuben. He was being treated as an outsider, perhaps because his status was so unclear; though he hadn't been accepted as 'one of us', he also couldn't be classified as a 'bad guy'.

Only Father Ramon seemed prepared to acknowledge his contribution.

'Mmmm. Yes. I take your point,' the priest said at last. 'But I do believe Barry might listen to us if we approach him from a position of advantage. You have to remember that we don't know how he feels about his son. There might be quite a deep connection.'

'In which case he'll want to shoot us for making his son a vampire,' Dave glumly observed. And Reuben endorsed this view.

'The only thing a McKinnon understands is a loaded gun,' he said. Then he jerked his thumb at the door. 'Like the one you left outside,' he warned me. 'You should probably bring that in, y'know.'

'Oh. Yeah. Right. Sorry.' I'd forgotten about the pistol, which was still lying on the back seat of Dave's car. Sanford's eyes widened.

'You brought a *firearm* with you?' he exclaimed. And Dave said, 'We didn't have much choice.'

'If we hadn't taken it off Barry, he would have used it on us,' I confirmed. 'It belongs to him.'

'No, it doesn't.' Reuben spoke with complete authority. 'It belongs to whoever owns that scummy little flat we were holed up in.'

There was a general gasp. Even Mum winced. I'm pretty sure most of us realised that if the gun in question did indeed belong to Nefley, it had probably been fired at Casimir's head.

'You mean it's Nefley's gun?' asked Dave. 'Oh, man.'

'We should get rid of it,' Sanford decided.

'Get rid of it!' Reuben was clearly appalled. 'Are you joking? You're gunna *need* that gun! Without that gun, you're defenceless! The McKinnons will eat you alive!'

It was an unfortunate choice of phrase, which reminded those of us who were still conscious (and not sprawled on the floor, or draped across the stairs) that we had a werewolf in our midst. Reuben must have realised this, because he flushed.

Sanford frowned.

'Violence begets violence,' he said stiffly, in his most pompous manner. 'It's the last resort of any rational human being. You should understand, Reuben, that as vampires we've spent most of our lives battling against the violent compulsions borne of our diseased instincts. So we don't believe in using brute force where persuasion can be just as effective.'

'Yes, but –'

'We have a murderer in our custody upstairs,' Sanford pointed out, 'and he's already demonstrated a noticeable shift in his outlook since he arrived here several hours ago. Thanks to the power of reasoned argument.'

'Really?' This was news to me. 'Are you talking about Nefley Irving?'

'I am.'

'You mean he doesn't hate vampires any more?' asked Dave, his face a study in disbelief.

'He doesn't *fear* vampires any more,' Sanford corrected. 'He's received medical treatment from a vampire, he's been nursed by a vampire, and he's enjoying the gracious hospitality of a vampire's relative. He's beginning to realise that we're no threat either to him or to the human race.'

'Are you sure?' Knowing that Sanford can be something of an idealist – and that Bridget never has a bad thing to say about anyone – I looked at my mother. Mum has a pretty jaundiced view of humanity in general; you can trust her not to mince her words. 'Is he really changing his mind, or is he just pretending?'

'Maybe you should ask him yourself,' Dave muttered, to which Sanford's response was, 'That's not possible. He's asleep. It's three o'clock in the morning, don't forget.'

'I'm not likely to forget *that*,' Mum grumbled, before finally answering the question I'd put to her. 'If it's an act, it's a bloody good one,' she had to concede. 'And I wouldn't have thought a pathetic little bloke like Nefley would be smart enough to put on convincing show. Especially when you consider how dopey painkillers can make you.'

'But what did he say about Casimir?' Father Ramon interjected, before Reuben suddenly hijacked the conversation.

'Okay – you know what? I'm glad you talked some sense into this guy . . . whoever he is. That's great,' Reuben said, all clenched fists and restless feet. 'But I'm telling you right now, if you convince Barry McKinnon that you're harmless, you'll be *annihilated*.'

'Reuben –'

'Wait. Just listen.' He cut me off. 'If you're not gunna shoot him, you've only got one choice. You'll have to pay him to go away. Because he *will* listen to money.' Peering around at the array of bad haircuts and thrift-shop clothes that surrounded him, Reuben seemed to lose heart. 'But I don't reckon you've got a hundred grand to spare, eh?' he inquired, without much hope.

'A *hundred thousand dollars*?' yelped Sanford. Mum nearly

choked on her own indrawn breath, and Bridget said, 'Oh, dear.'

'That's what I'm worth to him,' Reuben insisted. 'A hundred grand. That's what he was gunna sell me for – the dirty rotten yellow scumbag *arsehole*.' When his fierce gaze alighted on Barry McKinnon's defenceless beer gut, I wasn't the only one who started forward. Even I could see that Barry's paunch constituted a very tempting target.

Fortunately, Reuben was able to restrain himself; Dave didn't have to do more than grab his arm, and murmur a warning. It was just as well, because a scuffle in that tiny space would have left more than one person injured.

'Do you really think that if we paid him enough, Barry McKinnon would simply walk off?' Sanford had clearly been pondering the price on Reuben's head. 'Despite what happened to his son?'

Reuben shrugged. 'If you could beat Forrest Darwell's offer? Yeah, I reckon,' he said, instigating a brief discussion about Forrest Darwell. Mum wanted to know who Forrest Darwell was. Father Ramon reminded her that someone called Darwell was flying into Sydney that very morning. ('He talked to Barry on the phone, remember? I heard them,' the priest elaborated.) Reuben began to explain that Forrest Darwell was a millionaire fight promoter when Sanford brusquely interrupted him.

'That's all very well, but we can't stand around here for ever. Those drugs will be wearing off soon,' Sanford barked. His gaze swept the overcrowded vestibule. 'Dave, you can go and get George out of the basement – he'll shift Horace with you. Tell Gladys she'll be going home with Father Ramon. Nina, I want you to fetch that gun from Dave's car; when

293

you're done, you can help me to move Dermid. Father, you and Estelle can take Barry up to his room –'

'Which room?' Mum interrupted. By this time she was very, very annoyed; I could see it in her baleful eye, and hear it in her grating voice. 'The guest room, you mean?'

'I think so.' Sanford gave a brisk nod. 'And Dermid can stay in Nina's room.'

'*Nefley's* in Nina's room,' Mum pointed out, with dangerous calm.

'Oh. Yes.' For the first time, Sanford sounded rattled. 'Um . . . what about your room, then?'

'*My* room?'

'It wouldn't be for long,' Sanford promised. 'If you need a rest, you can use the daybed in the living room.'

'For Chrissake!' Mum was about to explode. The veins throbbed on her forehead as her face assumed a congested, purplish colour.

I hastily tried to intervene.

'Surely it wouldn't be safe for Mum to have Dermid around?' I objected, and was immediately given a short lecture as to why Dermid's predatory instincts would only become really dangerous during the second night of his transformation. 'You might recall what happened to Dave,' Sanford concluded, 'and how he resisted the urge to infect, that first morning. Am I right, Dave?'

Dave nodded. But I wasn't satisfied; I still felt that my mother needed a break.

'Dermid can have a sleeping bag in the basement,' was my next suggestion. 'After all, he's a vampire now.'

'Not yet, he isn't.' Sanford refused to yield. 'And before he becomes a vampire, he's going to be quite ill. Which is why he needs a proper bed, close to the bathroom. Where you can keep an eye on him, Estelle.'

'Oh.' Mum was talking through clenched dentures. 'That's *my* job, is it?'

'I'm afraid so. Just for the day.'

'And what about the other two?' she demanded. 'Am I supposed to be looking after them all day, as well? While everyone else is fast asleep?'

'*I* won't be fast asleep,' Reuben volunteered. When we all looked at him, he squared his shoulders and lifted his chin, defiantly. 'I'm not a vampire,' he continued, 'so I can help, if you want. It's the least I can do.'

'*You're* planning to stay, as well?' said Mum. Her voice was faint, and had a visible effect on Reuben – who began to deflate like a balloon.

'Or I can leave,' he mumbled. 'Whatever.'

'No!' I couldn't understand why Mum was being so dense. (It didn't occur to me that she was completely exhausted.) 'Reuben will be *really useful*! Can't you see that, Mum? He'll take some of the load off! He can make sure that Barry doesn't escape!'

'But not by breaking Barry's legs,' Sanford warned quickly. 'If anything happens to either of these men, Reuben, you'll have to answer for it. Physical violence will *not* be tolerated.'

'I know that,' said Reuben, sulking.

'Are you sure you can cope?' Sanford pressed. 'Are you sure you can resist the urge to attack?'

'Better than you can, probably,' Reuben retorted, 'since there won't be a full moon. Like I told you, I'm not a vampire.'

It was a snappy little comeback, and I couldn't help

295

admiring it. Even Mum seemed impressed; it's not often that anyone leaves Sanford tongue-tied, and she surveyed Reuben with a glimmer of approval. Bridget looked embarrassed, while Dave threw me a sidelong glance, as if trying to gauge my reaction.

At last Horace broke the spell. Blinking up at us from the bottom of the staircase, he groggily asked, 'What's going on?' At which point everyone remembered that we didn't have all the time in the world.

There was a sudden flurry of movement. Sanford seized hold of Dermid; Mum shuffled over to Barry; Dave tossed me his car keys, then headed straight for the basement. I was about to go outside when a plea from Father Ramon made me pause on the threshold.

'If you do end up talking to Barry McKinnon,' he said plaintively, to the entire gathering, 'could someone please ask him where he's put that orange van? Because if we don't get it back, there'll be hell to pay. As it is, I don't know *what* I'm going to tell Saxby's Hire and Haul.'

'It's all right, Father.' Oddly enough, Reuben was the one who replied. He had clearly gained confidence from his exchange with Sanford, and was now cheerfully helping to rearrange Dermid's legs. 'Whatever you tell 'em, they'll believe you. Because you're a priest.'

Sanford, however, felt obliged to add a qualification.

'Just as long as you don't tell them the truth, of course,' he said.

Then he hoisted Dermid's torso off the floor, as I went to retrieve Nefley's pistol.

Chapter Twenty-five

Once again, I'm going to have to cheat – because I can't say that I was really around, on Monday. While events unfolded above my head, I was locked in my mother's basement, dead to the world.

I'll have to tell you what I was told by other people. Like Reuben, for instance.

Reuben passed out before I did. He grabbed a sleeping bag from the basement, hauled it upstairs to the top landing, and dozed off outside Barry's room, just like a guard dog. Not that Barry needed guarding, at that precise moment; he was still heavily drugged, and had been chained to a bedpost using handcuffs presented to my mother on the occasion of her retirement. (They had her name engraved on them – together with the words *Time, Gentlemen* – and had come in a presentation box with miniature cricket bat, a bottle of Guinness, and a night stick.) Since the guestroom window was barred, and the guestroom door had been locked, most of us felt that Barry was well secured.

Nevertheless, Reuben took a few extra precautions. He jammed a chair under the guestroom doorknob, before positioning himself in a carefully chosen spot between the chair and the staircase. Then he fell asleep, well satisfied, with

Nefley's pistol hidden inside his sleeping bag. I had given him this pistol myself, despite Sanford's protests, and Mum had backed me up. 'It's safer with Reuben than it would be with any of us,' she'd insisted. 'At least Reuben's actually *fired* a gun before.' Mum had gone on to say that it was her house, and that if Sanford wanted to turn it into a high-security prison, she had every right to a fully armed response team.

I think she may have been a bit worried about Dermid, to tell you the truth.

Unlike his father, Dermid wasn't tethered to anything. Nor was the door to his room locked. Sanford had maintained that such measures would be ill-advised, since Dermid would feel as sick as a dog upon awakening, and would require prompt and ready access to the toilet. Mum wasn't about to argue; not once she had seen the colour of Dermid's face.

She also had to concede that, with a broken arm and a sprained ankle, Nefley Irving wouldn't be much of a threat. That's why his door wasn't locked, either. Mum did, however, lock the basement, once Sanford and I were safely bedded down in there. And she made sure that every rake, spade, broomstick and mop handle was locked away in the outside laundry. She didn't want Nefley sharpening any stakes, you see.

After doing all this, Mum went to sleep herself – and for a while there was peace in the house. But at 8:36 a.m., Reuben was awakened by the trilling of a cell-phone. It was Barry's phone, and it was tucked into Reuben's pocket (along with Barry's wallet, car keys, and sunglasses). Anyone else would probably have ignored the call; Reuben, however, decided to indulge his reckless streak. Adopting a deep, rough, flattened voice, he answered as Barry McKinnon. At which point he found himself talking to none other than Forrest Darwell, who had just touched down at Sydney airport.

Forrest wanted to organise an 'exchange' with Barry. For one hundred thousand dollars (cash), Forrest was keen to take possession of Barry's werewolf. This would have to be done in a secure and isolated spot, where the transfer of a drugged teenager from one car to another wouldn't be noticed. Forrest would bring a briefcase full of money; Barry would bring the werewolf. Neither man would bring a gun, a companion, or any form of ID.

Forrest didn't explain how he was intending to smuggle his purchase out of Australia. He did, however, admit that he was having a hard time accumulating enough cash to complete the proposed transaction. 'I couldn't have got that kind of money through customs,' he explained, 'and any kind of transfer over ten grand is tracked through the system like a goddamn rogue elephant.' Nevertheless, he was hoping to have the required sum by the end of business that day, after negotiating with 'a third party'. Would Barry be able to meet him afterwards and hand over the goods?

Gruffly, Reuben said 'yes'. He agreed to wait for Forrest's next call, which would confirm that the cash was available. Together, they would then decide on a suitable location for the rendezvous. Since Forrest himself knew nothing of Sydney, he wouldn't be able to pick a good spot. 'But *you* can make that decision,' he said, just as the real Barry McKinnon began to moan and curse behind the guestroom door.

Luckily, Reuben happens to be a very smart guy. When Forrest asked what the noise was, Reuben told him that the 'delivery' was 'causing trouble', before promptly signing off. By the time Mum had staggered upstairs, about fifteen minutes later, Reuben had devised a clever plan for dealing with Forrest Darwell. And Barry was roaring like a newly caged lion.

'I told you,' Reuben said, as he and Mum both winced at the muffled *crash* of a stainless-steel bedpan hitting the floor, 'we shoulda tied his hands behind his back.'

'And let him piss all over my good sheets?' Mum objected. 'He has to be able to use the bedpan.'

Reuben shot her a pitying look. 'He won't use the bedpan. You'll be lucky if he doesn't piss all over the walls. Like I said – he's an animal.' Listening to the frantic rattle of steel against brass, Reuben frowned. 'I just hope your bed's heavy enough, or you won't have much of a spare room left,' he finished.

As it happened, he was right. Barry demolished that guestroom. Even with a brass bedstead attached to his ankle, he managed to smash the light fitting, topple the bedside cabinet, pull the doors off the wardrobe, tear up the sheets, rip down the curtains, and piss on the rug. He also punched a hole in one wall, and cracked a pane of glass in the window.

But Mum only discovered this much later, when she able to inspect the damage. She couldn't risk entering Barry's room while he was still in residence, or he would have killed her. Instead she had to stand by while he vented his fury with a series of cracks and thuds and wild, incoherent yells that seemed to shake the whole house.

As Reuben remarked, it was very fortunate that Mum lived in a freestanding terrace. Otherwise someone might have called the police.

I suppose it hardly needs to be said that Nefley woke up once the shouting started. (Only a vampire could have slept through that racket.) He was confused, at first, and quite scared; when Mum heard a scuffling sound, she went into my room and found Nefley trying to arm himself with the lava lamp. But she soon persuaded him that there was no immediate danger, since the howling captive next door was none other than Barry McKinnon, handcuffed to a bedpost.

'We're waiting for him to tire himself out,' she explained, 'and then we'll see what he might do in exchange for a cup of coffee. It's not that we mean him any harm. It's just that he's a bit of a handful – as you know.'

By this time, of course, Mum was well aware that Barry had attempted to kill Nefley Irving. So she felt sure that Nefley wouldn't object to Barry's imprisonment. In fact she was convinced that Nefley would come to sympathise with the vampire cause, just as soon as he realised that we all – werewolf, vampire and average person alike – shared a common enemy in Barry McKinnon. That's why she decided to turn on the charm. That's why she helped Nefley downstairs, cooked him breakfast, and cut up his bacon for him. That's also why she gave him such a full and detailed account of recent events, including the silver bullet quest, the visit to Cobar, and the werewolf fights.

She cooked breakfast for Reuben, as well; he practically inhaled it while he described how a bunch of vampires had saved his life. 'They're just like normal people, only sicker,' Reuben informed Nefley. 'In fact *they're* the ones who need protection, not us.' He then appealed to my mother. 'Not one of 'em has ever tried to bite *you* – eh, Mrs Harrison?'

'Nope,' said Mum.

'The priest told me all about it,' Reuben continued, shovelling scrambled egg into his mouth. 'They have these rules they have to follow, and medicines they have to take, and therapy they have to do. It's like they've got AIDS, or something. You just have to take a few precautions.'

'What about the man upstairs?' asked Nefley, in his rather high-pitched voice. As if on cue, a huge *thump* sounded from the room above them; they glanced up at the ceiling, as Mum sighed. 'The other man, I mean, not Barry,' Nefley amended, after a brief pause. At that stage he was wavering, but not fully convinced. 'You just said that he was bitten last night.'

'So? You got a problem with that?' Reuben's tone was scornful. 'Because *I* don't.'

'Horace did it,' my mother intervened, from the kitchen sink. 'He's a piece of work, I'm afraid – always has been. I never had any time for Horace.' She turned to face the two men. 'Thirty years ago, Casimir did what Horace just did, and got buried alive for a quarter of a century. If you ask me, the same thing's going to happen to Horace.' She pulled a face. 'And about time too.'

'You reckon? *I* think he deserves a bloody medal,' Reuben replied. 'Dermid's a killer. You can't help wanting to bite him. I bit him myself.'

'How do I know you're not just servants of the coven?' Nefley interrupted, in a manner that was both anxious and fretful, yet strangely avid as well. According to Mum – who later described the whole conversation to me in microscopic detail – Nefley was quite obviously a bundle of nerves beneath all his extra padding; she classified him as the type who becomes a 'hysterical' drunk. (Having worked in a pub for so many years, she still analyses people like a barmaid.) Sitting there at the kitchen table, with his fluffy hair on end, and his arm in a sling, and his small eyes puffy with sleep,

302

Nefley was a perfect candidate for Mum's Hysterical Drunk category. 'How do I know I can believe you?' he went on, when his reference to covens drew a complete blank. 'How do I know you're not just familiars dedicated to luring new victims into the vampires' lair?'

Mum and Reuben exchanged glances. 'Well – I dunno, Nefley,' Mum said at last. 'I mean – this is the lair. Here you are. What's your objection?'

'You've been here since yesterday, and no one's taken a bite outta you yet,' Reuben reminded him. 'It's been thirty years between victims, mate. I reckon you're more likely to get hit by a car than bitten by a vampire.'

'And you're free to go any time,' Mum added, 'as long as you think you can handle things on your own, with that leg playing you up. It won't be easy. Sanford's left a stock of painkillers, but if there's anyone who can take care of you for a few days . . .' Mum trailed off at this point, because it was somehow perfectly obvious that Nefley didn't have anyone to take care of him. You only had to look at the stains on his clothes, she said later.

Nefley stared at her in astonishment.

'You're – you're not going to keep me here?' he stammered, whereupon Mum shrugged.

'How can we?' she asked. 'I've got enough on my plate as it is.' Another huge *thud* from upstairs confirmed the truth of this claim. 'In fact, you'll be making things a lot easier if you do go.'

'And if you don't come back,' Reuben added. 'At least, not with a sharpened stick, or nothing.' He leaned forward, exuding a kind of manic intensity. 'See, these people saved my life,' he said. 'So I've got a *duty* to save theirs. And if you decide that you still want to get rid of 'em, then you'll have to go through me first. Which you don't wanna do. Because I'm no vampire, Nefley – I'm more than a match for you, mate.'

This hardly needed saying, in Mum's opinion; the contrast between Reuben and Nefley was almost ludicrous. She reckons it was like watching a muzzled greyhound contemplating a generous bowl of vanilla custard. As Reuben narrowed his eyes, Nefley blanched, then offered up some feeble excuses. He'd been misinformed, he insisted. There was too much sensational coverage, out there. The facts weren't being publicised as they should be – vampires weren't arguing their case well enough. If he'd known the truth, he would never have . . . have . . .

'Killed Casimir?' Mum concluded. And Nefley's face crumpled.

'Your friend *wanted* to bite me,' he shrilled. 'That's why he answered my message!'

'Yeah, but it was entrapment, wasn't it?' said Mum (who's watched a lot of TV cop shows). 'Besides, he wasn't *my* friend. I didn't like him.' Remembering the task she'd set herself, she quickly changed tack. 'Still doesn't mean he deserved to die, though.'

'Look.' Reuben was getting impatient. He addressed Nefley in a more forceful manner. 'There are some screw-up dickhead vampires, just like there are screw-up dickhead people. But most vampires are okay. Like Nina, for instance. She's a really nice person.'

'Which one is Nina?' Nefley quavered. 'Is that the knitting lady?'

'Nina's the little one with all the hair,' Reuben said. 'The

304

one who lent you her room. She wouldn't hurt a fly.'

'Oh. Yes.'

'Her life seems pretty awful, if you ask me,' Reuben went on. 'She can't go out in the daytime. She can't go to parties. She's always sick. Isn't that right, Mrs Harrison?'

'That's right.'

'The last thing she needs is some idiot trying to stab her with a fence-post – which is why you have to keep your mouth shut about all this.'

'But –'

'There are lots of idiots out there, Nefley. Lots of 'em.'

'But if you tell everyone the truth, no one will *want* to kill vampires!' Nefley exclaimed. And Reuben gave a snort.

'Oh, yeah?' he said.

'There's always going to be people who'll try to kill vampires, love.' Having seated herself at the table, Mum began to quote Sanford, word for word. 'The press has been so bad, over so many years, that you wouldn't be able to change things fast enough. Every vampire on earth would be wiped out long before the truth really sank in. Because some people are just phobic about vampires – like they are about spiders.'

'And werewolves,' Reuben added. He then went on to explain how hard it had been for him, and how he simply wanted a quiet life, and how there would always be McKinnons dedicated to exploiting the weaknesses of other people. After which he confessed that he'd never had a job, while he quizzed Nefley about finding employment in the postal service. Would there be an opening for someone like Reuben in mail-sorting, or delivery? Because he wanted to start a new life – as a normal person – and the first step would be to look for paid work.

It's possible that Nefley found this appeal quite flattering. Being an impressionable sort of bloke, he would also have been heavily influenced by the free meal, the borrowed towels, and the friendly domesticity of Mum's kitchen. In any event, according to her, he really loosened up after that. He even offered to stay and help her with the McKinnons, though (as she later remarked) what kind of help he could have provided, with a broken arm and a sprained ankle, was anybody's guess.

So she thanked him, but rejected the offer. Instead she asked him to vacate my room as soon as possible. If he did that, she explained, Dermid could be moved into it, and her own bed would be restored to her. 'I'll call a cab to take you home,' she promised, 'and give you a ring later on. To see how you're coping.' Then she gave him some of her shepherd's pie to heat up for dinner, because it was going to be hard for him to cook with only one arm.

I don't know if it was the shepherd's pie that converted Nefley, or Reuben's testimonial, or Barry's frantic cries for help. It may even have been my diary, which Nefley secretly pocketed when he returned upstairs to fetch his pistol. But whatever the cause, I can attest to the fact that he left Mum's house a changed man that morning.

And I'm not just talking about the broken arm.

Meanwhile, Dermid was really beginning to suffer. By the time Mum had said goodbye to Nefley and traipsed back upstairs, Dermid was on his knees in the bathroom, puking his guts out. I mean, *literally* puking his guts out; there's something very nasty that happens to the lining of your stomach when you turn into a vampire – but you probably don't want to hear all the symptoms. Let's just say that it's painful, and terrifying, and almost worse to watch than it is to experience. (Personally, I don't remember much about my own transformation; it's poor Mum who's still having nightmares about bloody discharges, thirty-five years on.)

Anyway, Dermid was a mess. And so was my mother. For one thing, she hadn't had enough sleep. For another, as Dermid's metamorphosis progressed, she found herself troubled by memories of my own first day of infection – when Sanford had been obliged to lock her in the basement, to stop her from summoning an ambulance. Nor did Barry make things any easier. He continued to rant and rave in the guestroom until he drove my mother from the house; she had to pop down the road to get some money and cigarettes and a bottle of gin before she had strength enough to go back inside.

Fortunately, Reuben was around – and he didn't give a damn about the McKinnons. Being totally unmoved by Dermid's distress, he was able to wipe up blood and listen to heartrending groans with perfect equanimity. Barry's tantrums also failed to disturb him. And when at last Barry fell silent, Reuben refused to let my mother open the guestroom door. 'He hasn't hurt himself,' Reuben assured her. 'He's probably lying there, waiting to throw a lamp at whoever sticks their head in.'

'If he's quiet, he might listen,' Mum speculated.

'Yeah, but he won't listen to *you*.' Reuben was trying to be patient. 'Not until you've got something concrete to offer.' Seeing Mum frown, he took a deep breath, then tackled the subject even more fervently. 'Look,' he said, 'I know this guy. He's too dangerous to mess around with. Just wait a few hours before you talk to him, because I've got an idea that'll give us a lotta leverage. It'll give him a *reason* to walk away.'

'What idea?' asked Mum. Reuben, however, wouldn't tell her. Not at first. He waited until Father Ramon arrived, at about eleven o'clock, before laying out his carefully conceived plan for revenge.

First of all, a meeting would be arranged with Forrest Darwell, just as soon as the American called to confirm that he had a hundred thousand dollars in cash. Disguising his voice, Reuben would specify a rendezvous point not far from a railway station. Here the priest would leave Barry's truck, then catch a train back home. Long before the American showed up, an anonymous tip-off would alert the police to a possible drug-related transaction. Forrest would be nabbed with a suitcase full of suspicious money, and there would be hell to pay – for the McKinnons, in particular.

'Whatever happens, Darwell's gunna be furious,' Reuben opined. 'He'll think that Barry set him up, and he'll try to get even. God knows what he'll tell the coppers. And Barry will be lucky if *they* get to him before Darwell does.'

'But how's that going to help us?' Mum wanted to know.

Reuben explained. He reminded her that Barry would be deprived of his hundred thousand dollars at the worst possible time – and would therefore take pretty much whatever we decided to hand over. (A few hundred dollars and a ticket to New Zealand would probably do the trick, as far as Reuben was concerned.) When Father Ramon proceeded to make inquiries about Dermid, Reuben shrugged. There could be no telling how Barry would react to news of his son's transformation. It was possible that he might lose control. It was equally possible that he might become more cooperative. But Reuben was willing to bet money that Barry

McKinnon would put his own interests above those of his son, and skip town without a backward glance.

'Which would suit you just fine . . . wouldn't it?' Reuben guessed.

Mum said that she supposed so. Father Ramon asked how he was meant to get hold of the McKinnons' truck. Reuben suggested that the priest take his own car to Nefley's flat, where the truck was parked in a visitors' spot. 'While you're at Nefley's,' Reuben added, 'you should pick up that rifle. It doesn't belong to him, and we might need it.'

'We won't need it,' Father Ramon said firmly.

'We will if Dermid blows his top.'

'If that happens, I'm afraid a rifle won't help us.'

'Then we'll wave it at Barry,' Reuben proposed. 'To stop him from getting any stupid ideas.'

In the end, Mum endorsed the notion of having a gun nearby; she was becoming quite rattled by Barry's explosive outbursts, I think. So Father Ramon capitulated ('Perhaps it's better that Mr Irving doesn't have access to something so dangerous,' was how he rationalised his decision), before he agreed to follow Reuben's directives.

After that, it was just a matter of waiting.

Chapter Twenty-six

I woke up at the usual time, feeling lousy. It was very dark. When I pushed open the lid of my Iso-tank, I wasn't surprised to see Sanford across the room, struggling out of his sleeping bag. But I *was* surprised to see my mother leaning against the basement door.

Normally she doesn't come down to watch me emerge from my daily coma.

'Mum?' I said feebly. 'What are you doing here?'

She jumped, then pressed a finger to her lips. Almost at the same instant, Father Ramon addressed her from out in the hall. 'Estelle?' He sounded upset. 'Are you all right?'

'Yes!' said Mum. 'What about you?'

'Oh, I'm fine,' he assured her, as she fumbled with the lock. 'But Barry isn't.'

Sanford was on his feet, by then; though he looked dishevelled, and was still a little shaky around the knees, he'd obviously grasped that something was wrong.

'What is it?' he croaked. 'Estelle?'

Mum didn't reply. Instead she jerked open the door to admit Father Ramon, whose face was as almost as white as a vampire's. 'You mean Barry's still in the house?' she squawked, clutching at the priest's arm.

'He's upstairs.' Father Ramon turned to Sanford. 'I'm – I'm afraid he's been infected.'

'*What?*'

'And Dermid's gone,' the priest finished, his voice cracking.

I stood there with my mouth open and my head in a spin. Sanford reeled. He might have lost his balance altogether if he hadn't propped himself against a wall.

Nevertheless, he managed to stagger upstairs in pursuit of my mother, his demands for an explanation growing stronger and sharper with every step. I followed him, but only after donning my slippers and dressing gown. Father Ramon took the lead. I heard him say, 'It's a long story, Sanford,' before entering the kitchen.

Reuben was there, waiting for us. He wore a pair of Sanford's lace-up shoes, and was cradling the rifle in his arms. On the floor at his feet lay Barry McKinnon.

The smell of blood hit me before I'd even spied the fang marks.

'Oh, my God.' I froze. Sanford had to stop as well; it's not easy to fight the fanging urge when you're still groggy and disoriented. We stood in the hallway for a moment, taking deep breaths, while Mum eyed us doubtfully.

'Are you two feeling it?' she asked. 'Shouldn't you be going back to the basement?'

'No.' Sanford shook his head. 'I'm perfectly well, thank you.'

'So am I.' But I was still confused. 'Mum, what *happened*?'

'It's a long story,' she replied, echoing Father Ramon. Then she noticed something under the kitchen table. 'Is that my purse?' she said. 'Who's been going through my purse?'

'Give you three guesses,' was Reuben's rather sour

311

response. He fell back a little as she passed him, and his feet immediately caught Sanford's attention.

'You're wearing my shoes.' Sanford's tone was more dazed than accusatory. 'No wonder I couldn't find them.'

'Sorry,' said Reuben, who seemed genuinely apologetic. 'I had to go out. Nothing else would fit.' With more honesty than tact, he added, 'If I'd had any kinda choice, I wouldna picked these.'

'Is that Barry's rifle?' I queried. And Father Ramon said, 'Yes.'

'He brought it back from Nefley's,' Reuben revealed, as if this explained everything. Whereupon Sanford seemed to snap out of his trance.

'Where *is* Nefley?' he wanted to know. 'Where's Dermid? What's been going on?'

'I tell you what's been going on!' cried Mum, who had retrieved her handbag. 'Dermid's taken my money! *A hundred and twenty dollars!*'

This news hit Father Ramon particularly hard. He groaned, then churned up his silver hair in consternation. Reuben growled, 'That figures.' I stared at them both, all at sea.

'That was my housekeeping money! I just got it out this morning!' Mum wailed. She was hugely upset, and had to be helped to her feet by Sanford. 'What am I going to do now?'

'We'll work something out,' Father Ramon promised. 'I'm sorry, Estelle.'

'You should check *his* pockets, to start with,' Reuben advised, poking at Barry's midriff with a leather-clad toe. 'Just in case. It's this bastard who calls the shots, not Dermid.'

But when Mum went through Barry's pockets, they were

empty. Her housekeeping money was nowhere to be seen.

And that, as Father Ramon said, was very bad news.

'If Dermid took it, he could be anywhere,' the priest exclaimed, in despairing accents. 'These days you can buy a plane ticket for that kind of money!'

'He won't have bought a plane ticket,' Sanford insisted. 'He's not – he can't – he's not thinking straight.' Though his own powers of concentration also appeared to be slightly compromised, Sanford was very firm on this point. 'Dermid's entered the second phase. He's able to move around, but his cognitive abilities will be affected by a profound drop in his blood-sugar levels. It's going to be making him very erratic. Very disoriented.'

'He can't be *that* disoriented,' said Reuben. 'I mean, he knew enough to take a wad of money when he saw it.'

'Possibly,' Sanford rejoined, 'but not necessarily. He might have recognised the money as something desirable, without actually remembering how to use it.'

'So in other words, he's out of his mind,' said Mum.

'You could argue that.' Sanford gestured at Barry. 'After all, he just fanged his own father. Isn't that the scenario, here? In which case, he must be seriously disturbed.'

'So he might not be doing the logical thing,' Mum continued. 'In fact he might have gone back upstairs, for all we know.'

Sanford swallowed. He probably would have turned pale, if he hadn't been snow-white already.

'You mean you – you haven't checked?' he stammered.

It hardly needs saying that we immediately checked the first floor. At least, Sanford did. He wouldn't allow any of the non-vampires to risk an encounter with Dermid, and he wanted me to search a few of the likelier ground-floor hiding places – such as the cupboard under the stairs, for instance. Sanford even shone a torch around our attic area, just to be on the safe side. Only when we were convinced that Dermid wasn't anywhere in the house did we finally transport Barry McKinnon up to my room.

We couldn't return him to the guestroom, because of the damage he'd done to it.

Poor Mum received a very nasty shock when she saw what Barry had accomplished. He'd done a pretty thorough job of trashing just about everything within reach. Nevertheless, the trail of destruction that he'd left behind told us exactly how he'd managed to get out.

First of all, he had applied so much pressure to one particular bedpost that a weld had snapped. He had therefore been able to slip a handcuff over the top of the post, having first unscrewed the knob. From the enormous dents in its solid oaken panels, we deduced that – once free – he had tried to kick down the bedroom door, without success. So he had then climbed onto the wardrobe, using the bedside cabinet as a kind of stepladder, and knocked his way through the plaster-and-lathe ceiling with an old marble lamp-base that he'd found in the bottom drawer of the dressing table. ('Dammit,' Mum said gloomily, when this lamp was discovered. 'I forgot all about Auntie Vera's stuff.') After squirming through the rough-edged escape route that he'd made for himself, Barry must have located the nearest access panel, and dropped onto the landing – because when we looked, we saw that the aperture most commonly employed by electricians and exterminators hadn't been covered up again.

'That's where he would have come down,' Father Ramon

314

decided. 'And from here he must have gone straight in to rescue Dermid.'

'Because the door wasn't locked,' Mum agreed, adding, 'I was *told* not to lock the door.'

'You shouldn't have had to.' Sanford was quick to defend the decisions he'd made. 'Barry's mistake was to cut himself while he was breaking into the roof. He blooded his own son. It's as simple as that.' Irritably, he rounded on the nearest available scapegoat – who happened to be Reuben. 'Why weren't *you* here?' Sanford snarled. 'I thought you were going to keep an eye on things?'

'I was. I mean, I did,' said Reuben. 'But I had this idea. It was a *good* idea.'

Suddenly Mum's phone rang. The noise made everyone jump; even Reuben was startled. After a moment's pause, my mother went off to answer it, leaving Father Ramon to recount the day's events.

That's when Sanford and I heard about Forrest Darwell's first call. The priest also told us about Nefley's conversion, and Barry's violence, and Reuben's carefully laid plans. According to the priest, Forrest had phoned back at about four o'clock. Afterwards, Father Ramon had driven Barry's truck to a deserted inner-city laneway lined with skips and bins and garage doors. (Father Ramon's pastoral duties had taken him there once, when he was searching for the runaway child of a widowed parishioner.) On his way back to Parramatta, the priest had notified Reuben of the truck's exact whereabouts. At which point Reuben had left Mum's house to find a public phone box.

'I didn't want to ring the police from here,' he explained, 'just in case they ended up tracing the call.'

315

He also hadn't wanted to use the *nearest* phone box, and had spent about forty-five minutes wandering the streets of nearby suburbs. Meanwhile, Father Ramon had returned to Nefley's apartment, where Nefley himself was already halfway through my diary. Any normal person, of course, would have tried to conceal this diary before answering a knock on his door. Any normal person would have been ashamed of getting caught with his nose stuck in someone else's private papers.

Nefley, however, isn't exactly what you'd call a normal person. As soon as he had admitted Father Ramon, who was there to collect the rifle, Nefley began to babble on about the insights he'd gained from my diary, and how he'd never realised how fragile vampires actually were, and how sorry he felt for me – now that he knew the kinds of difficulties I faced – and why he wanted to do something that would make amends for the crime he'd committed. 'I'll spend the rest of my life in the service of the very people I once tried to destroy!' he had announced, in the manner of a comic-strip hero.

Father Ramon had been torn. On the one hand, Nefley's change of heart had been gratifying to witness. On the other hand, it's always a shock to encounter someone who can't understand the concept of privacy. According to Father Ramon, Nefley seemed to view reality as an extension of his own, personal fantasy world. 'He's very immature,' the priest reported, in worried tones. 'I'd have to recommend that we keep him under surveillance, or he might do something stupid.'

After expressing himself very strongly on the subject of stealing, Father Ramon had persuaded Nefley to hand over my diary – and had been on the verge of mentioning Barry's rifle when his mobile had rung. It was my mother, calling with bad news.

Barry had managed to free himself.

At that stage, she wasn't quite sure how he'd done it. All she knew was that he had managed to climb into her attic. And since Reuben wasn't carrying a phone, she had immediately rung Father Ramon – who had told her to lock herself in the basement. 'Get down there *now*,' he'd instructed. 'Take your mobile with you. If anyone tries to get in, just contact the police. I'm on my way.'

In fact, he had been on his way with the rifle. He might even have entered the house with it, if he hadn't picked Reuben up in the street. (Reuben had made his anonymous call, and was retracing his steps along a main road when Father Ramon spotted him.) After conferring together, they had decided to enter Mum's place from the rear, sneaking in through the kitchen fully armed. And they had both agreed that Reuben should be the one to carry the rifle, since Father Ramon didn't even know how to load it.

They hadn't expected to find the back door standing open. Nor had they expected to find Barry already in the kitchen, sprawled on the linoleum with fang marks in his neck.

'We realised that *you* weren't responsible,' Father Ramon hastily assured me. 'You and Sanford weren't even awake, then. We knew that Dermid must have done it – since he can still get about during daylight hours.'

'And now he's on the loose.' It was a terrifying thought. What could we possibly do? 'We have to find him,' I said. 'He'll attack someone else, otherwise.'

'Possibly,' Sanford had to concede. 'Though I suspect he

won't be plagued by very strong urges. Not after what happened downstairs.'

'You mean he'll be racked with guilt?' Father Ramon inquired, eliciting a surprised look from Sanford.

'Oh, no.' Sanford dismissed the possibility. 'I doubt he'll even recall what he did, with any sort of coherence. But *physically* he'll be satisfied. If you take my meaning.'

'Oh.' The priest lost even more of his already depleted colour, and I took advantage of his sudden silence to interrogate Sanford myself.

'Where do you think someone like Dermid might actually go?' I asked. 'Do you think he'll go to a hospital, or – I dunno – the police?'

Sanford shrugged in hopeless kind of way.

'Your guess is as good as mine.'

'Yeah, but look.' Reuben broke in with his usual excess of energy; it was like being buffeted by a powerful gust of wind. A nerve was twitching in the corner of his left eye. 'This only just happened. Maybe a quarter of an hour ago? He can't have got far.'

'Yes, he can,' I retorted. 'He has money, remember?'

'Money's no good if you don't know how to use it,' Reuben reminded me, before addressing Father Ramon. 'Anyway, even if he *can* use it, how often do the buses actually stop, around here? How often do the trains run? Maybe we can catch him, if we're quick enough. Maybe we should form a search party.'

'Oh, no.' Sanford shook his head. 'Not you. You won't be going anywhere *near* Dermid. Not in his current condition.'

'But –'

'*No*. You wouldn't be safe. Neither would Father Ramon.

318

This is vampire business. I'll ask Dave to conduct a search of the area.'

Sanford had barely finished speaking when Mum reappeared, holding her cordless phone. 'It's Dave,' she announced. 'He wanted to know what's going on, so I told him. Now he's asking if he should come over.'

'Yes. I mean, no. Wait – give it here.' Snatching at the receiver, Sanford began to pepper poor Dave with instructions. He told Dave to leave Horace locked in the bank vault and to bring George along for the ride. According to Sanford, George would be able to keep an eye on passing pedestrians while Dave was watching the road. 'And if you see Dermid, give me a call. We need to handle this very carefully; we can't just abduct him off the street, with a pubful of people watching.'

He then went on to describe, in great detail, the exact location of his 'emergency knockout kit', before passing the phone back to Mum. 'Dave recommends that we warn Nefley Irving, and I agree with him. Because there's an outside chance that Dermid might be heading for Nefley's place. So I'll leave that to you, Estelle.' When my mother opened her mouth, Sanford anticipated her protest. 'It's probably best that you ring him, since you're the one he spent most of his time with. Just call Directory Assistance for the number.'

'But why would Dermid want to go to Nefley's place?' I'm ashamed of myself for having made this inquiry; my only defence is that I still hadn't had my evening guinea pig, and was therefore feeling more than usually wiped out. Sanford must have been similarly afflicted, to judge from the longsuffering manner in which he began to massage his eyeballs.

'You need to get some blood into you, Nina,' he remarked, leaving Reuben to answer my question.

'Those pricks parked their truck outside Nefley's place,' said Reuben, kindly jogging my memory. He was shifting from foot to foot, like someone desperate to relieve himself. 'Which means that old Dick-face might go back there to get it.'

'Except that it's not in Parramatta any more.' Father Ramon was looking more and more like a vampire: not only pale, but ill and haggard. 'It's sitting in a laneway near Central Station.'

'In which case,' Sanford declared, 'you should get on to Nefley as soon as you can, Estelle. If I were him, I'd vacate the premises. It's hard to know *what* Dermid will do, if he can't find his car.'

There was a brief pause. From the glum expressions around me, I deduced that ghastly visions of possible worst-case scenarios must have been flitting through a lot of neighbouring minds. Father Ramon, in particular, seemed to be strongly affected. 'Maybe I should go over there and help Nefley,' he proposed at last. 'Since he probably can't drive –'

'No,' said Sanford.

'His arm's broken. He can barely walk –'

'He can catch a cab, Father.'

'Anyway, if the worst comes to the worst, he's got a *whole heap* of sharpened stakes in his living room,' I pointed out. As everyone turned to stare at me, I expanded on my argument. 'Plus he's got a gun full of silver bullets, and a notch in his belt. There's no need to worry about *him*, Father. I reckon if Dermid does show up there, he'll be lucky to get out alive.'

Sanford blinked. The priest swallowed. Then they

exchanged a long, grave, resigned sort of look, before Sanford finally cleared his throat.

'I think we'd better ring Nefley right now,' he mumbled, 'and tell him to come straight back here.'

But when Mum dialled Nefley's number, no one answered her call.

Chapter Twenty-seven

Though Sanford was reluctant to leave Barry McKinnon in my mother's care, he didn't have much choice.

'I can't let Father Ramon go to Parramatta all by himself,' was Sanford's reasoning. 'It's bad enough that he has to drive there in the first place. I'm not about to make him get out of the car as well – not if Dermid's anywhere about.'

My suggestion that Dave be sent to Nefley's flat was treated with something very close to contempt. Dave had a job to do, Sanford informed me. Dave would be looking for Dermid in the immediate neighbourhood. 'Which means that someone will be close at hand, if you need any help,' Sanford advised my mother, as he was exiting the house. 'Not that I think you will. There's not much you can do for Barry, at this stage – not now that his wound's been dressed. Just keep his feet elevated and make sure he isn't too hot.'

'You've already told me all this,' Mum rasped, exhaling a cloud of cigarette smoke. She was standing at the top of the stairs, glowering down at Sanford. 'I'm not deaf, you know.'

'If you're not deaf, why are you still smoking?' was Sanford tart retort. 'I must have warned you off it a hundred times.'

'And I've told you a hundred times to mind your own business.' Mum's gaze shifted across the chequerboard tiles of the vestibule, until it came to rest on Father Ramon. 'Take care, Father.'

'I will,' he promised.

'Sure you guys don't want the gun?' asked Reuben, who had stationed himself near the front door, rifle in hand. 'You can have it if you like.'

Sanford shook his head. Father Ramon murmured, 'I don't think so, Reuben. Thanks all the same.'

'You might need some firepower,' Reuben warned. 'We still don't know what's been going on back at Nefley's.'

Sanford heaved an impatient sigh. 'A gun will cause more problems than it will solve,' he said.

'But –'

'Out where you come from, Reuben, you might be able to lug small arms around with impunity. Here in Sydney, it's a perfect way of attracting far too much unwelcome attention.' Sanford turned back to Mum. 'We'll keep you posted.'

'Don't be too long.'

'If you hear from Dave, tell him to call my mobile,' was Sanford's final directive, before he donned his sunglasses and disappeared into the night. Father Ramon followed close on his heels; when the door closed, Mum gave a sniff and said, 'Right. I'm off to bed, now.'

'Are you?' I still wasn't dressed, so I hadn't strapped on my watch – but the cuckoo clock on the landing told me that it was only seven fifteen. 'Isn't it a little early for that?'

'Not when you've had about four hours' sleep in the last three days,' Mum growled. I was draped over the banisters at this point, and as she trudged past me towards her bedroom, she added, 'You can keep an eye on Barry yourself. I've had my fill of gastric cases. And don't wake me up unless it's an emergency.'

'You don't think *this* is an emergency?' I called after her. 'There's an unreformed vampire on the loose, Mum. It's serious. I mean, it's *really* serious.'

Mum paused on the threshold of her room, twisting the doorknob with one hand while her other hand was occupied with her cigarette. 'Nina,' she replied, 'over the last week, I've had a basement full of vampires using up all my hot water, I've had a killer jumping out of an upstairs window, I've had a mad bloody kidnapper knocking holes in my ceiling, and I've had a werewolf eating me out of house and home. Not to mention the damage to my downpipe, and my bathroom door. It's getting so that I can't tell the emergencies from the daily routine, around here.' Suddenly she erupted into a fit of coughing, which left her limp and teary-eyed. 'Tell Reuben if he wants dinner, he can open a tin,' she said at last. 'And tell him to go easy on the bread, or we won't have any toast for breakfast.'

'Mum –'

'There's only one guinea pig left downstairs. You'd better grab it before someone else does,' she finished. Then she retreated into her room, slamming the door behind her.

I suppose that I could have said 'sorry', but I didn't. There are only so many times you can apologise for being a vampire. I did, however, take her advice about the last guinea pig, which was looking decidedly unwell – listless and mangy, and much too thin. Sometimes guinea pigs in that sort of condition can leave you feeling a bit off-colour; there are vampires of my acquaintance (Gladys, for instance) who wouldn't have touched the thing. But I always find that the relief of being able to tell yourself that it was 'a merciful release' far outweighs any physical side-effects, when you fang a sick guinea pig. So I shut myself in the bathroom and did what I had to do, conscious all the while that Reuben was prowling around the house, his ears pricked and his curiosity inflamed.

'I guess you've gotta be really careful with the dead ones,' he remarked, as I thrust my zip-lock bag full of lifeless guinea pig into Mum's freezer. 'Or someone might call the RSPCA.'

I grunted.

'Where do you get them from?' he inquired, and I said, 'We breed them. *George* breeds them.'

'Oh. Right.'

'Speaking of dinner, Mum says you can open a tin,' I continued, trying to change the subject without being too obvious. 'There are tins over there, in the pantry.'

'As long as they're not in the freezer!'

'Ha-ha.' (I'd heard that joke before.) 'So do you know how to . . . you know . . . do everything?' It had occurred to me that Reuben probably hadn't used a stove, or washed a dish, or seen a refrigerator since he was fourteen years old. 'Do you want me to open a tin for you?'

The flush that mantled his face made his eyes look greener than ever.

'I'm not a *complete* retard,' he snapped, before regretting his sharp tone and proceeding in a more conciliatory fashion. 'What I mean is that I used to live in a normal house, once.'

'Sure.'

'I can remember what to do. I can remember how to use a tin-opener.' He set his gun down on the table, then padded across the cracked linoleum towards the pantry cupboard.

'My mum was such a lush, I've been cooking since I was six,' he continued, peering at my own mother's selection of tinned soups and stews. 'My brother just wanted to eat corn chips all the time.'

'When are you going to contact your brothers, anyway?' I asked. 'Soon?'

Reuben didn't answer immediately. He kept his gaze fixed on our selection of tuna. 'Maybe,' he said at last.

'Are you going to tell them what really happened to you?'

'Maybe.' His voice was strangled; he ducked his head, as if he were surveying the condiments on a low shelf, and I suddenly caught a glimpse of the fourteen-year-old boy lurking beneath his hardened, prickly, nineteen-year-old carapace.

I realised that, after being imprisoned in an underground tank for all of five years, Reuben hadn't been given a chance to grow up properly.

'No offence, or anything,' I went on, choosing my words with care, 'but I think you should get some kind of counselling. Because what you went through – it's bound to have messed you up a bit. It would have messed *anybody* up a bit.'

He stiffened. 'You think I'm messed up?' he said, glaring at me.

'No more than I am.' When this failed to appease him, I decided to elaborate. 'Why do you think I go to a vampire therapy group every Tuesday night? I'm not there for the laughs, Reuben.'

He snorted. 'No,' he agreed. 'Even though – well, it's pretty funny, isn't it? A vampire therapy group.'

'I only wish it was.'

'Dermid won't join something like that,' he assured me.

'Not in a million years.'

'If a million years is how long it takes . . .' I replied, with a shrug. When Reuben frowned, I reminded him that Dermid had all the time in the world to change his mind. 'He's not the same person. Not any more. He's a vampire.' I tapped my bony chest. 'Do you think *I* used to be like this? No way. I was completely different. *Completely*. I used to have *fun*.'

'You do seem really old, sometimes,' Reuben conceded. 'I mean, the way you talk, and stuff.'

'That's because I am old. I'm fifty-one.'

'*Fifty-one?*' His expression almost made me laugh. 'Jeez, I didn't . . . I thought . . .' He trailed off, then rallied bravely. 'Well, you don't look it,' he avowed. 'In fact I hope I look as good as you do when I'm fifty-one.'

'No, you don't.' I probably sounded more abrupt than I'd intended, because he gave a little start. 'You might think you do, but you don't.'

'I was just kidding, Nina.'

'It's always the same thing, day after day. Year after year. The fatigue, and the pain, and the nausea – they never let up. You always feel hungry. You always feel thirsty. You never go anywhere or meet anyone –'

'Whaddaya mean?' he interrupted. 'You went to Cobar, didn't you? You met me!'

'Yeah, but –'

'Seems like you've had a much better time than *I* have, lately!'

'I guess so, but –'

'Try being a werewolf, and see what that's like!'

The phone rang, then; it made us jump, and put a stop to our exchange. Sanford was on the other end of the line. He told me that he had reached Nefley's place, but that no one was answering his knock. What's more, Nefley's garage door was standing open.

'It has his number painted on it, so it must be his,' Sanford explained. 'And it's empty. There's no car inside.'

'Maybe he doesn't have a car,' I hazarded.

'Oh, he has a car. He mentioned it to Father Ramon.' There was a brief exchange that I couldn't hear properly. Then Sanford said, 'Ah.'

'What?'

'According to Father Ramon, the McKinnons kidnapped Nefley at Dave's house. So the car might still be parked near Dave's.'

'Then maybe he's gone to fetch it,' I speculated. 'Nefley, I mean.'

'In his condition?'

'Well – he hurt his left leg and his left arm, didn't he?' I was thinking back to my brief glimpses of Nefley Irving, trying to work out whether he was right- or left-handed. 'He could probably drive it back, if he's got an automatic.'

'Don't be ridiculous, Nina.'

'I'm not being ridiculous!' It irked me that Sanford was falling into his old habit of treating my every utterance as if it were the babbling of a three-year-old. 'He's probably right-handed! And you only need one foot!'

'Don't you think it would be a lot simpler if he asked a friend to bring it back for him?' Sanford asked, in the kind of wearily patronising tone that he always adopts when he thinks I'm being dense. It raises my hackles every time – especially when *he's* the one who isn't thinking straight.

'What makes you think he even has any friends?' I demanded, before it occurred to me that we were being side-

328

tracked into yet another bout of vampire-ish bickering. And since I was determined not to fall into that trap, I made a heroic effort to change the subject. 'So are you going to stay there, or what?' I asked.

'Maybe for a little while.' After a long pause, he added, 'If Nefley's gone to fetch his car, why leave the garage door open?'

I pondered for a moment. 'Because it's hard for him to get in and out of the driver's seat?'

'Good point.'

'Sanford – what are we going to do if Dave can't find Dermid?'

This time the pause was so long that I was afraid he hadn't heard me, and was opening my mouth to repeat the question when he finally said, 'Well . . . in that case we'll have to start watching the news, I suppose.'

'You don't think he might go back to Wolgaroo Corner?'

'It's possible.'

'He could sleep in one of those underground tanks, but what would he do about shopping?' I was intrigued despite myself. The notion of an outback vampire wasn't entirely implausible; I had a sudden mental picture of Dermid driving around the desert plains at night, setting traps for kangaroos and ordering his supplies over the Internet. But of course he wouldn't feel well enough to go trap-setting a lot of the time. And he wouldn't restrict himself to kangaroos, either – not unless he had some kind of emotional support. He would start to prey on campers, and shearers, and stranded motorists.

He'd start arousing suspicions soon enough.

'I'm going to call Dave,' Sanford remarked, interrupting my train of thought. 'Keep me posted, all right?'

'All right.'

'*You might want to alert Bridget, as well. She'd probably like to know what's going on,*' Sanford concluded. Then he broke the connection abruptly.

I was about to dial Bridget's number when Reuben said 'Nina!' in a strangely high-pitched voice. Turning, I saw that he had opened a tin of baked beans, and was standing at the sink with the tin in one hand and a plate in the other. But he set down his plate with a rap.

'Look,' he croaked, pointing out the kitchen window. I looked – then gasped.

Dermid McKinnon was tottering through the back gate, dragging Nefley Irving along with him.

Chapter Twenty-eight

I'd been right, you see. Nefley *had* gone to retrieve his car. He didn't have any friends who could fetch it for him, so he'd caught a cab to Dave's house, then driven his own vehicle back to Parramatta with one arm in a sling.

It hadn't been easy. He'd been forced to stop once or twice when his nerves had failed him. But he'd managed the journey somehow, despite his handicap. And he hadn't caused any accidents along the way.

Unfortunately, however, his good luck hadn't lasted. Upon arriving home, he'd pulled up in front of his garage, heaved himself out of his car, and hobbled across a crumbling stretch of asphalt to push open the roller door. He hadn't seen the shadowy figure lurking nearby. And since he'd left his pistol on the front passenger seat (in plain view of anyone with highly developed night vision), he'd soon found himself being compelled – at gunpoint – to drive Dermid McKinnon back to my mum's place.

Don't ask me what Dermid's motives were. Having lost his truck, he certainly needed transport. But I still don't understand why he suddenly felt the need to rescue his father. Was it guilt? Or fear? Or something to do with money? Perhaps there wasn't any logic to it at all; he certainly wasn't making much sense when he yelled at me through Mum's kitchen window.

'*You let go of my dad right now, or I'll blow your friend away!*' he screamed.

It was an odd sort of threat, because Nefley was no friend of mine. We hadn't even been formally introduced. I recognised him, of course, despite the fact that his empurpled, sweat-soaked, badly illumined face was contorted with fear. I also felt sorry for him – as I would have felt sorry for anyone trapped in a headlock, with a pistol jammed against his skull. Nevertheless, I didn't feel like hurling myself out the door to save him.

If he had been Mum, or Dave, or Father Ramon, it would have been different. But Nefley?

'Oh, shit,' Reuben hissed, out of the corner of his mouth. He cut a glance at the table.

'Don't move,' I warned.

'*Get Dad!*' Dermid was still yelling, his bulging, bloodshot eyes just centimetres from the glass. '*Bring him out here! Now!*'

'You go up,' said Reuben, under his breath.

'No. You,' I replied.

'Nina –'

'He can't kill me. He can't infect me, either.'

'But –'

'Call Dave. Go now.' Raising my voice – and my hands – I addressed Dermid. '*He's just going to get your dad! Okay? Your dad's upstairs. Can you hear me?*' As Reuben started to back away, I added (with more than a trace of anxiety), '*Maybe you should come inside, eh? Before our neighbours call the police?*'

'*DON'T TOUCH THAT!*' Dermid's hand jerked, and suddenly his gun was aimed at the window. Glancing over my

332

shoulder, I saw that Reuben had been edging closer to the rifle.

'Leave it!' I snarled. 'Get going!'

Reuben hesitated.

'We're sitting ducks, you moron!' I shrilled, and the insult seemed to shock Reuben into a state of heightened awareness. His gaze flitted across the wide expanse of glazing in front of us; he must have realised that we were silhouetted against the light, as vulnerable and exposed as goldfish in a bowl. At any rate, he abandoned any notions that he might have entertained concerning the rifle. Instead he made for the stairs, his chiselled features drawn tight with tension, his green eyes blazing.

'I'll be back,' he promised. 'Just . . . just be careful, okay?'

'I know.'

'Don't do anything stupid.'

Before I could thank him (through clenched teeth) for this vote of confidence, he had disappeared – leaving me all alone in the kitchen. For a few seconds I simply stood there with my hands up and my heart pounding. Then it occurred to me that Dermid didn't look well. Though he'd clearly recovered a lot of his strength, he wasn't by any means a raging bundle of energy. And it crossed my mind that fresh human blood might not have quite the same explosive impact on a half-formed vampire as it has on someone who's already undergone a full transformation.

I began to move sideways, very slowly and carefully.

'*Do you want to come in?*' I asked Dermid, trying to project my voice through the glass. '*There's only me in here now!*'

Dermid shook his head. Though his tattooed arms were still brown and muscular against the grubby pallor of his T-shirt – though his scarred cheeks were still plump and his hair hadn't lost its gleam – the infection had already left its mark on him. I could see traces of it in his yellowing irises, and his pinprick pupils. His mucus membranes were turning a livid, unhealthy colour; dark patches were forming near the wound on his neck.

'*Don't come any closer!*' he cried. '*Or I'll shoot your friend!*'

'*He's not my friend! He killed my friend!*' I was feeling safer, by this time, because Dermid had once more aimed his gun at Nefley – who whimpered as I inched my way towards the exit. '*Listen, Dermid. We don't want the police involved! Can you come inside? Before the neighbours get interested?*'

'*You'd better not call the police!*' was Dermid's strangled response. '*You'd better not do that!*'

'Shh! Keep it down!' I pushed open the back door, adjusting my volume as I did so. You might be wondering where I found the courage. You might be thinking: *She's just like Zadia Bloodstone.* Well, you'd be wrong. Because I had already spotted something that told me exactly what I needed to know.

Most people would have missed it – I realise that. Most people don't have my night vision, and wouldn't have seen Dermid swallowing, over and over and over again. But I saw it. And I understood what it meant.

Dermid was feeling bad. *Really* bad. He was on the verge of throwing up.

'Just come inside and we'll talk,' I pleaded. 'You're confused because you're sick –'

'I'm not sick!'

'Dermid –'

'Stand back!'

'Okay.' I lifted my hands again, to show him that I didn't

mean any harm. 'I've stopped. Don't worry.'

'Where's Dad?'

'He's coming. He's sick, too.' I took a deep breath, to steady myself. 'Don't you remember what you did to him?'

Dermid swallowed, three times in succession. His eyes widened until they almost sprang from their sockets. His gun was beginning to shake.

But he didn't speak. Perhaps he *couldn't* speak.

'You bit him, Dermid. You drank his blood.' Ignoring Nefley's groan, I pressed on, as quietly as possible. 'Don't you remember doing that? It happened just here, in the kitchen.'

Dermid made an odd noise. Then he said, 'No.'

'You're a vampire now. Like me.'

'*Bullshit!*' Dermid's grip on Nefley must have tightened, because Nefley coughed, turning an even darker shade of mauve as he pawed at the tattooed forearm that was pressed against his windpipe. Anxiously, I took note of the veins standing out on Nefley's forehead. And I was about to suggest that Dermid ease up a little when the back gate squeaked.

Dave had arrived. He'd been summoned by my mother, and had parked in the alley behind the house.

George was with him.

'*Freeze!*' Dermid yelped, yanking Nefley around to face the newcomers. Dave froze. He stood quite still, his fingers clamped to the top of the gate.

In the dimness, his chalk-white complexion had an almost phosphorescent glow to it.

'They're not going to hurt you, Dermid,' I said quickly. 'They're vampires. Like you are. We're all in the same boat.'

'Shut up! *Shut up!*' Dermid's voice cracked. All at once, the pistol was pointing straight at me. 'You're crazy! Where's

335

Dad? I'll count to ten!'

'He – he's coming,' I stammered, not even daring to glance around. It's amazing how big a small hole can seem, when there's a bullet somewhere down the other end of it. And though I knew that a shot to the head wouldn't kill me, I also knew that life with half a brain would be more uncomfortable than ever.

'Could you please just think about this? For one minute?' I begged. 'You were bitten by a vampire. You *are* a vampire.'

'I am not!'

'Nina, *don't*.' Dave's frantic plea was almost unrecognisable; he sounded like Bridget, all breathy and high-pitched. 'For God's sake, be quiet!'

'Hey, Dermid!' someone barked. Dermid jumped, and I was lucky he didn't shoot me. The gun-barrel wavered, then swung off to my left. When I looked in the same direction, I saw that Reuben had returned.

He'd entered the kitchen with my mother. She was wearing her nightgown. Between them they were supporting Barry McKinnon, whose arms were draped around their necks, and whose feet were dragging.

Dermid stared at his father through the kitchen window, in a kind of horrified bewilderment.

'You see?' I whimpered. 'Your dad's sick. You bit him. He's going to need help, all right, but not *your* kind of help, Dermid. We're the only ones who can help him, now.'

'*It's finished!*' Reuben declared loudly, with far too much relish. '*You! Him! The whole damn deal! You're done and dusted, mate!*'

'*Shut up!*' snapped Mum, who looked about a hundred years old. Reuben actually flinched away from her glare, which could have stripped the paint off wood, like a blow-torch.

Dermid licked his dry lips. He staggered slightly, turning pale beneath his tan.

'Actually, you're not finished,' I assured him, with as much certainty as I could muster. 'Being a vampire doesn't mean that you're *finished*. I used to think so myself, but I don't any more.' Though I was talking simply to keep him occupied – to stop him from forming any kind of firm resolution – I was also speaking straight from the heart. 'You can still live like a human being, even if you are a vampire,' I continued. 'Even if it is a lot harder to be energetic, and excited, and involved, it can still be done. I've *seen* it done.' Glimpsing a peripheral movement, I realised that Dave was creeping forward, and surreptitiously flapped my hand to make him stop. 'It's an infection – that's all. You can rise above it, like Dave has. You wouldn't think that Dave was a vampire. He's just like a normal person, except that he can't go out in the sun, these days.'

'*Dad? Can you hear me? Are you all right?*' Dermid bellowed. His gun was trained on my head once more, though his aim was far from steady.

'*You've run out of options, arsehole!*' Reuben's delivery was sharp and fierce and high-pitched. '*Forrest Darwell's in the clink, by now! So's your truck! We faked a meeting – tipped off the police! You can say goodbye to your hundred grand!*'

'Reuben, *shut up*! You're just confusing him!' I could see that Dermid was in no condition to absorb complex ultimatums; he was too fuddled and frightened to think in a logical way. 'You don't have to worry, Dermid. We'll find somewhere for you to go – you and your dad. We have to. Because you're one of us, now, and we always help each other.'

Then – without warning – Dermid threw up.

There was a retching gasp as his head snapped forward. Suddenly my shoes were covered in tar-black vomit. At the same instant he relaxed his hold on Nefley, who broke free with a tortured howl. Reuben and Dave dashed towards me, one from each side. Though still doubled over, Dermid began to wave his gun about, wildly.

He pulled the trigger when I caught his arm.

Click.

Mum screamed. Dermid fell to his knees, gagging. I wrenched the gun from him, holding it aloft as I retreated. Though quick, however, I was barely quick enough. Reuben rushed through the back door, jumping on Dermid with such an excess of energy that he almost knocked me off my feet.

'You didn't *load* it?' I asked Nefley, who was cowering nearby.

Before he could answer, I was engulfed in a bear-hug. While Mum struggled with Barry's dead weight, and Reuben pinned Dermid to the ground, and George stood slack-jawed and goggle-eyed near the fence, I found my nose rammed against Dave's chest.

'Did you mean it?' he said hoarsely.

'What?' I wasn't processing questions; I was too busy trying to absorb what had just occurred. When I struggled to free myself, Dave's hands dropped to my elbows. 'I'm all right.' I assured him. 'There were no bullets in the gun.'

'*Did you mean it?*' His tone was urgent. 'What you said? About being a vampire?'

You probably won't believe this, but my mind was a blank. It was the shock, I expect. You don't recover quickly from having a gun fired at you, even if it isn't loaded.

I stared at the thing: it was heavy and dull in my hand.

'What?' I murmured. (What *had* I said?) 'Could you remind me . . .?'

'You said I'd risen above it. You said I wasn't like a vampire.'

'Oh.' I could vaguely recall making some such comment – a very long time ago, it seemed. 'Well, you aren't,' I confirmed. 'I mean, you're not like a *typical* vampire. You do things. You make a difference. You're brave, and you care about stuff, like a regular guy.' I glanced around, distracted by all the activity in our immediate neighbourhood. Reuben had Dermid in an arm-lock. Mum was yelling at George, telling him to come inside and call Sanford. Nefley was apologising tearfully to anyone who would listen. 'Nefley,' I said to him, 'what's wrong with you? The gun wasn't *loaded*.'

'I'm sorry. I'm really sorry. I forgot . . .'

'You *forgot*?' I couldn't believe it. 'That's a pretty big thing to forget, don't you think? You let Dermid drag you all the way here, and you forget that the gun has no *bullets* inside?'

'I forgot to check! I thought maybe *you'd* loaded it!'

'Why on earth would we have loaded it?' I exclaimed. 'We wouldn't even know how!'

'In that case,' Reuben interrupted, from down on the ground, 'you'd better make damn sure it's empty.' He stretched out a hand, reaching for the pistol; his other hand was clamped around Dermid's wrist. 'It might have been a misfire. There might still be bullets in the chamber.'

'Really?' This was alarming news. Hurriedly I relinquished the weapon. Though Reuben took it, however, he wasn't able to inspect it without letting Dermid go.

Instead he gave it to my mother – who had abandoned

Barry McKinnon, and was now hovering on the back steps.

She held the gun as if it were a dirty sock, dangling from her thumb and forefinger.

'What the hell am I supposed to do with this?' she said.

'Just put it next to that rifle,' Reuben advised, nodding towards the house. 'That rifle in there is loaded, for sure.'

'Nina?' said Dave. His grasp tightened on my elbows when I didn't immediately respond. '*Nina!*'

'What?' I was reluctant to drag my attention away from Barry, who was now lying flat on Mum's linoleum. I could just see one of his legs if I craned my neck and peered through the back door. George was stepping over this leg on his way to the telephone. 'What is it?'

'Are you trying to say that you've changed your mind about vampires?' Dave asked. 'Are you telling me you don't hate them any more?'

'What do you mean? I never *hated* vampires. I just – I dunno, I just had this stupid idea that all vampires are a bunch of do-nothing losers. Which they aren't.' *Speaking of losers*, I thought, as my wandering gaze snagged on Nefley. He was standing there like a fence-post, sweaty and moon-faced. 'Hey, Nefley,' I suggested, 'why don't *you* go and see if that pistol's loaded? It would be really nice to know for certain.'

'What?' He blinked at me, before abruptly snapping out of his daze. 'Oh! Yeah. Right,' he said. Then he waddled inside, following my mother.

I could see them both quite clearly through the kitchen window, as the pistol passed from her custody to his. She must have said something to George, too; though I couldn't hear exactly what she told him (not from where I was standing), I did observe the way George obediently surrendered the telephone, then crouched beside Barry McKinnon.

Clearly, Mum had decided to call Sanford herself – while George took Barry upstairs.

'Right!' Reuben gasped. He reared up suddenly, catching me by surprise.

'What'll we do with this one?'

'Um . . .' I gazed at Dermid, who seemed dizzy and disoriented. He was groaning softly, though I couldn't tell you exactly what was troubling him. It might have been nausea, or despair, or simply the pain of Reuben's arm-lock. Whatever the cause of his distress, however, it was certainly debilitating. He was barely able to stand up straight, and sagged against Reuben's chest.

'I guess . . . I guess we should wait for Sanford,' was my advice. 'Sanford can give him a shot of something. To calm him down.'

Reuben sniffed. 'If you say so,' he spat, hustling Dermid towards the kitchen. 'Personally, I'd give 'im a shotta lead in the brain. That would calm him down, all right.'

'Reuben –'

'I know, I know. Vampires hate violence.' Adjusting his hold on Dermid, Reuben made his captive yip like a dog. 'But isn't *Dermid* a vampire now? And he tried to shoot you, Nina. I reckon he deserves whatever I can dish out.'

'He's not a vampire yet, though. Not quite. Not fully,' I rejoined. 'And when he is one . . . well, he'll change. Like I said before, he won't be the same person.' After a moment's inner struggle, I was finally compelled to admit the truth. 'He might – you know, he might even be a *better* person. It's possible. Becoming a vampire might improve his character.'

'Well, he certainly couldn't get any worse,' Reuben

341

muttered, pushing Dermid up the back steps. At which point somebody yelled, from the house next door, *'Can't you people keep it down, over there? My family's trying to sleep!'*

I recognised the voice. It belonged to one of our neighbours, Mr Kyrillis, who was leaning out of his bathroom window.

For at least five years, he and Mum had been engaged in a vicious feud about tree-roots. So he was never shy about complaining – not when he felt justified in doing so.

'Oh! Sorry!' I exclaimed. 'Sorry, Mr Kyrillis! We're just going in!'

'Buncha drunks!'

The window above us slammed shut, as I tried to break free of Dave's grip.

'Hurry! Get inside!' I whispered. 'Before he throws something at us!'

But Dave wouldn't budge.

'So what you're saying,' he murmured, 'is that I'm in with a chance. Even if I am a vampire.'

'What?' I didn't understand. 'What do you mean?'

'I mean that if you've changed your mind about vampires, then maybe you wouldn't hit the roof after all,' he said, leaving me none the wiser.

'Hit the roof about what?' I queried, in utter confusion.

Whereupon he swooped down and kissed me, full on the mouth.

Chapter Twenty-nine

Well, that was exactly one year ago, and a lot's happened since then. In fact there have been so many changes, I hardly know where to start.

Perhaps I should begin with Nefley Irving, and move on from there.

Nefley is no longer our fiercest opponent. Instead, he's our staunchest ally. I suppose it makes sense, because he's one of those obsessive and single-minded people who can only make friends if they're part of a campaign, or a club. The trouble is, he's not interested in sport, or religion, or politics, or computer gaming. He is, however, interested in vampires. As a matter of fact, he now knows more about vampires than most vampires of my acquaintance. And he's become an unofficial member of the Reformed Vampire Support Group.

Every Tuesday, he's always the first to arrive at our 9:30 meeting. He's taken to picking up Gladys and Bridget on his way in, and dropping them off on his way home. Sometimes he goes shopping for us. He'll make guinea pig deliveries, on occasion, and he also tends to hang around St Agatha's quite a bit when he isn't at work. Father Ramon says that he likes to discuss the moral implications of avoiding death by becoming a vampire.

Nefley has a great many ideas about vampire websites, and vampire medical research, and vampire documentaries. He keeps raising these subjects at our meetings, only to be shouted down. In fact I can't help worrying that Nefley might one day succumb to his own, peculiar brand of loopy idealism, and launch some kind of Vampire Appeal, complete with newsletter, walkathon, and charity Christmas cards.

But that's not going to happen as long as Reuben's around. While Nefley has dedicated himself to the cause of vampire welfare, Reuben's mission is to keep Nefley on a short rein. They spend a fair amount of time together, and it isn't because Reuben enjoys Nefley's rambling monologues about on-line support networks, viral mutations, and medieval family trees. It's because Reuben doesn't want Nefley shooting his mouth off to other people.

'Somebody's gotta listen to him,' Reuben's said to me, more than once, 'and he's not the worst guy in the world.' According to Reuben, Nefley won't go spilling his guts over the Net while he has a werewolf to converse with. 'He just needs to vent,' is Reuben's opinion.

Personally, I think there's more to it than that. I think that Nefley hasn't done anything ill-advised because he's a little scared of Reuben. We all are, really; there's a dangerous quality about Reuben that can't be expunged by a quiet, regular, nine-to-five existence. Although he's doing his best to live a normal life, working as an apprentice mechanic as he finishes high school, Reuben has a wild and hard-edged side to him that keeps everyone off-balance. For one thing, he's moody – especially during the waxing phase of the lunar cycle. For another thing, he can't always control his temper. Despite the fact that he manages to keep pretty cool most of the time, certain people invariably set him off: like his brother Dane, for instance.

I don't know if you remember Dane. He's the brother who made a home for Reuben after their mum died. Dane was understandably shocked to hear that Reuben wasn't dead after all; it's perhaps not surprising that Reuben's vague remarks about 'going off to find himself' and 'getting hooked up with the wrong people' weren't good enough for Dane. I keep telling Reuben that you can't *blame* his brother for getting angry – that our need to keep the whole werewolf business under wraps has inevitably made Reuben look like a bit of a selfish bastard. 'Consider it from Dane's point of view,' I pleaded, just the other day. 'He must have been devastated when you disappeared. He must have thought you'd been murdered. And now he's hurt because he thinks you wandered off without trying to contact him. He doesn't know that you *couldn't* contact him. So you can't expect him to be entirely sympathetic, can you?'

Unfortunately, Reuben seems to have anticipated a prodigal-son kind of welcome from his family. He's suffered so much that his perceptions are slightly skewed, and he can't understand why Dane won't simply forgive and forget. Dane's disapproval came as an enormous shock. It hurt Reuben almost as much as his apparent disloyalty must have hurt Dane. So there was a huge fraternal row, and now the two brothers aren't talking to each other. In fact you can't even mention Dane to his brother, at the moment. If you do, Reuben will practically burst a blood vessel.

We have to keep him well away from the McKinnons, too. It doesn't matter that they're sick, and skinny, and shell-shocked. It doesn't matter that they're having a hard time adapting to their supplements. The minute Reuben lays eyes on their bleached and bony faces, you can see the wolf unleashed inside of him. His fingers curl, his colour changes, his breathing speeds up. He'll bare his teeth when he talks, and his voice will take on an oddly gruff timbre. That's why we never see Reuben at our Tuesday meetings. Even Father Ramon agrees that the McKinnons aren't safe while Reuben's around.

It's a pity, because those McKinnons aren't the men they once were. If Reuben would just put himself in their shoes, for three seconds, he'd soon understand that. Their lives have been completely overturned; they're even living under assumed names. (Though not because they should have been dead years ago, like some of the other vampires in our group.) Barry and Dermid are in hiding because they're on the run from Forrest Darwell – who seems to be under the impression that they were involved in a police conspiracy against him. Although he wasn't actually arrested, Forrest can't have been thrilled at the way he was expelled from the country. So it's perhaps not surprising that he's made the McKinnons his target. When Father Ramon returned to Wolgaroo – in order to retrieve the hired van from its hiding place inside an old mine shaft – he found Barry's house ransacked. Cushions had been ripped open and linoleum torn up. The whole place had been thoroughly searched, no doubt in the hope of finding some clue as to where Barry and Dermid might have gone. Clearly, Forrest Darwell is very nervous about their intentions. He must be wondering if they're about to blow the lid off his entire werewolf-fighting racket.

They aren't, of course. They couldn't risk attracting that

kind of attention. In fact they can't even rent out their property, since the underground cells are bound to make people curious. There's been a lot of discussion about turning those cells back into water tanks. Meeting after meeting has been devoted to the thorny issue of how this might be done without hiring nosy contractors. But the problem remains: where would the McKinnons sleep, if they didn't have underground cells any more? And what if Forrest Darwell is somehow keeping an eye on their old address? And how will they cope with all that physical labour if they feel like death warmed up most of the time? As it is, Barry's had to miss a lot of meetings. His transformation was especially hard – perhaps because he was infected by a blood relative. He can barely stand up, let alone pour concrete, or wield a nail-gun. That's why he and his son are both living with Sanford at present. They need constant medical supervision.

That's also why they have to be kept away from Reuben Schneider. These days, Reuben could cripple them with sharp glance, never mind a sucker punch. We're far more worried about what he might do to them than we are about what they might do to him.

Gladys maintains that Reuben's a threat to the rest of us, too. She continues to distrust the werewolf in our midst, despite the fact that there hasn't been a single unfortunate incident since we met him. What we've found is that it's easy enough to deal with a werewolf, if you have access to a bank vault. Reuben simply spends every full moon locked in Sanford's windowless concrete vault, behind a reinforced steel door. Though poor old Reuben will occasionally emerge looking bloody and defeated, the vault itself never suffers very much damage. And Father Ramon has confirmed that you can't hear a thing from outside. Not even when you're directly overhead, in what was formerly the manager's office.

Needless to say, this means that Sanford and the McKinnons have to sleep somewhere else for a night every month. But they don't mind. They simply move in with George, who's grateful for the company. It's been pretty lonely for George, I'm afraid. Though he might not be especially talkative, and his favourite activity is watching television, and his guinea pigs occupy a lot of his waking hours, he still misses Horace.

Things have been tough for George, since Horace was interred.

It was Sanford who closed the lid on Horace. Nobody else would have had the stomach for it. Even *I* couldn't help thinking: *there but for the grace of God* – and I'm positively pitiless, compared to some of the others. Bridget doesn't believe in judging people for behaviour that is, essentially, the symptom of a chronic disease. George is under the impression that Horace only fanged Dermid in self-defence, though I've insisted over and over again that Dermid was asleep during the attack. Dave's too soft-hearted to approve of someone being forcibly detained for a *day*, let alone a decade. And Gladys feels that, if Horace has to be punished, then Dermid should suffer the same fate – since he fanged his own father.

'I don't see why Dermid should get away with it,' she's often remarked, in the presence of both McKinnons. Nothing that Sanford's said about the physical effects of the transformation process has made the slightest difference to Gladys. She still doesn't agree that Dermid's disoriented state, at the time of his blooding, can be offered up as any kind of excuse.

'We're all of us sick,' she's complained. 'We all feel dizzy and tired and confused – Dermid's not the only one. But that doesn't mean we go around fanging people, does it? If you ask me, we should either let Horace out or stick Dermid in there with him.'

Sanford disagrees. He's overruled Gladys. Nevertheless, Dermid must be frightened that Gladys will one day prevail, because he's lodged his own objection to Horace's interment. No doubt Dermid is willing to put up with anything – even the company of his attacker – in preference to ten years underground. 'If *I've* forgiven Horace, I don't see why everyone else can't,' he's declared, in fretful tones.

As for Barry, he's far too sick to contemplate anything as hideous as being buried alive. Right now, Barry can't look at a freezer full of dead guinea pigs without throwing up; the mere thought of what Horace must be going through, trapped in his subterranean casket, has more than once sent Barry rushing to the toilet.

I have to admit, I've suffered the same reaction myself, occasionally.

It's lucky that I don't dream when I go to sleep. If I did, I'd be having nightmares about Horace. I know that what he did was a terrible crime. I know that the deterrent has to be harsh, because the urge is so strong. I know that Horace will survive his sentence, and that, with any luck, it will transform him into a wiser, humbler, less dangerous vampire (who won't dress in black leather and purple satin any more). Nevertheless, even after a year, I'm still haunted by feelings of guilt and dread. I can't help wondering if Horace was somehow influenced by Zadia Bloodstone.

Dave tells me that I'm being foolish. He insists that Horace would have fanged Dermid no matter what. According to Dave, Horace was only using Zadia as an excuse to justify his actions.

'You know how often we've talked about this in group,' Dave said to me, a few months back. We were in his living room, at the time; I was opening his mail while he picked out tunes on his guitar. 'Sanford never *stops* talking about it. You can come up with a million rationalisations: they deserve it, they asked me to, they were about to die, it was self-defence –'

'Yeah, yeah. *A million rationalisations, and not one good reason.*' I was quoting Sanford. 'But I still think Zadia influenced Horace. The whole crime-fighting scenario –'

'Was his excuse for chewing on someone's neck,' Dave finished. He set aside his guitar, before coming to sit beside me. 'Horace was thinking like a vampire, Nina. He was thinking about himself.'

'Are you sure?' Because I wasn't. 'I mean, what would have happened if he hadn't done it? How would we have handled the McKinnons? What if we're all better off, thanks to what Horace did?'

Dave snorted. 'Are you kidding?' he rumbled, with a sideways look. 'Nina, we've had to sit through something like ten hours of Dermid's childhood traumas –'

'I know.'

'Maybe *you're* enjoying it, but I'm not.'

'I just worry that Horace might have been punished for doing something helpful.'

'There was nothing helpful about it,' said Dave. He put his arm around my shoulders. 'The police had been tipped off, remember? Reuben's plan would have worked out fine.'

'You really think so?'

'Yup.'

'And you don't feel bad?'

'Not any more,' he replied, then gave me a squeeze.

It's true that Dave's much, much happier now. He's beginning to write songs again, for one thing. And he cracks a lot more jokes than he used to, despite having to put up with Dermid's childhood traumas, Nefley's over-enthusiastic friendship, and a lingering sense of unease about Horace. Sanford claims that it's a natural progression: that Dave has moved on from the 'depression' to the 'acceptance' stage of the Kubler-Ross Grief Cycle. But the explanation is much simpler than that.

For a very long time, Dave was convinced that I hated vampires. *All* vampires. And now he knows that I don't.

You won't believe how much more cheerful he's become, since making this discovery.

I can't deny that I'm in pretty good spirits myself. It was such a *relief* to find out that Dave was actually pining after me, all those years, instead of his former girlfriend. But I'm still not quite as upbeat as he is. I keep worrying that Zadia's melodramatic existence might have exerted more of a negative than a positive influence on the world. In fact I'm starting to wonder if Sanford might be right after all. Perhaps Zadia always was an act of repudiation. Perhaps she was my attempt to deny the truth.

That's why I've spent the last year writing this memoir: because I want to set the record straight. Not that *everything* in this book is accurate. I have to protect the anonymity of my family and friends, so you won't find an Estelle Harrison living in Surry Hills, or a Wolgaroo Corner near Cobar. Nor will I even hint at the current location of Horace Whittaker;

there might be someone out there who could track him down, if I carelessly let slip a single clue. But I've done my best to be clear, and honest, and straightforward. I've told as much of my story as it's safe to tell. I've given you an unvarnished account of what it's *really* like to be a vampire, so that you'll know enough to discount just about everything else you might hear on the subject.

At our last meeting, I finally mentioned this book to the others. I'd been keeping the whole project a secret, because I wasn't sure that it would ever be finished; even Dave wasn't told, until yesterday. Having reached the final pages, however, I decided to come clean. So I told everyone that I'd been writing an autobiography.

The immediate response was a stunned silence – which Gladys was the first to break.

'What do you mean?' she whined. 'How could you be writing an autobiography? You haven't *done* anything.'

'Yes, she has,' said Dave. 'She's done lots of things. She rescued Reuben. She was nearly shot by Dermid –'

'No she wasn't,' Dermid objected. 'That wasn't me. That wasn't *really* me. I was in a semi-schizoid state, remember? Sanford said so.'

Dave rolled his eyes, as Father Ramon interjected soothingly, 'We're not blaming you, Dermid. No one's blaming anyone, here. This is a blame-free zone.'

'At any rate, I daresay Nina's referring to her mood journal,' was Sanford's contribution. 'She's taken my advice – haven't you, Nina? You've been plotting your emotional landscape, and keeping a diary of your thoughts and feelings. To share with the group.'

'N-n-no-o-o,' I replied. 'Not really. I've been writing about what happened last year. When Casimir was killed.'

Nefley winced. George said, 'Am I in it?'

'Yes.'

George looked pleased. But Barry didn't.

'*I'm* not in it, am I?' he asked.

'Of course you're in it.' Seeing him scowl, I launched into a spirited defence of my actions. 'How could I have left you out of it, Barry? You're going to have to accept responsibility for the part you played.'

'It's got nothing to do with responsibility!' he spat. 'This is all about *confidentiality*. I'm supposed to be incognito! I'm living under a false name!'

'Oh, the names have all been changed,' I assured him – whereupon Sanford stiffened.

'What do you mean, the names have been changed?' he demanded. 'Why would you want to do that? You're not intending to *publish* this book, are you?'

'Well . . . yes.' I was surprised at the way his brows snapped together. 'Sanford, you're the one who said that I should stop writing fantasies. You're the one who said I was only making things worse. So I'm trying to make things better now. I'm telling the truth.'

'About *me*?' Nefley squealed in alarm. 'About what *I* did?'

'Why not?'

'Because I'll go to jail, that's why not!'

'No you won't. People won't find out who you are. I've said that you work as a mail sorter.'

'As a *mail sorter*?' Nefley was horrified. Before he could protest, however, Bridget cut in.

'You haven't put Reuben in it, have you?' she inquired, with obvious concern. 'He wouldn't like that, Nina. You know how he feels about public exposure . . .'

'I told you, I've used *false names*.'

'And descriptions? What about false descriptions?' Gladys seemed very anxious to clarify this point. 'You didn't make me too skinny, did you? You didn't mention my scar?'

'Gladys –'

'I want to see what you wrote about me!' she cried. 'Sanford, tell Nina she has to show us her book before she does anything else with it!'

Sanford took a deep breath, just as Father Ramon lifted an admonitory hand.

'Sanford can't tell Nina to do anything, Gladys. You know that,' the priest gently reminded us all. 'But I do think that a book like this merits some very serious discussion. And we can't discuss it unless we have some idea of what's in it.'

'I'd kinda like to read it myself,' Dave mumbled. When I threw him a reproachful glance, he hastily added, 'If I promise not to change anything.'

'*I'll* make no such promise,' Sanford declared. 'The safety of this group is of paramount importance. If the book compromises our security in any way, then changes will have to be made to the text.'

'Not too many changes,' I warned. 'This is supposed to be the truth, Sanford. You've always told me to face up to the truth. To stop denying what I am.'

'Which doesn't mean you have to go round telling every-body *else* what you are!' Dermid chimed in. And Bridget said, 'He's right, dear. You really do have to be very careful – for all our sakes.'

'It's not like we want to pretend that we're Zadia Bloodstone,' Dave agreed, albeit in a shamefaced manner.

'We don't want people to think we have superpowers, or anything. But – well – if you stick in all that stuff about blooding, and vomiting, and dead guinea pigs, and bad breath, and haemorrhages, and dizzy spells . . .' Dave sighed. 'I mean, who's going to want us around, for God's sake? We'll be treated like lepers, Nina.'

So there you have it. I've tried to tell the truth, and I might have succeeded. Or then again, I might not. You'll never know, will you? At least, I *hope* you'll never know.

One thing, however, you can be absolutely sure of – and that's the fact that I've done my best.

What more can you expect from any normal human being?